BOUND
TO
YOU

ALSO BY
Christopher Pike

THE THIRST SERIES
REMEMBER ME
THE SECRET OF KA
UNTIL THE END

COMING SOON

WITCH WORLD

BOUND
TO
YOU

INCLUDES *SPELLBOUND* AND *SEE YOU LATER*

Christopher Pike

Simon Pulse

New York   London   Toronto   Sydney   New Delhi

This book is a work of fiction. Any references to historical events, real people, or real locales are used fictitiously. Other names, characters, places, and incidents are the product of the author's imagination, and any resemblance to actual events or locales or persons, living or dead, is entirely coincidental.

SIMON PULSE
An imprint of Simon & Schuster Children's Publishing Division
1230 Avenue of the Americas, New York, NY 10020
This Simon Pulse paperback edition August 2012
Spellbound copyright © 1988 by Christopher Pike
See You Later copyright © 1990 by Christopher Pike
All rights reserved, including the right of reproduction
in whole or in part in any form.
SIMON PULSE and colophon are registered trademarks
of Simon & Schuster, Inc.
For information about special discounts for bulk purchases, please
contact Simon & Schuster Special Sales at 1-866-506-1949
or business@simonandschuster.com.
The Simon & Schuster Speakers Bureau can bring authors to
your live event. For more information or to book an event contact
the Simon & Schuster Speakers Bureau at 1-866-248-3049
or visit our website at www.simonspeakers.com.
The text of this book was set in Adobe Garamond.
Manufactured in the United States of America
10 9 8 7 6 5 4 3 2 1
Library of Congress Control Number 2012932332
ISBN 978-1-4424-5971-7
These books were previously published individually.

Contents

SPELLBOUND

For Eileen

Chapter One

The morning was brisk as Cindy Jones stepped from her house to fetch the newspaper at the end of the driveway. She had grown up in the Rockies, but still the first breath of early mountain air always filled her with an invigorating freshness that was both surprising and pleasant. Dew glistened on the thick green branches of the many surrounding trees, evaporating swiftly in the bright sun. The sky was that special cerulean blue that longtime city dwellers could hardly imagine. It was going to be a beautiful day, she thought as she knelt and collected the paper, pulling off the rubber band and glancing at what was new in the small community of Timber, Wyoming.

An article that began in the lower right-hand corner of the second page changed her mind about what a beautiful day it was going to be.

HOW DID KAREN HOLLY DIE?
BY KENT COOKE

Seven weeks ago today, on August 2, seventeen-year-old Karen Holly died. The circumstances surrounding her death, as reported by Jason Whitfield, her boyfriend at the time, are as follows.

Jason picked Karen up at her home at approximately six p.m. Neither of Karen's parents was present; they were visiting a relative in Laramie. The kids left the house to attend a seven o'clock showing at the Rest Theater in downtown Timber. The young man taking tickets at the door, Ray Bower, was later able to verify that Jason and Karen did indeed see the movie. Although it was an unusually busy night, Ray remembered them well because Jason had gone out of his way to ridicule Ray's haircut. After the show, which ended at nine o'clock, Jason and Karen rode up to Castle Park. It was Karen's idea, according to Jason. She wanted to see Crystal Falls in the moonlight. They parked in the H lot not far from Snake Tail River and began to hike up along the Pathfinders Trail to the falls. During the hour it took them to reach the top of the falls, they saw nobody. Once at the top, they "hung out," doing nothing in particular.

Near midnight, Jason's attention was drawn by a "strange sound" coming from the other side of a mound of granite that juts up not far from the waterfall. To Jason, the sound was reminiscent of a bear on the prowl. Telling Karen to remain where she was, he went to investigate. He was no sooner on the other side of the mound than he heard Karen scream. Immediately he ran back to where he had left her.

He was greeted with a horrible sight. A large bear was on top of Karen, mauling her as she lay helpless on the ground. Jason reached for a stick and began to beat the animal from behind, trying to force its attention away from Karen. To an extent, he was successful. The bear turned away from Karen long enough to smack him in the face with a paw. He was thrown to the ground where he "remembers" striking his head on a rock and blacking out.

When Jason came to, Karen was dead. Her body had been ravaged beyond recognition. At first, he tried to carry her back down the trail, but because of the seriousness of his own injuries—a swollen left eye and a bruised skull—he had to abandon the idea. He went on alone, and somehow managed to reach his car and drive to the police station in Timber.

At this point our source of information switches to Lt. James Baker, who had just completed his shift and was returning to the station to check out for the day. It was Lieutenant Baker who first heard Jason's account of the death. The officer later described Jason as being in a very agitated state. After listening to his story, the lieutenant quickly headed for Castle Park. Because of dizziness caused by his wounds, Jason was unable to accompany Baker. But he was able to describe specifically where the bear attack had taken place, and where

Karen's body lay. Jason was taken to Timber Memorial by a night clerk, where he was examined by Dr. Harry Free. A neurological examination and X-rays showed evidence of a mild concussion. Jason was treated for this condition, and for slight scalp abrasions, and was released to the care of his parents.

Lieutenant Baker reached the top of Crystal Falls at precisely two-thirty. Although he searched the spot Jason had described, he was unable to find Karen's body. He did, however, discover evidence of a struggle. There was a significant amount of blood staining the ground, so much, in fact, that he had no doubt someone had died that night.

At three-thirty the lieutenant was joined by Deputy Jeff Pierce, a part-time employee of the Timber Police Department. Together they continued the search of the area, with no success. It was only when they had taken the trail back down the mountain, and were walking along Snake Tail River, in the vicinity of parking lot H, that they found Karen's body. She was lying in the rushing current, held in place by a large branch that had fallen across the edge of the river. She was, in Baker's words, "a mess."

An autopsy was performed the next day by Dr. Gregory Adams, a coroner out of Cheyenne. His initial findings were made public the following day. To quote: "Karen Holly's rib cage was shattered across the entire right side. Her head had suffered from what appeared to be an extremely powerful blow—the top of the skull was cracked in several places.

Whether she died from the former or the latter wound is diffi-cult to say, and of only academic importance. Either injury was sufficiently severe to terminate her life. The blood loss alone from her numerous lacerations would have been enough to kill her."

Dr. Adams concludes by saying Karen Holly had "prob-ably" been the victim of a wild animal attack. The doctor does not offer the type of animal.

I would like to ask the reader to forgive my rehashing the details that have already been adequately reported in these pages on the days following the death of Karen. But I feel it necessary to have the events fresh in your mind before I pres-ent new facts that have recently come to light, and before I offer an analysis of the implausibilities in Jason Whitfield's account.

I caught up with Dr. Adams in Cheyenne two days ago. This took some doing, for he is a very busy man, or rather, I must assume he is. In the last three weeks he hasn't had time to return a single one of my calls. When we finally met, I can't say he appeared eager to satisfy my curiosity. He did, however, reveal a couple of interesting details that had come out during Karen's autopsy and that had not been previously released to the press. The first was the discovery of small amounts of human skin under the girl's fingernails. The sec-ond concerned the nature of the scratches covering her body; they didn't resemble those normally found on the victim of a grizzly attack. Indeed, it was this point, the coroner confessed, that had made him reluctant to specify that the culprit had been a grizzly. On the other hand, he was quick to assure me it must have been a bear. No other animal would have had the strength to do what had been done to Karen. But when I asked if a person, say a young man with a sledgehammer and a rake of some type, could have inflicted such damage to Karen's body, the doctor would not rule out the possibility.

That surprised me. With all the sophisticated forensic tests that can be done these days, I had assumed a coroner could tell the difference between a murdering bear and a murdering human. If nothing else, I figured a bear would leave quite a few bear hairs lying around. I told the doctor as much. It was then the gentleman suddenly had another appointment to keep. As he was walking away, I called, "Would a grizzly first kill a person, leave the area, and then return and drag the body three hundred yards to a river and throw it in?" The coroner must not have heard my question. He did not answer.

The experts say it was a bear. Jason Whitfield says it was a bear. So what's my problem? And why am I spoiling your breakfast going on about an incident you would all rather forget? Frankly, I'm not sure. It's just that there's something scary about experts who don't want to talk and an eighteen-year-old boy who may have talked too much. It was Karen's idea to hike up to the top of the waterfall, Jason reports. Karen's sister says Karen hated exercise of any type. Then Jason says he heard a strange sound, and thought it might have been a bear, and went to investigate, leaving his girlfriend all alone and unprotected.

Now I don't know Jason personally, but he must be either very brave or very stupid. Why didn't he simply grab Karen's hand and get the hell out of there? Plus, there is the manner in which the grizzly treated Jason. From the sound of things, the boy got off awfully light, especially when you consider that this was a kid who was beating the blasted beast with a club. When I spoke to the doctor who had treated Jason that night, he told me that boy must be one of the luckiest people in the world. He also answered affirmatively when I inquired if it was possible that Jason's wounds were self-inflicted.

I'll leave you with a few more points to ponder. The police will neither confirm nor deny something as basic as whether or not there were grizzly tracks in the vicinity of the incident. A hunt was made for a grizzly, but it was conducted by a few men and lasted only three days. As far as I know, no one has compared the skin under Karen's nails with Jason's skin.

Jason is scheduled to appear next Monday at a preliminary hearing in Cheyenne. This hearing is to determine whether he should be tried in connection with the death of Karen Holly. I have it on good sources the hearing is only a formality, that the state is already prepared to drop the case. As we all know, Carl Whitfield, Jason's father, is mayor of Timber.

Do I believe Jason killed Karen? I'll say again, I don't know.

I'll go so far as to say I think the chances are against it. I prefer to think this way because the alternative makes me feel sick.

But maybe this is the reason so little is going on to solve this mystery. None of us even wants to consider this alternative. Maybe we should. Odds were that Karen Holly would have been Timber High's homecoming queen this year. She was only seventeen.

Cindy refolded the paper and tucked it under her arm. She was familiar with this reporter and the slant of the article had not surprised her. Kent Cooke was the small-time investigator type who was always looking for the big conspiracy. He was fanatically liberal, always lashing out at the local government, the police department, authority in general. For years he had been carrying on a personal vendetta with Mayor Carl Whitfield, who was doubly hexed in Mr. Cooke's eyes, not only because he was in a position of power, but because he was rich.

Cindy was also familiar with the Whitfields' wealth. She saw signs of it every time she went out on a date. She was Jason Whitfield's new girlfriend.

But I am not Karen's replacement.

The article was dumb. A rake and a sledgehammer? Wouldn't Karen have noticed those little niceties as they hiked up to the top of the waterfall? "Hey, Jason, what are you doing with that hammer?" "Just going to crack some rocks, babe." Then there was that point about why the bear hadn't hurt Jason worse when everyone knew a grizzly usually let you alone if you lay perfectly still, which Jason, being unconscious, would have been doing. Finally there was that feeble attempt to create a mystery about the absence of bear tracks. Kent Cooke must have known the area near the waterfall was more rock than dirt, and that it had rained heavily right after Karen had been attacked. Chances were the tracks had been washed away. It was pretty shabby reporting not to mention that tiny detail. No, Kent Cooke wouldn't be getting a Pulitzer prize for this piece. He would probably be getting sued.

You'd deserve it. You ruined my breakfast. And I've already eaten.

Cindy had not known Karen well. Cindy's best friend, Pam Alta, had been Karen's cousin, and the two cousins had not gotten along. Consequently, it had been impossible for Cindy to talk to Karen in a normal way after having listened to Pam tell her what a self-centered weasel her cousin was. Of course, Pam sure felt awful when Karen had died.

Karen had been beautiful, a striking redhead. And despite Pam's words to the contrary, she had not seemed a bad sort. Certainly, she had been popular. Her boyfriend had, after all, been the best-looking guy in the school. The reporter had gotten one point right. Karen probably would have been homecoming queen.

Cindy turned toward the south. Crystal Falls was just visible between the trees, five miles away—one of those miles being straight up—its early-autumn waters fanning a white veil over the hard brownish-gray cliffs of Castle Park. As she watched, Cindy saw a drifting cloud hug the mountain, and the place where Karen had come to her horrible end was covered in mist. The symbolic quality of the scene, taking place as it did moments after the reporter's dark questions, did not sit well with Cindy.

Jason loved Karen. You just had to listen to his voice when he talked about her to know that.

"Wolf," Cindy called to her big silver dog who had suddenly appeared from the side of the house. He was one dog who fully deserved his name. Wolf had so small a percentage of *real* dog in him that Cindy had had the worst time getting him shots and a license. He was really a civilized monster. It was only when he heard the word *sic*—spoken by her lips and no other's—that his wild heritage emerged. Then he went for the throat. Having him around made her feel sort of invincible.

Wolf licked her right hand, his warm tongue making her realize how cold her fingers had become. She had meant to dash outside, collect the paper, and hurry back in to make her brother breakfast. Alex was probably wondering what had become of her. It wouldn't be good to tell him about the article. As it was, he was not crazy about Jason.

"You wouldn't have any trouble handling a grizzly, would ya, sweetie?" Cindy asked, petting an appreciative Wolf on the head before she turned back toward the house. Wolf followed at her feet, and as she opened the front door, he hurried inside.

Alex was in the kitchen beside the toaster. He was making his own single-course breakfast with a loaf of brown bread and a cube of butter. She gave a disapproving look. Their parents owned a hardware store in downtown Timber and had to be up early and out of the house. As a result, Cindy was accustomed to preparing Alex's breakfast, a task she didn't mind. She enjoyed cooking and usually felt good about doing her younger brother a favor in the morning, since usually he had helped her the previous night with her homework.

"Wouldn't you rather have an omelet or some bacon?" she asked.

"Don't bother," Alex said, retrieving a couple of slices of bread from the toaster and reaching for the knife.

"It's no bother. I meant to have something fixed already."

Alex began to dig into the butter. "You're forgetting what day it is."

"Oh, yeah, race day." Her brother ran cross country for Timber High. Although only a junior, he was the best—or the second best, depending on whether he had a good day or not—runner in the school. He took his sport seriously. On race days he ate only complex carbohydrates for breakfast; in this case, about eight slices of whole grain bread. He wouldn't be eating lunch that afternoon. He skipped the meal because he said there wasn't enough time to digest the food before he had to run. Cindy knew it was because he got so tense imme-diately before a race that he'd throw up if he had anything in his stomach. "Why don't you at least have a glass of milk with it?" she asked.

"Milk's mucous forming. It could affect my wind."

"Would an apple affect your wind?" She was keen on bal-anced diets.

"It would if I tried to run with it in my mouth," Alex replied, biting into his toast, glancing out the window. "Looks like a pretty day."

"That's what I thought," she muttered, grabbing a carton of milk off the table and pouring some into a bowl for Wolf, who didn't know about balanced diets and who wasn't worried about winning races. Wolf lapped up the milk hungrily.

He wasn't their only weird animal. Alex owned a blind par-rot that had to be a hundred years old. Her name was Sybil, and she could recognize a dozen different people by their voices alone and clearly pronounce each of their names. The one thing that annoyed Cindy about Sybil was that she didn't know *her* name.

"Say hello to Cindy, Sybil," Cindy said, tearing pieces off the front page of the paper and feeding the old bird portions of Kent Cooke's article. Looking at the parrot, you'd swear she could see. Her wide-open soulful eyes possessed a keenly penetrating gaze.

"Mornin', Alex," Sybil chirped, enjoying the article more

than Cindy had. Sybil would often chew on a piece of junk all day without swallowing it.

"Cindy," she pronounced carefully. "Cindy."

"Mornin', Clyde."

"Who the hell is Clyde?" Cindy wanted to know.

"He's a friend of Bill's," Alex said. "They were up here the other day, talking to Sybil."

"Mornin', Bill," Sybil said.

"Stupid bird," Cindy scowled.

"Mornin', stupid," Sybil said.

"I suppose she's getting closer." Cindy sighed. "Finish your toast. I want to get out of here." She threw the remainder of the paper in the garbage.

Alex wanted to drive. He had just gotten his license. To Cindy that meant it was time he started asking girls out. Alex was so shy around girls she was afraid if he didn't start dating soon, he never would. But it wasn't as though she was trying to force him into anything he didn't really want to do himself. Her brother was a great romantic at heart. That was part of his problem; he elevated girls he had a crush on to such stratospheric heights he was unable to ask them out. His current flame was an English girl new to the area. She was in Cindy's psychology class. Her name was Joni Harper. She was rather reserved, *very* pretty. She was also a senior. This chick didn't need elevating.

"I think you should do it today," she said as they rolled

away from the house down the winding road into town. Turning the first corner, they had a glorious view of valley open before them. With so much green life all around, it was hard to imagine how anyone, old or young, could have died in Timber.

"You mean, win the race? I intend to."

"No. I think you should ask Joni out. Today."

Alex concentrated on his driving. "I should probably wait. She hardly knows me."

"How many times have you talked to her since school began last week?"

"Seven times."

Boy, he's counting. "Do you think any other guy in school has talked to her that many times?"

"Probably not."

"Then you know her better than anyone. Just ask her out."

"But when I've talked to her, *I've* done all the talking. I hardly know anything about her."

"You know she likes your voice."

"I think I should wait."

"How long do you think a chick who looks like Joni will go before being asked out?"

Alex considered that. Logic worked wonders on him. "How should I approach her?"

"Depends on the situation. You have to be natural. Strike up a conversation. Then just ask her if she'd like to go to the game with you tonight."

"What if she doesn't like football?"

"She won't turn you down because she doesn't like football."

"You think she might turn me down?"

"No. She's new here. She hardly knows anybody. Why would she turn you down?"

Alex shrugged. "Being new to the area doesn't mean she's feeling desperate. Maybe she doesn't like the way I look."

Cindy studied her brother for a moment before answering. He was a shade under six feet, thin but with wide shoulders and a way of moving that made it clear he worked out often. The last quality was perhaps not a virtue. By nature, Alex was very controlled, and it showed in his physique as an overall tightness. Then again, as Joni herself appeared somewhat cautious, she might appreciate the quality.

His face reflected his intelligence. His blue eyes were deep set and his mouth, though usually set in a pondering line, was wide and could break into a warm grin if given sufficient provocation. He had a head of thick brown hair that any half-witted English girl should enjoy running her fingers through.

"*I* like the way you look," she said.

Alex glanced over at her and smiled. "Want to go to the game with me tonight?"

"Yeah. We'll make it a double date. Jason and I, and you and Joni."

"Jason's playing."

"We could all go out together afterward. It's an early game."

Alex paused. "How did Jason ask *you* out?"

Well, he called me up to thank me for the flowers I sent to Karen's funeral and we got to talking and . . .

It sounded worse than it was. He had thanked her for the flowers, but it had been two weeks after the funeral and who said a period of mourning had to last a certain length of time and to hell with those who talked about it behind her back. They hadn't been married, for god's sake.

"I don't remember. See how spontaneous it must have been?"

Alex frowned. "He probably asked you if you wanted to go to a motel."

Cindy paused. "That's not fair," she said coolly.

Alex glanced at her. "I'm sorry."

"Apology accepted." There was a moment of silence. "Want me to ask the girls on the squad if they'll come to the race today?"

She was a member of the cheerleading team. Last year, being on the squad had been a big deal, but lately, especially since school had begun, she'd been wondering if she shouldn't hang up her pom-poms. Wiggling her butt in front of the crowds who came to the games no longer appealed to her, and she no longer felt she had much in common with the other girls on the team. Outside of practice, she never talked to them. They were all still into gossiping about their bodies, and their boyfriends' bodies, and what a rush it was when the two of them got nice and close. This didn't mean she wasn't interested in sex; her fantasy life was so disgustingly rich that Pam had several times accurately accused her of blushing while staring off into empty space. It was just that she was dissatisfied with her life as a whole, while her peers didn't seem to be. She was beginning to realize that everything was *not* going to change when she graduated. Unlike Alex, she had no plans to go away to college. She wasn't dumb, but school didn't do a thing for her.

The way her parents were talking lately, they assumed she'd be working full-time in their hardware store. She'd done that all summer. It was going to be news to them, but she had no intention of going back to those fifty-hour weeks. She had quite a bit saved; she figured she'd travel in June. She hoped seeing other places would give her an idea of what she wanted to do with her life. It was a secret hope of hers that a flying saucer would pick her up on some lonely desert road and make her a galactic ambassador. There just didn't seem to be anything in the world that really thrilled her.

Except a pretty face. I still do love them boys.

She was presently wearing her uniform and knew she could turn a few heads in it. The colors were blue, white, and gold, and complemented her tan skin and light blond hair nicely. The skirt was cut short, which allowed her to flaunt her long legs and shapely hips. She had a nice figure—she could admit it to herself without having to be an egomaniac—and her face wasn't bad, either. Her eyes were a deep blue and she shared Alex's clearly defined chin. Jason had once told her she looked like the girl next door. The compliment fit. She was the wholesome type.

"I don't want those phonies there," Alex said.

"Why not? They should be there to support you guys."

"If they wanted to support us, they wouldn't have to be reminded that there's a meet today."

"Suit yourself." Alex had his pride. "What about Joni?"

"I'll think about it."

"Great." Cindy decided if he hadn't asked her out by psychology class, she would invite Joni to the race.

Chapter Two

Alex Jones's physics class was small. He was the only one in it. Biology was usually enough for the students at tiny—five hundred students during a good year—Timber High. A few hardy minds would go so far as to take chemistry, and this year Chem A had eight people in it. But *physics*—there was a limit to how much preparation an adolescent should have to make for college; at least, that was how Alex's contemporaries saw it. But to Alex, the class wasn't even an elective. He planned on applying to an Ivy League school back East—Yale or Princeton—where he knew the competition would be fierce. He'd need all the preparatory education he could scrape together. Nevertheless, he liked physics and probably would have taken it even if he had planned on working in his parents' hardware store for the rest of his life. He'd always been curious about why the universe worked the way it did. He studied his physics texts alone during fourth period. These, with occasional input from Mr. Magnuson, who taught all the science classes, satisfied many of his questions. But next year he was going to see if he could take an advanced psychology class. There were questions about himself he wasn't finding the answers to in the books he was reading.

Alex didn't know why he worried so much. He didn't know why he felt he had to prove himself. When he looked around, no one was asking him to excel. When he had told his parents he'd asked Mr. Magnuson to set up a special physics program for him, they told him to take a fun class, like sculpture or something, and not put so much pressure on himself. What they didn't realize was that sculpture probably would've been more of a headache. His GPA was a big concern to him, and in art and stuff like that he couldn't be sure of getting an A no matter how hard he tried. For example, he was already no longer a candidate for valedictorian the next year. As a sophomore, he had been required to take creative writing, and the teacher, an irritable old lady who didn't understand the difference between what appealed to her and what was good, had given him two Cs. That had dragged his average down a few tenths of a point and had practically handed Ray Bower the top spot on a silver platter.

The thought of Ray filled Alex with double layers of anxiety. Ray was on the cross-country team with him and had been running strongly. Last week, during the time trials to see who'd run on varsity during the first meet, Ray had finished only five seconds behind him in a three-mile race. And the guy hadn't even looked that tired, whereas Alex had felt exhausted. This was particularly worrisome to Alex because of what had happened the previous fall. Through the first part of the season, he had beaten Ray repeatedly. Then he had developed a nasty case of shin splints, where the muscles of the inner shin began to tear away from the bone. This was particularly bad because the injury produced no sign of being there, outside of what he felt in his own pain centers. Alex knew that a few guys on the team had thought it was all in his head. He wouldn't have minded their talk so much if they hadn't been partly right. The injury was there, that was a fact, but it had affected him more than it should have. Subconsciously, he had to admit to himself, he had probably used it as an excuse to take pressure off himself. In either case, Ray had ended up being the most valuable runner on the team, even though—as far as the whole year was concerned—Alex had out-scored him by a large margin. When the vote was taken, the guys' memories had been short.

Alex was also worried about Ray Bower because Mr. Magnuson was having the biology class in the next room choose lab partners, and at the start of class, Ray had been sitting in the back next to Joni. On top of everything else, Ray was a ladies' man. Recently, he had dumped Pam Alta, Cindy's best friend. He was on the prowl.

If Cindy were here she would tell me to get to Joni first.

Alex closed his book, standing. A lot of chatter was coming from biology. That meant the teacher had finished his formal lecture and was letting the kids pair off. Alex stepped through the small equipment area around which the two science rooms were grouped. Mr. Magnuson was inside, taking a hamster out of a cage.

"Alex," the gentleman greeted him, "how are the laws of thermodynamics coming?"

"They seem to be functioning fine, sir, without the benefit of my understanding."

Mr. Magnuson smiled. A pudgy old guy with unkempt gray sideburns that made him look a shade wild, Alex had incorrectly assumed he wasn't serious about what he taught when they'd first met because he had such a jovial personality. In reality, Magnuson was a genuine scientist. Even in hole-in-the-wall Timber, he performed sophisticated immunological experiments on animals. He, in fact, regularly published the results of these experiments in the most prestigious scientific journals in the country. Once, when Alex had asked what he was hoping to discover with all his research, Magnuson had laughed and said, "The secret of immortality, of course!"

"When I get done here," he said, "we can talk about entropy and maybe plan a few practical experiments for you to perform."

"Fine." Alex nodded. "Are you going to kill the hamster?"

Magnuson tied the squirming ball of fur onto a small Formica table that was inclined at a slight slant toward a narrow groove, which was used to drain off the blood into a two-gallon metal tin. "Sorry to say I am. He's already hemorrhaging inside."

"Why?"

"Because of an injection of AT-Seven, an extremely powerful carcinogen, that I gave him two months ago."

Alex occasionally had trouble reconciling the price these little animals had to pay in order to further man's knowledge of disease. But the autopsies never seemed to bother Mr. Magnuson. "I think I'll excuse myself," Alex said, inching toward the biology class.

Magnuson nodded, picking up a scalpel. "Give some of the newcomers inside help with their microscopes, would you? I probably shouldn't have left when I did. I'll be there in a few minutes."

"That's exactly what I was going to do, sir."

Joni wasn't around when Alex entered the class. He was amazed at how much this minor fact caused him to relax. He wasn't looking forward to asking her out. Actually, he was terrified of the prospect. Yet he felt it was something he had to do. She was quite simply the most fascinating thing he had ever seen in his life. He was ninety percent sure she was going to turn him down.

Ray Bower was sitting alone at a corner lab table. Alex wandered over, trying to look casual. Ray brightened at his approach. It was a source of frequent guilt to Alex that Ray didn't realize how much he bugged him. Ray thought they were great friends.

"Looking forward to busting a lung today?" Ray asked as Alex sat down across from him. This was an example of how the dude could get under your skin. The meet that afternoon was all fun and games for him.

"Should be a cake walk," Alex replied. "Brea's got no one who can keep up a five-minute-a-mile pace."

Of course, Timber had two people who could, and looking at Ray, Alex wondered how the guy did it. Ray was on the short side, stout. With his chubby face and long brown hair, he didn't look like an athlete.

"Don't fool yourself." Ray smiled. "I'm going to be on your ass the whole way. Till I pass you at the end, that is."

Alex shrugged. "I always like a good race." He glanced around. "Where's your lab partner?"

"She had to go to her locker."

"She?"

"Joni Harper. You know her."

Damn. Damn. Damn.

"Oh, yeah, Joni. Nice-looking girl."

"Tell me about it. I'm in love with her. You think I should ask her out?"

"Let her get to know you first," Alex muttered, disgusted. He could see it now, a whole year of watching Ray strolling around campus with one arm around Joni and the other around the cross-country trophy.

"I'd rather she got to know me while we were making out in the front seat of my car."

Alex resisted the impulse to grab a nearby bottle of formaldehyde and throw it in Ray's face. "She's a senior, you know."

Ray nodded. "You're right, I'll have to vacuum out the front seat of my car so she'll know I'm no slouch. Oh, here she comes."

Alex turned his head quickly and swallowed. Seeing her again each time, he always had the irrational fear he would discover she wasn't really as he remembered her. She seemed too perfect. Her figure was sleek, and she walked with a fluid grace, an almost animal deftness, that left him bewildered when he glanced up and saw the delicate lines of her sweet red lips, the pale smoothness of her innocent face. She was like a wild lamb, if there was such a creature. Her hair was long, black, and curly. He had stared into her eyes a half-dozen times and still wasn't sure what color they were, only that they were dark.

"Joni, hi," he said stiffly. She nodded and slid into the chair beside Ray, placing a notebook she had been carrying on the countertop. Her long-sleeved green dress looked expensive; it was clasped at the neck with a silver broach of a bird in flight. "How are you today?" he asked.

"Obviously, she's in excellent form." Ray grinned. "Joni and I are going to have a great time this year, aren't we?"

She smiled faintly. "I think so." Her voice, in spite of its soft accent, sounded a bit hoarse. Indeed, each time he had spoken to Joni, he had thought her voice strained, as if she had recently exhausted it singing or something.

"This class can be a lot of fun," Alex said.

"Biology always is," Ray agreed heartily, his sexual innuendo going right by Joni.

"Are you going to be coming into our class regularly, Alex?" she asked.

"I'm supposed to be learning physics during this time." He added awkwardly, "But I'll probably be stopping in on occasion."

"We'll be lucky if he does," Ray said. "Alex's a genius with the kind of stuff we'll be studying."

Ray was being sincere. Had the positions been reversed, Alex wouldn't have wanted Ray stopping in.

Joni's gaze had strayed to the equipment room. "What is our teacher doing in there?"

Magnuson generally didn't reveal the details of his experiments to his average student. "You don't want to know," Alex said.

"He's disemboweling some poor little rabbit, isn't he?" Ray asked with his usual measure of tact.

"Nah," Alex said.

"But I smell blood," Joni said, still eyeing the center room.

Ray stood. "There's only one way to solve this horrible mystery. Let's go see."

"Ray, I really don't think this is the sort of thing Joni wants to see," Alex said hastily.

"Sure she does. Better she know what a murderer Magnuson is right from the start." He took an unprotesting Joni by the arm as she slid off her stool. Alex didn't know what to do but tag along.

They couldn't have picked a worse time to interrupt Magnuson. He had just sliced the animal lengthwise down the chest, and the blood was still draining off. Alex would have left if there hadn't been the distinct possibility Ray would jokingly shout out what a coward he was.

"Not a pretty sight before lunch, I grant you," the teacher remarked, glancing up, apparently unannoyed at their intrusion.

"God, that's disgusting," Ray said. "Mr. Magnuson, I hate to say it, but there's probably a special hell somewhere for those who were cruel to animals."

"I'll send you a postcard if there is, Bower," Magnuson said, used to Ray's ways.

"If you put all the blood back in," Joni said suddenly, "and sewed the animal together, and had everything just the same as before, it wouldn't get up and walk away, would it?"

"If I could get the hamster to do that, I'd be preparing my Nobel prize speech right now," Magnuson said, taking his hands away from the bloody mess and giving Joni more of his attention. "The main obstacle to bringing about that miracle is the sensitivity of the animal's brain cells. Like our own, they can only survive for a few minutes without oxygen. When you take away the blood, you take away the oxygen."

"But if you could fix each of the brain cells?" Joni asked.

"I still don't think the animal would get up and walk away," Magnuson said wistfully. "Something would still be missing. Some sort of precious ingredient. You could call it life itself."

Joni nodded, apparently satisfied with the explanation.

"I think in that hell for animal murderers there'll be some cute bunny with a pitchfork that'll keep shoving you back into a boiling pool of black oil," Ray said.

"I didn't know you were a vegetarian, Bower," Magnuson said.

"I'm not," Ray admitted before he realized that meant he was pretty much in the same boat as the teacher. Then all of them laughed, including Joni, at the ridiculousness of a bunny with a pitchfork.

The bell rang a moment later. Class was over. Alex had left his books in the other room, but he was reluctant to leave Joni alone with Ray in case Ray extended her an invitation to go somewhere in his car. Ray was quick to justify Alex's paranoia as they walked back into the biology class.

"Doing anything this afternoon, Joni?" Ray asked.

Joni stared at him a moment. "I don't think so."

Ray smiled. "Great. Come to the cross-country meet. I'll be running. So will Alex. Having you at the finish line will give us a big incentive to hurry and get there."

Joni seemed uncertain. "We'll see."

"You'll be glad you came," Ray reassured her. He punched Alex in the arm. "See you at the tape, buddy."

"I'll be waiting for you," Alex said. Ray thought that was funny. He laughed as he walked away.

Joni collected her books slowly. She appeared lost in thought. Alex didn't know if it was about the invitation she'd just been extended. He glanced around. The class had emptied quickly, and Magnuson was still in the equipment room with the hamster. Alex was alone with Joni. If he was going to ask her out, he'd have no better opportunity.

"I hope the blood didn't bother you," he said. "I would never have taken you in there."

Joni glanced up. "I should go."

"Okay," he muttered, trying to remember the things Cindy had told him that morning in the car. Naturalness, spontaneity—

"Do you like football g-games?" he stammered.

"Do you play football, too?"

"No."

"I didn't think so," she replied with a slight frown, turning to leave.

"Wait. Joni?"

She paused and faced him, watching, waiting. Her eyes were black, he could see that now. And they had tiny flecks of purple in them. Or maybe those were green flecks. They were such pretty eyes. "Yes?" she said.

"I was just wondering, you know, if you'd like to go?"

"I don't think so."

Alex nodded weakly. "I was just wondering," he repeated.

He should never have listened to his sister. He should have listened to his intuition, which had been telling him all along he would be lonely all his life.

Joni suddenly set down her books and reached out and touched his left shoulder. The feel of her hand on him sent all kinds of strange currents going in his body. "You're nice," she said seriously.

He forced a chuckle. "I think you're nice, too. But if you don't want to go, it's fine, you know. What I mean is, it's no big deal."

She squeezed the top of his arm before letting go. "I'll come to the race," she said.

"Huh?"

"I'll watch you run," she said. "I'd rather do that."

Then she picked up her books and walked away.

I'd better win, Alex thought. He didn't know whether to celebrate or not. In the end, he just worried some more.

Chapter Three

Cindy Jones and Pam Alta were sitting in their favorite spot at their favorite time of day. Set in the northwest corner of Timber High's courtyard was a tree stump from a pine that must have once been the pride of the valley; the thick knob of wood was easily six feet across. What made the stump especially appealing to Cindy and Pam, and which kept practically everyone else away from it, was the fact that the tree had been felled six feet above the ground. Neither of the girls was afraid of heights. They loved the view from their perch, especially at lunchtime, when they could sit and swing their legs in the sun and watch the entire student body bustling beneath them.

At present, Pam was doing more talking than watching. She was raving about Bala, a foreign exchange student from

Kenya. In America for the school year, he was staying at Pam's house. From their Olympian vantage point, they could see Bala standing to the side of the snack-bar line, apparently searching for somebody. Cindy thought he looked like the direct descendent of an exotic African king. Pam was already in love with him.

"He's so polite," Pam said. "He says 'please' and 'thank you' when you ask him what's new. Last night at the dinner table, when I finished my milk, he immediately jumped up and got the carton from the fridge, just in case I wanted some more. I hadn't even said I wanted more. You know, Cindy, how I only drink milk 'cause of all those doctors on TV talking about calcium deficiencies and your bones falling apart when you turn thirty. I really can't stand the stuff. So what could I do? Here he's flown halfway around the world to serve me milk, and I don't want any more? Nah, I just couldn't turn him down. I ended up polishing off another couple of glasses."

"Bad for your wind," Cindy muttered, spooning down a cup of strawberry yogurt.

"What?"

"Nothing."

Pam stopped and thought a moment. "You know what's bothering me about this whole relationship?"

"That it doesn't really exist?"

"No. That it's kind of incestuous."

"Bala's visiting for a while. He's not your brother." Cindy

laughed when she thought about it some more. "God, he's six and a half feet tall. You look like someone stepped on you. Anyway, he's black. How could you even imagine you were related?"

Pam was reassured. "So you think I should make a pass at him?"

Cindy raised an interested eyebrow. Pam was no one's choice for Miss Timber. She looked too much like her old boyfriend, Ray Bower. She was a head shorter than Cindy and her backside was chunky. She also had a big nose. Yet Pam somehow avoided being a dog, and Cindy thought it was because she always seemed so ready for a good time. She was not all talk, not when it came to sex. Every time she'd been alone with Ray, Cindy had received a full report. It was no wonder Alex was having trouble beating Ray if half the stories Pam said were true. The guy had endurance.

Cindy was still a virgin. Pam thought the condition was akin to having bad acne. Cindy was in no special hurry. Not this very minute, anyway.

"I don't see why you shouldn't make one," Cindy said.

"I don't know. It would be neat to walk around campus with him holding my hand. Then hopefully Ray would see what a woman of international appeal he'd given up."

Cindy noted Pam's choice of words—*"he'd given up."* Initially, Pam had tried to lead people to believe she'd dumped Ray, and not vice versa. For a few weeks there, happy-go-lucky

Pam had been one miserable dog. Only Cindy knew how much she still wanted him back.

Pam changed the subject. "Have you seen Jason today?"

Cindy felt a stab of uneasiness. "No. Have you?"

Pam nodded. "He's breathing fire."

"That damn article. You read it, too?"

"The whole school read it."

"It's just a bunch of crap," Cindy said defensively. "Kent Cooke's only using Jason to get at Mr. Whitfield. You didn't believe any of it, did you?"

"I believe the part where Karen died."

"Pam!"

"All right, don't get excited. No, I didn't believe that Jason suddenly developed a grizzly's strength and tore Karen apart. Or that he had a sledgehammer hiding in the bushes. None of the other kids does, either. But Cooke makes one point I think most of the school *does* believe. Jason's not being totally up front about everything that went down that night."

"Be specific," Cindy said in an even tone.

"I can't be," Pam said, looking genuinely puzzled. "But he took her up there at night. You'd think he could've looked after her better."

This was a familiar point of view. In the days following the funeral, Cindy had heard it discussed in bits and snatches by the townsfolk when she'd been working at her parents' hardware store. Since, at the time, she hadn't been going out with Jason, she hadn't given the talk much heed. But even then it had struck her as unfair. The end result was that he was seen as a coward. Why hadn't he done something, for god's sake? People would gossip to one another. He was *the man,* after all. Of course, they never said what he could have done.

"Swell," Cindy muttered. "You pick any guy in the school and put him in a cage with you and a grizzly and we'll see how well he protects you. I bet you wouldn't even find a guy who'd have the guts to try to hit the bear with a stick."

"Exactly. None of us think Jason hit his grizzly with a stick. The common consensus is he took one look at the beast and put his ass in gear. That's what I would have done."

"Then how can you accuse Jason of being a coward?"

"'Cause I'm a coward, myself. Look, don't get all bent out of shape. I'm just telling you what people are saying. I still think Jason's a babe, and I think you should try to make him a happy man one of these nights soon." She added, "What are you guys doing tonight after the game?"

"I don't know. We might be going out with Alex and Joni Harper." She hadn't seen Alex since they'd parted in the parking lot that morning, although she had searched for him at the beginning of lunch. There was a lot of stuff they'd done in Algebra II that wasn't clicking. Her brother was always so much better at explaining things than her math teacher. He had a lot more patience. And she'd wanted to see if he really had asked Joni out.

Despite what she'd said in the car, she was worried Joni might turn him down. But she hadn't been able to find him. He often went for a walk at lunch on race days.

"Alex asked Joni out?" Pam said. "That's great. That's absolutely wonderful. I'm happy for him. She's a doll."

Cindy looked at her suspiciously. Her enthusiasm was out of place, even though Pam really did like Alex. Last year, she had gone to every one of the cross-country races and shouted her support for him instead of Ray, despite the fact Ray was her boyfriend at the time. Her kind remark about Joni was what lacked sincerity. Ray had broken up with her not long after Joni had appeared in town, and Pam had insinuated several times that Joni was partly responsible. This appeared to be nothing but pure paranoia.

Before she could respond to Pam's comment, she noticed Bala walking away from the snack bar in the company of Joni. Apparently, Joni was the one he had been waiting for. Watching them together, Cindy was strangely affected. Her mind started to draw a connection her eyes could not support. Bala was a powerfully built black guy. Joni was a trim fair-skinned girl. Yet in some way, they looked the same to her, somehow closely related. The impression seemed to emerge from the way they moved. Cindy couldn't pinpoint it any closer than that. Indeed, a moment later, she was wondering what had caused her to find a similarity at all. They were both new, she told herself, that's what they had in common. That was all. Bala's walk was completely different from Joni's. She had to take two steps to his one.

"I didn't know Bala knew Joni," Cindy said.

"He was here only a couple of days when they met. I got the impression Joni wasn't crazy about him. Bala was going too far out of the way to be nice to her—even by his standards. And that's saying a lot."

"How did they meet?" Cindy asked. Bala was smiling, talking freely. Joni was chewing on an apple, nodding occasionally.

"I don't remember. Maybe Karen brought her over. Karen and Joni were pretty good friends."

"Really? How did that get started?"

"They lived next door to each other. I think Karen sought her out. Once she saw how beautiful Joni was, I think she figured she'd better get on her good side. But then Karen seemed to end up really liking her."

Pam's observation about Joni's lack of interest in Bala appeared correct. Already, Joni seemed to be trying to break off her conversation with him. A moment later she did so, walking away with her apple, leaving Bala staring at her back.

"Let's go talk to him," Cindy said, collecting her lunch bag.

"Bala? Why?"

"Because I want to, that's why."

They climbed down from the tall stump and headed through the mass of loitering students. Cindy could feel her pulse quickening. This wouldn't be the first time she had spoken to Bala.

They had talked on several occasions during the last few weeks, usually when she was visiting Pam at her house. She'd been doing more of that lately, going over to see Pam, or maybe Bala himself, if she wanted to be entirely honest with herself. He held a totally new attraction for her. A minute ago she had compared him in her mind to a king. There was something noble in his demeanor. Yet his real allure for her was something more abstract, something she had yet to figure out. He seemed more than human, as if he were surrounded by a magnetic aura.

Pam had no idea Cindy felt this way. And it wasn't as though it would ever go anywhere. Jason was her boyfriend and he was the mayor's son and Bala was just a beautiful body passing through on his way back to Africa.

I'm so superficial.

Bala greeted them with a bright smile. "Good afternoon, girls," he said in his deep voice, a velvety concoction of back bush accent and impeccable British English. She briefly wondered if the accent similarities had triggered her association between him and Joni.

"Hello, Bala." Pam smiled. "Cindy wants to ask you something."

"Yes, Cindy?"

Talking to Bala, she always had to incline her head toward the heavens. This didn't add to her confidence around him. "Yeah," she muttered, "I wanted to ask if you had—ah, a last name. And how you spell it?" Pam was always pulling pranks like this on her.

"I have several last names. One relates to the tribe I am part of. We are called the Mau Dogan. Another is what you would call my family name. It is Retala."

"So your full name is Mr. Bala Mau Dogan Retala?" Pam said.

Bala smiled. "Bairavee Bala Retala of Mau Dogan is closer."

"Where's the Bairavee come from?" Cindy asked.

Bala hesitated a moment before answering. "I am directly descended from a shaman, or what you might know as a sorcerer. My grandfather is considered a mighty shaman. As a show of respect for him, my people call him Bairavee. This can't be translated directly into English. It means approximately "he who gathers the soul." Because we are related, I am also sometimes called Bairavee."

"I'll just call you Bala," Pam said. "But you better write down all those names for Cindy 'cause she is *so* curious about how they're spelled."

Bala looked doubtful. "Is this important to you, Cindy?"

"You don't have to bother," Cindy said, intrigued with his reference to shamanism.

"It is no bother at all," Bala said, taking a pencil from his back pocket, searching for something to write on. "In my fascination with all aspects of your lives, I forget my cultural background must be as intriguing to you."

"Everything must be completely different for you," Cindy

said, handing him a scrap of paper torn from her lunch bag. His command of their language never ceased to amaze her. It was as though he had been born to it. "Don't you feel homesick?"

"In many ways, I feel more at home in your country than in mine. You do not realize how fortunate you are. Reason predominates here. People do not decide what they are going to do next because of the ways the birds arranged the leaves on the ground in the morning. My tribe is sunk in superstition. I have rebelled against it all my life."

"Is that why you were chosen to be a foreign exchange student?" Cindy asked.

The question seemed to catch Bala off guard. He didn't answer immediately, and then they were interrupted by Jason. The timing was unfortunate. It looked like she had just asked Bala for his phone number. Jason apparently saw it that way.

"Hey, what's going on here?" he asked, trying to sound only mildly interested, unable to hide the edge in his voice.

"We're picking names for Christmas gifts," Pam said. "Cindy's got to get Bala something."

"Jason, you know Bala, don't you?" Cindy said quickly. "Bala this is my—friend, Jason Whitfield."

Friend, not boyfriend. What am I thinking?

"Pleased to meet you," Bala said, extending his hand. Jason was six feet tall and no sissy, but his fingers almost disappeared in Bala's grip.

"Yeah, I've seen you around," Jason said. He turned to Cindy. "But where have you been? I've been looking all over for you."

"She's been with me," Pam said.

Jason glanced at his watch. It was Swiss, and if he was ever down on his luck and had to hock it, he would have food to eat for a long time. "The bell's going to ring in a few minutes," he said. "Let's go out to the parking lot. I want to talk."

"I'll see you both in psychology," Cindy called over her shoulder as she hurried to catch up with Jason, who was already walking away. There was no doubt about it, he was in a foul mood.

They didn't speak until they were out in the lot and standing next to Jason's new motorbike. He'd once gotten it up to a hundred with her on the back, and she hadn't spoken to him for two days. He only purchased the cycle after Karen had died. He always drove like a nut, which worried her. It was as though he were trying to show people he wasn't scared of anything.

"I read it," she said, deciding to get right to the problem. "It was so unfair."

Jason sucked in a breath and Cindy braced herself for an abusive tirade directed at Kent Cooke and possibly the rest of Timber. But he held his breath a moment and then let it out slowly, turning in the direction of Castle Park. The waterfall wasn't visible but she imagined he could see it, anyway, in his memory, running with red waters. He sighed, now looking more sad than bitter. She wanted to hug and comfort him but hesitated for reasons that were themselves unfair. His sorrow looked somehow incongruous on his black-haired, gray-eyed movie star face. Jason was the kid who'd had everything: the best-looking girl in the school, an expensive sports car, and a carefree future fat with daddy's money. But now he had lost the respect of his peers, and that he couldn't buy back. And he knew it.

"Thank you," he said finally. "I think those were the first kind words I've heard all day."

"Aren't the guys on the team rallying around you?" Jason was the school's starting fullback. He was pretty good.

"Yes and no," he said, looking at her. "They'll come up and say something supportive and then they'll have to add a little joke about bears or bumps on the head. You know what bugs me the most about that article? It was the phony pain that jerk tried to make you think he felt over Karen's death. But he didn't know her. He didn't feel a damn thing when he heard she was dead, except the satisfaction that Carl Whitfield's son was involved."

She put an arm around his shoulders. "After the hearing next Monday, when the facts are reviewed by the court, everyone will see you did everything you could."

"I wished I believed that," he said, shaking his head. "No, I think something's got to be done."

"There's nothing you can do. You did all you could that night. You've got to get on with your life."

He stared at her for a moment. "Let's go up there tonight."

"Where? Up to the top of the falls?"

"Yeah, after the game. It'll still be early."

"But—why?"

"I haven't been up there since Karen died. I need to go. I need to get something out of my system. Will you come with me?"

"But my brother was going to ask this girl out. I thought maybe we could do something with them. He's never gone out with a girl before, and I think he could use the moral support."

"We could bring him and his date along."

"You wouldn't mind?"

"No, I always like having Alex around. He's a good kid."

Cindy considered a moment. "Do you think it would be safe?"

"The chances of the grizzly still being around is about one in ten thousand. Will you come?"

The area around the top of the waterfall had always been one of her favorite places. But like Jason, she had stayed away from there since Karen had died. Psychologically, for him especially, there might be a value in returning to the spot. It would be like confronting the problem head on, she reasoned.

"Sure, I'll go with you. And if you want just the two of us

to go, that would be okay. Alex might want to be alone with the girl, anyway."

Jason leaned over and gave her a quick kiss. "Thanks. You're the only friend I have. But invite your brother. I want him there. Who's his girl?"

"Well, she's not really his yet. But he's working on it. Her name's Joni Harper. Do you know her?"

"I've seen her."

"She's pretty, isn't she?"

"Not next to you," he said, kissing her again on the cheek, before throwing his leg over his motorcycle. He gunned the engine. In the distance, she could hear the bell ringing, signaling the end of lunch.

"Are you ditching?" she asked.

"Yeah, got some stuff I've got to take care of."

"What?"

"Just some stuff."

"That's too bad. I was hoping you could come to Alex's race after school."

Jason showed interest. "Ray Bower's running against him, isn't he?"

"Yeah."

Jason gunned the engine again, his eyes cold. "Tell Alex for me I hope he kicks Ray's ass. You know how the article said Ray remembered me 'cause I ridiculed his haircut? That really pissed me off. I've known Ray since we were ten years old. And that night, I didn't say a blessed thing about his haircut. Ray just told Kent Cooke that so the two of them could establish right away in the reader's mind what a violent dude I am." Jason shook his head. "Ray's got some real bad luck coming to him."

"He's just got a weird sense of humor. He went with Pam for too long." She patted him on the back, trying to sound cheery. "If I don't see you before the game tonight, score five touchdowns for me."

He nodded grimly. "I think tonight's going to be a good night."

She waved as he drove away, still curious about where he was going. Jason never ditched.

Miss Clemens taught psychology. She was young, had large breasts, and often bent over in her short skirts. All the boys liked her, and most of the girls, including Cindy, who had observed with an appreciative eye all the times Miss Clemens had counseled the kids that were going through rough times.

Cindy arrived at class a few minutes late and took a seat across from Joni, who didn't turn to acknowledge her. Cindy took that as a sign Alex hadn't asked her out. It seemed to her most girls would give some reaction to the sister of a guy who had just approached them.

Miss Clemens was apparently introducing Bala as a speaker. She wanted him to discuss how daily life in his village differed from life in Timber. Cindy thought this a fortunate coincidence. She could finish the conversation she'd started at lunch without fear Pam would try to embarrass her.

"Unless you have something in particular you'd like to begin with," Miss Clemens said, sitting behind her desk, which always frustrated the guys' view of her fine legs, "you could start by accepting questions."

She was trying to relax Bala, which was obviously unnecessary. He sat up front on a stool, and it was as if, without speaking, he already had command of the room. His size alone wasn't responsible for creating the effect, Cindy thought. There was something else.

Bairavee Bala.

"I would appreciate any question," he said softly. Pam immediately raised her hand. Bala smiled. "Yes, Pam?"

"Do all the guys in your village look like you?"

"We are all black," he replied with a straight face.

The room broke up. Bala smiled again. Another hand was raised. "Could you tell us exactly where your village is in relationship to Kenya's big cities, how many people it holds, and what degree of Western influence you guys get?" a fellow named Ken asked.

"Those are good questions. Mau Dogan is sixty miles west of Nairobi, the capital of the country. Until ten years ago, our population was close to two thousand. But with the famine we've been having, we're down to less than half that. Our main source of Western influence has been a doctor and his wife. His name was Herbert Stevens and he used to care for the people of our village and those in neighboring villages. It was his wife who taught me how to speak English. Her name was Valerie. I was a favorite of hers. She used to get me tapes and books." He added quietly, "But they don't live in Mau Dogan anymore."

"The drought must have been hard on your people," Miss Clemens said sympathetically. Bala responded in a surprising fashion. His voice took on a stern note.

"It was, but it was largely our fault. We had plenty of water. It was right beneath us. All we had to do was dig wells and develop storage facilities. Do not misunderstand me, not all of Africa could have escaped the effects of the drought so easily. But we could have. We just would not listen to Dr. Stevens and other representatives of UNICEF. We had our 'customs' that said you could anger the soil by digging too deeply into it."

"But these customs must be deeply ingrained in the psyche of your people," Miss Clemens said. "It must be difficult to overcome them."

Bala would have none of this rationalization. "It was more difficult for my people to die," he said.

Cindy raised her hand. Bala nodded in her direction. "Do some of these old-fashioned ideas come from the shaman in your village?" she asked.

Bala hesitated and Cindy recognized why. She had, after all, just asked about his grandfather. "Yes."

"But doesn't this person know things that, say, a Western doctor has no knowledge of?" Cindy asked.

"Maybe," he answered reluctantly.

"You're not sure?" she asked, surprised.

"I am not."

"Could you give us an example of abilities or knowledge your shaman *might* possess that we would consider extraordinary?" She'd always had a deep fascination with things mystical. Alex said it was because she didn't realize how interesting science could be. She thought her interest sprang from the realization of how much scientists didn't know.

Bala scanned the room. He appeared to come to a decision. "Very well. At lunch I told you our shaman is referred to as Bairavee, 'he who gathers the soul.' Our Bairavee has given demonstrations where he has taken a person, a young boy, and put him in a trance by chanting softly in his ear. When the boy was ready, an animal was tied directly in front of him. The choice of animal varied. Sometimes it was a monkey, sometimes it was a snake or a lion. Once even a fish held in a bowl of water was used. Then our Bairavee used an ability people in the West definitely do not have. He put the *animal* in a trance, using a different sort of chant. This was only the beginning. With the boy and animal staring into each other's eyes, our Bairavee— you will have trouble believing this and I can understand how you feel—transferred their spirits. The spirit of the animal went into the boy, and the spirit of the boy went into the animal. The experience of the boy was that he was indeed in the animal. If a lion was being used, he would feel the strength of the lion's claws, even understand what it was like to *think* like a lion. But at all times he never lost the awareness he was still a boy. Therefore, I suppose you could not call it a complete transfer, but a merger of some type. Of course, how the animal felt during these demonstrations, I could not say."

"That's nothing new to us," Pam said. "Merlin was doing that to Arthur centuries ago."

There were a few chuckles, not many. Bala was apparently unaware of the reference. "Pardon?" he said politely.

"Never mind her," Miss Clemens said. "Bala, were there any side effects from these *spirit journeys,* or whatever you want to call them, on the people who went into the animals?"

"The boy did not feel he'd been harmed in any way," Bala said carefully.

"Did he feel he'd grown from the experience?" Cindy asked, not bothering to raise her hand.

"I do not understand," Bala said.

"Did he take away with him a better understanding of what it was like to be the animal he'd just gone into?" she asked.

Bala was beginning to look as if he wished he had never brought up the subject. "To be frank, I cannot say if these experiences were anything more than hallucinations brought on by an elaborate form of hypnosis."

"Do *you* think it was only hypnosis?" she asked.

Bala looked down. "Yes."

The subject was changed. Someone asked for details on the relief efforts being made throughout Africa. Bala answered with more enthusiasm than he had shown for sorcery. Cindy's mind began to wander. She was worried about starving children, but at the moment the topic just didn't fire her imagination. She wondered what it would be like to go into an eagle and soar high above the mountains. One day, she thought, she'd like to meet Bala's grandfather. "Hypnosis" was a convenient word she felt was too often used to explain the inexplicable.

When the bell rang at the end of class, Pam hurried to Bala's side and threw Cindy a look that said she wanted to be alone with him. Maybe she did know, Cindy thought, about a "certain someone's" attraction to him. Oh, well, that was life in relationship lane.

She remembered her self-made promise to invite Joni to the race. The English girl sure could move. Cindy only caught up with her after Joni had made it halfway across the courtyard.

"Joni," she called. The girl slowed and glanced her way. "You remember me, Cindy Jones?"

Joni nodded. "You're Alex's sister." A slight smile touched the corners of her mouth, but her large black eyes remained impassive.

"That's right." No sense beating around the bush. "Did you know Alex has an important race today?"

"Yes. I'll see you there."

"You're coming?"

"Yes."

"Do you know where it is?"

"Yes," Joni said, returning to her original pace. Cindy slowed to a halt.

"Great," she called.

Joni nodded without turning around.

Chapter Four

Their warm-up was complete. The race started in less than ten minutes. And Ray Bower was eating a package of Hostess miniature chocolate doughnuts and drinking a carton of milk.

"I need the sugar to fuel my body for the upcoming ordeal," Ray said when Alex warned him he would probably cramp. "Besides, I'm hungry." He offered him a doughnut. "Are you sure you don't want one?"

"I'll pass," Alex said, feeling he might be the one who was getting a cramp. He had a minor stitch in his left side, under his rib cage. But he had to wonder if he didn't usually have a bit of tightness there, that he wasn't simply making an issue of it because this was the first race of the year.

Alex scanned the stadium field for Joni Harper, and didn't

see her, feeling as relieved as he did disappointed. He did catch sight of his sister, however, and Pam. They were standing next to the bleachers, not far from where the exhausted junior varsity were finishing. He had no reservations about their presence. Cindy was still wearing her uniform, naturally; she was required to wear it the whole day before a game. She was the only one from the squad who had taken the time to come. That was fine with him. Most of those rah-rah girls had about as much upstairs as a Ping-Pong ball. That was what he liked about Joni. She didn't talk much, but there was obviously a lot going on behind those deep black eyes. He searched again for her.

"Looking for Joni?" Ray asked, stuffing a doughnut in his mouth.

"No."

Ray took a swig of milk, spilling several drops on his gold warm-up jacket. "I wish she was here."

"And what if you run badly?"

"If I do, so what? It won't change a hair on her great body." He crumpled up his doughnut wrapper, showing a trace of disappointment that they were all gone. "Besides, I'm probably going to win."

Alex nodded toward the finish line. "Our JV's sure getting their butts kicked. Brea's stronger this year."

"Nah. They're probably running their varsity now. We'll have no problem." He laughed. "I can't wait to hear Pam screaming for me to trip. I'm glad she's here." He paused. "You know, Alex, I think I'm going to try to get back together with her. I really miss her whining in my ear."

"Then what's all this talk about Joni?"

"Joni's a fantasy. I'm going to ask her out. I'm going to try to get her in the sack. I think it would make my junior year. But I could never have her as a girlfriend."

Alex was curious in spite of the disgust he felt at how casually Ray could talk about having sex with someone he felt he would have been willing to give his life for. "Why not?" he asked.

"She's too different from me. She's too refined. I can't see laying around the house and watching TV with her. Can you?"

"I don't watch much TV," Alex said. "So why even ask her out if you feel this way?"

"I can't help myself. She's cast a spell on me. Just once, I've got to know what that soft white skin feels like under my fingers." He stopped, squinted at him. "As long as that's okay with you, buddy?"

The question caught Alex off balance. Was Ray serious? Of course he was, the blind fool. He would back off if asked. But Alex realized he could never ask. He couldn't admit he was unwilling to compete fairly with Ray in this area any more than he could ask Ray not to race against him to his fullest ability.

"I don't give a damn what you do with your hairy fingers," he said.

Ray smiled. "I'll shave them before our date."

A few minutes later the last of the JV runners staggered in. They had been crushed. Alex took it as a bad sign. Cindy and Pam walked over to give him a last word of encouragement.

"How do you feel?" his sister asked, brushing a hair off his shoulder.

"He's not very hungry, that's for sure," Ray said, finishing his milk.

"I hope you barf those doughnuts up all over yourself at the second mile," Pam told Ray.

"I feel strong," Alex lied.

"Varsity!" the starter, Brea's coach, called. Their own coach was stationed at the midway point, where he would be giving them one of the split times.

"Just do your best," Cindy said seriously, giving him a kiss on the cheek. "That's all you have to do."

"Where's my kiss?" Ray asked Pam, belching.

Pam whacked him on the top of the thigh. "There's a charley horse to slow you down."

"See you in less than fifteen minutes," Alex told Cindy, referring to the time he planned to break, his throat bone dry. He almost wished he could have had a sip of Ray's milk.

They gathered at the starting line, pulling off their sweats. "Ready!" the coach shouted, raising the gun toward the sky. Alex crouched down, taking a deep breath.

"Hey, I forgot to tie my right shoe," Ray said casually.

The gun went off and Alex sprung forward with the crowd. It was a jumbled start, which was often the case at the beginning of the season, with runners bumping into one another. As Alex hurried down the first straightaway of the track, before exiting the stadium, he was distracted by a thin dark-haired girl standing in center field.

Joni.

A Brea runner, a tall blond Alex did not recognize from last year, set the pace. It was fast. Staying with him, Alex could feel the rest of the pack falling back. He didn't know what Ray was doing and wondered if he had stopped to tie his shoe. A quick glance over his shoulder told Alex nothing.

The course was three miles long and it was rough. It led out the rear of the school onto a dirt path that wound through the forest for two miles, following an initial gradual downgrade before slamming into two steep hills. The last mile consisted of a loop around the school, with the finish in the stadium.

As they passed into the shade of the trees, Alex wondered if he wasn't making a mistake. He knew he was going too fast too early. What he didn't know was if the guy he was following was going to burn out or keep up this pace till the end. Because the guy was not familiar, he thought it prudent to stay close in case he was an iron lung new to Brea High. On the other hand, if that were the situation, he probably couldn't beat the guy, anyway, and he would just be setting himself up for his own burn-out, virtually assuring Ray second place.

When they reached the first mile, Alex knew for a fact he had chosen the wrong strategy. The time was four minutes and forty-two seconds. He was eighteen seconds under his pace! Plus the blond-haired dude was already faltering. Alex passed him as the path dipped into a grassy meadow and the sun glared from behind the tree branches. He risked another brief glance over his shoulder, but didn't see Ray. That counted for nothing. With the turns in the path, Ray could be five seconds back and he'd never know it until too late.

With his running companion slipping behind, Alex tried to will himself into his usual rhythm, without much success. He was breathing too hard; he felt as if he had already tackled the hills, and it depressed him to know that they were still to come.

Coach Tyler was waiting at the midpoint with his scratchy voice and ticking stopwatch. "You're looking good, Alex," he called. "Seven-seventeen—seven-eighteen—Looking good."

The man was gone in a blur. That was the trouble with people who were there to support you. They couldn't take away a morsel of fatigue. Coach Tyler always said he was looking good, even when he was dying inside. The time was all that was important. He was still pushing too hard too soon. And, God, did his body know it. Stinging sweat dripped into his eyes. A cramp began to form in his *right* side.

The first hill was upon him a minute later. Leaning forward slightly, he drove with his arms. He wasn't a good hill runner. Ray, with his short legs, was better. Nearing the top, Alex could feel a heavy lactic acid debt accumulating in his shoulders, spreading into his arms. He was literally gasping for air. At least now he would be able to see where he stood. For the third time, he threw a glance behind. But what caught his attention was not the other runners, but a bank of thick black clouds gripping the mountains behind Castle Park. Lightning sparked in their midst and he spotted a hazy band of shadow shifting over the peaks. Rain was falling heavy up there. By tonight, Crystal Falls would be gorged.

Alex shifted his gaze to the path he had just covered. What he saw was not totally unexpected, and yet, he was shocked. Ray was at the foot of the hill. And the blond dude hadn't faded much at all; he was on Ray's shoulder. Alex had at best fifteen seconds on them. That should have been a lot with just over a mile to go. But with the lead in his legs, a minute lead wasn't safe.

Why do I put myself through this?

Joni and Cindy were waiting for him at the finish line, that was why. He plowed forward.

The second hill, shorter and steeper, did not drain him as badly as he'd feared. Indeed, as he emerged from the forest and raced along the sidewalk at the west side of the school, hearing shouts of encouragement from the stadium above, he began to believe he might pull it off. He was still running against steadily increasing fatigue but he suddenly felt more in sync. His wind had settled into a decent rhythm.

The stadium was close at hand but before he could enter it he had to head away from it for a couple of minutes. At the southwest corner of the school, he plunged into the campus proper, racing along a path that had been cleared of traffic by other members of the team. Their shouts mixed with the echoing pounding of his feet. Someone called out that his lead was seventeen seconds.

He was rounding the gym when disaster struck. Two cheerleaders were painting a poster for the night's game directly on top of the gold chalk line that marked the course. Maybe his teammates had forgotten to tell them to move. Maybe the girls had figured the geeks on the cross-country team should run around them. It didn't really matter. He saw them too late. His left foot caught on one girl's arm. His right foot slipped on the drying blue poster paint. He didn't have a chance to brace his fall with his hands. He hit the asphalt hard, his left knee taking the brunt of the impact.

"We're sorry!" one of the redfaced girls cried as he rolled on his belly and tried to get to his feet. He wasn't angry, not yet. His left leg was stinging something awful. A wad of flesh had been scraped away. Blood oozed from the cut. He had to get going.

The fall had an insidious effect on him, but not because of the physical damage it had done or the time it had stolen from his lead. Back in stride, he realized the wound was superficial. It looked nasty but it hadn't weakened his strength. Also, between going down and getting up, he had sacrificed at best five seconds. No, his problem was with the excuse the fall had given him, and the one half of his personality that was always looking for an excuse so he wouldn't have to feel so much pressure. By no means did he intend to quit. He still wanted to win just as badly. The only real difference inside was he began to entertain the thought of saving his strength for the finish. He was nearly exhausted. The cramp in his right side felt like an appendix ready to burst. Suddenly it seemed wiser to play it conservative. Besides, no one would question his slowing down after such a terrible fall. It was really quite simple, as simple and handy as the shin splints had been last year. He slacked his pace a notch.

But you're not hurt! You only have to gut it out for another two minutes! Joni is here!

It was strange how what was surely his stronger side wasn't nearly as persuasive. He eased back some more, taking a welcome breather.

Ray caught and passed him a hundred yards before the stadium, and with him, the tall blond. He watched them go by with a mixture of detachment and despair. Their lead widened as they ran onto the track and began to round toward the finish line. He watched and did nothing till he saw Joni standing beside Cindy and Pam in the center of the football field. Cindy and Pam were bouncing up and down and screaming at the top of their lungs. Joni had her hands clasped behind her back.

She was not yelling or moving. And yet, he could feel her eyes on him. He remembered what it had been like to stare into them that morning. Such pretty eyes, watching him lose.

Now, you idiot!

Alex accelerated sharply, a rising panic flushing every trace of fatigue from his limbs and every indecisive thought from his mind. He realized the precariousness of his situation. How could he have squandered a hundred-yard lead! But all was not lost. Ray had thirty yards on him, the blond twenty. Alex had a superb kick. He had half a lap to close the gap.

He almost made it. Had the course been a few yards longer, he would have won. He had burst past the guy from Brea and was close enough to reach out and touch the tape when Ray hit it. He stumbled against Ray's back and slipped around him as they went into the chute. The girl at the end of the flimsy funnel handed him the number one position stick. She probably thought he had won. He took a look at it and broke it in half.

"Nice race, buddy," Ray said, bent over, sweat pouring off his brow. "Can't believe you finished after going down like that."

"Yeah," Alex croaked, his heart shrieking in his chest. He wanted to congratulate Ray on his outstanding victory. But he didn't know if he could bear the sound of the words.

Ray coughed and straightened. Hands patted him on the back, lines of praise flowing over him. He glanced around with a big smile on his face. "I hope they have another pack of doughnuts in the machine by the snack bar. I'm starving. Hey, Alex, want to go eat somewhere after we shower?"

Alex shook his head and walked away. The entire lower half of his left leg was covered with blood. In the days to come the whole school would probably talk of how Alex Jones rose from the dead to finish the race. What heart. What a man. What a bunch of crap.

"Alex?" Cindy said, hurrying to his side, pain in her voice. He wouldn't look at her. "Stop, let me see your leg. Oh, Lord, you've got to get to the hospital. Alex!"

"I'm all right."

She tried to grab his arm. He shook her off. "What's wrong with you?" she pleaded.

He stopped, stared her in the eye. "I'm a loser."

Her mouth dropped open in amazement. "I saw how you got tripped. Those silly bitches were right in your way! It's a miracle you were able to finish."

"Right, a miraculous second place."

"Listen, Alex, you did the best you could. You were amazing, you really were. But now you need to get to a doctor."

"My leg is fine, Cindy," he said bitterly. "It's my head that needs a doctor."

He ignored her cries for him to come back and left the school through a hole in the fence, walking into the woods where he could despise himself in private. Beside a tall fern, he plopped down and buried his face in his arms.

He was sitting there for approximately twenty minutes when he felt a warm hand touch his injured leg. He looked up, expecting to see his sister. Instead, he found himself staring into a wide-open pair of dark eyes.

"Joni," he muttered, surprised.

She took a new, clean white handkerchief from her pocket and began to wrap it around his cut. "Your sister wants you to have this cared for," she said.

"Did Cindy send you here?"

"No."

"Then—why are you here?"

Joni sat back on her legs. She had changed into a plain white T-shirt and red pants. Her long black hair was tied up in a ponytail. There was blood on her right hand from where she had touched him. "I enjoyed watching you run, Alex."

He lowered his gaze. "I hope you didn't enjoy watching me lose."

"I think you run better when you are chasing than when you are being chased."

He raised his head. "Huh?"

Joni smiled, her top teeth playing over her lower lip. "You should be the hunter, not the hunted."

"You mean, I shouldn't try to run in front?" He'd always done that. It was his style.

"Yes. I think you're going to win next week."

He brightened. "Maybe I will."

Joni touched his hand, squeezed it gently. Her skin was soft and warm. "Do you like me?" she asked shyly.

He blushed. "Yeah."

Joni nodded to herself, suddenly serious. "I thought so."

"Do you like me?" he asked, astounding himself.

She paused, stared at him intently for a moment. The flecks in her eyes seemed to have changed color from that morning. "Yes."

Alex began to forget about the race and the end of the world and other such nonsense. "Would you like to go to the game with me tonight?"

She pulled back slightly, glanced in the direction of the school. Alex had the impression she was considering Cindy before deciding how to answer. Her lower lip trembled slightly. "I do like you, Alex," she said.

He laughed. "Then we should go to the game together."

She hesitated. "It would be all right?"

"Sure. It would be fun."

Her smile returned. "Good."

Chapter Five

In the end Alex let Cindy take him to the emergency ward at Timber Memorial. He did so only under the condition she not tell their mother. His mom freaked when the least little thing happened to him. He was her baby. He never could understand why she didn't worry about Cindy in the same way.

A Dr. Harry Free put eight stitches in his knee. Cindy stayed in the room during the entire procedure—she had a strong stomach—and Alex kept his eyes glued to the ceiling. Had he not been going out with Joni that night, he probably would have gotten depressed by the whole situation. As it was, he felt fine.

The fee was one hundred and fifty dollars for twenty minutes of treatment. Their family had insurance, but they opted against using it; their parents could find out that way about his fall. Cindy had to dash over to their bank to get the dough. They were lucky it was Friday and the bank was still open. They both had solid savings accounts; their parents paid them hefty allowances for all the time they put in at the hardware store. But Cindy used her own money, insisting he didn't have to pay her back. She was real excited about his going out with Joni. When they left the hospital, they stopped at Peter's Pants, where she bought him a new shirt and pair of slacks, again using her own money. She jokingly told him that he had better get some "action" from Joni after all this trouble.

Cindy also mentioned the possibility of Joni and him accompanying Jason and herself up to Crystal Falls that evening. He wasn't enthusiastic about the idea. He didn't care for Jason, though he didn't know why exactly. Certainly, he didn't believe Jason had been responsible for Karen Holly's death. There was just something about the guy that didn't feel genuine. To dissuade Cindy, he told her about the thundershowers he had spotted way back in the mountains. She'd tell Jason about that, she said. Maybe he wouldn't want to go, after all.

The game started at six. He'd told Joni he'd pick her up at five-thirty. They didn't get back to the house until close to five. He barely had time to run into the house, stuff a roast beef sandwich in his mouth, brush his teeth, and throw on his new clothes. Cindy would be getting a ride with Pam.

"Don't treat her like she's a goddess," she warned him as he went to drive away. He assured her he'd be cool.

He was shaking when he got to the address Joni had given him. Less than two hours had gone by since he'd last seen her, and he was worrying she'd changed her mind. His leg ached as he stepped up to the front door.

You should be the hunter, not the hunted.

A kindly grandmother type answered the door.

"Mrs. Harper?" She was old to be Joni's mother.

The lady smiled. "I'm Mrs. Lee, Joni's aunt. You must be Alex. Please come in."

They went to the kitchen. He took a seat at the kitchen table. Mrs. Lee was clearing away dishes.

"We only finished dinner," she said, without a trace of her niece's accent. "Joni's still getting dressed. I'll tell her you're here in a moment."

"I'm probably early," he said, noticing Joni's schoolbooks next to him on the table.

"Joni's told me you're a runner, Alex."

"Yeah, I'm on the cross-country team."

"She also told me you're an excellent student."

"Well, I'm all right, I guess." He liked the idea of Joni talking about him. But a dark thought suddenly entered his mind. "Mrs. Lee, are you new to Timber?"

"Gracious, no, I've lived here the last twenty years with my husband. Mr. Lee's at work now, perhaps you'll meet him later. He always works late."

"Is Joni—just visiting?"

Mrs. Lee glanced over from her place at the sink. "No. Joni will be living with us from now on." She turned away, putting on the faucet. "She didn't tell you about her parents?" There was an edge in the woman's question.

"No."

Mrs. Lee stood still for a moment, then quieted the water, drying her hands with a dishtowel, returning to the table to take a seat beside him, her face pinched with concern. "It's not a matter she ever talks about. I don't know if it's something I should talk about now. But I feel I should warn you in case you were to accidentally bring it up."

"Is it something to do with her parents?"

"Yes." She paused. "They're both dead."

"That's a shame." The news did not surprise him. Since meeting Joni, he'd felt there was a shadow across her past. She possessed a "haunted" quality. It was a quality that had seemed to draw him to her. Nevertheless, he was saddened to hear the news.

Growing up without parents couldn't be easy. "When did they die?" he asked.

"Not that long ago. They— There was an accident. We were all shocked. Joni's mother was my youngest sister."

"Was Joni an only child?"

"No. She has a brother. He's—still in England." Mrs. Lee clasped her fingers together nervously. "It was a terrible accident."

"What happened?"

The woman twitched involuntarily. "It happened twice," she whispered, before suddenly twisting around to check the clock. "Oh, dear, what time does your game start?"

"Six o'clock. But that's okay, we can be late."

"I'll go see what's keeping her." Mrs. Lee stood. "I think she must have taken a shower. Wait here just a sec."

Alex decided *parents* was the last topic he would bring up that evening.

While waiting, he took a quick peek in Joni's notebook to see what she was doing in her other classes. What he found was confusing. Her Algebra I notes were a shambles. She mustn't have a mind for math, he thought, before turning to her biology papers and discovering they were in worse shape.

Mrs. Lee was back swiftly and caught him with his nose in Joni's notebook. He closed it suddenly, feeling a shade guilty. But the woman wasn't angry. She nodded sadly.

"The trauma she's been through hasn't helped her studies," she said. Then added wistfully, "And she used to do so well at school."

"I can see how losing both parents might make you lose interest in books."

"Yes, that's the problem," Mrs. Lee said hastily, again taking a seat at the table beside him. He sensed a question that she was reluctant to ask.

"Maybe I could tutor her a couple of days a week until she gets caught back up," he offered.

Joni's aunt perked up. "Could you? You have no idea how much that would be appreciated." She lowered her voice. "Joni would never directly ask for help, you understand. Perhaps you could help her in an informal setting, here and there." She added, "We could pay you for your time."

Alex smiled. "If Joni wants tutoring, it would be my pleasure to give it to her." He was somewhat surprised at how quickly the woman had taken to him. There was a slightly desperate tone in everything she said. The grief over her sister's death must still be weighing her down.

"Alex," Joni said.

He hadn't heard her entering. She'd changed into a baggy blue skirt, and loosened her thick black hair so it twisted and curled practically to her waist. He'd never really seen her legs before. They were very shapely, and tone. She was probably a fair runner. She'd caught him easily enough.

"You look marvelous," he said, responding spontaneously, getting to his feet.

"Thank you."

Mrs. Lee hurried to Joni's side. "Did you use my dryer?" she asked, touching her niece's hair. "Can't have you catching cold."

"Yes."

"But you can't be going out like this without a coat," the aunt said. "You've seen how the mountain air changes once the sun goes down."

"I won't be cold," Joni said.

"I have a wool sweater I want you to take," Mrs. Lee said, turning for the hallway. Joni stopped her.

"I'll be fine," she said.

"I have an extra coat in the car, Mrs. Lee," Alex said.

The lady fussed nervously before forcing a big smile. "Very well, then. I do hope you kids have a good time."

Joni smiled at him. "We will," Alex said.

Cindy's legs were cold and so was her butt, even though she'd been waving the latter around all evening. Halftime was always a pain; they had to stand around the stadium in their cute little skirts while the football team got to relax in the warm comfort of the locker room. The cheerleaders did not participate directly in the halftime show. The score was tied at fourteen. Both sides were running on every boring play and Cindy was thinking it was going to be a long season.

"I told you to quit the squad this year," Pam said as she handed Cindy a hot dog and coffee through the fence that separated the bottom row of the bleachers from the track and playing field. "Then you could be in the stands where all the action is."

Cindy sipped her coffee. "So what's happening in the stands?"

"I've got Bala with me and Alex's got Joni."

"Are you sitting with Alex?"

"A couple of rows behind them."

"How's he doing with her?"

"I saw him put an arm around her."

"For how long?"

"Just for a moment," Pam said. "It was kind of a hug."

"That's not bad, though, for a first date. Don't you think?"

"Ray was out with me only an hour and he had his hand under my bra."

"I saw Ray walk by here a moment ago."

"Don't mention that guy's name," Pam swore.

"Sorry. Where's Bala got to?"

Pam made a face, which was easy for her to do with the sort of face she had. "He wanted to go for a stroll. I don't think he's finding my company completely captivating."

"Let him go through a half dozen other girls in the school and then he'll know what he's got in you."

Pam regarded her suspiciously. "Starting with who?"

Bala walked up at that moment. Standing on the planks above Cindy, he looked about ten feet tall. The way she smiled at him, Pam could probably guess who he could start with.

"Having fun?" Cindy asked, taking a sexy bite out of her hot dog.

He filled his lungs, glancing to the right and left, at the bowl of the stadium, the bright tungsten lights and the colorful crowd, and said with a note of awe, "I have never seen anything like this in my whole life."

"Wait till we play a team that has a quarterback that can throw the ball," Pam said.

"I love those little dances you do," he told Cindy. "And those songs you sing."

"That's just lewd suggestive squirming and jock-stroking squealing," Pam said, disgusted. Cindy put on her sweet innocent expression.

"Thank you, Bala."

"Oh, Cindy, dear," Pam said in the same sugar-coated voice, turning her head toward the north end of the field. "Our young gladiators are returning to the appointed battlefield, and I do believe your personal champion is heading this way for a kiss of encouragement."

She was right. Jason, carrying his helmet, was jogging over to see her. He'd fumbled the ball twice in the first half. He might not be keen on finding her flirting with Bala for the second time in the same day. "Bala," she said. "Could you do me a favor? Could you go tell Alex I'd like to speak with him?"

Pam recognized her discomfort. "I'll go. Bala can stay here and chat with you and your *boyfriend*."

"Bala, you go," she said. "Please?"

"Certainly," he said, leaving. She hoped he knew who Alex was.

"I think we're going to end up hating each other before Africa gets him back," Pam growled.

Jason arrived a minute later. He'd painted black chalk underneath his darling gray eyes to cut down on the glare of the lights. It made Cindy think of zebras.

"Can I have a bite of that hot dog?" he asked. Cindy gave it to him. "Brea's defensive line's got some big bastards," he remarked, stuffing the wiener in his mouth.

"I think they've been hitting you low," she said sympathetically.

"Ain't that the truth," Jason agreed, starting to give her the hot dog back. She gestured for him to finish it.

"I think they've been hitting your football too often," Pam remarked.

"Huh?" Jason said.

"That was a great run you made at the end of the first quarter," Cindy said quickly.

"I've got to make more of them in the next two quarters if we're going to win," Jason said.

Oh, no, Cindy thought. They had a new arrival.

"Hey, Jason! My man! Love the way you squirt that ball out of your hands when you're carrying it."

Ray Bower, a large Pepsi in one hand and a gallon of popcorn in the other, leaned against the rail beside his old girlfriend. Pam's eyes widened. Jason's narrowed. "If you took a single one of the hits I've been taking all night, Bower," Jason said, "you'd be in a hospital bed."

"Yeah, you're right." Ray grinned. "You're a mean hombre. You're like your namesake in *Friday the 13th.* You get up no matter how many times you're knocked down. I bet an old grizzly couldn't put you out of action."

Jason slammed his helmet onto the track. He began to climb the fence to tear Ray's head off. Cindy grabbed hold of his jersey. Pam moved in front of Ray.

"You take that back!" Jason screamed, unable to fit his cleats into the meshed wire, slipping hopelessly against the fence.

"You should be in the movies," Ray went on, taking a sip of Pepsi. "In a new series: *Jason's Younger Brother.*"

"You're dead, Bower!"

"Guys, stop it!" Cindy shouted, yanking on Jason's team number, spilling her coffee on her nylons. "Everyone's watching. Ray, you should apologize."

"I'm sorry if Jason took *personal* insult in what I just said," Ray replied, enjoying his popcorn.

"Hey, let's cool it," Pam said, obviously worried what Jason might do, now or later. Jason's face smoldered with blood.

"I'll remember that remark," Jason swore, letting go of the fence, fighting to calm himself.

"I doubt it," Ray said. "According to the papers, you've got a lousy memory."

"Stop it!" Cindy pleaded, getting upset as Jason made another lunge at the fence. She was not a crier, but she purposely let tears fill her eyes, hoping she could make the guys feel ashamed. It worked, to an extent. Jason backed off.

"There'll be another time, Bower," he muttered, picking up his helmet.

"There's a week from Monday at your preliminary hearing," Ray said ominously.

Bala returned with Alex and Joni. That sure had been quick; her brother must have been sitting in the lower bleachers. She'd sent Bala away because she didn't want him around when she was with Jason. Now she felt the reverse; if hostilities erupted again, his strong arms would be able to restore order. Alex noticed her eyes were red.

"What's wrong?" he asked.

"Jason's been playing basketball with his helmet," Ray said. "Almost brought tears to my own eyes."

Alex scowled at Ray. "You been starting a fight again?"

"Actually, I have, yes."

"Let's ignore him and maybe he'll undergo spontaneous human combustion," Pam said.

"Good idea," Jason said, turning to her. "Is tonight still on?"

"Alex said he saw a thunderstorm brewing back in the mountains," Cindy said.

"Were the clouds over Castle Park?" Jason asked Alex. A couple of teammates on the bench called for Jason to come over. He waved them away.

"No, they were way back. But the park will be getting the run off."

Jason smiled. "That's good. The falls will be full of water. You should come with us, Alex. Show your girl Wyoming's most scenic spot."

"Where is this?" Joni asked. Cindy noted with pleasure how close Joni stood to Alex, making it clear to everyone she was with him. And she was wearing his jacket.

"There's a national park about half an hour drive from here," Alex explained. "There's a waterfall there you can hike up to. Does that sound like fun?"

Joni nodded. "I like the outdoors."

"We would be out late if we go," Alex warned.

"It doesn't matter," Joni said.

"I have never seen a waterfall," Bala said.

"But they show lots of them in movies." Pam said in disbelief.

"I have never seen a movie," Bala said innocently. "Could we, too, go to this place?"

"Sure," Jason said. "We'll all go."

"I hope you won't mind me riding with you, Jason," Ray said.

"Ray," Pam told him, "if Jason took you, you'd probably end up walking home."

"With two broken legs," Jason agreed.

Ray lost his carefree snicker. "I couldn't complain about that," he said seriously. "Not after what happened to Karen." He turned, preparing to leave, when he seemed to notice for the first time that Joni was with Alex. He went to speak again, thought better of it, and then simply walked away.

"Who's Karen?" Bala asked.

"Just a girl." Cindy sighed, feeling a chill.

Chapter Six

Jason fumbled once more in the third quarter, but all was forgiven when he broke through in the last two minutes of the fourth quarter for a five-yard touchdown to put Timber High up to stay: 21 to 20. He was in a much better mood after the game than he had been at halftime.

The three pairs ended up going in separate cars to Castle Park; that way, on the trip home, they wouldn't have to return to the school. Since her legs were yelling for a pair of warm pants, Cindy had Jason swing by her house. The others would just have to wait. They had arranged to meet at Lot H.

Inside, her parents were enjoying the latest episode of their favorite sitcom. Her dad got all excited when he heard about Jason's run at the end of the game. He promised he would be at the game next Friday. Cindy was not overjoyed at the prospect. She always felt inhibited cheering when her father was watching.

Cindy did not tell her folks about Alex's fall and subsequent visit to the hospital, but did mention his hot date. Her mother was delighted and started pumping her for information about Joni. Cindy warned them Alex might be bringing Joni back to the house for a snack, and that they should remain in bed like good little parents. She didn't say exactly where they were all going that night.

Wolf needed walking and Cindy wanted his protection, so the big dog joined their party. Jason began to wonder about her paranoia when they were walking to his Camaro—his Jaguar was in the shop—and she suddenly jogged into the garage and returned with a rifle and a box of cartridges. The caliber of the gun was high enough to stop an elephant.

"If you tried firing that thing," he said as they pulled away, "you'd probably take your shoulder off."

"I'm an expert shot," she said honestly. "I could hit a Coke can at a hundred yards with this rifle."

He knew she wasn't one to brag, and was impressed. "Where did you learn to do that?"

Wolf perched over from the backseat and licked the side of her face. She patted him on the top of the head and pointed out the window. A week-old moon hung above the treetops, its light shining like a peaceful celestial tonic over the whole valley. "See that target up there?"

"What? The moon?"

"When I was in about fourth grade, my dad would take me outside at night with a rifle and a pair of binoculars and have me shoot at the moon. After each shot, I would check in the binoculars to see if there were any new craters. That would mean I had hit it. I must have known I wasn't really shooting the moon, but it seemed after each shot, I'd see an extra crater."

"Why did he have you do that?"

"I think it was his way of telling me at that impressionable age that the moon was the only safe thing to shoot at. Of course, later we practiced on cans and bottles. My dad has always been big on me being able to protect myself. He helped me train Wolf."

"I'm glad you told me all this." Jason smiled. "I'll be sure to move carefully around you."

She touched his leg. "I don't want you being too careful," she said slyly.

He shook his head. "You amaze me, Cindy. I don't know how you've put up with me lately. I've been so disgusted with all the talk that's been going on at school, I've been perpetually pissed off. Tonight was a perfect example. If you, and the fence, hadn't been there, I don't know what I would have done to Ray."

A feeling of warmth for him flowed through her. Caught in the light of the moon, she thought his profile adorable. He was much more relaxed, going to this place where all his troubles had started, than he had been since school had begun. It was easy to remember all the reasons she liked him: his great eyes, his confidence, his sharp mind, his great mouth. She leaned over and kissed him on the cheek. "Let's not worry about any of that stuff tonight," she said.

The toughness of the soles of Joni's feet amazed Alex. They were almost to the top of Pathfinders Trail—with Cindy and Jason ahead, and Pam and Bala bringing up the rear—and she had yet to complain about a sharp pebble or jagged pine needle. He was still mad at himself for his lack of foresight. But it had only been when they had reached Lot H, and were waiting around for the others to show, that he had realized Joni couldn't possibly hike to the top of the waterfall in high heels. No problem, she had said, taking off her shoes. Apparently, she liked to go barefoot.

The night was beautiful and Alex was happy. Off to their left, falling a steep and rocky two thousand feet, was the gorge the swift and patient Snake Tail River had cut over the last couple of ice ages. And the waterfall was not far ahead, its cold water sparkling in the moonlight, the roar of its crashing foam filling their ears.

"We're almost there," he told Joni. Their path was partially protected from the harsh surroundings, with intertwined tree branches creating a natural ceiling above their heads. Joni was holding his hand and her fingers were delightfully warm. "Are you getting tired?"

"No," she said.

He was. The race that afternoon and the stitches in his knee had slowed him a spell. But it was a pleasant fatigue. He was thinking of the look Ray had given him when he had realized Joni was with him. It was rare to see Ray shocked.

"Did you enjoy the game?" he asked. She hadn't appeared to understand the rules.

"The boys looked like they were trying to hurt each other."

He laughed, quickly changing his mind. She had understood in one night what most people in the audience never did after years of watching, he thought.

Cindy was slowing and they caught up with her and Jason a few minutes later. Wolf was giving Cindy an awful time; the dog was unusually nervous and kept darting off the path.

"I should never have brought him," she grumbled, searching the foliage. "Wolf! Wolf!"

The dog did not appear, and they waited for better than two minutes. Cindy started to worry. "Jason, could something have happened to him?" she asked.

"If he slipped and broke a leg, you'd hear him howling," Jason said.

"There he is." Alex pointed. Wolf was trudging happily beside Bala, who, along with Pam, was finally catching up with them. Alex was surprised; the dog didn't normally take to strangers.

"If you don't start behaving," Cindy said, scolding the dog, "you're eating dog food for the next two weeks. Now keep beside me."

Wolf was not impressed. As they continued their hike, the dog continued to stay near Bala.

They reached the top of the falls not long after, and took a breather on a boulder next to where the river went over the edge. The view was glorious. Had Jason not been keen to press on, Alex thought, they would've been content to stay where they were.

Looking straight down over the falls was enough to get one's head spinning. The mighty shower fell nearly two hundred feet into a churning rock-rimmed bowl that gave the impression of having a giant creature deep within its bowels, fighting to enter the world of the living.

"How deep is that lake down there?" Bala asked.

"That isn't a lake," Pam said, unusually quiet, probably because she was tired from the hike. "It's a whirlpool."

"It's deep enough that one guy thought he could go over the falls in a barrel and live," Jason said.

"When was that?" Cindy asked.

"Five years ago," Jason said.

"Did he drown?" Bala asked.

"He broke his neck," Jason said and then he did a very unexpected thing. He had carried Cindy's father's rifle from the car, and now, suddenly, he raised it to his shoulder, reaching for the trigger. "This gorge has incredible acoustics. Listen to this. I'm going to shoot Cindy's moon."

"Jason, no!" Cindy screamed.

Her warning came too late. The gun was fired, and before the boom could even begin to reverberate through the rocky valley, Wolf attacked Jason.

Seeing the dog come, Jason immediately threw up his arm. Wolf went for that instead of the throat. Since the dog couldn't finish Jason by ripping out his arteries, it decided to finish him by shoving him over the side of the cliff.

"Heel! Heel!" Cindy shouted, moving quickly to grab Wolf by the neck. The dog had gone wild. Guns always had that effect on him. He ignored Cindy's command, and Jason staggered backward, moving closer and closer to the edge, a row of teeth clamped around his right elbow.

Then the crisis ended almost before it began.

A small miracle happened. A high-pitched shrill whistle sounded above the roar of the falls. And Wolf let go of Jason.

Come again? Alex thought.

Wolf turned and ran to Bala, who grabbed the dog by the thick fur at the back of the neck. It had been Bala who had made the strange whistle. Wolf licked his face to show he could whistle more if he wanted.

Cindy snatched her boyfriend back to safety. "Are you okay?" she asked anxiously, hugging Jason. "I should've warned you sooner. Oh, God, you could have gone over the side! How's your arm? Are you bleeding? That damn dog."

Jason was shook, but no one was going to say he didn't have good reason. "I'm fine," he said, feeling his arm while keeping an eye on Wolf. "Your dog's got violent reflexes."

"Those sure are incredible acoustics, Jason," Pam said with a nervous laugh. Standing to her left, Joni appeared unmoved by the incident.

"Hey, Bala," Alex said. "What was that you whistled?"

"Yeah, how did you do that?" Cindy asked, quickly regaining control of herself. She let go of Jason and stepped toward Bala. He knelt and fluffed Wolf's hairy head.

"It was nothing," he said.

"It was definitely something," Cindy said. "I've raised this dog since he was a puppy. Why did he react so quickly to your whistle?"

Bala smiled. "I have always had a way with animals."

"Did your grandfather teach you this *way*?" Cindy asked.

Bala lowered his head. "Yes, he did. When I was young."

Cindy leaned over and gave Bala a brief hug. "Well, thank your grandfather for me. He just might have saved Jason's life."

The hug appeared to embarrass Bala. "I will, when I see him," he said.

"Yeah, thanks Bala," Jason said with an eye on Cindy. "You've got to teach me that whistle someday."

"It is not something you can learn in a day," Bala said.

Pam turned away, shaking her head. "Since when does Wolf understand bush language?" she muttered.

Cindy would have preferred to call it a night. She was tired and it wasn't getting any earlier. But Jason was adamant about going on. There was a cave he wanted her to see.

She couldn't remember any cave in the area.

The gang had been reshuffled. The guys were walking on ahead, as guys are prone to do when their female companions start to get tired. Wolf was sticking with Bala. Cindy had been surprised Alex had parted from Joni's side. Perhaps he felt a responsibility to scout on ahead and make sure all was safe. No one knew this place like Alex. He was carrying the gun now.

Rain clouds continued to linger over the distant mountains, from which could be heard an occasional rumble of thunder. The river was two hundred yards off to their left, fat with the storm's fresh downpour. Few trees could be found at this elevation, and the light of the moon shown unobstructed. A roughly chiseled granite mound protruded on their immediate left. Cindy remembered Kent Cooke's article.

"Do you know where we are?" Cindy asked Pam.

"I'm not sure," Pam said uneasily.

"This is the spot," Joni said, her voice a bit heavy, as though she were just getting over a cold.

Cindy looked at her. "Are you sure?"

Joni nodded. "Karen died right here."

Cindy wasn't inclined to question her sources. "Ray didn't sound like himself when he mentioned Karen tonight," she said to Pam.

"I suppose he had his reasons," Pam said, obviously not wanting to discuss this in front of Joni. She'd made her point, anyway. It had been a strange match, but Ray and Karen had actually dated for several months. This had been before Ray and Pam had become an item. This was probably another reason Ray and Jason were not bosom buddies. Joni must have sensed the undercurrent of the discussion.

"Karen was a wonderful friend to me," she said suddenly.

Cindy felt slightly ashamed. She had known Karen— known *of her*, at least—for years and couldn't say the same. "It must have been a terrible shock for you, to just meet her and all, and then to have her taken away?"

Joni regarded her thoughtfully, the large moon reflecting with uncanny clarity in her big black eyes. "I often dream of Karen in this place." She lowered her thick lashes. "It makes me sad."

They were heading due north, cutting directly in between a loop in the river. Consequently, it wasn't too long before they were again beside the water. The guys had stopped and were waiting.

"Almost there," Jason said, holding their unused flashlight.

"Where exactly is this cave?" Alex asked, scrutinizing the narrow bank of the river as it wrapped precariously between the water and the stone walls, the latter rising higher and higher the farther you went back into the mountains.

Jason nodded. "Around this bend. I'll show you." He stretched out his hand to Cindy. She still felt self-conscious holding Jason's hand in front of Bala. The demonstration of Bala's ability to handle Wolf—and she had a sneaking suspicion he could handle *any* animal—made her even more reluctant. His aura of mystery had deepened in her eyes; she knew this was making him more enticing to her.

She shoved the thought away and took Jason's hand.

"The bank is smooth and narrow here," Alex said. "It may even be wet. I don't know if this cave is worth it."

Jason was thinking. The rest of them were waiting for another opinion. Bala spoke next. "I'll go first. I'm quick on my feet. I'll be able to see how safe it is."

"No," Jason said firmly. "I'll lead the way. I'm familiar with the terrain." He chuckled. "We're beginning to sound like we're going off to war. Come on, Cindy." He tugged on her hand and then dropped it.

She was wearing a pair of leather high-top basketball shoes. She'd found them preferable to ordinary hiking boots; they supported her ankles over rough ground while still being flexible enough not to throw off her natural stride. The soles of the shoes had an excellent grip. Following Jason along the narrow stone path that ran about ten feet above the rushing water, with Bala at her back, Cindy felt secure. If her balance were to waver, there were ample branches sticking out from the wall on her right to grab. But she was concerned about Joni in her bare feet.

Cindy was turning to check on Joni when she slipped.

Instinctively, Cindy's right hand shot out and grabbed a thick branch. It must have been dead and dried. It snapped, and she was falling. For the tiniest instant, just before the icy water engulfed her, Cindy thought she felt Bala's fingers touching her wrist.

Oh, God, no!

The cold was black and strong. She was going down and being swept backward. The fall had caught her without a solid breath. Her lungs screamed for air. She flailed blindly with her arms, her flesh cringing in the grip of the current. Her leg slapped a rock, then another. She kicked upward. Her head broke the surface.

"Alex!" Cindy screamed.

They were receding from her at a frightening speed, but even with her hair plastered over her face, she could see them clearly. Her terror sharpened her eyesight, so that the moonlight appeared far more brilliant. The group got jammed on the narrow bank as they all tried to chase after her. Alex was the first to emerge from the tangle.

"Swim toward the side!" he yelled, running downstream at approximately the same speed she was being swept away. Almost as soon as she had entered the water, she had been sucked to the center of the river. She tried to do as he suggested. Her soaked sweatshirt made her feel as though she were swimming in molasses. The bank was getting no closer. A crosscurrent was resisting her.

"Alex!" she cried, water splashing down her throat, making her gag.

"I'll catch you downstream, Cindy!" Jason yelled, drawing up beside Alex. She thought she understood what he meant and had her guess confirmed when she saw him beginning to cut inland, away from the water. The river looped. He was going to run across the ground they had just covered, going downstream way ahead of her, and wait for her to come to him. She didn't like that plan. If he were to miss her there, only a few seconds would be left before she'd go over the falls.

"No!" She coughed, continuing to flail with her arms, her strength draining. The intense cold was to blame. There was snow back in the mountains that hadn't melted all summer. The rain water must have run over it. Her muscles were literally freezing up.

"I'll save you!" Jason promised, breaking away from Alex and Bala—who had joined in the pursuit. He disappeared into the night. Alex and Bala were running side by side. They were no longer shouting to her but were talking between themselves. First Alex shook his head, then Bala shook his. It was an awful time, Cindy thought, for them to be unable to come to an agreement. More submerged stones struck her feet and legs, one so hard she felt it must have shattered her ankle. But the pain up her leg did not last long. Her feet were going numb.

"Help!" she wailed.

The river was picking up speed, narrowing. Up ahead, she could hear the roar of Crystal Falls.

"Alex!"

Alex and Bala both vanished. A cluster of trees and boulders had forced them away from the edge of the water. Cindy began to panic. A shrewdly calculating part of her brain was telling her that the odds were that she would be going flying very soon.

Karen went this same way.

But Karen had been dead before she had been thrown in the water. Cindy strove harder with her leaden arms. She was not going to give up.

A couple of minutes went by—and *a lot* of ground. Alex finally reappeared. He was alone. He was pulling off his coat, preparing to dive into the water.

"Stay! Stay!" she yelled. All the time she had been screaming for her brother to save her, she had meant that Jason and Bala should do it. "Don't, Alex!"

He wasn't listening, striding swiftly into the water, being picked up off his feet and sucked into the current. He was much closer to the bank than she was, and at least a hundred feet farther upstream, but suddenly she had hope. Alex was an excellent swimmer. He plowed toward her.

"Hang on!" he said.

The force of the current appeared to be split down the middle of the river. Alex drew even with her but was unable to make it across a vicious invisible eddy.

"Cindy! Try swimming toward the other side!"

She understood the logic of his advice. Yet it was next to impossible to convince her exhausted limbs to head away from her only source of help. The approaching falls sounded like thunder in her ears.

"Get back to the side!" she shouted.

"Turn! Go the other way!" Alex shouted back. "Use your legs as well as your arms!"

She decided her only choice was to do what he said. But as she turned, a tall dark figure caught her eye.

Bala was standing on a cliff above where Alex and she would soon pass. He was removing his shirt. How he had gotten all the way up there in so short a time was beyond Cindy.

As she watched, he retreated from the edge of the cliff, vanishing. For an instant her heart stopped beating. A second miracle from him in the same night would have been too much to ask. She asked, anyway.

God, please!

Suddenly he reappeared, running at an incredible speed, leaping off the cliff. He seemed to hang in the air forever, falling in slow motion. He hit the water not ten yards from her. But he did not resurface, and she waited, and waited—

A strong arm wrapped around her side and a large head popped up a few inches from her gasping mouth.

"My grandfather also taught me how to swim," Bala said.

"And how to fly?" she choked.

"Alex, I have her," Bala called. "Return to your side."

Alex waved, turning away from them. Bala tightened his grip on her, actually lifting her several inches above the water. He must have had incredibly powerful legs. He began to take long even strokes with his free arm.

"Hurry," she whispered. The point where the river transformed into Crystal Falls had become visible. Between them and it lay a huge fallen tree. To her further amazement and horror she saw Jason was hanging from the tree *by his knees,* waiting to swoop them to safety. Bala saw him, too.

"Jason, get off there!" he yelled.

Jason checked in the direction of the falls, then appeared to mentally measure the distance between them and the opposite side of the river. "You won't make it!" he yelled back. "Swim more toward the center!"

Cindy wouldn't have known which option to take: hope Jason would catch them as they whisked by or hope they could make it to the shore. Bala had no doubt about the matter; he was going for the opposite shore. He ignored several pleas of Jason's to reverse directions. A few seconds later, they floated beneath the tree, far beyond Jason's hanging reach.

"You're crazy, Bala!" he swore. "Cindy!"

Bala didn't reply. He was saving his breath, moving them toward the side, foot by blessed foot. The water of the river had quickened, anticipating the big plunge that was coming. For Cindy, it was like drowning at the edge of the world. She squeezed her eyes tightly shut, wishing she could wake up in her bed at home.

I cannot die. I will not die.

An eternity of slow seconds went by. Then a wave slammed against her, and kept slamming.

"Cindy, open your eyes," Bala said.

She did as she was told. He had reached the side, and was hanging on to a narrow crack in the stone wall. The wave was from the force of the river; while moving with it, she hadn't truly felt its pressure.

"I am going to have to let you go," Bala said.

Cindy glanced over her shoulder. The floor of the gorge was waiting with wide-open arms. "I think that would be a very bad idea," she said.

Bala was firm. "I have to let you go to climb up this rock. See, there are many places you can hold. When I reach the top, I will be able to pull you up."

She nodded. "Okay." He was right; there were many places to grab hold.

"Keep a good hold, Cindy," he cautioned, reaching to pull himself up.

"You be careful, yourself," she said between chattering teeth.

Bala could not only talk to dogs and swim like a fish, he could climb walls like a fly. He was up and over the top in the blink of an eye. His head poked over a moment later.

"Cindy, you're going to have to move down about thirty feet."

"Why?"

"I need a place to wrap my feet around in order to pull you up."

"Do you mean I have to move in the direction of the waterfall?" The edge was only fifty feet away.

"Yes."

"Maybe I should just try to climb up. You did it easily enough."

"You are not me."

She couldn't argue with that. The rock appeared equipped with ample handles. Carefully, more carefully than she had ever done anything in her life, she crept toward the brink.

We should have just gone for pizza.

The river made one last stab at her life. She was in position and reaching up, with Bala leaning over the side with practically the entire length of his body, when a log—it was really lousy timing on the log's part—hit her flush on the shoulder. The jolt made her anchoring fingers slip.

"Bala!" she cried.

His hand closed on her wrist like a vise. Seemingly without effort, he pulled her up to the point where she could make it the rest of the way on her own. When she was safe, she saw that his toes were dug around a sharp ripple in the stone. His entire weight was being supported by the equivalent of a thread. Yet he waved her away when she started to grab his legs. He could manage very well on his own, thank you. You'd think she would know that by now.

"Does your grandfather like to go for late-night swims?" she asked when he was upright once more. She was trembling violently, her breath coming in ragged gulps.

Bala laughed, loud and deep. "Not as much as you do, Cindy." *I'm alive.*

The truth of the simple thought filled her with wonder. She collapsed against him, pressing into the warmth of his body. Hesitantly, he wrapped his arm around her. He had stripped off his shirt for her rescue. He was as wet as herself. But he was not shivering, nor did he even seem to notice the cold.

"I owe you my life," she said.

He shook his head, glancing at the moon. "Do not feel in my debt. One day, you never know, you might feel you have to pay me back. And that would not be good."

Alex did not go careening by and Cindy therefore knew he must have made it to safety. Jason appeared shortly after, on the other side of the top of the falls, and confirmed that her brother was indeed fine. Jason did this by arm gestures. Talk across the deafening noise of the water was impossible.

An exhilarating euphoria began to fill Cindy. She'd read

about such experiences from people who had just missed meeting the Grim Reaper. A shame you had to go to such extremes to get the happiness hormone flowing. She wouldn't mind feeling this way all the time—as if she could fly.

Alex and Joni arrived beside Jason a few minutes later. Joni had removed the coat Alex had lent her earlier and wrapped it around his shoulders. Alex appeared to be sharing her joy at their near escape from the clutches of death; he kept bouncing up and down. Or maybe he was just trying to stay warm.

Pam was the last to put in an appearance. She'd thoughtfully collected Alex and Bala's coats, plus the rifle Alex had dropped when the mad chase had started. Her excited waves were easy for Cindy to decipher. Pam was glad she was alive, too.

Not far from where they had parked was the sole bridge over the river. It was obvious to both sides they would have to split up until they reached it. Cindy thought the others might be waiting for a while. The blow her ankle had taken from the underwater boulder appeared serious. As their two groups went their respective ways, she was limping badly. Bala immediately offered to carry her.

"It's four miles back down," she said. "You couldn't possibly carry me all that way."

He crouched over and swooped her off the ground. "I have carried heavier women," he said.

"Whoa! You mean, I'm not your first?" she teased, leaning her head against the smooth hardness of his chest.

"I used to carry my mother to her bath. That was three miles in the heat. Even when she was sick, she weighed more than you do now."

"She was sick? What was wrong with her?"

"Cholera. We had an epidemic of it. Killed many of my people." He added, "But my mother was spared."

"She's still alive today?"

"Yes."

"Do you miss her?"

"When I think about her, I feel close to her; I know she is thinking of me, too."

"How about your father?"

"He died. But not from cholera. It happened when I was much younger. When I was a boy."

His voice wavered when he spoke of his father. She decided to change the subject. "I loved that story you told in class today," she said.

"I did not tell much."

The noise of the waterfall was receding. The air was still, without a trace of a breeze. "Yes, you did. And you told me more tonight. I've watched you. You have magic. That boy who went into those animals, that was you, wasn't it?"

Bala didn't answer immediately and she worried that she had tread where she was not welcome. "Why do you say this?" he asked finally.

"Bala, I didn't mean to pry. I—"

"No, your question is not offensive. But why do you say I was this boy?"

"You speak English as well, if not better, than I do."

He smiled. "And which animal taught me this?"

"I mean, you have an extraordinary mind." *Not to mention an extraordinary body.* "Why do you sometimes sound ashamed of being a Bairavee?"

The moon had slipped behind a cloud and the landscape had darkened. Bala's stride was long and tireless. Cindy wasn't worried he would stumble.

"You said I have magic, Cindy. I have read your definition of that word. I do not believe in it. No one is magically given what he wants in life. Even my grandfather has to earn what comes to him. Or pay for it."

"What do you mean?"

Bala took a deep breath. "My father died trying to learn my grandfather's craft."

"I'm sorry," she muttered, not knowing what else to say.

Bala shifted her in his arms. "You love to hear of Bairavees, Cindy. That is unusual in this country. I think *you* have the extraordinary mind. I will sing you a Bairavee song. Listen closely; you can learn more that way than by asking questions."

"Bala?"

"Shh. Listen."

He began to sing. His voice, though soft and deep, was very powerful. She imagined it carrying far, over and around the trees and rocks, into the sky. In some way it seemed to her his song was *coming* from the outside, and that he was merely reciting it back to an earth that already knew its meaning.

She hugged closer to his body. He had magic, the fool, he just didn't know it. His skin was as warm as if a bright sun were beating down upon it. And the warmth was seeping into her, into her blood. The stinging in her ankle receded, as did the rest of the world. She could hear his song, that was enough. Listening and floating, she knew she could learn a lot.

She didn't remember when she fell asleep.

Chapter Seven

I don't know if my nervous system could take many more days *like this,* Alex thought as he pulled into his driveway, still dripping wet, Joni still by his side. He had run his legs off, crash-landed on the asphalt, been humiliated by his friend, gone out with the girl of his dreams, and fought to save his sister from death. He was surprised when he checked his watch; it was only one in the morning.

"Are you sure you're not tired?" he asked Joni before turning off the ignition. "I could take you straight home?"

"I feel fine."

Alex had to agree she looked fine; the long walks and the evening's drama had not ruffled her feathers in the slightest. "Your aunt won't be worried about you?"

"My aunt worries about me when I'm home in bed."

Alex turned off the engine and opened the door, letting Wolf out, who, to his surprise, promptly ran into the trees and disappeared. Probably had to attend to a call of nature, he decided, not giving the matter a second thought. He was anxious to get out of his soggy clothes. "Let's go in, then. I don't think my parents will still be up."

He was glad his guess proved accurate. His mom would've wanted to know why he was all wet. His dad would've been winking at him after taking one good look at Joni. The first thing Alex did was close the door to the hallway leading to their bedroom.

"Do you like tea?" he asked, turning to look at Joni as she stood silently in the kitchen. The lower hem of her dress was damp. When he had pulled himself gasping from the river, she'd been there to help him. That had been a terrible moment; he hadn't known if Bala would be able to rescue Cindy. He shuddered at the memory.

"Very much."

He stepped past her, feeling her eyes on him. "I'll put on the kettle. The water should be boiling by the time I get back. I'm just going to make a quick change."

Upstairs in his bedroom, with his pants off, he discovered he had reopened half the stitches in his knee. He decided that was a small price to have paid for Cindy's safety, though of course he realized he hadn't done a damn thing to help. Bala and his incredible athletic ability were to thank. Bala might not know it yet, but he had a friend for life in Alex Jones.

Bala versus Jason? My sister's blind.

Alex hadn't been too pleased with Jason's behavior once the crisis was over. Walking back down the mountain, with Cindy and Bala on the other side, Jason had rambled on about what a fool Bala had been not to let him pluck Cindy up to safety from the overhanging tree. Alex had finally had to tell him to shut up. Then, when they had joined up with Bala, and discovered Cindy asleep in his arms, Jason had reacted with typical immature jealousy. He'd insisted Cindy be awakened, that she could walk the rest of the way. He'd only backed down when Bala had explained how painful her ankle was, and how much the experience had worn her out. It had sure burned Jason up watching Bala carry Cindy all the way to the car, knowing he didn't have the strength to do it. Then, finally, at the parking lot, Jason had ignored Bala and Alex's recommendation that Cindy be taken straight home.

Jason's probably trying to convince Cindy right now that it was Bala's idea to go to the cave.

Cindy sure had been zonked. She hadn't even awakened when Jason had strapped the seat belt across her chest. It was as though she had been sedated.

Alex got a roll of sterile gauze from the bathroom next to his bedroom—his knee was bleeding slightly and beginning to sting a lot—and began to worry whether he should try to kiss Joni. He wanted to; he had sure thought about it enough since school had begun. But he didn't know how to get started. He sort of doubted the opportunity would simply present itself. He didn't even know if he would recognize the opportunity should he be so fortunate. He wondered if he should brush his teeth again.

Joni was pouring the boiling water into the teapot when he returned to the kitchen. Watching her complete the simple task, he realized again why he found her so attractive. Her beauty was only a part of it; she had grace. She only had to walk across the room and anyone could tell she came from a different universe from the other girls at school.

He smiled. "How did you find the tea?"

"The container gives off an aroma." She glanced past him. "You haven't introduced me to your girlfriend."

Alex turned. "You mean Sybil? She usually introduces herself." He stepped over to his old yellow parrot, Joni coming up at his side, her long hair brushing against his arm. "Sybil, say hello to Joni."

"Hello, Sybil," the bird chirped.

"Sometimes she can learn a new name in a single session. Except my sister's. For some reason, she refuses to say Cindy's name." Alex bent again to the cage. "Joni—Joni—She's really old, really smart." He didn't see any point in saying she was also blind; it might make Joni sad. "Say Joni, Sybil. Joni—Joni—"

"Hello, Alex," the bird replied.

Joni smiled, a larger smile than he had ever seen on her face. "Can I talk to her?"

"Certainly, just don't put your fingers—"

Through the wire. Damn it!

Like Cindy's warning earlier about her pet, his was too late. Joni had poked her hand inside the cage and Sybil had immediately pecked at it. A dark red drop spilled over the long nail of Joni's index finger.

"Joni, are you okay?" he asked, feeling like the entire evening had probably just been ruined. "I was going to warn you to keep your distance, though she seldom bites anybody." He scolded Sybil. "You are a stupid bird!"

"Hello, Joni," Sybil said.

"Don't get upset, Alex. It's her nature."

Alex went to fetch a bandage—they seemed to be needing a lot of them lately—but Joni didn't use it, preferring to hold the cut until it stopped bleeding, which it did a moment later. Leaving the kitchen with their cups of tea, Joni patted the top of Sybil's cage.

"Joni," the bird said again.

They ended up on the couch. Joni sat down after him and she sat very close. She would've had to have sat on his lap to get any closer. Her skirt was riding up over half of her thigh. Alex sipped his tea and wished it was whiskey. And he didn't even drink.

"Quite a night we had," he remarked for something to say.

Joni nodded, trying her tea. "I had fun."

"So did I." He chuckled. "Except when my sister went in

the water. Boy, I have to admit, I was scared. If anything had happened to her, I don't know if I could have taken it."

Joni took another drink of her tea and then placed the cup on a saucer on the coffee table. "I wasn't worried. I knew Bala would save her."

The remark surprised him. He'd received the impression she wasn't crazy about Bala. "How could you be so sure?"

She casually brushed at something in his hair. "Because he is so sure of himself."

"What do you mean?"

Joni's fingers lingered near his ear. "Let's not talk about him."

"Okay." Her touching him tickled. "What would you like to talk about? Ah, do you have any hobbies?"

"Yes. My hobby now is doing all the things every other girl my age does."

She must be referring to the period of mourning she had just gone through, he thought, and of her desire to start again on a normal life. "I hope I can help you practice that hobby," he said, feeling pleased at the gall of the remark. Joni nodded seriously.

"I hope so, too." She slipped her hand onto the back of his neck.

"How are you doing in your classes?" he asked quickly.

"Not good." She placed her other hand on his knee.

"I could help you, maybe, if you want?"

"That would be nice." She paused. "Alex, let me see your eyes."

He looked directly at her, something he had hesitated to do

while sitting so close. There was a lamp on over her left shoulder, the only light on in the room. It cast a shadow across most of her face. She moistened her lips with the tip of her tongue.

"You have a lot of feeling in your eyes," she said.

He chuckled again. "Me? My eyes are very plain. It's yours that are exotic. I bet if you tried, you could become a successful model."

Joni shook her head, still serious. "My eyes are flat. They have no personality. They have only what—" She stopped herself, suddenly grinned. "I was going to say something, but I think I'll say something else."

"What?"

She moved so close he could feel her breath. "Kiss me."

"What?"

"I want you to kiss me."

Alex decided he wouldn't get a better hint all night. He kissed her and it was *something*. He had heard that nothing could compete with your imagination, but a priest had probably said it. The real Joni had a mile and then some on his fantasy Joni. Their arms went around each other. Her mouth pressed against his and she pulled him toward her and they slowly sank into the couch. Her lips were incredibly warm; it was almost as though she were hot with a fever. They stretched out on the couch. A part of him could not believe what was happening. Minutes of delight went by. The smell and taste of her filled his senses. He ran his fingers through her hair, down her back. She sighed softly, finally drawing her head slightly back.

"You're nice," she whispered. "Too nice."

He smiled, his courage growing in quantum leaps. "I might not be everything I appear."

She thought about that, gave him a quick peck, then leaned back again. "This is dangerous."

Was she referring to the possibility of them going all the way? Yes, that could be dangerous. He could have a heart attack. "This whole night has had its dangers," he said.

"Your sister loves you very much."

He caressed her cheek. "Why do you say that now?"

"Because I—I thought of it," she said, burying her face in his chest so that the top of her head pressed against his chin. "Alex, do you ever get hungry for something you can't have? Something you're not supposed to have?"

At the moment, he was in touch with that kind of hunger. "Yes."

"What do you do when that happens?"

"Usually? Usually I don't do anything."

"Then what happens?"

"Nothing. And my life always goes on. I suppose it always will."

She tilted her face up, touched near his right eye. "When I do nothing, I feel like—"

"Alex, is that you?"

Splendid! Splendid! Damn it!

It was his mother. He rocketed into a sitting position, almost tossing Joni onto the floor in the process. With relief, he saw his mother hadn't actually entered the living room. She was standing on the other side of the partially open hallway door, the door he had closed all the way when he had entered the house.

"Yeah," he croaked.

"Is Cindy back yet?"

"She should be in soon."

"Okay, dear, just checking. Have a good night. Sweet dreams."

"Good night, Mom." Cindy must have told her he might be bringing a girl back to the house. That was the only explanation he could think of for his mom not bursting in on them. He would have to thank Cindy in the morning.

The spell had been broken. He could sense it without having to ask. Joni was sitting quietly on the couch, fixing her skirt. Her face had regained its normal distant expression.

"What were you going to say, Joni?"

She smiled faintly, sort of sadly. "Nothing."

It was a pity; she had really begun to open up. Well, there would always be another time. On the whole, the evening had exceeded his greatest expectations. "Would you like me to give you a ride home?"

Joni nodded.

She felt hot and sticky. Warm air was circulating over her legs, but at the same time she seemed to be sitting in a puddle. The awakening was a strange one. Not only did she at first have no idea where she was, she had no idea *who* she was. Opening her eyes, she glanced about, feeling a stiffness in her neck. The world came into focus slowly. She was in a car. The heater was on. The car had just stopped in a driveway. It belonged to Jason Whitfield. He was her boyfriend.

Yeah, this is the right planet.

"Are you awake, Cindy?" Jason asked.

"Yeah, I'm here," she mumbled, sitting up, her back cracking. "How long have I been asleep?"

"Bala said you blacked out a few minutes after leaving the waterfall. Don't you remember?"

"I remember him singing—" And she remembered almost dying. "Did he carry me all the way back to the car?"

"We both did. You didn't even stir. What did he do, hit you over the head with a club?"

"Huh?"

"Nothing." Jason opened his car door. "Let's get inside."

Jason's house was the biggest in Timber. The architecture was simple and beautiful; two stories set in a rectangle around a large central pool. Old red bricks made up the exterior walls, with ivy clinging from the flower beds to the eaves, giving the residence a traditional eastern flavor. Jason's rooms—yes, he had more than one—were on the south corner. Her ankle throbbed as she limped up the driveway.

"Can I help you?" he asked, offering his hand.

"No, I can manage."

"You might want to have that X-rayed."

"I'll be all right. Why are we here? What time is it?"

Jason opened the door to his well-lit game room. He smiled. "I thought you could use some hot chocolate after your cold bath."

"That sounds good." She nodded, staggering inside, searching around for a frumpy chair she wouldn't mind getting all wet. Naturally, she didn't find any; there was no second-hand furniture in the Whitfield residence.

"Why don't you get out of those clothes?" Jason asked, watching her.

"I've nothing to change into."

Jason smiled again. "Wear one of my robes. Then I can put your things in the dryer. They'll be ready in a jiffy."

That sounded reasonable. Better to dry her clothes here than to try to put on the dryer at home. Her parents might hear it. She had no intention of telling them about her spin through the rapids. She knew Alex would automatically keep the incident secret.

Jason directed her to his bedroom and went to prepare their hot drinks. The place was full of "stuff." There was a computer, a telescope, a TV hooked up to a DVD player with wires leading to a couple of speakers that were each as big as her own chest-of-drawers.

Show me your platinum-plated charge card, why don't you?

Cindy had been in Jason's room before. They'd made out on his bed only last Tuesday. His many toys had never annoyed her before. Quite the opposite, she'd always seen them as evidence of a place she would someday like to reach. But now she was thinking of Bala's village, Mau Dogan, where you couldn't even take a bath without having to walk three miles. Bala was fascinated with Western society, but she couldn't imagine him ever having a room like this, even if he were to move to America and become fabulously wealthy. He might argue this point with her but he'd be wrong. There was a part of him she felt she knew better than he did. That part didn't need "stuff."

Cindy stripped off her clothes and dried herself with a towel she found in a drawer. Standing naked in Jason's room, she began to feel uneasy. She was tired and she was sore. Her exhilaration over being rescued had worn off. She didn't know what excitement Jason thought the night might still have in store. But had she been fresh, her uneasiness would probably have still been there. All of a sudden, Jason was the last person in the world she wanted to be with.

Something happened tonight that I'm missing.

The coolness of her feelings made no sense. Just that morning she had steamed over the newspaper article; her loyalty had come instinctively. Why, on the drive to the park she'd told herself how lucky she was to have him as a boyfriend. What had happened between then and now? Was it Bala's heroic rescue? Maybe her feelings had not disappeared, just been redirected.

No, that was not it. Her affection for Bala was a totally new thing. The way her heart had changed toward Jason had to do with Jason himself. Something he'd done, or something he'd neglected to do.

Something Karen might have missed, too?

The latter thought came as she caught sight of a photograph partially hidden in the corner behind a sweatshirt. Jason had quickly gone through his room before letting her in to change. Obviously, he had tried to hide the picture, but the shirt had fallen away. It was of him and Karen at the prom last year.

So he keeps her near his bed.

There was a robe in the closet she was able to tie tight enough at the waist that her breasts didn't pop out. Gathering together her soggy clothes, she returned to the game room. Jason was waiting for her. He took the clothes, disappeared for a couple of minutes, then reappeared with the hot chocolate. They sat together on the couch beside a pool table and a giant aquarium. Cindy let the cup warm her hands before taking a drink.

"I set the dryer to max," Jason said. "I hope you weren't wearing anything that can shrink."

"Just my underwear."

"I didn't see any underwear."

"Oh, I must not have been wearing any."

She had not intended to drop a suggestive remark. Jason brightened. "You're not wearing any this minute, that's for sure."

He put down his cup, placed his hand on her shoulder. "You know, Cindy, you look very beautiful right now."

She took a gulp of the hot chocolate. The taste was too sweet. "I don't feel beautiful," she muttered.

His fingers played with the top of her arm. "How do you feel?"

"Tired. And grateful. I don't know how I'm ever going to repay Bala."

Jason glanced at the fish. "That was a nice jump he took off that hill," he agreed.

"It was absolutely awesome."

"But I think he made a mistake not letting me pluck you up from the tree." She did not respond. He added, "What did you think when you saw me up there?"

"I thought you looked like you were about to fall off."

Jason nodded gravely. "It wasn't the safest place in the world to be."

"Yeah."

He put his arm around her. "What's the matter, Cindy?"

"Nothing."

"You seem far away."

"I'm thinking."

"About what?"

"Nothing."

He forced a laugh. "All right, I understand. You don't want to talk. I don't want to, either."

He started to kiss her. With her fatigue, it was easier to cooperate than resist, although she was feeling about as romantic as she did when her seventy-year-old dentist cleaned her teeth.

But then Jason's kisses became insistent. He was pulling her down on the couch, tugging at the knot she had tied in the robe's belt. She snapped her head back. "No," she said.

His wide eyes were inches away. "Are you still shook from the fall in the water?"

"I—yes. I just want to rest here until my clothes are ready." She leaned her head into his chest. "Okay?"

"Sure, whatever you want." He stroked her hair, which was not a particularly soothing thing to do with all the knots in it. "I don't know if I told you how relieved I was when you made it to the side safely."

"It was scary," she agreed.

His hand moved from her hair to her lower back, rubbing. "I don't know if I ever told you how important you are to me."

There's a lot of things you don't know if you've told me.

The sarcasm felt out of place in her own mind. She was glad Jason did not have ESP. "You don't have to say anything, Jason."

For a while he did as requested, and she began to doze. Her breathing deepened, developing a slight snoring sound, and she vaguely realized she was listening to herself falling asleep. That was fine; when she awoke her clothes would be dry and she would be able to get to her own bed.

But then, all of a sudden, Jason started kissing her again. These were hungry passionate kisses, never mind that her response was almost nonexistent. He yanked open the knot in the robe belt, running his hand up her side.

"Jason, stop, it's late."

"It's almost a new day," he said, excited, continuing to paw at her.

"But I'm tired."

He pulled at the top of her robe. "You're amazing."

"Jason."

"Come on, Cindy, don't be such a tease."

"Get off me!" she shouted, coming fully awake, sitting up forcefully and retying her robe. "Don't you ever call me a tease!"

There was blood in Jason's cheeks. "Well, what do you expect? You take off your clothes and put on that thing that doesn't hide a damn thing and you get all pissed that I start getting interested."

"I took off my clothes because they were wet, not because I was trying to get you excited. What do you think I am?"

Now he was mad. "I think you're just like all the other girls at school. You're all talk. You wiggle your ass in front of the whole city at the stadium to support the guys on the team, but in private you'd rather make it with some geek on the cross-country team who—"

Cindy slapped him across the face. An instant after she

did so, she realized he couldn't have possibly been talking about her brother. He was referring to Ray, who used to go with Karen—

Something Karen missed— His temper?

Jason leapt to his feet and raised his arm to strike her, his handsome face almost unrecognizable because of his fury. Cindy made no move to protect herself. Or maybe she made the best move. She just stared him straight in the eye. Jason paused, then slammed his fist into his leg, turning away.

"You had no right to hit me," he said, disgusted, taking a deep breath.

"You had no right to say what you did."

He whirled. "What did I say!?"

She nodded slowly. "A lot. Enough." She stood. "I'm going to get my clothes."

"Cindy, wait, please!" He grabbed her by the shoulders, suddenly worried. "Look, I'm sorry. I apologize. You know how much pressure I've been under lately? I don't know why I said that. I don't feel that way."

He looked so totally miserable, her sympathy came against her better judgment. "Okay. We'll forget it. I accept your apology. I'm sorry I slapped you."

Jason smiled. "So we're still friends?"

"Yeah. Sure."

They were great friends. When he took her home, she couldn't remember ever feeling so glad to get out of his car.

Alex pulled in the driveway while she was busy unlocking the front door. He limped from the car to the porch. His knee must be hurting. Her own ankle wasn't exactly in bliss. They made a great pair. Except Alex was smiling.

"How was Joni?" she asked, trying to sound upbeat for his sake.

He sighed. "I think she's in love."

Cindy chuckled. "I get the feeling she's not the only one. Did you kiss her good night?"

"Till our lips caught fire. How's your ankle? Bala told us you'd bruised it."

They entered the house. Wolf must still be outside; he usually came to greet her. Well, she wasn't going to go looking for him now. "I'm fine. You didn't tell Mom?"

"No."

"Good." She yawned. "I'm going to want to hear every last detail about Joni's combustible lips tomorrow, but right now, I've got to go to bed."

Alex was sensitive to her unspoken moods. "But you're okay?"

She nodded wearily. "I'm more than okay. I'm Cindy Jones."

He surprised her with a tight hug. "Thank God I didn't lose you tonight," he said.

"I knew you'd try to save me," she replied, squeezing him back, feeling her eyes burn. Then she laughed. "A pity you couldn't swim any better than me!"

Alex stepped back, grinned. "Ain't that the truth." He patted her on the side. "Sweet dreams, sis."

"You, too."

Cindy went to her room and lay down and fell into a sleep so deep she didn't remember dreaming at all. Alex had a different experience, though in the morning he was to recall nothing more than his sister. But for the time he dreamed, if it could be called that, he witnessed a scene so vivid and so awful that it seemed to scratch his very soul.

He was caught in the current of a warm river rushing toward a cliff. A blazing sun hung in a rusty sky. He could feel its heat in spite of being all wet. And he could hear a noise coming from the approaching cliff, not the sound of water crashing on hard rocks, but the cries of many animals, and maybe people, in terrible pain. As he listened, he realized that on the other side of the cliff was a thing whose nature it was to rip the life out of the living. How he knew this, he wasn't sure. But he was convinced if he didn't escape the river soon, he would come face-to-face with this thing, and that it would show him no mercy. He would become just another one of the victims whose death agony wailed in his ears.

He tried swimming for the sides of the river. The way was difficult and his time was short. Yet somehow he managed to reach the edge, only to discover that its walls were smooth, impossible to scale.

There never had been a way to escape. Everyone who entered the river was doomed to go over the edge. He had been born and he was going to die. He saw that the river flowed not with water, but with blood.

He began to panic. He began to cry for help. The sound of his pleas mingled with the sound of all those who had already taken the awful plunge. He would be one of them. It was his destiny.

Yet he did not fall when the river came to its end. He was instead lifted up into the air, where he floated on a hot dry draft. And then everything changed, and it could not be said to have changed for the better. The cliff remained, but the river vanished, and he himself was no longer the same. He could fly, and his path swooped him past the very base of the cliff. There he saw no people and heard no cries. He saw only animals, quick-footed and sharp-toothed predators, feeding on other animals that weren't so quick, or so cruel.

And he watched, feeling a great horror, because the feeding animals filled him with envy; the sight of the bloody carcasses were making him hungry.

Yes, he had changed.

Chapter Eight

Cindy didn't go to school on Monday. Her ankle was still sore—she told her parents she had twisted it getting out of Jason's car—and she didn't want to be seen hobbling around on crutches. Fortunately, the foot was feeling much better on Tuesday.

On that particular morning, as she had done the previous Friday morning, she stepped out of her house early to collect the local paper, delivered twice weekly. There was another article by Kent Cooke starting on the second page, and she read it from beginning to end, standing in the cool sunlight at the end of her driveway.

KAREN HOLLY'S STRANGE GRIZZLY
BY KENT COOKE

I received a lot of mail Saturday morning. Much of it was delivered to my office, not by the mailman, but by those who had written the letters. Apparently, a few people were concerned I might not hear their opinions in time to respond in today's edition. Not all the mail flattered my reporting abilities. Some of it was outright hostile. It was probably good that I'd decided to take Saturday off.

But the majority of the mail was encouraging. People were curious. They wanted to hear more. They wanted me to dig deeper. I must confess, I had anticipated their desires. Since my previous article probing into the unusual circumstances surrounding Karen Holly's death, I have been busy sniffing around. I hope I won't be accused of having purposely withheld information last week so that I could have more to talk about today. Practically everything I will relate today I learned early yesterday morning.

First I spoke to Lieutenant James Baker. He was the gentleman who arrived at the scene of Karen's death before anyone else, with, of course, the exception of Jason Whitfield. I had been trying to talk to the lieutenant for some time; it was only after my article appeared a few days ago that he consented to meet with me.

Lieutenant Baker seemed a troubled man, maybe even an angry one. But he wasn't angry at me or my work. The investigation into Karen's death was troubling him, too. Certain things didn't make sense, he said.

Rain had fallen the night of the tragedy, between the time Jason left Karen's body and the time the lieutenant reached the spot he had been directed to by Jason. In my hate mail many people said the rain was the reason there were no bear tracks. Lieutenant Baker dismissed this explanation. When he arrived at the top of Crystal Falls, he said the rain was nothing more than a light drizzle. It is true that within the hour, a heavy downpour was to start, but in the interlude the officer had plenty of time to scout the area. Even equipped with a special high-powered flashlight designed for police work, he found not a single bear track. Of course, as previously stated, he didn't find Karen's body, either, not until much later in the night, when he was returning to his car in the company of Deputy Jeff Pierce, walking along the lower level of Snake Tail River, miles from where Karen had supposedly met the grizzly.

Those who knew Karen personally will have to forgive what is said in the following paragraph. They may even want to skip it. Lieutenant Baker paled when discussing the matter. It has to do with the nature of Karen's head wound. The coroner's report stated, and I quote, "Her head had suffered from what appeared to be an extremely powerful blow—the top of the skull was cracked in several places."

The lieutenant didn't directly dispute the coroner's statement. But he did add something. When he pulled Karen from the river, he said, it looked as though her head had been grabbed by the ears and squashed together.

The only way I can imagine a grizzly creating this effect is if the animal had trounced on Karen's head while she was lying on the ground. It would be physically impossible that the damage was done by a single blow while she was standing or sitting. But, somehow, I can't see the bear jumping up and down on the poor dead girl, nor can I see the grizzly dragging her body to the river and tossing it in.

Lieutenant Baker wasn't worrying about his job when he told me these facts. He's leaving the Timber Police Force in a couple of weeks. He's moving to Los Angeles, where he plans to go into real estate. He says he no longer feels good about raising his kids in this town. The place is too dangerous.

Last week, when I mentioned a sledgehammer and a rake, I was implying they'd been previously planted in the vicinity, that the murder—if there was one—had been planned. But let's play pretend and let's keep things simple. Say we had someone who wanted to kill this girl. Say the desire to do so came to him on the spur of the moment, in a fit of anger perhaps. What can you kill a girl with in the mountains? Big rocks would be handy enough. And let's further imagine that this murderer, when he was done smacking Karen on the head, suddenly realized that he'd made a terrible mistake, that he was in big trouble. What could he do?

Maybe he could make it look like a grizzly attack. By getting a bigger rock, by getting a sharp branch, he could cave in her rib cage and tear her flesh and so mutilate her body that it would be hard to tell what had gotten her. Then, to further confuse the situation, he could carry her to the river and let her go over the falls.

Do I think Jason Whitfield killed Karen Holly? I keep asking that question, don't I? I'll tell you one thing, I don't think a grizzly did it.

The preliminary hearing into Karen's death is next Monday. My spies in the district attorney's office still say there isn't a chance Jason will go to trial. This strikes me as incredible considering the "reasonable doubt" any sane person must have about Jason's innocence. Why doesn't the state have access to the information I have? Could it be because Jason's father plays golf on Saturdays with people who represent the state?

What do I know, I'm just a hack reporter who's always dreaming up conspiracies.

I went to the game Friday night against Brea High. I'm a big football fan, as you're probably all aware, but the game was slow and sloppy even by my modest standards. Things got kind of interesting at halftime, though. A fight broke out between a player for Timber and a spectator. I don't know what the fight was about or how it got started. All I can say was that the player was Jason Whitfield, and that he yelled out a threat to kill one of his classmates.

That kid's got a hell of a temper.

The bell signaling the end of lunch had rung, and Cindy was walking across the courtyard with Pam before going to Miss Clemens's psychology class, when Bala stopped her. She had not seen him since she had fallen asleep in his arms. He looked worried.

"May I talk to you in private?" he asked her, glancing at Pam to indicate he also wanted her approval.

"Whatever Cindy talks about in private," Pam said, "I hear about on the phone that same night."

"Sure," Cindy said. "Pam, I'll catch up with you in a couple of minutes. Okay?"

Pam nodded with exaggerated patience. "I suppose I must learn to deal with the rejection." Giving a theatrical swirl, she walked away.

"Did I offend her?" Bala asked.

"No," Cindy said, not sure if he had. "She's always saying stuff like that." She smiled. "I was searching for you during lunch."

Bala glanced around. "Can we talk where there are fewer people?" he asked, serious.

"All right. Let's go sit on the stump."

This was the first time she didn't have to climb up the back of the tree. Bala simply lifted her onto the stump after leaping up himself. Settling herself, she could see the courtyard emptying quickly.

"What did you want to talk about?" she asked.

Bala withdrew the morning paper from his back pocket and her heart sunk in her chest. The article had been on her mind all morning. She hadn't talked to Jason about it yet. He didn't appear to have made it to school.

"Did you know this girl, Karen Holly?" Bala asked.

"Pam knew her better. She was Pam's cousin. Did you talk to her about the article?"

"I wanted to talk to you first."

"Why?"

"Because you are Jason's girlfriend."

She looked down. "What do you want to know?"

"How Karen died."

"A lot of people want to know that. Jason says a bear killed her."

"Do you believe him?"

She shrugged. "What else could it have been?"

"Cindy?" His hand touched her hand. His skin appeared so dark against hers. She must try to get more sun. "Do *you* believe him?" he repeated.

She looked into his big luminous eyes. "Why do you want to know?" she asked uneasily.

"It is important to me. I cannot explain why." He paused. "I cannot tell you all my reasons, at least. But when I read this"—he tapped the paper—"I was worried about you."

"I don't think I'll be spending much time alone with Jason from now on. You don't have to worry."

You could even try to take his place, if you wanted. I wouldn't stop you.

"Did something happen between you since last Friday?"

She ran her hands over her legs, glancing at the ground again. "Yes. It's a long story, and sort of private." She stopped. "We should be getting to class soon."

Bala was studying her. He was not the same person she thought she knew. He seemed confused. "How is your ankle?" he asked absently.

She wiggled it for his benefit. "Fine, thanks to you." She paused again, undecided whether she wanted to probe. "You have a lot on your mind?"

"The death of this young girl, particularly the way in which she died, disturbs me."

She nodded. "It's no fun reading about, that's for sure."

"Where is Jason today? I have not seen him."

"He may have taken the day off. You weren't thinking of asking him directly about Karen?"

"Yes, I was."

"That would be a bad idea, believe me. He hardly knows you, and I don't think you're one of his favorites."

"Does he have this bad temper the man in the paper mentioned?"

"He wouldn't kill anybody, if that's what you're asking."

"That *is* what I am asking," he replied, showing uncharacteristic impatience. He leaned close, gripping her arm. "Cindy, please? This is important."

"But *why*?"

"I cannot tell you why."

"And I can't tell you whether he did it or not!" she shouted, the words out of her mouth before she realized. Bala let go of her arm and sat back.

"He could have?" he asked quietly.

She hung her head miserably. "I don't know." She sniffed. "I don't think so, but I don't know."

Why doesn't this death go away? Why does it hang around like it had a life of its own?

Bala thought about what she said for a moment. "How is Alex?" he asked suddenly.

"What?"

"Your brother? How is he doing?"

"Alex is fine."

"Good." He seemed on the verge of asking more, before deciding against it. He jumped off the stump, then helped her down, his massive hands practically encircling her narrow waist. His strength continued to amaze her.

If he wanted, he could snap me in two.

Where had that thought come from?

He let go of her. "You are different from any of the girls in my village," he said, staring down at her, his voice solemn, as though the difference were not something he necessarily would have wished for.

She forced a smile. "Because I have blond hair?"

He went to touch her hair, stopped himself with an effort. He nodded, averting his eyes. "That must be it, Cindy."

Cindy wasn't the only one in her family who was late to fifth period class that Tuesday afternoon. Alex had spent the entire lunch period looking for Joni, and had not found her. He had done the same thing the previous lunchtime, with the same result. He had ended up calling her house. Her aunt had answered. Joni was not feeling well, Mrs. Lee had said, and was resting in bed. Alex had been angry with himself for having kept her out so late Friday that she'd gotten sick. And now, with her second absence in a row, his disgust with himself had changed to concern for her. For some reason, Joni had struck him as the last person in the world who would get sick.

The second lunch bell had rung already, and the bulk of the school was busy expanding their minds with knowledge they would probably forget before the day was over. Alex put a quarter in the pay phone at the back of the gym, not ten steps from where he had skinned his knee during the race. Joni's aunt answered again.

"Mrs. Lee, this is Alex."

"Alex, how are you today?" She sounded happy to learn it was him, almost relieved. It had been the same the day before.

"I'm fine. How are you?"

"Wonderful." She was definitely exaggerating. "I suppose you're wondering why Joni hasn't been at school. The poor girl's still not herself."

"There is a bug going around." He hadn't actually heard of one in particular, but it seemed the thing to say. "What are her symptoms?"

The question stumped Mrs. Lee for a moment. "She just feels kind of lifeless, you know, like she can't do anything."

"Is she in bed now? I'd like to talk to her, if that would be all right."

The woman paused. "I'll check. Could you hold a moment?"

"Yes."

He waited two long minutes before Joni came on the line. There was a lifting and putting down of receivers. Joni was talking from a different phone.

"Alex?" Her voice was devoid of energy.

"Yeah, it's me. I've been worried about you. How are you doing?"

"Good."

"You don't sound so good. Do you have the flu or something?" He had to wait for an answer.

"I don't know."

He wondered if her problem might not be emotional, if the grief over the death of her parents might have resurfaced and knocked her whole system out of whack. "Are you drinking plenty of fluids?"

"Huh?"

"Have you been drinking orange juice and grape juice and stuff like that?"

"Yes, my aunt has juice in the house." She coughed, making a strange sound in her throat. "I'm glad you called, Alex."

"You know, I sat in on your biology class today and took a few notes. If you'd like, I could bring them by. You don't want to fall too far behind while you're out sick."

"No," she said quickly, her voice gaining a measure of life. "I don't want you to come over."

He tried to sound light. "I don't care if you're not looking as wonderful as usual. And I never get sick. I'm not worried about catching what you've got."

A faint note of humor entered her tone, and yet, strangely enough, it only served to deepen the gloom of the conversation. "What I've got isn't catching."

"Then there's no problem. I'll stop by after practice."

"No," she said again, anxious now. "I don't want to see you."

Alex felt a painful stab in his chest. The way they had kissed—she must care about him. "But why not?"

Joni's words descended to a faraway whisper. "My aunt is here, but we don't really know each other. There's nothing between us. It's like I'm in an empty house. That's the way I want it right now." She coughed again, her vocal cords sounding as rough as sandpaper. "Stay away, Alex, just stay away."

He swallowed. "Okay, if that's what you want."

They said their good-byes. Alex stood for a while holding the silent phone in his hand.

Chapter Nine

Joni Harper wasn't seen at school that week, but Jason Whitfield returned on Thursday. Cindy ran into him during the break between second and third periods. They made a date to have lunch together at the McDonald's a block away from the campus, or rather, Jason made the date. All through the morning Cindy wondered if she should use the time to tell him the romance was over. What made her hesitate was that she had still to figure out what had soured Jason in her mind. All she knew, for certain, was that her feelings for him had changed up at the waterfall, before he had gotten rough in his game room.

She had to wonder if Bala's song hadn't planted shamanic seeds deep in her mind. The world looked different than it had the previous week. Pam's gossiping was no longer as interesting.

Jason took her to McDonald's on the back of his motorcycle.

He drove fast, as usual, scaring her, and making a mess of her hair in the process. But he was kind enough to pay for her food. With his dad's money.

"You hear the game's on a Saturday this week?" he said when they were seated in a booth. He took a bite of his hamburger, reaching for his fries. A small box of Chicken McNuggets and a carton of milk had made up her order. Her appetite was off.

"Yeah."

"We're playing Hope. They only lost twice last year. But I think we'll kick their butts, if we don't put the ball in the air more than half a dozen times. The game's at their stadium."

"So I heard."

"I hope I get the ball if the game's on the line like it was last week."

She opened her milk. "I don't see why they wouldn't trust you with it," she muttered.

He looked at her. "What's wrong?"

"Nothing."

"Are you still mad at me for Friday night?"

"No. I hardly remember it."

"Then what's bugging you?"

"Nothing. What time's your hearing on Monday?"

He stopped, with a french fry hanging out of the corner of his mouth. "Why do you bring that up?"

She shrugged. "I think it's more important to talk about that than the game. But if you don't want to, that's fine with me."

He began to chew slowly. "In a way, I'm glad you mentioned it. I might need some help from you. I was talking to my lawyer yesterday, and he said, after all the B.S. press this thing's been getting, it might not be a bad idea to have a few character witnesses present." He paused, adding, "He thought my current girlfriend would be a good one."

Cindy sighed. "I don't know, Jason."

"What don't you know?"

I don't know if you're a good one.

"I have school on Monday."

His tone sharpened. "So what's one day of school? My ass is on the line."

"I heard the hearing was just a formality."

"Who told you that?"

"You did."

He was annoyed. "It was, last week. But with that jerk's articles, the D.A.'s going to have to act like he's hot on my tail."

"He's just going to act?"

Jason did a double take. "He's going to do his job," he said carefully. "Will you help me, Cindy?"

She almost told him, right then, that it was finished between them. What stopped her was a peculiar intuition that there might be a value in attending the hearing, a value outside of what Jason was counting on. Analyzing the feeling, she failed to find the rationale behind it.

"Can I think about it?" she said.

"Sure. Can I have my lawyer call you?"

"Sure."

Hope High's cross-country course was a piece of cake next to Timber's. It was also unimaginative and boring. There was a fine park adjoining the school, but they'd chosen to construct a route completely within the campus, using the track, various playing fields and an assortment of loops through the buildings. By squeezing a three-mile course into a school that could hold less than a thousand students, they'd created a situation where the runners had to cover the same ground again and again. Alex didn't care. There were no hills. He hated hills.

As usual, Cindy and Pam were there to cheer for him. Alex wished Joni had been able to come. Here it was Friday and she still hadn't returned to school. He was going to call her after the race, he'd decided, and he was going to go see her no matter how much she felt she needed to be alone. The more he'd thought of it, the more obvious it'd become she was depressed. She needed a friend. She needed him. He would call her after he won.

The hunted, the hunter.

They had removed their sweats and were walking over to the starting line. Cindy had just given him a good-luck kiss and Pam had just kicked Ray in the shins. Alex was surprised at his lack of tension. He'd lost last week and still his confidence was high. He kept thinking about how it'd been on the couch with Joni, how her mouth had seemed to almost swallow him. That had been nice.

"Going to trip over any cheerleaders this week, Alex?" Ray asked in his usual jovial way.

"Only if they throw themselves at my feet. Going to remember to tie your shoes?"

"Damn, I shouldn't have quit Boy Scouts when I did." Ray laughed, kneeling to take care of his laces. They had both been loose. Alex waited for him patiently, reflecting that Ray and he had not talked once about Joni all week.

"Hurry," he said after a minute. "Their coach is loading the starting pistol."

Ray stood, brushing off his chubby knees. "What kind of pace are you going to set, buddy?"

"A merciless one," Alex lied.

He was taking Joni's advice. When the gun went off, he didn't rush to the front. He tucked in behind Ray, who was in turn following a short redhead whom Alex knew to be Hope's strongest runner. He had barely defeated the guy last year.

They circled the track twice, then headed onto the baseball field. The grass under their feet was thick and made for a slow surface. Alex didn't mind. He had fallen into an excellent rhythm. This lagging behind wasn't so bad. He realized he'd always been afraid to use this tactic before because of his lack of confidence. He'd always been so afraid of losing that he'd felt he had to win every blessed yard of every course. In reality, with his kick, it made sense to take it easy at the beginning. Joni had taught him more in a minute than his coach had in three years.

Alex thought of Joni as he ran. He would buy flowers before he visited her. Roses, yeah, what girl didn't like roses? The thing was, he had to get her out of that house, away from her aunt. The woman was nice enough but it was a fact it had also been her sister who had died. How could being around Mrs. Lee not help but depress Joni?

As they entered the third mile, Alex knew he was in good shape. The redhead had led most of the way, with Ray occasionally pressing the pace. Alex had allowed them a thirty-yard lead, but now he began to close that gap. With a half a mile to go, he drew even, noting with pleasure how hard his two opponents were breathing. His own breathing was heavy but didn't feel strained. He remembered the speed the redhead had showed in the final stretch last year. Feeling how much spring he had in his own legs, he wasn't worried.

Ray charged to the lead as they reentered the track. The Hope runner hung close and Alex stayed on his heels. He could hear Cindy shouting his name. The fatigue was there, but he had it under control. He switched to his reserves and found them waiting to be used. Half a lap from the finish, he accelerated in a burst, passing the others. He knew he had it at that point. But hitting the tape a few seconds later still felt divine.

Ray finished third. Sweating like a bear, he gave him a

congratulatory hug as they exited the chute. "Nice kick at the end, Alex," he gasped. "If only I'd had my doughnuts this week, I might have made it closer."

Alex smiled. "Fast on them for the next week and you'll be back on top." It was easy to be the nice guy when you were a winner. He let his head fall back, drinking up the air, tasting the sweetness of victory. For the rest of the season, he swore, he was going to enjoy this sensation after every race.

"Alex!"

Cindy was as happy, if not more so, than he was. One of the main reasons he always wanted to win so badly was to give her something to cheer about. She squeezed him tightly, not minding the fact she was staining her uniform with his sweat. "You were magnificent!" she said.

"You stunk," Pam told Ray, who had bent back over, trying to catch his breath. "You choked. Alex stomped your ass. You should quit while you're only third rate."

Ray smiled, letting himself fall over onto his butt on the ground. "I love you, too, baby."

Alex came back to earth hard and quick after they'd showered and were walking to the bus for the ride home. He was alone with Ray. They'd changed quickly and were ahead of the others. Alex spotted a phone attached to Hope's administration building. He went to excuse himself.

"Who are you calling?" Ray asked.

He saw no point in lying. "Joni Harper. You must have noticed she hasn't been in this week. I think she's going through a rough time."

"She sounded all right to me."

Alex stopped in midstride, glancing back at him. "When did you talk to her?"

"Yesterday."

"But she wasn't at school yesterday."

Ray shrugged. "We talked on the phone."

Alex's heart skipped a beat. "You called her? When did you get her number?"

"We exchanged numbers the first week of school. But I didn't call her. She called me."

"*What?* Why would she call you?"

Ray couldn't understand his amazement. "I'm her friend. Maybe she was bored. She wanted to know if I wanted to do something this weekend."

Alex went very still. He had not calmed down. He had gone into mild shock. "What did you tell her?"

Ray was beginning to realize this wasn't a casual situation. "I told her, sure," he said slowly. "I didn't think it was any big deal."

Alex had to fight to keep his voice from trembling. "But you knew I was going out with her. You saw us together at the game, for god's sakes."

"What of it? You went out on a date. You didn't exchange vows."

"It wasn't just a date. We— How can she go out with you? She's sick."

"Like I said, she sounded all right on the phone." Ray paused, ran his hand through his hair. "You're not mad, are you?"

Alex looked away. She told him to stay away. Then she had called Ray. Lord, *she* had asked Ray out! This did not make sense. She cared about him. She had made that clear. They had held hands and kissed and made plans to do things together.

But maybe she would just as easily do all those things with Ray. Maybe she would do even more with him.

"Just once I've got to know what that soft white skin feels like under my fingers."

"I'm not happy about it," he said quietly.

Ray looked uncomfortable. "Hey, that's your own fault if you're not. I told you earlier I was going to hit on her. You didn't tell me not to."

Alex considered a move he had sworn he would never take. "And what if I told you now?"

Ray took a step back, folded his arms across his chest. "I can't do that, Alex."

He raised his voice. "Why not?"

"I told her I'd go out with her. I hate going back on my word."

"Your *word*? You're stabbing an old friend in the back, and you're worried about your word to a girl you hardly know?"

Ray was insulted. "I'm not stabbing you in the back."

"Have you got another name for taking a guy's girl?"

"She's not your girl. If she was, she wouldn't be going out with me. She wouldn't have *asked* me out."

"I don't believe she did ask you out. I think you just weaseled her into doing something she doesn't really want to do!"

Ray's tone sharpened. "Call her."

"Why should I call her?"

"To ask her what I weaseled her into. Go ahead. What are you afraid of?"

That she'll hang up on me.

Alex shook his head, the fight suddenly going out of him. "I'm not going to call her," he muttered.

Ray also softened. "I'm sorry, Alex. I guess I did know you liked her. But I couldn't resist."

"It's that hard?" he asked wearily. Stupid question; who knew better than he how hard it was not to want Joni Harper.

Ray appeared thoughtful, even perplexed. He stared at a group of young children who were playing on a swing in the park across the street. "I don't know what it is. I told you I'm going to try to get back with Pam? Right after the race, I asked her if she wanted me to drop by Sunday afternoon. She just laughed at me. But I know she meant, yes. I miss Pam, you know? I really do. But I feel I've just got to go out with Joni this one time."

"You're not making sense."

Ray glanced his way, trying to smile. "I told you before, it's like she's cast a spell on me. She's called and I have to follow." He put his hand on Alex's shoulder, spoke seriously. "It'll just be this once. And nothing will happen, buddy, I promise."

He nodded. "All right, Ray, whatever you say."

Alex ended up driving back to Timber in the car with Cindy. He did not take the bus. He never saw Ray alive again.

Chapter Ten

Cindy was doing the laundry when the reporter Kent Cooke came to the door. With the hours her parents put in at the store, there wasn't much time left over for them to take care of household chores; for that reason, Cindy didn't mind washing the dirty clothes. Normally, she took care of them Sunday night; but with Jason's hearing, she'd decided to take Monday off, and had postponed the chore until Monday morning. Jason's lawyer had called her Saturday afternoon, and that cat sure had been persuasive. He should've been a used-car salesman. He'd not only tried to convince her to appear as a character witness, he'd tried to program her as to exactly what she was supposed to say. But she had a mind of her own. She might just stay home all day.

Jason's the most thoughtful and sensitive boy I know. He has never once tried to take advantage of me nor has he ever raised his voice in my presence— Come on, give me a break. He's as horny and as loud as any guy I know.

At the knock at the door, Wolf rushed to her side and Sybil said hello to Joni. That stupid bird really had taken a liking to Alex's friend. Sybil had been calling for Joni for the last week.

"Cindy," Cindy said as she swept past the bird cage. "Hello, Cindy Jones."

"Hello, Joni Jones."

"Dumb, dumb," Cindy muttered.

"Hello, Dumb Jones."

The newspaper always ran a miniature black and white of Kent Cooke at the top of his column. As a result, Cindy recognized the man instantly. That didn't lessen her surprise.

"Can I help you?" she asked warily, standing with the door only partway open. He had to be close to forty, but there was something in his face and the way he held himself that made him seem younger. His big ears would have done better with a thicker head of hair, and his sports coat needed pressing.

"Are you Cindy Jones?"

"Yes."

"Do you know who I am?"

"You write for the paper."

He nodded. "I'm Kent Cooke, yes. May I come in?"

She hesitated. "I'll be off to school in a few minutes."

He consulted his watch. "Are you sure you're going today, Cindy? You're already late."

"What do you want?"

"If I may come in and have a seat, I'll tell you."

"All right." She opened the door all the way. Wolf sniffed the man's hand, and Mr. Cooke patted the dog on the head, making himself comfortable on the couch. Cindy sat on the edge of a chair directly across from him. "Go on," she said.

He smiled briefly. "You don't seem overjoyed to see me, Cindy. Have you read my articles about Karen Holly and Jason Whitfield?"

"I've seen them."

"I understand you're Jason's latest girlfriend?"

"We're friends," she said cautiously. Mr. Cooke noted her tone.

"I hear you're going to appear at his hearing today as a character witness?"

"Who told you that?"

He shrugged. "Reporters have to protect their sources. And does it matter? Are you going to the hearing?"

"I might."

"What are you going to say? If you go, that is?"

"Are you going to be there, Mr. Cooke?"

"Certainly."

"Then you'll find out then."

He leaned forward, studied her. "Let's not fence with each

other. You're Jason's girl, and he can't have helped give you a favorable impression of me. He's probably told you I'm on his case just so I can make his father, the mayor, look bad."

"I form my own opinions of people, Mr. Cooke. What is it you want?"

He sat up. "The truth. I want to know whether Jason killed Karen. I would want to know this no matter whose son he was."

"Why don't you let the police and the courts decide if he killed her?"

"If they were free to go about this investigation in a normal fashion, I would. But they're not; they're being obstructed. Before you dismiss this possibility, let me tell you who appoints the sheriff in this town—Jason's father. It's Timber's sheriff who's been overseeing the investigation since the night Karen died. And things have not been going by the book. Karen's own parents have been unable to obtain a full report of the autopsy. That alone would indicate that outside 'influences' are at work."

"What does any of this have to do with me? Do you want me to take the stand today and tell the judge that Jason has tried to kill me a couple of times?"

He stared at her a moment. "Has he?"

"No! What kind of question is that?"

Mr. Cooke paused. "As I mentioned in my article, I went to the game a week ago last Friday. I saw Jason fighting with

Ray Bower. I saw you trying to break up that fight. I heard threats shouted."

"It was just a silly argument. It was nothing serious."

Mr. Cooke shook his head sadly. "I'm afraid it's very serious, Cindy. How well did you know Ray?"

Her heart began to pound silently. "I've known him a long time. Since I was a kid. Why?"

"Then I'm sorry I'm the one who has to bring you this news." He cleared his throat. "Ray's dead."

She almost laughed, the remark sounded so absurd. Ray couldn't be dead; he'd just run against her brother on Friday and he'd never looked more alive.

"What?"

"The police found his body at three this morning at the national park, though it appears he'd been dead at least twenty-four hours. Apparently, he went out with a girl Saturday night. He dropped her off about eleven but never made it home."

Cindy closed her eyes, moaning inside. All those great gross jokes, those loud obnoxious laughs—no more. "How did it happen?" she whispered.

"Whatever or whoever got hold of Karen appears to have gotten hold of Ray. In fact, the officer I spoke to said Ray's body was in worse shape." He added, "It was difficult to make the identification."

"A grizzly," she mumbled.

"It was no grizzly, Cindy. Ray was murdered. He was

murdered by the same person who murdered Karen."

"But what does the girl say? My brother said Ray was going out with Joni Harper."

"She doesn't know anything."

"But isn't she a suspect?"

"Joni Harper is a ninety-nine pound seventeen-year-old."

"But Jason couldn't have done this. How could he have? If what you say is true, he wouldn't have had the strength."

"I know this is not easy. I hate talking about it. But since we must, if you think about it, once Jason had Ray unconscious, or dead, he could, with suitable tools, do just about anything he wanted to his body."

Cindy bent over, her stomach heaving. "No!" she cried. "Jason would have no motive."

"An angry man doesn't need a motive. Outside of his anger. He'll do anything."

"You're saying Jason's a psychotic? Is that what you're saying?"

"Yes."

Cindy sat upright, put her arm over her eyes. "I want you to leave."

"I will, in a moment. But first I want to ask you something. Has Jason ever given you a hint of being badly disturbed?"

"No," she said flatly. Alex would have no one to run against. Pam would have no one to make fun of. . . .

"Are you sure?"

"Yes. Now please, go."

"But surely you've seen signs of his temper?"

She grabbed the arms of the chair, glaring. "So what? Lots of people have tempers. That doesn't mean they cut people up. Do you think I would've gone out with him if I thought he might kill me? Why, just last week we were up at the mountains and he—" She stopped.

Tried to save my life? Why did my life need saving?

Kent Cooke was watching her intently. "Please continue, Cindy."

"It was nothing," she muttered, thinking. Jason had dragged her up to Castle Park. He had dragged the whole group up there. And he'd insisted they go to a cave, a cave Alex thought didn't even exist.

"But you were saying you were up at the mountains and Jason did something. What did he do?"

"Nothing," she said evenly. "He didn't do a damn thing."

Mr. Cooke stood reluctantly, sighing. "It's a terrible thing that happened to Karen. It's even worse that it had to happen to Ray, too. I hope this is the end of it. I pray that it is. But frankly, I'm worried it's not. Jason's lying. If he had nothing to hide, he'd be telling the truth. His hearing is in five hours. I've already learned that Ray's death will not be brought into the proceedings. Don't ask me why not. The D.A. doesn't even have anyone lined up to question Jason's story. But Jason's lawyer has you scheduled. Think about it, Cindy, would you? I've been watching you. Each time I've mentioned Jason's name, even before I told you about Ray, you didn't react like a girl who didn't have doubts. A lot depends on you. Up on the stand, you might be the only voice Karen and Ray have got."

Cindy stood, composing herself, gesturing toward the door. "I can't talk anymore. I have things I have to do."

He nodded sympathetically. "You strike me as an intelligent young lady. I know you'll carefully consider the situation. See you at the hearing." He opened the door, took a step outside. "Once again, I'm sorry I had to be the bearer of bad tidings."

"So am I," she said softly.

When Mr. Cooke was gone, Cindy began to make plans. Alex had taken the car to school. He'd said he'd call at lunch to see if she still wanted to go to the hearing, which was in Cheyenne, two hours away. She could call the school now and have him return home immediately, but then she'd probably have to be the one to break the bad news. It appeared the reporter was several steps ahead of the general public when it came to local news. It was her responsibility to try to console Alex, she knew, but if she got involved in that at the moment she'd lose the time between now and the hearing. And if she called her parents at the store, they'd ask too many questions and probably not let her out of the house for fear she might drive into a tree or something in her distressed state.

There was really only one choice. She'd have to take her dad's seldom used motorbike sitting in the garage. She'd only had a couple of lessons on the thing. Jason had given them to her.

Cindy put on a leather jacket she never wore and stuffed a camera in the inside pocket. Outside, the bike started up without a hitch. In a way she might be better off with it than a car. She should be able to run the cycle pretty far up Pathfinders Trail.

Alex didn't learn of Ray's death until break, between second and third periods. He was hanging out near the science building, talking to Bala. It had been Bala who had started the conversation. He seemed sort of down and Alex could relate to that; Alex had spent the entire weekend dialing Joni's number on an unplugged phone.

But I didn't really call her. If she can call Ray, she can call me.

Bala seemed to be having girl troubles of his own.

He was asking about Cindy and Jason, how close they really were. Looked like Superman was falling for his sister. At least, that's what Alex thought was going on. Bala was beating around the bush. He also kept bringing up Joni, maybe trying to impress upon him that their situations were very similar.

"Just a minute, Bala," Alex interrupted. "I'm the last person who can give you advice. Believe me, I don't understand a thing about women. And that includes my sister."

Bala appeared taken aback. "I am not asking your advice, Alex, although I would welcome it if the situation called for it.

What I am seeking, without wishing to pry, is information."

Alex felt Bala was just too embarrassed to come right out and say he had the hots for Cindy. Alex was somewhat relieved to see these problems were international in scope. "Ask me something specific. Then maybe we can make some progress."

"How well does Cindy know Jason?"

"Pretty well."

"Would she try to protect him?"

"Are you referring to his hearing? You don't have to worry about that. Jason didn't kill Karen. All this talk going around is just hot air. A bear got that girl."

"How can you be sure?"

Alex shrugged. "What else could it have been? Anyway, I thought you wanted to know about Cindy? Look, I'll tell you what I'll do. Next time I see her, I'll bring you up and see how she reacts. This will be between you and me."

Bala frowned. "Why would you do this?"

Alex smiled. "Bala, you like her, admit it. You may as well find out if she likes you."

Bala turned away. "It is true I find your sister an extraordinary human being."

"Extraordinary human being—that's a great way to put it. I'll have to remember that when I think of Joni."

Bala eyed him. "How do you feel when you are with Joni?"

"On our date I felt fine. Better than fine. But now I'm

wondering where it all went. How do you feel when you're with Cindy?"

Bala didn't seem to hear the question. "Did you ever feel uneasy?"

Alex blushed. "Well, there were a few moments, here and there, you know?"

"Tell me."

"I shouldn't be talking about these things."

"Did you feel scared when her body touched yours?"

"Hey, now hold on! I'm not saying we did anything."

Bala was insistent. "Did her mouth touch yours?"

"Bala, listen, in our society you don't ask people of integrity questions like that. Sure, I kissed her good night. We don't have to go into how much anatomy was involved."

"And you did not feel scared?"

Alex sighed. "How did all this get started?"

Bala's brow was furrowed in concentration. "If it were so, there would be signs," he muttered to himself.

"Huh?"

"Alex, have you been having any dreams? Nightmares about awful bloody things?"

Alex shook his head, getting more confused by the moment. "And I thought I was going through a rough time with Joni. Look, Bala, Cindy is easy to get to know. All you've got to do is—"

Alex spotted Pam at that instant. He almost didn't recognize her. Pam wasn't the prettiest of girls, but she usually had a spark to her. Such was not the case now. She was weaving like a drunk, apparently searching for someone she couldn't find. Bala saw her, too. They hurried to her side.

"Pam, is something wrong?" Bala asked, concerned. Pam took a moment to recognize him. Tear stains dampened her cheeks. Bala grabbed her by the shoulders, shook her gently. "Pam?"

"Bala, I'm looking for Cindy. I need a ride home."

"Why do you need a ride?" Bala asked.

Pam looked down, squinted her eyes as though something irritating had lodged in them. "Because my head is screwed up. I don't think I can drive."

"Why do you have to go home?" Alex asked.

Pam gazed at him in wonder. "Alex, do you know where Cindy is?"

Pam phasing in and out like this was unbelievable. She was usually as steady as a rock. "Never mind, Cindy," Alex said. "We can give you a ride. Tell us, what's wrong?"

"It's Ray," she said. Then her whole face crumbled and she began to cry. "He's dead."

"Ray's dead?" Alex said in disbelief. "No, he's fine. What are you talking about?"

Pam continued to sob and it was only Bala who was keeping her on her feet. "My mother called the school," she said. "She wants me to come home. Something killed Ray."

"What?" Bala asked sharply.

Pam sniffed. "They think it was Mr. Bear. He got Karen and now he's gotten Ray."

"Mr. Bear?" Alex chuckled, though he felt far from happy. "Pam, what exactly did your mother say?"

Exasperation pierced through her grief. It appeared to help her get a grip on reality. "She said Ray was dead! What else do you want to hear? Some animal got hold of him. Now just shut up and take me home!" Her face fell on Bala's chest. "Damn this world," she moaned.

Bala backed away from Pam slowly. Alex had to move to support her. Bala's face had undergone a complete metamorphosis. His aura of quiet strength had disintegrated. Pure cold horror had replaced it. So frightening was the change in him, Alex didn't even have a chance to assimilate that Ray really was gone.

"Bala, what is it?"

"It is true," he whispered. "What I was told is true."

"What's true? What's going on? Do you know what has happened to Ray?"

Bala turned away, leaning his head on the wall of the science building. "I was warned."

Alex was having to fight too many things at once. Pam was collapsing in his arms. Bala was mumbling gibberish. "Who warned you about what?"

"My grandfather warned me about the girl."

"Bala, I need some help here. We've got to get Pam home. We can talk on the way." Alex winced. "God, I hope none of this is really happening."

Bala stood abruptly upright, turning toward them, trying to master himself. "Alex, you told me Ray went out with Joni last Saturday?"

"Yes."

Pam broke suddenly from his arms, spoke savagely, "I'm going to find Cindy. You guys don't know what's happening." She began to hurry away. Alex moved to follow.

"Cindy's not at school today," he called. Bala grabbed his arm.

"You're going to have to take Pam home."

"Fine, let go of me and I'll do just that," Alex said, shaking loose.

"Give me the keys to your car first," Bala said, blocking his way.

"Why?"

"I will explain later."

Alex removed them from his pocket and Bala snatched them up. "Do you know how to drive?" Alex asked.

"I have watched Pam do it. Listen to me, Alex, I have something important to tell you. Do not call Joni to ask what happened to Ray."

That was exactly what he'd planned to do. "Why shouldn't I? She might know something."

Bala's voice was urgent. "That does not matter. What I have to say does. Have no contact with her whatsoever. Do not talk to her. If she should call you, hang up the phone. And do not go see her. Alex, a dozen times you have said you did not know how to thank me for saving your sister's life. This is how you can thank me. By doing what I say and not asking me why you should do it."

"But this could be a terrible trauma for Joni. She might be distraught, and need my help."

Bala closed his eyes for a second and took a hissing breath. "Joni is not distraught. That would not be possible."

"Bala—?"

"I have said too much. I have stalled too long. Go to Pam, take care of her." He gave Alex a quick hug, a sad note entering his tone. "Perhaps some time you can ask Cindy about me. Another time, perhaps."

He sounds like he thinks he's going to die, too.

Alex wasn't given the opportunity to ask if that were true. Bala, running at a pace Alex could never have matched, disappeared in the direction of the parking lot.

Cindy was fortunate. The motorbike got her to within a mile of the top of Crystal Falls. But while racing up the trail, she'd almost flattened a ranger on foot. She was worried he might try to write her a ticket on the way back, or worse, confiscate her bike. For that reason, when the path suddenly hit a rocky step that was meant to be tackled by carefully placed feet, she hid the cycle off the path behind a bush.

It was only eleven. The point where she had entered the water was an hour away, maybe less if she could jog part of the way. She should be able to get up and down in time to make the hearing.

Depending on how long it takes to get rid of my paranoia.

That was the problem. She didn't know what she was looking for. Perhaps she should have invited Kent Cooke. If nothing else, that guy didn't miss much. Five minutes talking to her and he'd known she didn't trust Jason.

Hurrying up the trail, panting on the crisp forest air, she thought of Ray—not of anything specific they'd done together, or of anything in particular he had said—she just thought of his face, and his laugh. It seemed to give her strength.

When she reached the place where Wolf had tried to eat Jason, where the falls tumbled into the wide churning bowl two hundred feet below, she decided on a short detour. The quickest route to the narrow path that led to Jason's supposed cave was to cut between the loop of the river. But she chose to stay close to the water. She wanted a look at that tree Jason had been hanging from.

The current wasn't quite as strong as when she'd gone for her swim. Nevertheless, rainstorms farther back in the mountains must be continuing to stock the river; the level was considerably higher than it normally was at that time of year.

She hesitated as she stepped onto the overhanging log. If she went in now, there would be no apprentice sorcerer to pluck her out. What finally gave her the courage to proceed was the sight of a short piece of rope sticking out from close to the spot Jason had been. Going down on all fours, she crept toward it.

Initially, a closer view didn't tell her much. It was rope, maybe even from her parents hardware store, and it appeared to have been cut at both ends by a sharp knife. The only surprise was that a gust of wind hadn't knocked it into the water; it wasn't attached to anything.

Not now at least.

Leaning forward, she noticed there were friction marks on the thick branch Jason had been hanging from. They'd been created by a larger piece of rope, wrapped several times around the branch, under pressure. That was very interesting. She pulled out her camera and took a picture.

The branch had been fortified to keep it from breaking.

Cindy took more pictures when she reached the spot where her trusty basketball shoes had failed her. What was left of the branch she had grabbed at the start of her ordeal had been cut—by a sharp knife, probably—from underneath, over three quarters of the way through. In other words, it had been left in place as a false reassurance of safety.

But it was the ground that made her realize beyond a shadow of a doubt that her deepest fears were true. Going down on her knees, brushing aside the gravel that had been hurriedly thrown over this portion of the path, she gathered together a slimy substance that rolled with calculated smoothness between her trembling fingers.

Someone had previously oiled the spot.

Nothing was making sense. When Alex finally got Pam home, and the girl had finished exchanging a tearful hug with her mother, disappearing into her bedroom where her sobs could still be heard coming through the walls, Alex learned from Mrs. Alta that Bala had just been there.

"But he insisted I take Pam home because he had something he had to do right away," Alex said. He desperately needed a moment to himself where he could let the grief—and, yes, guilt—over Ray's death come to the surface. Choking it back inside, he felt ready to burst.

"He was here two minutes when he was back out again," Mrs. Alta said, nervously rearranging the apples and bananas in the fruit bowl for no apparent purpose. A homely, older version of Pam, she had known Ray as long as any of them. "He didn't even turn off his car."

"That was my car." Alex rubbed his head, trying to assemble all the bizarre things Bala had said into a meaningful framework. Something about a warning that had been true about a girl. Then he had started on him to stay away from Joni. Was she this girl? "Mrs. Alta, what did he do when he was here?"

"Nothing that I know of. Except that he took a blanket when

he left." She wiped at her eyes. "I don't know if I should call Ray's mother or wait for a couple of days. That poor woman."

"A blanket? That's weird. Wait a second. Could he have been carrying something in this blanket?"

"I don't know. I've never seen Bala so anxious. He's always so calm. I didn't think he knew Ray at all."

"He only knew him in passing. Can you remember anything, anything at all, he did besides grab the blanket?"

"Well, he went into the basement. But just for a minute."

That was not what Alex wanted to hear. He knew Pam's dad was a greater gun enthusiast than his own father, and that he kept his rifles and pistols downstairs in a locked cabinet. Alex quickly excused himself.

"Joni is not distraught."

The basement was gloomy. Alex didn't need the lights on, however. Bala's haste was again in evidence. There was glass on the floor, from where he had smashed into the cabinet. Mr. Alta had a collection of fine handguns, six of them to be exact, each with its own special place. One of the places was empty.

Alex took four steps at a time going back up the stairs.

"Mrs. Alta, may I use your phone? Thank you, I've got to make a call." Alex punched out Joni's number from memory. Joni's aunt answered.

"Hello?"

"Hi, Mrs. Lee. Is Joni there?"

"Alex?"

"Yes, it's me. I must speak to Joni immediately."

"She's not here."

"Where is she?"

"That tall African boy came over. They went out together."

"In the neighborhood?"

"Well, they took the car. It looked like your car."

"It is," Alex muttered, leaning against the wall, a weakening despair rising up his legs into his chest.

Bala had gone off the deep end. He blamed Joni for Ray's death. And he was carrying a gun.

"I'm glad you called, Alex. A lot has been going on. The police were over earlier asking Joni about the boy she went out with Saturday night. I understand he hadn't been back home. That's what Joni told me, at least. Then this other fellow came by." Her voice lowered, becoming confidential. "Between the two of us, I don't much care for her being around that foreign sort. She's had trouble with them in the past."

Alex's ears perked up. "What sort of trouble?"

"It was a long time ago," Mrs. Lee said reluctantly. "I'd rather not discuss it now." Her tone brightened. "At least Joni's feeling better. She woke up Sunday morning looking wonderful."

"I'm happy to hear that, Mrs. Lee," Alex said. "Are you going to be there? I think I should come over."

There were few people at the courthouse. Cindy was surprised. She'd figured, with all the publicity, the curiosity seekers would be out in droves. Then again, this was a hearing, not a trial. And Timber and Cheyenne weren't exactly next-door neighbors.

She was hanging out near the courtroom Jason's lawyer had told her about on the phone when the lawyer suddenly appeared through the doors. He had a large black moustache and pale brown eyes. The smoothness in his voice sounded phony.

"Cindy, I'm Michael Kenner. I'm glad to see you could make it."

"Am I late?" The hike back to the bike had taken longer than anticipated. Her discovery had worn her out. All the times she'd spent alone with Jason, kissing him, talking with him about her future, kept crowding uncomfortably into her mind. All those times he hadn't given a damn about her.

The lawyer smiled. "The hearing has been on for a while but they've only been covering material that wouldn't be of interest to you." He took her by the arm. "I'll be calling you to the stand soon. Do you remember what to say?"

"Yes. I have a good memory."

"Just keep it short. Answer my questions as I give them to you. It's not necessary to go overboard praising Jason."

Cindy forced a laugh. "Oh, I won't do that."

The lawyer settled her into a wooden pew several rows behind Jason. Her "boyfriend" turned and gave her a wink. She smiled, and he would have shook in his seat if he had known what was behind that smile. On the other side of the room, she spotted Kent Cooke. He, too, noted her arrival. He held her eye for a moment before turning back to listen to the proceedings.

The district attorney, a short elderly man of Japanese descent, was questioning Timber's sheriff. Cindy half listened. They were probably all lying.

Jason's lawyer called her to the stand not long after. They gave her a Bible to put her hand on and she swore to tell the whole truth and nothing but. The judge leaned her way from his position behind his high desk. He had the shiniest head of silver hair she had ever seen.

"Miss Jones, how long have you known Jason Whitfield?" the lawyer asked as he paced confidently in front of her.

"I've known him casually since I entered Timber High three and a half years ago. We've only been dating seriously for the last four weeks."

"In this four-week period, how often have you seen Jason?"

"Almost every day."

"So we could safely say you know him well?"

Cindy glanced at Jason. He nodded to let her know she was doing a good job. "I feel like I know him better than his parents do." Then before the lawyer could ask another question, she said, "I'd like to relate a story that tells just what kind of guy he is. It'll only take a few minutes."

The lawyer glanced at her in surprise, though without alarm. Cindy turned to the judge, who appeared to check with the lawyer, and then shrugged. "Please go on, Miss Jones," the judge said.

In a concise methodical fashion, she told the court about the hike up to Crystal Falls, starting with Jason's suggestion in the parking lot at lunch, and ending with Jason's criticism of Bala's tactic in rescuing her. It was at this point Jason's lawyer interrupted. He'd been dying to do so since she'd told of falling in the water.

"This is all very interesting, Miss Jones, and I'm sure you had a night you'll not soon forget. But the fact that Jason was unable to rescue you, despite making a valiant attempt, isn't of direct relevance to the issue at hand."

"But it is," she said. "What went on that night could explain why Karen Holly died."

Jason began to fidget. His lawyer lost his pleasant smile. "Really, Miss Jones, we know why Karen Holly died and we have had numerous testimony by experts to that effect. Now if you will just—"

"I have to finish my story," she said quickly, appealing to the judge. The man raised his eyebrow.

"There's more?"

"Yes, your honor. This morning I went back up to the place where I almost drowned. I made a few discoveries. First, the branch Jason had been hanging from had been supported by a rope. Second, the branch I grabbed when I was falling had previously been doctored so that it couldn't possibly support my weight. Third, someone had put oil on the path at the exact place where the weakened branch was, where I slid into the water. I've pictures of all of this. You see, I remember that night. Jason insisted on going first, and he took my hand so that I would be right behind him. Just before I went down, he took one big step. He knew that oil was there. Why shouldn't he? He'd put it there!"

A commotion went through the courtroom. Jason buried his face in his hands. Kent Cooke leaned forward in his chair, nodding slowly at her revelations. The lawyer lost all pretense of friendliness.

"I'll remind you, young lady, this is not a stage where your dramatics are appreciated. For you to state, based on the evidence you have presented, that Jason purposely arranged for you to drown is absurd. Especially in light of how he risked his own life to save yours. Now—"

"He didn't want me to drown," she interrupted. "He wasn't going to weep if I did, but it's obvious that he wanted to rescue me."

The lawyer laughed at her. "You are confused, girl. Why would he do all these contradictory things? What was his motive?"

This lawyer was a fool. He'd asked a question he didn't realize she had the answer to. "To look like a hero," she said bitterly. "To get rid of the cowardly image he deserves. He is a coward, and a violent jerk. He almost took my head off that same night 'cause I wouldn't put out for him. I guess Karen wouldn't put out for him, either!"

The lawyer spoke to the judge. "Your honor, I ask that this young lady's testimony be stricken from the record. It contains numerous self-contradictory statements."

"Overruled." The judge looked down at her. "Miss Jones, would it be possible for you to return tomorrow at this same time? I would like to give the district attorney an opportunity to cross-examine you, and to see your pictures."

She nodded. "I'll be here, your honor."

The judge called for an overnight recess. The district attorney asked for her phone number as she was leaving the room, saying he would be talking to her that evening. Kent Cooke stopped her in the hallway.

"You weren't exaggerating when you told me this morning you had things to do," he said. "You've given me a lot of material for my next column."

"I'm glad," she said flatly.

Her tone caught him offguard. But then he nodded his head sympathetically. "That was pretty stupid what I just said. I'm sorry." He squeezed her arm. "Please give my condolences to Ray's family."

"I will."

When he had gone, she looked around for the exit, anxious to get back on the road. Jason caught her before she could get to the door. There were tears in his eyes.

The poor baby bastard.

"Cindy, why are you doing this to me?" he cried.

"I swore to tell the truth, the whole truth, and nothing but the truth. Now get out of my way. I get nauseated around scum like you."

"Wait!" he pleaded, grabbing her arm.

"Don't touch me," she said, her breath cold.

He let her go, backed up a step. "Give me five minutes, Cindy. You owe me that much."

"All I owe you is a good spit in the face."

"Two minutes. Just let me explain. Please?"

She put on an expression of infinite boredom. "Start your lies."

Jason glanced around nervously. "Not out here in the open." He pointed to an empty room across the hall. "Let's go in there."

"No way I'm going in there alone with you."

"For god's sakes, Cindy, I'll leave the door open."

"*All* the way open," she said, agreeing reluctantly.

Once in the room Jason put on the same phony tone as his lawyer. "I honestly care about you. I would never do anything to harm you. When you fell in the river, I did everything I could to get you out."

"You did everything you could to put me in the river! Now you admit that right now or I'm leaving this instant! Right after I kick you in the balls!"

"Is this off the record?"

"I'll decide that. Speak."

Jason humbled his stance. "All right, all right, I did set it up so you would slip. But you were never in danger. I checked out the movements of the current thoroughly that afternoon. I threw in tiny Styrofoam balls and watched where they went. I knew if you were still in the water when you reached the overhanging tree, you'd pass directly beneath where I'd be waiting."

"Tiny Styrofoam balls?" She punched him in the chest. "I am a human being! I would have died if I'd gone over those falls!"

"I would have caught you first, Cindy."

"You don't know that! Your grip could have slipped!"

Jason shook his head, looked pained. "I didn't intend for anyone to get hurt."

"I don't believe that. What if more than one of us had gone in the water? What would you have done then? Choose who to save? What if my brother had slipped?"

"That could never have happened. As soon as you went in, I knew everybody would turn and go after you."

Cindy nodded grimly. "You had it all figured out. Well, you should've spent more time cleaning up your oil. Now you'll have to excuse me. I have to go home and cry about what you did to Ray."

Jason appeared puzzled. "Ray? What's wrong with Ray?"

She glared. "I hope you go straight to hell after you're executed."

Jason grabbed her again as she tried to get away. "What's wrong with Ray?" he demanded.

"The same thing that's wrong with Karen!" she yelled, slapping away his hands. "He's dead!"

"That's impossible. When did he die?"

"You should know!"

"But I didn't kill Ray. I didn't kill Karen! Cindy, you don't think I'm capable of murder?"

"Capable? I think you enjoy it."

"I didn't kill anybody! Listen to me!"

"No! You're sick!"

He stared at her for a moment, appalled at the hate he was seeing, and then the last visage of strength seemed to go out of him. "I'm not sick," he moaned, turning away and burying his face in the wall. "I was just scared."

Cindy was curious in spite of herself. There had been an uncanny ring of truth in his last words. "What were you scared of?"

He was weeping. He wouldn't look at her. "We were hanging out by the waterfall. We'd brought a blanket. Karen had brought it. I thought she was trying to tell me something. I knew she wasn't a virgin. I'd heard the stories about her and Ray. I figured we'd make it. We had fooled around enough. We were fooling around that night. But Karen got mad at me.

She had a temper. She hit me in the face, scratched me with her nails. I chewed her out, told her she could walk home, and stalked off."

"This is B.S." But this did explain where the flesh under Karen's nails, that the coroner had uncovered, had come from.

Jason took his head off the wall, rubbing his red eyes. "No, this is the truth. And I wouldn't have really left her. I planned on heading back to the car and waiting for her to show."

"And she never showed?"

His lips trembled. "I'd just left her. I was on the other side of that granite mound I'd told the police about. I heard Karen say something. It sounded like she was talking to someone. I didn't know what was going on. There was no one else up there. Then I heard—I heard this shriek. It was awful."

"Karen?"

"It wasn't Karen. It was some kind of animal. I'd never heard anything like it before. Then Karen was shouting for me. She was screaming my name over and over again. But I couldn't go to her."

"Why not?"

He was having difficulty breathing. "I told you, I was scared. The shriek was getting louder. It was like a high, shrill strangling sound. There's no way to describe it. When I'm in bed at night, I still hear it. And I have these horrible dreams."

"Go on."

"I ran. I didn't know what else to do. I couldn't help Karen.

I could hear the thing tearing her apart. Then Karen stopped screaming my name, and I knew she was dead. I ran all the way to the car."

"And the bump on your head?"

"I did that to myself."

"Why?"

"Can't you see why? I'd acted like a coward. No one would be able to understand why. No one would believe me if I told them what I'd heard. I had to make up an excuse."

"There was no bear?"

"I didn't see one."

Cindy considered. "Your excuse didn't fool many people."

"Because that damn thing didn't leave Karen where it had killed her! How was I supposed to know it would throw her in the river?"

"That *thing*? What was that thing?"

Jason shivered. "I don't know."

"How convenient."

His eyes were pleading. "You believe me, don't you, Cindy?"

"I believe in an awful monster. But you're him. You're a sick dude. You need to be locked up. I'm going to make sure you are."

"But I'm telling you the truth!"

"If what you said is true, you'd never have gone within a hundred miles of Crystal Falls again. But you dragged us all up there in the dark."

"I knew the thing must be gone. The entire area had been searched by the police. I felt safe going back up there with all my friends."

"And I felt safe being with my boyfriend," she muttered sarcastically.

A police officer, who'd been in the courtroom, was calling for her out in the hallway. Leaving Jason in his self-inflicted anguish, she hurried to find out what the gentleman wanted.

"There's a call for you, Miss Jones. It's a Pam Alta. She says it's urgent."

"Pam? Where can I take it?"

"This way."

The policeman led her to an office where a number of secretaries were typing furiously. She had to cup the phone to her ear to hear. "Pam?"

"Cindy, thank God I found you. I've been calling all over. Your mom told me you might still be at the hearing."

She could hear people being paged in the background. "Where are you, Pam?"

"At the hospital."

"Ray! Is he still alive?"

"No," Pam said weakly. "It's something else. It's Bala. He's been attacked, too. They're operating on him now. But before they wheeled him in, he told me I had to get ahold of you and Alex. He said your lives are in danger."

"In danger? How?"

"I don't know. He wouldn't talk to me. He seemed especially worried about your brother."

"But what attacked Bala?"

"It must have been some kind of animal. It messed him up pretty bad. Cindy, you have to come here. I can't handle all this by myself."

Some kind of animal.

Cindy closed her eyes. Was the whole world going nuts? There couldn't be a monster on the loose in Timber. The town was too straight to have one. "Have you been able to get hold of Alex?" she asked.

"No. I've tried everywhere. He's not at school. He's not at home. He's not at your parents' store."

"Keep trying. I'm on my way."

Cindy broke the connection and got hold of the operator. She had her dial the Lee residence, charging the call to her home phone. It was Joni who answered.

"Hello?"

"Joni, this is Cindy. Have you seen my brother?"

"No."

"Have you talked to him today?"

"No."

"If he should stop by, could you have him call my parents' store or our house?"

"Yes."

"Good. Thank you."

"You're welcome."

Cindy put down the phone. That girl was weird. Alex should stay away from her.

"Who was that?" Alex asked.

"No one," Joni said, hanging up the phone, returning to her seat beside him at the kitchen table. Mrs. Lee had been right; Joni was looking wonderful. Her cheeks were flushed with life. She had on a beautiful white dress, and her shiny black hair hung over her shoulders with natural abandon. He was having a hard time taking his eyes off her.

From Pam's house, he'd driven straight to Joni's. He'd had to sit and listen to Mrs. Lee for almost two hours, all the time asking himself why he wasn't calling the police. In the end, what had probably kept him from such drastic action had been the rising conviction that he must have misunderstood Bala. The guy was as gentle as a butterfly. Why would he want to hurt Joni? And his patience had been rewarded when Joni had shown up safe and sound. Though Alex was still a bit confused as to what had gone on. Joni had returned, driving his car, without Bala.

Mrs. Lee was a case. The whole time he'd been waiting with her, she hadn't stopped talking about how worried she was. But then, ten minutes before Joni had returned home, she'd run off to do her shopping. Alex was beginning to think the aunt didn't really like Joni.

"Was it a wrong number?" he asked.

She nodded, regarding him curiously. "Why did you happen to come over just now, Alex?"

"I was concerned about you. Last week you didn't come to school. Then when I learned about what happened to Ray, I thought you'd be feeling bad."

She sipped her tea, which she'd prepared for both of them. She made it strong and drank it plain. "It was sad about Ray," she said.

"Does your aunt know what happened? I got the impression she just thought he'd disappeared."

Joni shook her head. "I never told her the details."

"I see. Well, do you know what happened?"

She continued to stare at him. "How should I know?"

"He dropped you off and you didn't see him again?"

"Yes."

"That's how I thought it probably went." He sat back in his chair. He couldn't quit thinking about the way Ray had died. Torn to pieces like Karen. He hoped to God it had been quick, that he hadn't suffered.

"What are you thinking?" Joni asked.

Alex played with his spoon and cup. "About Ray. He was my pal and I never—I never treated him with the same kindness he treated me." He sighed. "I still can't believe this has happened."

"He seemed like a nice boy."

"I'm glad you got a chance to know him a bit." Alex chuckled, a lump in his throat. "He was such a character."

"He was very attached to me."

"Yeah, he was. He had a crush on you. I didn't know you knew."

Joni's eyes watched him above the rim of her cup. "I can always tell."

"Can you?"

"Always."

Alex began to fidget, thinking he should leave, not sure why. "So you left my keys in the ignition?"

"Yes."

"Did you drop Bala off at home?"

"I dropped him off, yes." Joni put down her cup. "Alex, tell me why you are here."

"I told you."

"But Bala spoke to you. I know this. What did he say?"

"He said, ah—just a bunch of weird stuff."

"Tell me?"

"Why?"

Joni's eyes were more exotic and more fascinating than even he could remember, so black and deep with their hypnotic flecks of color; greens and purples floating around wide pupils. Her cold or flu or whatever had been bothering her must be completely gone. Except for maybe in her throat. She sounded more hoarse than usual. "Because I want to know," she said.

Alex laughed nervously. "He said I had to stay away from you. He was talking like a madman."

"Did he tell you why you should stay away?"

He picked up his spoon again. It felt strangely heavy. "I don't like talking about this. Bala's a great guy."

"Did he tell you I killed Ray?"

Alex shrugged, trying to keep his gaze down, not succeeding. "He implied it, yes. Like I said, he seemed to be very confused."

Joni closed her eyes for a moment, sitting so still she could have stopped breathing. Then she appeared to come to a decision. Standing suddenly, she began to clear away the dishes. "Alex, could you take me for a ride?"

"Sure. Where would you like to go?"

"Up to the waterfall, where we can be alone."

Chapter Eleven

The waiting lounge in Timber Memorial for the friends and relatives of those undergoing surgery was depressing. The decor was a harsh white and the few paintings cluttering the walls were so cheap and flat that it would have been better had no one bothered to hang them up. Of course, Cindy realized, you couldn't have posters of rock 'n' roll bands looking over your shoulder while you were waiting to hear if a loved one was going to live or die.

"So you didn't think the blow to his head was real serious?" Cindy asked Pam. She'd asked Pam the same question two hours before when she'd arrived at the hospital but she wanted further reassurance.

"He was conscious," Pam said, bags under her eyes. "Isn't that supposed to be a good sign?"

"They wouldn't have operated on his arm and his side if they were worried about brain damage," Mrs. Alta said. The short middle-aged lady sat across from them reading a *People* magazine. She had been studying the same page since Cindy had arrived.

"I wish Alex would call," Cindy said. And this, too, was something she'd said before. There was a west-facing window in the hallway outside the waiting room. The sun had recently set. Night was coming quickly.

"Did you leave a message at Ray's house?" Pam asked.

"Yes."

"Did you talk to his mother?" Mrs. Alta asked.

"No, his father. He could hardly speak. I felt bad for bothering them."

"I feel bad." Pam nodded vaguely. She wasn't totally with it yet. Cindy gave her a hug.

"Mrs. Alta?" a doctor said, appearing in the doorway of the lounge. Attired entirely in green, he must have come straight from the operating theater. "Bala's going to be all right. The operation went smoothly."

Pam's mother stood and squeezed her palms together. "Thank God."

"Can we see him?" Cindy asked, also standing.

"Not now, he's in the recovery room," the doctor said. "He should be there at least an hour, the operation was complicated. His left elbow was badly broken and we had to remove numerous bone splinters from his rib cage. He also has a concussion and has lost a lot of blood. But his vital signs are stable. The anesthesiologist said he's never seen an individual with such a hardy constitution." The surgeon glanced at the clock on the wall. "It's getting late. I would suggest all of you forget about seeing him this evening. When he gets back to his room, he'll be groggy. And, in either case, it will be better if he's allowed to rest."

"But I have to talk to him," Cindy insisted. "I can't wait until tomorrow. I can't wait an hour."

"Cindy," Mrs. Alta said, "let's do what the doctor says. Come home with us. You can stay for dinner. This has been a long day for all of us. And maybe later tonight we could talk to Bala on the phone, if he's feeling up to it."

The doctor nodded. He had a worn, hardened look and didn't appear the type who could be talked into anything. "That sounds like the best course."

Cindy took a step toward the surgeon. "You don't understand, Doctor. Before he was taken into the operating room, Bala said he had something very important to tell me. I must insist I be allowed to see him right now."

The doctor crossed his arms across his chest, assuming a slightly amused expression. "You must insist? I'm afraid, young lady, the policy of this hospital cannot be bent to conform to your wishes."

"But—" Cindy began.

"But if you won't be able to sleep tonight without seeing

him," the doctor interrupted, "you can wait until he is returned to his room. I will leave word with the nurse that you may have a few minutes with him. Please do not abuse this favor."

"But—" Cindy said.

The doctor raised his hand. "Don't argue with me." He looked at Mrs. Alta. "I have to go now, but I'll be in tomorrow afternoon. Call and make an appointment with my secretary. The name is Dr. Wheeler. We'll need to discuss the details of Bala's rehabilitation."

"Thank you, Doctor," Mrs. Alta said. The man nodded and walked away. "He seems a competent gentleman," Mrs. Alta remarked.

"He reminds me of that joke," Cindy muttered. "The one with the punch line, 'Oh, that's God, he thinks he's a doctor.'"

Naturally Mrs. Alta tried to talk her out of staying. But not knowing why Bala was desperate to speak with her, why he was specifically worried about Alex, Cindy felt she had no choice but to wait. Pam offered to keep her company, but Mrs. Alta said no, and so Cindy was left alone to watch the clock and the darkness outside, getting deeper and deeper.

When the better part of an hour had gone by, a nurse finally came for her and led her to a room on the second floor, instructing her not to tire Bala. Cindy promised she would not overstay her welcome.

The room contained a large window, which looked south

in the direction of Castle Park. The shadows of the mountains were clearly visible, cutting a jagged black line across the almost black sky. Inside, the only illumination was a red nightlight above the sink. Bala had the room to himself, his covered feet poking over the end of the bed, his face almost buried beneath a wad of bandages. He stirred as she entered and she quickly moved to his side. His left arm and shoulder were encased in a cast. Dried blood caked his lips. His open eyelids looked heavy.

"How do you feel?" she asked, taking his right hand.

He swallowed painfully, whispered, "I will live. Where is Alex?"

"I don't know," she said, the panic coming hard and fast. "We can't find him. What does Alex have to do with what happened to you?"

"Why can you not locate him?"

"I don't know," she repeated. "I thought you could tell me."

"Have you tried Joni's house?"

"Yes. I left a message there that if he comes by, he's to immediately call my parents. They know where I am."

"Who did you leave the message with?"

"Joni."

Bala winced. "Call again, now. See if the aunt is there. Find out what you can."

Cindy didn't question his order. There was a phone around the corner and change in her pocket. Information gave her the number—she'd forgotten it—and Joni's aunt answered on the second ring.

"Hello?"

"Mrs. Lee, this is Cindy Jones. I'm Alex's sister. Is he there by any chance?"

"No. He was here earlier, but he left."

"Did he leave with Joni?"

"I don't know. I had to go out for groceries."

"Was Joni there before you left?"

"No. I don't know if she's been home all day. If he comes by, should I have him call you?"

"I'd appreciate that. I'm at Timber Memorial. He can have me paged. Please have him, or Joni, call me the second they get there. This is very important."

"What are you doing at the hospital, dear?"

"A friend of mine has been hurt. I have to go now, Mrs. Lee."

Bala took the information hard. The flesh beneath the bandage that circled the top of his head paled, if that was possible. "Pray he did not leave with her," he whispered.

"What's the matter?" she cried, unable to bear the tension. "How can Joni harm him?"

Bala glanced at the cast binding his left arm. "It was she who did this to me."

"But that's impossible. She's just a girl!"

Bala rolled his eyes toward her. What she saw in those eyes, or didn't see, frightened her even more than his next words.

There was no hope there. It was as though he had already buried her brother in his thoughts. "She is not a girl, Cindy. She is not a human being. She is something else, something horrible."

Alex was glad the moon was full. Few people who lived in the city could appreciate how bright the moon was when it didn't have to compete with kilowatts of artificial light, how safe and comfortable it was to hike beneath its silvery orb. Joni couldn't have picked a better night for an impulsive stroll in the woods.

They were standing next to the top of the waterfall, on the exact spot where Wolf had tried to shove Jason over the edge. A stiff breeze was dragging up through the gorge, creating a dull echoing roar, which seemed to throb with a living beat, lifting a faint spray from the tumbling river and sprinkling it round their heads. Alex pulled Joni close, trying to keep her warm, hoping she would lean over and kiss the side of his face.

"Do you want to head back?" he asked after a long spell of silence between them.

"No," she said quietly, staring into the distance. "I want to fly. I want to fly away."

Alex glanced down, shuddering slightly. They were *very* close to the brink, much closer than he would have chosen to come himself. Heights seemed to have no effect on Joni. "That would be a handy talent to have on this ledge," he agreed.

She turned toward him, her face only inches away. That was a wondrous thing about her; no matter which way she turned, the moon always seemed to be in her eyes. "You're afraid of falling?"

"Well, I'm not really afraid." He laughed. "But I'd rather not fall, if that's what you mean."

"That's what I mean," she said.

"What?"

She swept her hand up his back, into his hair, tugging at the strands with a force that was close to painful. "I remember the first time I came up here. I felt at home, even though there was all this water. I'd never seen water flowing like this before, but it didn't scare me."

"Doesn't it rain a lot in England?"

"I suppose."

He frowned. "Don't you know?"

"I know more of a place I haven't told you of."

He would sort that one out later. "Did you come up here before I took you?"

"Yes. But I also remember that night with you. It was special for me. It was something a young girl would do, something she would enjoy. I was pleased I could enjoy it with you."

Alex cleared his throat, not sure if he was hearing her properly with the rushing water and the moaning wind. "I'm glad you had a nice time. But are you sure you don't want to start back? It's getting late."

Her stroking of his hair softened and deepened, so that she was now massaging his scalp. Alex had the amusing thought that this was something he often did to Wolf. He wasn't complaining. The sensation was relaxing; he was actually beginning to feel slightly drowsy. Everything that had happened during the day seemed nothing more than a collection of dream images that he would be able to awake from soon.

"We're not going back," Joni said.

"We have to. We can't spend the night up here."

Joni appeared to agree with him, contradicting her previous statement in the process. "I wish this night didn't have to be so short."

Alex swayed slightly on his feet. This was no place to forget where his shoes were planted. He took a step backward, pulling Joni with him. She lost her hold on his head. "We could do something else," he said. "I'm not big on junk food, but there's a coffee shop in town that serves the greatest doughnuts. Are you hungry?"

She glanced behind her at the edge, then stared at him, the cold light of the moon making her face appear deathly pale. The wind had taken ahold of her thick hair, and it flapped on the right side of her head like a single huge black wing. "Alex, I'm always hungry."

Bala had requested a glass of water. Cindy brought him a small cup from the hospital room sink, supporting the back of his head while he sipped it. His last statement had driven away all her questions. She no longer knew what to ask. She would have to listen first, for a bit, and see whether Bala was crazy, or if the world was. Pulling up a seat, she settled beside his bed.

"You were right," he began, his voice smoother with the gulp of water. "The boy I spoke of in psychology class was myself. Like my father, I was learning to be a shaman. Starting at such an early age, I was about eight at the time, is unusual. Traditionally, an individual has to wait until he has entered puberty. But my grandfather saw great potential in me. Many times he told me that one day I would be a powerful Bairavee.

"There were a number of things he taught me. I will not go into them all. It is only the ancient technique of transferring a human's soul into an animal's body that need concern us now. In this area my grandfather gave me a lot of experience. You must understand it was always he who took care of the details of the transfer. To this day, I do not know half of what he would do."

Bala closed his eyes. "I remember those days as though they were a part of last week. I remember the sound of my grandfather's voice as I sank deeper and deeper into myself. Stillness is a prerequisite for undergoing any shamic journey. The uniqueness of the silence he could induce was that I could experience it with my eyes open. Unless your sight is in use, no transfer is possible. This is true for the animal participant as well as for the human. You must be staring at each other.

"As I said in class, all types of animals were used. Once I was even sent into a snake. That was a strange day. I remember the feel of the dust on my scaly hide as I slithered over the ground. Yet that was only a small part of the phenomenon. I *was* a snake. I had snake thoughts and feelings. Do not ask me to explain what they were like. It was beautiful and it was horrible. You would need to know the reptile's language to even get the faintest idea of what I went through. And, yes, snakes have a language. My grandfather says every creature on earth does.

"These 'trips' all took place over a period of six months. At the end of that time, my father died and I lost interest. There, I am putting it mildly. Actually, I became furious with my grandfather. I would not speak to him. But it may not have been entirely his fault. My father had tried to use an esoteric skill he had yet to master. That was one of my father's weaknesses, and the reason my grandfather knew he would never be a true Bairavee. My father had no patience. He tried to dominate a spirit in the netherworld, and the spirit killed him. At least this was what my grandfather told me. Not that the details meant much to me then. My father was gone and my mother was a widow. I could see little benefit to be had from becoming a shaman, and much harm, and I wanted nothing to do with it. This upset my grandfather a great deal.

"The years went by and the famine started and it was hard just to stay alive. I had no time to worry about magic and whether I was depriving myself of important experiences. Then Dr. Herbert Stevens and his wife, Valerie, came to live in our village. I mentioned them in Miss Clemens's class. The doctor was a very busy man. I did not have a lot of contact with him. But his wife took a special liking to me. I liked her, too; she was a great woman. She taught me how to read and speak English. She had boxes of books imported from London, where the Stevens were originally from. I learned a lot from those books. I discovered that most of the suffering we were going through was our own fault. This was probably unfair, but I totally blamed our tradition of Bairavees for keeping us so backward. As a result, the distance between my grandfather and me became greater.

"One hot and hungry day, it was about a year ago, another doctor and his wife visited our village. They were friends of the Stevenses. They had come to Mau Dogan for the same reason, to help us, but planned on staying only a month. They had a beautiful sixteen-year-old daughter."

"Joni Harper?" Cindy whispered.

Bala opened his eyes and looked at her. "Yes, it was Joni. She was not like you know her now. She was vibrant, full of life. She was also headstrong, maybe even snobbish, but I found her quite charming. Oh, I did not tell you this. Despite my grandfather's disdain for the 'outside' world, he could speak English. This should not surprise you. He has perfect recall. Joni was always talking to him, always after him to show her magic, which would amuse my grandfather. Yet he gave her much of his time, and at first this did not make sense to me. But I was to learn the reason soon enough.

"Joni was a find for him. There were others in my village who had the potential to experience trance states. The ability is not that rare, not as rare as the potential to become a full-fledged shaman, which is quite another matter. Joni had the ability. And she had something else my grandfather thought could be used. She was not a product of our traditions. She was a skeptic. He knew I saw her that way. His plan was to prove to her that his powers were real. You see, by this time—this was years after my adventures in other bodies—I had come to the conclusion that the shamic experience was nothing but an illusion. My grandfather wanted to use Joni to respark my interest."

Bala paused. "It was a terrible mistake on his part to try these things on an outsider."

"Did Joni go into an animal?" Cindy asked.

Bala took a breath. "Yes."

Outside the window the silhouettes of the mountain peaks appeared to glow; the moon was rising swiftly. Cindy wasn't sure, but it seemed she could see Crystal Falls, sparkling faintly like a net of fine wires exposed to a shorting circuit. Had Joni taken her brother to that lonely spot, where Karen and Ray had died? She swallowed. "What was the animal?"

Bala's cheek twitched. "A vulture."

Cindy jerked as if she had been struck. "What happened?"

Bala sighed. "I saw the whole thing. I tried to stop it. But my grandfather is not one to argue with, and he had Joni on his side. She had not the slightest fear. Her parents were away visiting a nearby village. She wanted to do it before they came back.

"My grandfather lured a vulture out of the air. This was not a major feat for him; there were plenty of vultures about in those days, always waiting for another one of us to die. He tied the bird in front of the girl, sang his trance-inducing chants. Both Joni and the vulture went very still, staring into each other's eyes. Initially, all appeared to be going well. Then the bird began to thrash violently, shrieking with a noise that would chill your heart if you had heard it. Joni was inside, and she was terrified.

"What it was like for that poor girl, we can only imagine. During all the experiments I performed as a child, I had never gone into a vulture. You could not have forced me into one; they are disgusting creatures, always hovering about, want-ing you to die, wishing they had the strength and courage to kill you. I do not know why my grandfather did not choose another creature. But that was not his only mistake that day.

"Joni's fear was not totally unexpected. Quickly my grand-father moved to reverse the transfer. Unfortunately, the vulture had been bound at the foot with a simple string. In its fear, it bit through the string. My grandfather was able to grab it, for a moment, but it twisted free and flew away. Or I should say, Joni flew away."

Cindy trembled. "She was still inside?"

"Had you asked me at the time, I probably would have told you she was not. I still did not believe in soul transfer. But after what has happened in Timber in the last few days, I do not know. That vulture took off and headed directly to the next village, where Joni's parents were having lunch outside. It went straight to their table. Scared them badly, from what I was later told. The father reached for his rifle. He blew the bird's head off."

"He killed his own daughter?" Cindy asked, horrified.

"Perhaps. He killed the vulture she had supposedly gone into. There was a piece of string still tied around its leg."

"And how was Joni?"

Bala coughed painfully. "My grandfather said Joni was dead."

"You mean, her body died?"

"No," he said, wheezing. "Her body was still alive, though she was almost comatose. Valerie was there. She had seen the whole thing, too. She did not believe in my grandfather's powers, but she did not disbelieve in them, either. She knew something traumatic had happened to the girl, and she heeded my grandfather's command that no one be allowed near Joni, even her own parents. Do not ask me how he knew the vulture had been slain before the rest of us. There simply was something in Joni's eyes that told him there was no going back.

"When the parents returned to Mau Dogan that evening, they told everyone about the vulture attack at their lunch table. The news set off a stir, though the Harpers did not know the reasons behind it. Naturally, they wondered where Joni was. My grandfather wanted to stall them. He had Valerie tell them Joni had gone for an overnight hike with some of the village girls. The Harpers thought that was nice. They were not concerned.

"Joni seemed to be in shock. Along with Valerie and my grandfather, I stayed with her throughout the night. She kept looking about, turning her neck in strange ways, and making funny sounds in her throat. Not once did she show signs of violence. But her eyes had a peculiar glint in them. I felt uncomfortable when she looked at me. It was as if she was wondering if she could eat me.

"But I still honestly believed her problems were psychological in nature, brought on by her terrifying experience. I had read several books by English psychiatrists, and considered myself something of an expert on the mind—what conceit. I wanted her turned over to her parents, who could get her professional help. My grandfather dismissed the idea. He said we must not let the vulture out of our sight. Already, he had done away with Joni's name.

"Valerie did not know what to do. Her husband was away for a week, in a village two hundred miles to the south. For the most part, she agreed with me. Except when Joni looked right at her. Then she had her doubts.

"The Harpers did not stay long satisfied with the excuses they were fed to explain Joni's absence. They began to get suspicious. The following night my grandfather had Joni transferred to a village much smaller than Mau Dogan. It was located in some nearby hills. Valerie went with her. She was afraid to do so, but I think she felt a responsibility to look after the girl since it was obvious my grandfather was not going to relinquish her voluntarily. Oh, this is an important point. Valerie had known Joni since she was young, and had always loved her.

"I did not go. I never saw Valerie again."

Cindy's trembling refused to stop. She wished *he* would stop. But she had to know. "What happened?"

"The Harpers started to get angry. They became convinced that we had kidnapped Joni. They started to make threats. My grandfather finally told them the truth. Of course, they thought he was mad. When they saw they were not going to get past my grandfather, they went running to the authorities. In my country that is not an easy thing to do. The system moves slowly. It was several days before they returned with help. By then we had heard word that Valerie was dead and that Joni was beginning to talk again. Also, during this time, Dr. Herbert Stevens came back from his trip. It was awful telling him about his wife. They had been together many years."

"How did Valerie die?" Cindy asked.

"The same way as Karen and Ray."

Cindy nodded weakly, her eyes beginning to burn. "Go on."

"My grandfather was more anxious than ever about Joni. Hours before the government people arrived, he dragged me to the place we had hidden her. The change in her was dramatic.

She seemed much more *human*. She could even identify certain things by name. Although upset about Valerie—I did not yet know, or did not believe, it had been Joni who had killed her—I was relieved. Joni appeared to be improving. But my grandfather reacted differently. He said we had to kill the girl immediately."

Bala stopped, staring off into space for over a minute. Cindy finally asked, "Do you need to rest?"

He blinked, and resumed speaking in a softer voice. "I was thinking about what my grandfather told me then. Remember, although I was trying to be a logical scientific young man, I had been conditioned to the bizarre all my life. Yet what he said as we stood outside Joni's hut went beyond anything I had ever heard. Joni had killed Valerie, he said, and she had done so in order to steal the life from her *sheath*. I am using the closest English word I can find. The actual term he used was *manas*. You almost have to be a shaman to understand what your manas is. It is not an individual's spirit, nor is it the body; it is, rather, the immaterial substance that keeps the two wedded together. By killing Valerie, Joni had been able to *feed* on Valerie's humanity via her sheath. Do you understand?"

"No."

"We are more than animals. Your Western religions say we have a soul. A Bairavee would agree with that. But a Bairavee would add that we have a sheath that provides a connection between the physical world and the spiritual world. Apparently, when the spirit of the vulture got trapped in Joni's body, it inherited her brain and all the knowledge that was stored inside. But it could not use the knowledge. It lacked the connector. It lacked the sheath."

"Are you saying the vulture wanted to be human?"

"That's a penetrating question. Certainly, it could not be a bird anymore. But maybe it was the other way around. Maybe what was left of the real Joni wanted to be human again. Who knows? It could be that my grandfather created something that was neither animal nor human, but something different, something wholly unnatural. All I knew for sure at the time was that my grandfather insisted it must be destroyed before it destroyed others.

"But I was not going to let him kill her. I was still hoping she could be cured. Ignoring my grandfather's pleas, I picked her up and literally carried her all the way back to Mau Dogan, to her parents and the angry officials. And then she was gone, and we did not hear anything about her for a while. Dr. Herbert Stevens left the area shortly afterward.

"Joni had a younger brother. He was in England when the Harpers had first visited, but Joni had often spoken of him. His name was Jim. It must have been six months after Joni had been carried off by her parents that I met Jim. I was sitting outside my mother's hut, when he suddenly appeared and demanded to know what had happened to his sister. He was extremely upset. It seemed Joni had torn his mother apart."

Cindy jumped to her feet, unable to contain the pressure building inside. "I can't listen to this. I have to go."

Bala tried to sit up. "Where are you going?"

"I have to see about Alex." She hurried toward the door. "I have to know where he is."

"Come back!" Bala called. "There is much more."

She ignored him, for the moment, hurrying to the phone she had used earlier. She was wasting her time. There was no answer at her own house; her parents said he hadn't been by the store; and Joni's aunt had nothing new to report. Cindy trudged back to Bala's room, collapsing in her chair. "Go on," she said wearily.

"Alex has not come in?"

She shook her head. "What happened next?"

Bala settled back into the pillow. "Jim had not come to our village by himself. His father had also returned, and was meeting with my grandfather to see if anything could be done for his daughter. Mr. Harper was a changed man. He was scared. He was ready to listen. But my grandfather gave him not a shred of hope. He repeated what he had said originally; the girl had to be killed. The son heard this, and he was convinced my grandfather was right. Jim was spooked. But the father would not hear of it."

"Where was Joni at this time?"

"It was my understanding she was in a mental hospital in England undergoing observation. The doctors could not find a whole lot wrong with her, except that she was unusually withdrawn. I guess absorbing the mother's sheath had improved Joni even more."

"But didn't the doctors know this girl was a murderer?"

"No, they did not. Harper was not even sure Joni had killed his wife, though Jim swore she had. You can see why Mr. Harper had trouble believing his own son. Joni simply would not have had the strength to do what had been done to Mrs. Harper. Scotland Yard was out looking for an animal."

"How is it Joni didn't kill any of the doctors in the hospital?"

"Because Joni does not kill strangers. She only kills those who love her."

"What?"

"My grandfather says the emotional attachment is necessary for her to be able to absorb an individual's sheath."

"But her own mother— What if she loves someone in return?"

"If she is this soulless human, would she love anyone?"

"But Alex is completely attached to her!"

Bala sighed. "I know. I told him to stay away from her."

Cindy fought to calm herself. The more information she could get, the better chance she would have of saving Alex. Not for a moment did she disbelieve Bala's story. All the bizarre killings lately made it impossible to doubt him. "What happened next?"

"Mr. Harper and his son left. This time my grandfather

did not let the issue rest. Although he lives in a poor village in the middle of nowhere, he is fairly well known and respected in my country. There are even people in the government who have come to him for spiritual help. He went to such an official now, someone who owed him a favor, and said he wanted his grandson—me—sent to England to keep an eye on Joni. The official agreed; he was confident he could use the student exchange program to get me to London. But then this official learned Joni was being sent to America, to a city called Timber."

"But what happened to Mr. Harper and his son?"

"Mr. Harper was found ripped to pieces. This time the police suspected the son. He seemed crazy. He kept telling everyone that his beautiful sister was really a vulture. Jim Harper's now in a mental institution."

A disturbing realization hit her, and with it came anger. "But none of this makes sense. You knew Joni's history when you arrived here. You were nice to her. You treated her like she was a human being!"

"I thought she was."

"After all you'd seen and heard? I find that hard to believe."

"When I left Mau Dogan and came to this country, it was like a dream come true. I felt I had entered the real world and left the superstitions of my youth behind. When I rode in your beautiful cars past your tall glass buildings, I could hardly remember, much less believe, my grandfather's warnings."

"Are you serious? What of Valerie and Mr. and Mrs. Harper? These people were butchered. Surely you didn't think that was all due to bad luck on their part?"

Bala sounded defensive. "When I got here, the first thing I did was go to see Joni. Had she scared me the way she had that night after the accident, I might have done something. But she did not frighten me at all. She was not glad to see me—she knew who I was—but she was not rude. She seemed your typical teenage girl."

"That chick never seemed typical to me," Cindy said bitterly.

"But you encouraged your brother to go out with her?"

"I didn't know she had people for lunch!"

"I did not know that, either. When I looked at her, I could not imagine her killing anyone. Understand, everything I had heard about her violence had been secondhand. Also, you must remember, I still did not believe my grandfather's talents were genuine."

"But what about what happened to Karen? Didn't her death convince you?"

"I never heard about Karen until that day I asked you about her."

"It wasn't Karen who reintroduced you to Joni?" Pam had said that had been the case, although she'd been unsure. When Cindy thought about it, she figured Karen must have been dead at least three weeks before Bala arrived in Timber.

"No."

"Why did you bring up these spirit-swapping experiments in Miss Clemens's class if you thought they were all bunk?"

"You prodded me into discussing them."

"I think you had another reason. You were wanting to see if Joni would react."

"The idea did cross my mind," Bala admitted. "But I do not even think she was listening when I was talking."

Cindy shook her head in disgust. "You still should have warned Alex."

"How? I warned him today and he ignored me. He is infatuated with her. She could have drunk his blood, and he would have passed it off to bad upbringing. Until this morning, I was glad she was going out with Alex. I wanted her to have the chance to do the things normal girls do. She told me herself this is what she wanted."

"Why did your grandfather send you?" she asked. "Why didn't he come himself?"

"He is old, almost blind. He had faith in my abilities to deal with her."

"What abilities are these?"

"You spotted some of them. And you guessed how they came to me. Every time I went into an animal—I feel now this must have been the case—I took from it whatever special talents it possessed."

"So it was a fish who taught you how to swim?" she said sarcastically.

Bala stared at the ceiling. "You hate me. I suppose I cannot blame you. It was simply impossible for me to believe the impossible."

She went to snap at him again, stopped herself. He had his reasons for not warning them, but she believed he was omitting the most important one, although the lapse may have been unintentional. He had mentioned how he had been charmed by Joni. The truth of the matter, Cindy thought, was that he had loved her, as a sister perhaps, maybe as a good friend, but loved nonetheless. He had not warned them because he had refused to admit the truth to himself. She debated about confronting him with it, but quickly decided it didn't matter. "You became a believer today," she said instead. "What happened?"

"When I heard of Ray's death, I got a handgun and drove straight to Joni's house. I told her I wanted to go for a walk. I think she knew I intended to kill her. But she was not afraid. She has a cold confidence. She is aware of her strength and speed. She suggested we should go up to the falls, where we all went that night. This did not surprise me. Vultures are territorial. The national park has become her new hunting ground. The place could serve my needs just as well. I could kill her, I thought, and bury her, and, with a little luck, not be sent to prison.

"We parked in that place we had before, Lot H. We did not take the same path, though, but headed through the trees toward the river. She was a couple of strides ahead of me. I took out my pistol. I did not even have a chance to fire it."

"Why not?" Cindy asked.

"It was probably my own fault. I hesitated, for the same old reason. She was a beautiful young girl. I could not shoot her in the back. And then it was too late. She turned and stared at me. Her large black eyes seemed to fill the world. Having been shown the way to leave her body once, she apparently has not forgotten how to leave it again. This must be how she gets a grip on an individual's sheath; she lets a portion of herself wrap around the person. I could not move, for a split second, and then it did not matter. Her reflexes are incredible, at least the equal of her strength. She snapped my arms behind my back and, keeping them pinned with one hand, dragged me toward the edge of a cliff near the base of the waterfall. She threw me over the side without saying a word."

"Why didn't she ravage your body like she had the others?"

"I think she only does that when she is absorbing an individual's sheath. Obviously, she was able to affect mine, but since there was not a strong bond between us, she was not able to use it. You could say I was a meal she could not digest."

"I wonder," Cindy said doubtfully, thinking again of his initial affection for Joni. Bala seemed to read her mind, and quickly offered another explanation.

"She has inherited Joni's brain. She has not assimilated everything Joni knew, but she is not stupid. She probably did not want to add to the mystery that is developing. She probably wanted it to look like I had accidentally fallen over the side. If the two men fishing around the bend in the river had not been there and pulled me out, I would have drowned. Her plan was shrewd."

"So she thinks you're dead?"

"I would assume. But that is not necessarily a good thing. I told Alex that Joni was dangerous. If he is with her and spills that, she may feel she has to destroy him to keep the truth from spreading. Plus Joni might kill him for another reason."

"What? She can't want to suck on his sheath. She just had Ray's."

"But Alex is far more attached to her than Ray was. She stands to gain more from him than anybody since her own father."

"But you just said she doesn't want any more beat-up bodies lying around."

Bala nodded. "I hope that factor outweighs her hunger."

Cindy stood and went to the sink, splashing cold water in her face, noting that her eyes were puffy. She must have been crying while listening to Bala; she hadn't realized it.

I can cry later. If Alex is dead, I'll have the rest of my life to cry.

"What if we call the police?" she said.

"They will not believe us."

"But this reporter told me the coroner refused to release the results of the autopsy on Karen. The coroner would only have done that if he couldn't figure out what they were dealing with. Somebody already knows something weird is going on."

"There is not a chance, nor will there ever be, that the police will believe that a cute English girl has the strength of a grizzly. I am surprised you believe me."

"I was a born believer," she muttered. "Why *is* she so strong? And why does she behave like a predator and not a scavenger? Vultures don't go after the living."

"Vultures are usually a bag of bones and feathers. But they can pull a surprising amount of weight into the air. They are very strong for their size."

"And now we have a ninety-nine-pound vulture?"

"Yes, you see my point. And in a sense, I have already answered your second question. Joni hungers to be human. She needs to feed on human sheaths to stay human. She does not actually eat the flesh. The effect of each of her feedings must eventually wear off, forcing her to kill again."

"Then she won't need to kill Alex," she blurted out, knowing she was repeating herself.

Bala was grim. "There is the other consideration. You ask why she behaves like a predator? I will tell you something your encyclopedias might not agree with. Vultures are predators at heart. They would kill any living creature if they could, if they had the strength Joni has, and not only for food. They are hideous beasts."

"You're not giving me much hope."

Bala's face was sad. "Maybe it is better this way, Cindy."

She exploded. "Damn you! I have hope! I'm not writing

my brother off just like that!" She stepped toward his bed, glared down at him. "He's going to make it. He's smart and he's fast and he's not going to die! He might not even be with her!"

"I pray that he is not."

"I don't want your prayers! You're a shaman's grandson! I want magic! I want to know how I can waste this bitch!"

Bala was concerned. "I did not tell you this story so you would go after Joni."

"Then why did you tell me? So I would know not to invite her to my next slumber party?"

"I've been trying to warn you away from her. You are going to have to be patient. She has no idea I am here. Wait till I recover. Leave her to me."

Cindy stopped. "But she *will* know you're here. I told her aunt I was at the hospital, waiting to see a friend of mine who'd been hurt. She'll figure out who that friend is."

Bala frowned. "She could come here."

"I think she'll call first to speak to me, and see if I know anything. She wouldn't want to knock you off and not know if we'd talked about her past."

Bala nodded. "That is logical."

Cindy's voice shook. "It's also logical that if she has been with my brother, and calls instead of him . . ." She couldn't say it. She turned for the door. "I'm going up there."

"Where?"

"To her hunting ground, where else?"

Bala tried to sit up again. "Do not be foolish. That national park must cover thirty square miles. It is already dark. Where would you look? And even if by chance you did get close to her, she would see you before you saw her. And she would kill you, make no mistake about it."

She paused at the door. "I'll get someone to go with me."

"You are not going to convince anyone to help you search for a monster. Please, listen to me. Do not throw your life away. All we can do is wait for one of them to show up."

"All right," Cindy whispered, knowing he spoke the truth, looking out the window at the mountains. "But if she hurts Alex, that girl's going to wish she had stayed a bird. I'll kill her, I swear it."

They didn't go for doughnuts. Try as he might, Alex couldn't convince Joni they should start down the mountain. He was beginning to suspect she wanted to stay out past the time her aunt went to bed. She was stalling, that was for sure.

But he didn't let her have it all her own way. If they were going to stay outside, he told her, they were going to stay warm. He was going to build a fire. He had a Bic lighter in his pocket, and there were plenty of dry sticks to be found nearby. To his surprise, Joni was against the idea. It seemed she was afraid of fires. And she had always struck him as the fearless type. But he insisted, and once he had a small blaze going beneath the overhanging ledge Bala had jumped from while rescuing his sister, Joni finally began to relax, and curled up beside him and the flames.

The wall of stone at their back provided a shield against the wind, and the icy splashings of the nearby river couldn't touch them. Collecting the wood for the fire had been invigorating, but now Alex began to feel drowsy again. The warmth from the flames was sinking softly into his bones, and even Joni's throaty voice was beginning to sound soothing. She was talking about her childhood. He was only half listening, and he assumed that was the reason half of what she said made no sense. One moment she was reminiscing about playing in green meadows, and the next, about drifting over wide desert stretches.

"Now just a minute," he interrupted, though it was really a big bother to do so. "You're saying you didn't live all your life in England?"

"I've lived two lives," she answered, sitting on her knees before his outstretched legs, her dangling hair a dark shade of red in the fiery light. "It's difficult for me to put them together. But I wanted you to hear of both of them so you would know why we're here. I want you to understand me."

"I'd like to," he said, yawning, wondering if she were referring to her life before her parents died, and her life after. Another thing continued to puzzle him; that remark her aunt had made about Joni's previous contact with Bala's people. All the while he had been waiting with Mrs. Lee for Joni to come home, the woman had tactfully avoided explaining what she'd meant. "Have you ever been to Africa?" he asked suddenly.

"Places don't say where I have been. Or where I have to go."

"But have you ever visited there? Bala's always treated you like he knew you from before."

She nodded carefully. "His is the first face I ever saw, after I found my way back."

"What do you mean?"

She leaned closer, her hair lying across him. Despite the mountain chill, she seemed perfectly comfortable in her simple white dress. "Let's not talk about him."

She had reacted the same way on his living room couch. "But is he an old friend?" he asked.

She smiled. "He's nothing now. He's gone."

"Gone? Where did he go?"

"Far away, where he won't have to worry about me any-more." She placed her hand on his shoulder, pulled him slowly toward her. "Are you worried about me, Alex?"

He grinned. "Should I be?"

She lost her smile, nodded gravely. "Yes. I could eat you up."

His grin broadened. "That doesn't sound so bad."

She put her other hand on his other shoulder, her fingers spreading out, the nails digging into his flesh. "It doesn't have to be bad. For you, especially for you, I'd want it to be sweet."

Alex started to get excited. Yet, at the same time, his dreamy dullness did not leave him. Joni's suggestive words seemed at odds with her large dark eyes, which were soft with the warm reflection from the flames. "I'm game," he said.

She nodded again. "That's how it is in the wild. There is the strong and there is the game, the hunter and the hunted."

"And which am I?"

"The hunted."

Alex chuckled. "And all this time I thought I was chasing after you."

Her hands cupped the sides of his neck, squeezing into his hair. "In the beginning, I thought it could stay that way. You were different. You not only cared for me, you made me care for you. And I have never cared for anything, ever."

Alex was delighted, except that she was speaking in the past tense. "But do you still feel this way?"

Joni stopped her massage, her arms encircling his neck, her face inches away. It was then he noted the stain on her dress near her armpit. There was something about its color that he found disturbing, and he tried to pinpoint the reason.

"I feel you could've been my salvation," Joni said. "You made me feel like a girl should. I told Bala that was all I wanted. I thought he believed me. But he must have changed his mind."

"What did you and Bala do today?" Alex asked. The stain was a dirty brown, sort of crusty. He could have sworn it was a bloodstain.

"We went for a walk in the woods. Like you and I went for a walk."

"Did you go for a walk up here?" he asked, his excitement quickly turning to confusion. Joni had changed into this dress the moment she had returned to the house. This stain— Where had it come from?

"Near here."

Alex started to become aware just how firm Joni's grasp was, how strong her hands were. "Did you also go for a walk in the woods with Ray?"

"Yes," she said softly, beginning to tease her nails lightly into the back of his neck, and not so lightly; she was actually scratching him.

"Near here?"

"Very near, Alex. I like this place. I feel at ease here."

A cold thought entered Alex's mind. It was vague, more of an unpleasant sensation than an actual idea, and yet, it seemed something he should have thought of before, something that was as obvious as hell. He began to shiver. "Joni, did you wear this dress when you went out with Ray?"

"I wore a dress. Which one doesn't matter. Alex, let me see your eyes."

He looked up, in spite of a strong desire not to; the nearness of Joni's face made it hard to think clearly. "Yes?" he mumbled.

"You're not happy."

He forced a smile. "Sure I am. It's just getting late, that's all."

She nodded. "I'm going to have to go back in a few minutes."

"Good idea," he said, shifting uncomfortably. He couldn't be sure, but it felt as though the back of his neck was bleeding. A sticky warmth was spreading around his collar. "Joni, would you stop that?"

"You're such a nice boy."

He brushed at her arms. They didn't budge an inch. "You're hurting my neck," he complained.

She leaned closer, moistening her lips as she had done on the couch just before they'd kissed. "Look at me, Alex, and it won't hurt. You'll feel like you're inside me, like you're flying."

What she said seemed almost true. He could almost forget what was going on in his body, that he even had a body, when he allowed her eyes to hold him. Almost.

God, my neck is bleeding.

Moist trails were running down his back beneath his jacket; he could feel them distinctly now, and could vividly imagine how they were staining his T-shirt, staining it the same color as the spot on Joni's white dress. The image blurred the intensity of Joni's stare, her sharp black eyes melting into a nightmare of red. "Let me go," he said.

"I can't."

"Come on, Joni, it's late."

"I want to kiss you."

"Did you feel scared when her body touched yours?"

He tried to shake free but couldn't; it was as if his neck

were encircled in steel chains. His quiet anxiety instantly leap-frogged through many levels of previously unimaginable hor-ror. Joni was stronger than he, stronger than any human being had a right to be.

"Let's kiss later," he said, shoving at her chest without effect. It was then he realized what should have been so obvi-ous. Bala had been telling him the truth.

"Did her mouth touch yours?"

"But I need to kiss you," Joni insisted, shifting her grip from his neck to his cheeks, slowly pulling his face toward her mouth. Her lips parted slightly, and there seemed to be a dozen rows of teeth inside. Out the corner of his eyes, he could see her nails dripping bright red drops.

"No!" he shouted, searching with groping hands for any-thing he could use to ward her off. His fingers stumbled across a thick branch and, not realizing at first it belonged to the campfire, he whipped it up toward Joni's head. The flames had scarcely touched her hair when she let out a shout and threw him back, leaping to her feet. The base of his skull hit the ground with a force that brought stars to his eyes.

"Alex," she hissed.

He wasn't in the mood to apologize. Shaking off his dizzi-ness, keeping a hold on his burning stick, he stood up. "What's wrong with you?" he yelled.

Joni was quick to recover from her brush with the fire. "I need you," she said, taking a step toward him.

"Why are you doing this?" he cried, taking a step backward. He would have felt better if he had the campfire between them. But it was already too late for that. She had him cut off. He could hear the river at his back. "*What* are you doing?"

"I need what that teacher spoke of, the precious ingredient. I need to get close to you."

"But you're trying to kill me!"

"Yes."

There wasn't much left of the stick he was holding. The hot end was pretty well charred; the flame flickered in his trembling grasp. He was moving away from the shelter of the cliff wall, and the wind was doing its damnest to blow the thing out. "Did you kill Ray?"

"Yes." She was closing in, her eyes as steady as the cold moonlight, the smoke from the campfire billowing around her like a witch's aura.

"Did you kill Karen?" he asked, his voice cracking.

"Yes."

"What did you do to Bala?"

"I killed him. Put down the stick, Alex."

"But then you'll kill me."

"Yes." She stopped and took a deep breath. "You should have let me kiss you. I would be done by now. I don't take long."

Ten feet beneath the heels of his shoes was Snake Tail River. There was nowhere left for him to go. "How can you be like this, Joni?" he moaned.

"By forgetting who Joni was. By letting it all come at once, until the next time, until it comes again." She raised her right hand, her nails still dripping with the blood she had scraped from his flesh. Her eyes narrowed, and it was as though a tangible wave of insatiable hunger rolled over him. "Come to me, Alex."

A gust of wind slapped the night, and his torch died, and he was left holding ashes. Ice and ashes; it would be better than what had happened to the others. Tearing his eyes from the face he had dreamed he would always adore, he turned and jumped.

The shock of the cold was almost welcome. Her hypnotic hold on him seemed to snap. The current had him now, and though it would kill him as easily as she would have, it was not going to bleed him further.

The campfire was receding rapidly. As he resurfaced, he saw that Joni had vanished from its light. He knew his only hope was to swim to the other side, before he reached the falls. His chances were slim. He was not nearly the swimmer Bala was and the feathers lining his down jacket were already soaked, collaring him with a heavy burden. Rolling in the icy black, he fought for the zipper with freezing fingers. But when he got to it, he found the zipper jammed.

This damn jacket cost me two hundred dollars!

Submerged stones pounded his shins. Keeping his chin above the surface was consuming more of his energy than his feeble strokes. His muscles were cramping at an astonishing rate.

I can't drown. I'm supposed to be in too good shape.

He was choking on a lungful of water a minute later when he heard the scream. It seemed to emerge from every direction at once, a high, scratching screech, sharp enough to cut the bravest heart in two. He told himself that couldn't be Joni. Nothing human could make that kind of sound. Nothing living could.

But she always did sound like she had a frog in her throat.

The noise did not last, not that it mattered. He wasn't making progress. There definitely was a strong cross current preventing him from getting to the other side. And since he couldn't go back the way he had come, he was going to die. The truth of the fact rolled over him without reality. It wasn't that he couldn't picture himself dead, he just couldn't imagine Cindy at his funeral. He couldn't do that to her.

His sister was still on his mind a tumbling quarter of a mile later when he looked up and saw Joni stretching out her hand from an overhanging tree. Her eyes were on him again. There was simply no getting away from them.

"Stop, Alex," she said, and it was something of a miracle he heard her over the roar of the approaching falls. Or maybe her words were only in her mind. She was definitely inside there. He had decided with the last fiber of his being he wouldn't let her touch him again and still he accepted her offer without question, reaching out his hand to meet hers, feeling her fingers close around his with delicious warmth. He expected that she would pull him into her lap—and possibly bite his head off—but she continued to let him flail in the buffeting current.

"Alex," she said, staring down at him, her face deep with sorrow. "I really do love you."

Cindy was sitting by herself in Timber Memorial's waiting lounge when she heard the second page for her. Two hours had passed since the nurse had come to Bala's room and injected him with a solution that had sent even his extraordinary body into a deep sleep, leaving her alone with her fears. The first page had been for a call from her parents. They were still at the store, working on the inventory, her mother said. She didn't want Alex and her waiting up for them. We won't, Cindy had promised.

Alex, Alex, Alex—be on the other side of the line!

Cindy picked up the phone at the deserted nurses' station and identified herself. The hospital operator completed the connection. "Hello," Cindy said, her eyes tightly closed.

"This is Joni," the girl said without a trace of emotion.

Cindy's head dropped and she sagged against the wall. For a long moment she couldn't force a breath through her constricted throat. Joni waited patiently for her. "This is Cindy," she finally managed.

I have the rest of my life to cry! But not now!

"What can I do for you, Cindy?"

She swallowed. "Is Alex there?"

"No."

"Have you seen him today?"

"Yes."

"Do you know where he is now?"

"No. Why are you at the hospital?"

Tears poured silently over her cheeks. "I'm here with Bala."

Joni considered for a moment. "Is he hurt?"

"He's slipping into a coma. He might not wake up."

"That's terrible," Joni said flatly.

Cindy hoped vultures didn't know jack about comas. "Yes, it is. But before he blacked out, I had a talk with him. We talked about some things I would like to talk with you about."

"What sort of things?"

"Shamans. Do you know much about shamans, Joni?"

Joni paused again. "When would you like to talk?"

"Tonight, in an hour. I'll meet you by the river in the park, where Bala had his accident. Is that a good spot for you?"

"Yes. Will you be alone?"

"You can bet on it."

Chapter Twelve

Cindy was out in the parking lot when she realized she didn't have a car, neither here nor at home; and the motorbike wouldn't do for what she had planned. For a moment she entertained the perverse idea of having Joni pick her up. But in the end, she went back inside the hospital and called, of all people, Jason.

"Cindy?" he said, his voice incredulous. "What do you want?"

"I want you to go to my house and pick up Wolf, Sybil, a pair of binoculars, and that rifle we took up to the waterfall. You know where we keep the key. Wolf and Sybil are in the house. The gun and binoculars are in the garage. Also, get me a box of shells. You'll find them in one of the workbench drawers."

"You've got to be kidding."

"I want you to bring the pets and the stuff to Memorial. I'm here now. Oh, and I'm going to have to borrow your car."

"Cindy, have you flipped? You're trying to put me in jail. Why should I help you?"

"If you help me now, maybe you won't go to jail. Understand?"

He sounded doubtful, but interested. "What are you up to?"

"None of your business. But if you're not here in less than half an hour, my offer expires."

Jason could be reasonable when it suited him. After repeating her shopping list back to her, he hung up with a promise to be there in twenty minutes. Cindy waited on the front steps of the hospital and watched the full moon rise higher and higher in the sky. The power of Joni's eyes were on her mind. Perhaps she should have told Jason to fetch her sunglasses. It was too late now.

Jason was true to his word. She waved for him to keep the engine running when he pulled into the emergency unloading zone not long afterward. Wolf barked hello out the backseat window as she jogged down the steps to the red sports car. She didn't give Jason a chance to ask questions. She didn't even offer to give him a ride home. Handing him the keys to the cycle, she scooted him out of the front seat and slid behind the wheel, making a quick check to see that he had brought everything. Sybil was sitting quietly in her cage in the passenger seat, her sightless eyes watching her.

"Joni," the bird said.

"Don't you know it," Cindy swore, hitting the accelerator without saying good-bye to her old boyfriend.

She had a fairly good idea of where Joni must have thrown Bala over the cliff. He had spoken of Lot H, and of the path they had taken that cut directly through the woods to the river. That was rough terrain down there in the gorge, beneath the falls.

I should've told her two hours. I should've been early.

It was on the ride up to the park that the fear began to hit her. Her plan could be nothing but an elaborate suicide, made in haste before she'd really thought about what it was she was doing. Although she already missed Alex terribly, she didn't want to die. The steering wheel began to slip under her sweaty fingers, and she gripped it all the harder to keep her hands from shaking. All of a sudden she realized just how fragile a thing it was to be alive, to have your lungs breathing air, your heart pumping blood. If Joni was as strong as Bala said, she would only have to get a hand on her, a finger even, and Cindy Jones would be history. Bala was part Bairavee and the witch had swatted him as if he were a fly.

"Her head had also suffered from what appeared to be an extremely powerful blow—the top of her skull was cracked in several places."

A quarter of a mile down the mountain from Lot H, Cindy parked. With the giant moon and the howling wind, the silver trees jostling with each other in wild rhythms, the forest appeared possessed with an alien presence. Taking a string Alex always kept handy on the floor of the bird cage, she tied one end to Sybil's right leg, fastening the other end around a gold necklace Alex had given her for her birthday. Wolf watched the whole operation with the utmost curiosity.

"I'm going to be counting on you tonight, boy," she said, finishing with the bird and petting the dog on the head. It took her only a minute to load the rifle.

She was late but she took the hike up the road slowly, hugging the trees, staying in the shadows. Wolf's company was reassuring, and she kept a tight hold on his leash while the yellow parrot rode serenely on her right shoulder. Yet she was having trouble breathing, and she couldn't stop glancing above her, at the sky; she kept expecting a huge vulture to swoop down upon her.

Alex's car was sitting in the middle of the parking lot. Cindy considered leaving her cover to peek through the windows. What stopped her, more than the fear Joni would spot her, was the possibility she might find Alex's body inside.

My beautiful brother.

She didn't take the path Bala had described, but rather, continued to climb higher, until she came to a second path that she knew also led to the river. She wanted to come upon Joni unaware.

The waterfall was above and off to her right as she crept cautiously forward, and the rocky vale resounded with the noise of its white water. The path she was on was seldom traveled. Branches scratched at her arms and legs, and also at the barrel of her rifle, which she held low in front, her finger on the trigger. Bala hadn't commented on Joni's hearing and Cindy prayed it wasn't as extraordinary as her grip. The dried branches felt like so many claws trying to get under her skin.

"It looked as though her head had been grabbed by the ears and squashed together."

Whatever happened, she didn't want that damn reporter trying to describe what was left of her body.

A few minutes later she reached the end of the trees and was granted a wide view of the gorge. Crouching down behind a boulder, Wolf breathing on the side of her face, she spanned the area of the supposed meeting spot with her binoculars. It was only after a close search that she saw Joni. The girl was sitting approximately half a mile away, two hundred feet below, in the shadow of a sheer overhanging ledge, on a smooth stone a few feet from the water. If not for Joni's white dress, Cindy probably would have missed her.

"Bitch," she whispered.

Having Joni in view allowed her to relax somewhat. Joni's decision to wait away from the trees appeared to be a serious tactical mistake. Even in the shadow, she made a respectable target. Carefully, Cindy began to work her way closer, weaving around the jagged rocks and dry shrubs, watching where she placed her feet. The whole time Joni sat as still as a statue.

When she was perhaps two football fields away, Cindy

again went down on her knees behind a boulder. Her father kept the scope on the rifle well adjusted, and as she centered Joni's chest between the crosshairs, the barrel propped steadily across the stone, she knew all she had to do was pull the trigger and all the sheaths and all their owners in Timber would be safe. But she hesitated, and suddenly there were so many reasons why she should. It made no difference that the reasons contradicted each other.

First, she wanted to personally confront Joni. The girl had killed her brother, and she wanted her to know, wanted her to *see* what was coming before the bullet cut her down. The reason was savage and illogical and that made it all the stronger.

Second, she was worried about the police. Bala had commented about going to jail, and when you got right down to it, she probably would be tried for murder if she pulled the trigger. Nowadays, a slug could be traced back to practically any gun. Plus good old reliable Jason could always reverse the tables and act as a witness against her.

Third, her disgust at Bala's inability to deal with Joni had been unfair. It *was* next to impossible to believe the gorgeous creature resting on the boulder was evil. Joni even looked sad. Cindy took her eye off the scope. Her father's deep repugnance at the killing of any living creature was with her, and couldn't be ignored.

And finally, there was her brilliant plan that could satisfy all these objections to wasting Joni, and still get rid of the menace.

Shouldering the rifle, she decided she would have to try it.

Her brilliant plan had one major flaw. It would probably get her killed.

Cindy stood, stepping gingerly toward the base of the cliff where Joni waited. Halfway there, she stopped and undid Wolf's leash, whispering in the dog's ear.

"You're to stay, Wolf. Stay."

The dog did as told. But if all went as planned, he would disobey her command within minutes.

Grandfather Bairavee, if you can be in more than one place at the same time, please be here with me now. Please help me.

Petting the dog one last time, she started down.

Joni glanced up as Cindy waded through the shallow pool that was the final barrier between them, the icy water pouring over Cindy's high-top sneakers. Since Joni was still cloaked by the shadow, Cindy felt it should be safe to look directly at her. She could barely even see Joni's eyes, never mind be swept away by them. So she thought.

But before she could confront Joni, something off to her left caught her attention. Stuck in the water between a stick and a stone was Alex's jacket. The back had been torn to shreds.

No, no, no, no . . .

The will to live went out of her then, but not the fear of death. Her entire body began to shiver worse than when Bala had fished her from the cold river that now flowed at her back. Sybil stirred restlessly beside her head. Cindy tried to raise her rifle, tried to look at Joni and not see her. "Where's Alex?" she whispered.

Joni sighed, stretching her legs over the rock. "You know where he is."

"Did you kill him?"

"Yes."

A single powerful tremor went through her. "Why did you kill him?"

Joni slid effortlessly off the boulder, standing upright, glanced briefly in the direction Cindy had come from. "Didn't Bala tell you why?"

"He told me you're a vulture."

Joni took a casual step forward, the hair around her head a part of the inky black from which she was emerging. "I'm more than that, Cindy. I'm much more than that."

Cindy blinked several times. There was something obstructing her vision, as if a smoky haze were arising from the ground between them. Her breathing difficulty returned, and she began to pant rapidly. The air was full of strange odors, of things rotting. "You're nothing, Joni. You're dead meat."

"I saw you up there a few minutes ago, Cindy," she said, her approach steady but unhurried. "I think you could have shot me then. But I think you were afraid to. I could sense your fear."

"I'm not afraid," Cindy whispered, lying. This *thing* had killed God knew how many people, torn them to pieces so that their own families couldn't recognize them. Suddenly she realized the fool she had been to challenge Joni in this lonely spot. Suddenly she had no idea what she was supposed to do next.

This is a spell!

Hadn't Bala also been caught in an instant?

"But you are, you're scared you're going to die. And you are going to die. Or I am. We both can't live. You see, I'm scared, too. Bala probably didn't tell you that. I'm only trying to survive." She stepped out of the shadow, her white face appearing as lifeless as polished marble. "Look at me, Cindy."

Cindy looked; it was impossible not to. Not even the knowledge that it was her death to do so could make her stop. An invisible claw seemed to stretch out from Joni, enfolding Cindy from head to toe. Then the spell took a twist, coming at her from the inside rather than the outside. Cindy could no longer see Joni's eyes. But she could see *through* them. A swollen orange moon filled her universe, a moon from long ago, glimpsed from inside another body, a full moon hanging in a desert sky above a parched land too dry for even a vulture's empty thoughts.

Cindy's consciousness fragmented. There were three of her, and one of them was not human. Images of her life in the Wyoming Rockies, of a young girl's days in the English countryside, and of a beastly existence on the hungry plains of Africa bombarded her like a swirling kaleidoscope, the latter's memories convulsing her stomach in nausea. *She* remembered chewing on bloody fly-soaked carcasses!

I'm not dying. I'm being possessed.

But through all these memories was the moon, seen from different perspectives, but nevertheless remaining the same. Tilting her head back, she could see it still, and it seemed her only thread to reality. Different moments in time and space converged. As a vulture she had acute eyesight. She could see the craters of the moon without aid. And even though as a young girl she'd used binoculars, she'd thought the same as the vulture, *that it was full of holes.* And this single point in common created a single hole in the trance, a place where she could stand and not be bewitched.

Shoot the moon, Cindy. It's your only safe target.

Safe for all of them.

Cindy raised the rifle and shot the moon.

The roar of the gun came to her from far off.

Cindy came back to her body exactly where she had left it. Only now Joni was no longer fifteen feet away, but standing inches from her face, her black eyes twin silver mirrors of the moon above, her breath as cold as frost.

"Yes, I've always watched the sky," Joni said softly. "I watched it believing it was home, that I would one day return there." She raised her right hand, caught a lock of Cindy's hair, and slowly began to curl it around her finger. "Time for you to go home."

Cindy tasted blood in her mouth. She had bit her lip. "No," she pleaded.

"Don't resist me."

"Please."

"It hurts much more that way." Joni snapped her hand away, ripping the lock of hair from Cindy's scalp, sending a shearing pain slicing through her head, warm blood dripping round her ear. Sybil sat silent, unmoving. "It's like getting eaten alive."

"Don't, please." Cindy wept.

Joni smiled, cupping Cindy's chin in her hand. "You loved your brother, but you don't love me. I can't take you for my own. Don't cry, Cindy. It will be all right." Joni's fingers tightened, her nails pressing into Cindy's bones. "I will simply kill you."

Cindy squeezed her eyes shut, as Joni raised the other hand, placing it on the back of Cindy's skull, and began to squeeze the life out of her body.

Then there was a second roar in the night, unlike the sound of the rifle, but every bit as deadly. It had been part of Cindy's plan that the gunshot would have called him, and perhaps it had and he'd had difficulty navigating the steep rocky yards that separated them. Or maybe he had only thought to strike when he had seen Joni take hold of her. Whatever the case, Wolf was now attacking.

The bone-crushing pressure ceased. Cindy opened her eyes. Joni had leapt a dozen feet away, her soul-sucking eyes darting from her to the dog, back and forth. Wolf was less than fifty feet up the hill and closing fast. And as though their minds were still fused, Cindy could understand Joni's thoughts. She could take a few seconds to kill the dog, and leave Cindy free to put a bullet in her chest, or she could try to kill Cindy quickly, and leave the dog free to rip her throat out.

Joni had seen Wolf attack Jason when he had fired the gun, but Joni knew Wolf was never going to attack his master.

There's a way out, Joni. Take it! Take it!

Planting her right knee and using it to support the rifle, Cindy aimed directly at Joni's heart. Joni's attention continued to flash back and forth between her and the dog. A decision was going to have to be made fast. With all the noise and excitement, Sybil began to rock nervously. Joni appeared to become aware of the bird for the first time.

"Joni," Cindy said.

"Joni Jones," the bird chirped.

Joni's eyes suddenly settled in their direction. She nodded slightly, going very still.

Cindy quickly shut her eyes.

Sybil stopped her rocking.

Something brushed past Cindy's head, a cool mist that could be felt but never seen; the stuff of ghosts and spirits.

Sybil began to flap violently, trying to fly away, not succeeding. Cindy opened her eyes. "Heel, Wolf!" she shouted. "Heel!"

Her dog, making ready to leap, stalled in midstride. The command had hit home. Or maybe he'd halted because his prey had suddenly given up. Joni lay collapsed on the ground.

"Stay, stay," Cindy told Wolf, climbing to her feet, approaching Joni cautiously, keeping her finger on the rifle trigger, Sybil continuing to struggle for freedom on her shoulder. Wolf leaned over and licked Joni's peaceful face, half-hidden beneath her beautiful black hair. The girl was not breathing. Cindy knelt and felt at her neck for a pulse.

"My grandfather said Joni was dead."

The question was settled now. There was no pulse.

Cindy pulled her necklace over her head, worried that Sybil would scratch her face, and pinned the parrot to the ground with the help of a heavy rock set across the string attached to the bird's ankle. Then she looked around for something to do and realized there was nothing she could do. All the monsters had been slain. The genie was back in her bottle.

And my brother is gone.

Cindy rested her face on Joni's side and began to cry softly, not just for Alex, but for the others as well, including Joni Harper.

Time went by—ten minutes, perhaps an hour. Cindy finally stirred, as though awakening from a dream, and sat up, Wolf nudging her cheek with his wet nose. Wrapping her arm around the dog, she wondered if she had the strength left to walk to the car, if she should even bother.

A sound at her back made her whirl.

A panting young man limped around the bend, coming toward her, a huge stick in his hand. Cindy reached for her rifle, "What do you want?" she called.

"I'd like a ride home, if you've got one."

"Alex? Alex!"

"It's me."

Joni got me after all. I've died and gone over to the other side.

Cindy didn't care if that turned out to be the truth. In her excitement, she tried to jump up without realizing her soggy feet had gone to sleep while she had lain against Joni. She ended up flat on her face, laughing hysterically. "Alex, you're not dead!"

"I never said I was," he said, dragging through the puddle of water, using his stick as a cane. He stopped above her, dripping wet. "I'd offer you my hand but I think my leg's broken."

"What's a little broken leg?" she asked, making no sense and not caring. How was she ever going to thank God for this one? She would probably have to become a nun or something. "Sit down and tell me what happened!"

He accepted her invitation, except he sat next to Joni instead of herself, touching the fallen girl's hair. "Somehow, this doesn't surprise me," he said sadly.

Cindy stopped smiling. "I'm sorry, Alex."

He was silent for a moment. A single tear ran over his cheek. "Yeah."

Cindy put her hand on his back. "Who would have thought it would end this way."

Alex looked at her. "When did you find out about her—her—?" He didn't know what to say.

"Bala told me this evening."

Alex was surprised. "Then he's all right?"

"He's in the hospital, but he'll heal."

"Good." Alex turned back to Joni. "What did he tell you?"

Cindy hesitated. The whole truth might not be the best thing for him right now, if ever. "About a year ago, Bala's grandfather performed a shamanic experiment using Joni. It sort of ended badly." She paused. "Was she rough on you?"

Alex glanced up at the moon, then at his torn jacket stuck in the water, shaking his head. "Not as rough as the waterfall was."

"You went over the *falls*? That's impossible."

"I should have died," Alex agreed, touching Joni's head again. "I should have died twice. I was in the river, and she was hanging on to me from that log Jason used when trying to rescue you. I knew if she pulled me out of the river, she would kill me. It was like she wouldn't be able to help herself. And she knew it, too, and didn't want to do it."

"What happened?"

Alex smiled for a moment, then lowered his head. "She told me she loved me. And she held my eyes, and it was like she gave me a part of herself. I'm not sure if she actually said these words, but I remember them. 'Fly, Alex, you can fly.'" He took his hand away from Joni. "When I went over the waterfall, I seemed to fall forever. And when I hit, it didn't feel that hard." He shrugged. "But I still broke my leg. I guess now I've got a good excuse for not winning the next race."

Cindy hugged him. "Maybe you did fly."

And maybe she did love you. Maybe not all of Joni was taken that terrible day.

Alex noticed for the first time that Joni had not bled. "I heard a shot," he said, frowning. "I thought—how did you stop her?"

Cindy stood and carefully removed the rock that kept her brother's parrot from flying away, replacing the necklace and the attached string around her neck. Settling on her shoulder, Sybil stopped fussing. "Tell the police you fell off this ledge and broke your leg," she said. "And when Joni ran down here and saw you lying on the rocks, she must have thought you were dead. Tell them she just keeled over. There isn't a mark on her body. I can corroborate your story. They'll believe us."

"But what really happened?"

Neither she nor Alex could carry the body back; they would have to send the police for it. Ignoring the cold, Cindy removed her coat and gently covered Joni, thinking of the strong-willed girl Bala had described, who wanted to see some magic, and who saw more than she had bargained for. "That *is* what happened, Alex. She got scared. And it killed her."

Epilogue

I t was a day for funerals, and it seemed all wrong she was having to worry about what she was going to wear. But the reality of the situation was that she simply didn't have the clothes
for it; most of her things were bright colors. Flipping through
her wardrobe for the third time, she decided her gray pants suit
was her best bet, even though it needed pressing. Once, Ray
had told her she looked like a *real woman* in the outfit.

There was a knock at her bedroom door. "Are you decent?"
Alex called.

"I'm stark naked, just a sec," she called back, reaching
for her yellow robe. Her hair was still wet from her shower.
"Come in."

Alex had a midthigh-high cast on his left leg that he wasn't
letting *anybody* sign. Their mother had had to split his dress

pants to get him inside them. He lumbered into the room and plopped down on her bed. "You look clean," he said, meaning she had used up all the hot water and that their mother was complaining.

"I not only look it, I smell it. How much time have we got?"

"Ten minutes, at the most. Don't bother with makeup."

Cindy picked up her lipstick, facing the mirror above her chest-of-drawers. "Ray always liked a woman who knew how to fix herself up." She noted Alex was carrying the morning paper. "Does Mr. Cooke have another *mystery* article for us?"

"How did you know?"

"Let's just say I didn't have to use my psychic abilities to figure it out."

Alex opened the paper on his lap. "You might want to read it. Our names are mentioned twice on the front page."

Cindy took the paper and glanced at the article.

HOW DID JONI HARPER DIE?

She tossed the paper in the wastebasket by her desk, muttering, "I could've sworn he used the same title a couple of weeks ago."

"You're not going to read it?"

"Nope."

"Why not?"

"Why should I?"

Alex nodded, looked uncomfortable. "I need your advice."

"Take the money."

Now he was puzzled. "How did you know Ray willed me money?"

She messed up her lipstick. "I didn't, I was just being silly. What was Ray doing with a will?"

"His mom said he made it up as a practical joke. But now the thing is supposed to be legally binding."

"How much did he leave you?"

"His mother wasn't sure. It's a five-gallon water bottle stuffed with change. He'd been collecting it since he was a kid."

"Is it mostly quarters?"

"Cindy!"

"Just wondering. So what's your problem? Do you need help putting it in paper rolls so the bank will take it?"

Alex shook his head impatiently. "Mrs. Bower just called and said Ray had requested that I, Alex Jones, take care of the disposal of his remains."

"What? Didn't his mother have him cremated?" She knew Mrs. Lee had had Joni's body cremated. Having lived with the strange girl for a couple of months, the poor woman had probably been having nightmares of vampires. Cindy wouldn't have been surprised.

The funerals were actually simple memorial services, and no one would be going out to the cemetery. Cindy thought it was a nice touch that they were being held together.

"Yes, he was cremated. That's the problem. Ray wanted me to get rid of his ashes."

"What did he want you to do with them?"

Alex sighed. "He wanted me to mix them in with the chalk we use to mark off the cross-country course. He said in the will he liked the idea of all us guys on the team stomping on him all year."

Cindy smiled. "That's classic. Are you going to do it?"

"I'll get the chalk all dirty!"

"Nah. The stuffs bright gold, right? I bet you'll hardly be able to tell the difference."

Alex was unconvinced. "This whole idea is gross. I couldn't ever tell anybody."

"Well, you're good at keeping secrets."

He changed the subject. "While you were in the shower, Jason called."

Cindy hunted around for her blow dryer. "I hope you told him if he calls again I'll invent another nasty rumor to attach to his dirty name."

"You're not going to call him back?"

"Nope."

"He said he wanted to apologize."

"That guy's going to be apologizing for the rest of his screwy life."

Alex shrugged, standing. "Have it your way. Oh, Bala's downstairs."

"You kidding? Why didn't you tell me?"

"He just got here."

"Send him up."

"Don't you want to get dressed first?"

"He's still got his cast, too, doesn't he?"

"Yeah."

"Then what are you worried about? I should be safe. Send him up. And quit looking at me like that."

Alex gestured to the birdcage beside her bed. "Why are you keeping Sybil up here?"

Cindy stopped. "Do you mind? Lately, I've just felt like having her around, you know?"

Alex didn't understand, and didn't know it, and she wasn't going to explain herself. "Has she learned to say your name yet?" he asked.

"Not yet."

"As long as you feed her, it's fine with me." He moved for the door.

"Alex? How long do parrots live?"

He paused. "Some stay around over a hundred years."

"But Sybil was old when you got her, right?"

"Yeah. Why?"

"I was just wondering." She studied his face, concerned. He hadn't spoken much since that night. "Are you going to be all right today?"

"I don't mind remembering her," he said quietly. "There's very little that I need to forget."

She nodded. "We'll sit together."

Before Bala arrived, she quickly slipped on underwear beneath her robe. This would be, after all, the first time he had been in her room.

And the last time?

Like Alex, he knocked before entering. He had to lower his head to get through the door. His left arm was in a cast and sling and he appeared to have the ribs beneath his navy blue sweatshirt taped; there was a general stiffness in the way he moved—quite a change for him.

"I did not know you were dressing," he said shyly, averting his eyes. She laughed.

"Hey, you can look at me. I'm not naked."

He did so reluctantly, blushing. "I could wait downstairs."

"No, you have to stay. Sit on my bed. I'm glad you're here. I'm surprised that doctor let you out this soon. What's it been, three days?"

Bala sat, his legs reaching from the end of the bed to the wall. "Four, if you count Monday."

"That's right, today's Friday," she muttered. It went without saying that almost the whole week had gone by and she hadn't visited him. Sure, she'd called, but she knew he'd wait to see her before asking certain questions, ones she didn't want to answer. "How's your arm?"

"I am healing swiftly."

"I bet you are," she said thoughtfully.

Bala searched her face. "I did not think I would see you again when I awoke and learned from Mrs. Lee that you had gone to meet with Joni."

Cindy forced a laugh. "I'm a hard person to get rid of." Then she caught herself, softening her tone. "I suppose that isn't very funny. I had the same thought myself." She leaned against her desk, smoothed her hands over her legs. "But we're both here now and I suppose that's all that matters."

He nodded, spoke with feeling. "You look good, Cindy."

It was her turn to blush. "Alex just told me I looked clean."

"What I meant—"

"I know what you meant," she interrupted, looking him straight in the eye. "Thank you. I don't know if you have any idea how long I've been wondering if you thought I was attractive. I think you look good, too. Great, in fact." Then the question just burst out. "Are you leaving to go back home?"

"Yes."

She chewed on her lip. This pain in the heart didn't get any easier the more you experienced it. The pain just got worse. "Do you have to?" she asked, her voice quivering.

"I must tell my grandfather about Joni."

"Couldn't you write him?"

Bala glanced around the room. "I was wrong about him, about what he knows. It is all real. And he is getting old, and if he is going to teach me what I need to know, then it should not be delayed."

"You're going to become a shaman?"

He smiled faintly at the note of approval in her tone. "I would let you call me a magician."

To her immense embarrassment, she began to cry. The tears had a mind of their own and wouldn't stop, even when she held her arm across her eyes. Bala stood and tentatively reached out to touch her. She responded by burying her face in his chest, hugging him gently with both her arms. "Will I see you again?" she asked.

He ran the finger of his right hand through her wet hair. "On my eighth birthday I asked my grandfather how big the world was. When you are small, he said, it is huge. But when you are a master of nature, it is like a ball you can hold in your hand." He pressed his hand to the side of her head. "We will see each other again, Cindy, even if we have to meet in a dream."

She leaned back, looking up, still holding on to him. "I guess now I'll have something to look forward to when I go to sleep at night."

"I hope you recognize me in my true colors. I may not be the great warrior you once thought I was."

She hugged him again. "Don't say that. I didn't know what I was talking about in the hospital. You did what you could. You faced her alone. You're the bravest person I've ever met."

"Next to you." Then he asked *the* question. "How did you do it, Cindy?"

She closed her eyes. "I can't tell you."

"You do not know?"

She let go of him, wiped at her cheeks, and stepped to the window from where she could see the distant waterfall. "I gave her a choice. That's all I can say, Bala. Please don't ask me why."

He accepted that. "I will not be going to the service. I am afraid too many people associate me with the deaths. I never did give the police a clear account of what happened to me. I thought it would be best to just take a bus to the airport. There is a flight that leaves this afternoon. I have my things and I have already said good-bye to Pam and Mrs. Alta."

A faint rainbow had formed across the face of the waterfall, as sometimes happened when the light was right, and yet, it did not look beautiful to her. It just looked cold. "I'm glad I got a chance to say goodbye," she said softly, feeling sorry for herself.

Hey, if I don't tell him now, he'll never know.

Cindy suddenly turned and, inching up on her toes, kissed him warmly, catching him by surprise. "I'm counting on more than just a dream, Bala," she told him. "You're going to have to do better than that."

When he was gone, and she was finished getting dressed, she realized she hadn't given Sybil her breakfast. Picking up the feed jar, she leaned over the cage and stared at the bird.

She could have sworn it stared back.

"How long do parrots live?"

It was true she'd given Joni a choice, but it had been Bala who'd given her the choices, though he might not realize that until he was back with his grandfather. While lying in the hospital bed, he had told her he was certain the creature in Joni's body couldn't be a bird anymore. Then he had indirectly contradicted himself a few minutes later when explaining how she had immobilized him.

"She turned and stared at me. Her large black eyes seemed to fill the world. Having been shown the way to leave her body once, she apparently had not forgotten how to leave it again. This must be how she gets a grip on an individual's sheath; she lets a portion of herself wrap around the person."

Obviously, the spirit in Joni knew how to get around. The key, Cindy had realized, was to put her in a situation where she would *decide* to go into another body. And that was what Cindy had done, forcing the vulture to opt for a new landlord by placing her between a wild dog and a loaded gun.

Alex had told her the afternoon after his big date that he hadn't explained Sybil's blindness to Joni. He'd been afraid Joni would feel sorry for the bird.

Sightless eyes. You could go in, if you knew how, but you could never get out. No matter how long you lived.

And what happened to you, Sybil? Were you just shoved aside, out into the cold?

"Joni," the bird said.

"I know," Cindy whispered. Had Alex not convinced her

Joni really had loved him, that there really had been a portion of the original soul behind those beautiful eyes, she would've drowned the parrot. Certainly, if Bala had been told the truth, he would have insisted the bird be destroyed.

And now she was afraid to let the thing out of her sight. It was like the bird had cast a spell on her.

Sometimes she wondered if she wasn't taking a chance.

"Cindy," the bird said.

Sometimes she wondered if the bird was completely blind.

SEE YOU LATER

For Rob

Chapter One

I t began with a smile, or at least that's what I thought. But then, I didn't think much when I was eighteen. I just *longed* for things I didn't have, and *reacted* when they came to me and I no longer wanted them. But love . . . I always wanted to be in love, and to have love, and to pretend they were one and the same thing. I was like everybody else, I suppose, and I thought I was so different. I had to find that one girl who was so different, so perfect—who would accept me just the way I was.

I'm such a liar. I lie to myself constantly. The truth is I didn't know what I wanted back then. But when I saw her, I began to get an inkling.

She worked in an electronics store five miles from my house. I had been in the store a few times before but had never seen her. I love music. I had an MP3 player I had to scrape to buy and five thousand songs that made the plastic on my credit card peel on both sides. But I wasn't worried. I felt I could work my way out of any debt. In private I had tremendous self-confidence. The problem was outside my bedroom. There I was shy and awkward. When I opened the door to the electronics store and she spoke to me, I didn't know what to say.

"Hi," she said. "How are you?"

"What?" I asked. She was cute. I noticed that right away. But my heart didn't skip in my chest at the sight of her, even though I had been born with a congenital heart defect that caused my pulse to dance at the slightest provocation. It was not love at first sight. But I like to imagine that something did pass between us in that first moment, that destiny was at work. She continued to smile at me. Her teeth were white and straight, her eyes big and brown.

"I said, 'How are you?'" she repeated.

"I'm fine." I let the door close at my back, thankful for the air conditioning. Summer in Los Angeles didn't usually get off to such a fiery start, but that June was an exception. My car was like a furnace. "How are you?" I asked.

"Great," she said. "Can I help you find anything?"

"I'm just looking." I took another step inside. She was off to my right, behind a raised checkout counter; nevertheless, she was no taller than I was. I estimated her height at five two, her weight at a hundred even. I often do that—mentally record people's vital statistics. If a detective ever wanted to quiz me about the people present in any situation, I'd be ready. Her long dark hair possessed a remarkable shine. Her name tag read, "Becky."

"If you need help, give me a call," Becky said.

"All right." I surveyed the store. Except for one middle-aged lady, it was empty, which made sense. It was midday on a Monday, and school wouldn't let out for another two weeks. I was still officially a senior and waiting to graduate, but I had finished all my classwork by the January semester break. I doubted that I'd go back for the graduation ceremony. There had been only a few people at school I called friends. "Do you have a software department?" I asked.

"Yes." She pointed. "At the back, near the videos. Are you into computers?"

"I write computer games."

Her face brightened, and I asked myself if that was what I had been angling for—her approval. Ordinarily I don't brag to people about the computer games I've sold.

"Would we have any of yours?" she asked.

"It's possible."

Becky stepped down and out from behind the counter. "Let's see."

She led me to the software section. I walked behind her. She wore bright yellow pants and a short-sleeved shirt to match. For a few seconds I imagined what she'd look like in a bikini. She was on the thin side, but had enough curves to conjure up interesting images in my head. Still, she was just a girl. I was just a boy. I wasn't getting a crush or anything. It must have been the heat.

We stopped before the rows of games. Becky's store was part of a huge chain. The selection was excellent. I was happy to see they carried one of my games.

"What's your name?" she asked.

I pointed to the bottom row. "'The Starlight Crystal.'"

"Is that German?"

I glanced over. I hadn't really been listening. She grinned and I felt foolish. "My name's Mark Forum," I said. "That one's mine."

She picked the box up and studied the cover, which I thought was dreadful: two space-suited jocks beaming each other with phallic-shaped ray guns. No one in the game even wore a space suit.

"You really wrote this program?" she asked.

"Yeah."

"I sold one of these yesterday," she said.

"Good. I can use the royalties."

"Do you get royalties?"

"Yeah," I said.

"How much?"

"Ten percent retail."

She was impressed. "You must be rich."

I shrugged. "I get by."

I just got by. By the time I'd received the five thousand dollar advance on my last game—I'd sold three so far—I was down to my last five dollars. I no longer lived at home. I'd decided to leave after my dad hit me over the head with a gallon vodka bottle minutes after he'd drained the contents. Fortunately, when my hair grew back, after the doctors took out the stitches, it covered the scar. The funny thing was, my dad and I got along great when he wasn't drinking. Three years earlier we'd had a wonderful day together. I used to wonder how my mother put up with him. Then she finally left, the day before my fourteenth birthday, to marry a fire-and-brimstone preacher. On the rare occasions when I saw my stepfather, he talked continually, raving on and on about how only Jesus could save him. And you know, I agreed totally. I accepted the fact that my mother preferred bizarre men. My home life was pretty pathetic.

"Are you still in school?" Becky asked.

"Not really. Are you?"

"I graduated at the semester," she said.

"So did I."

She continued to study the game. "Did you really write this?"

"Yeah."

"But it says a Tom Cleary wrote it."

"Tom Cleary is a pen name. There's a Mark Forum who writes computer games." I shrugged. "I didn't want to get confused with him."

"So what you're telling me is that you can't prove this is yours?"

"I wouldn't lie about it," I said.

"How do I know that? I don't know anything about you."

"What do you want? I.D. saying Cleary is the same person as Forum?"

"Yeah."

I was a bit taken aback. "I don't care if you believe me or not."

She laughed. "I was just kidding, Mark."

Again I felt foolish. "Tom's my middle name," I muttered. "My mom used to call me that when I was young."

"Do you know what my middle name is?"

"Becky," I said.

She touched her badge, nodding her approval. "How did you know it wasn't my first name?"

"You wouldn't have asked me to guess."

"You're quick. I always go by Becky."

"What's your first name?"

"I'm not going to tell you." She glanced at the blurb explaining the game on the back of the box. "What's this about?"

"It's a quest game. You travel around the galaxy looking for different crystals to make up one huge crystal that has the power to destroy all the evil in the universe. Along the way you get chased by wicked aliens."

"Is it hard to solve?" Becky asked.

"Not if you know one secret."

"What?"

"I don't want to ruin it for you."

She pouted. "Come on."

"Tell me your first name first."

"No," she said.

"All right, then—no clues."

She put the game back on the shelf. "If I buy it, will you sign it for me?"

"People sign books. They don't sign computer software."

She smiled. "You're difficult. Did anyone ever tell you that?"

"You're the first." I added, "I have extra copies of the game at home. Don't buy it. I'll give you one."

"Thank you, Mark."

That was the end of our first meeting. A girl came into the store right then and needed Becky's help finding a song by a group she'd just heard of. They were called the Beatles. The girl was younger than I was and was to be forgiven. I browsed for a few minutes before deciding to hit the road. I waved to Becky as I left. She waved back. Nice girl, I thought. That was all. I didn't want to marry her or anything.

My life. It had no direction. I wanted to do a million things: be a doctor, an astronaut, a writer. But I couldn't stand the thought of going to college. I couldn't forget how it felt to sit in class and stare at the clock and wait for the period to end so that I could go to my next class and do the same thing. I had no illusions about programming computer games for the rest of my life, at least not alone. Hardly a month went by before a new game came out that left the competition far behind, particularly as far as the graphics were concerned. I knew I was lucky to have sold the games I had. I didn't have the artistic talent to create fantastic scenes. To continue in the field, I'd have to go back to school and study my brains out, or else join up with a whiz partner, who in all likelihood wouldn't need me. I couldn't stand the idea of getting an ordinary job bagging groceries or making french fries. I hated to have a boss, to take orders.

Not quite eighteen yet and I was worried about my future. Worried if I would have a future.

My health stunk. It was my heart. Walking up a flight of stairs made me gasp. Playing basketball or even catch turned me blue. I tried not to think about it, but it was like trying not to think of the fact that I had a body. Since I'd left home, I had only myself to rely on. I had no medical insurance. Naturally, both my parents knew about my problem; my defective aorta valve had been discovered when I was six. But whenever they asked—which was seldom—I told them I was feeling fine. And who knows? Maybe I was fine. I hadn't been to a doctor since I was sixteen. Maybe I had healed since then, I'd tell myself. What else could I do? The last cardiologist I'd seen tried to talk me into a new type of surgery that worked amazingly well on pigs. Getting sliced open and having someone stick his hands inside my chest didn't sit well with me, particularly when I saw that the surgeon who popped in after the cardiologist's explanation had a couple of nasty razor cuts from his morning shave. I told the docs I'd lay off the bacon and got the hell out of their office.

But listening to my heart making funny gurgling sounds as I lay awake late at night, I didn't know if my decision was right. My physical weakness had plagued me throughout my adolescence. I hadn't even had an adolescence—not really. The problems at home made it all but impossible for me to bring friends over. My defective valve ruled out sports. I went straight from being a young kid to being an adult. I knew I had a lot to be proud of, but I wasn't a man—not yet. Fighting to catch my breath in the early-morning hours before dawn, I sometimes cried for my mother.

But the night after I met Becky, I didn't wake once with chest pain. I dreamed of her. We were in a green place and we were happy. That's all I remembered. It was enough. The next day I promised myself I'd visit her again at the first opportunity. Unfortunately, I didn't get back to her record store for a couple of weeks, and she was off that day. The next two times I stopped at the store, she was off, too. A month after the day I had met her, I finally saw her again. By then I was an official high school graduate. I had gone to the ceremony after all, although neither of my parents attended—largely because I hadn't told them about it. I wasn't totally neglected, however.

After they passed out the diplomas, I got a few hugs, a few kisses—many of the girls were already drunk. No phone numbers, though. I didn't go to the all-night party. I went home to sleep. I needed my rest.

Becky hadn't forgotten me. Her eyes widened the moment I came through the door of her store. She quickly came down from behind the cash register. She looked cuter than I remembered, even though I did remember her well. Her eyes in particular impressed me with their warmth.

"Who is Chaneen?" she asked immediately.

"The queen of the universe," I said. "Who else?"

Becky slapped her leg. "I knew it! Do you know how many hours I've wasted on your stupid game since I saw you?"

I was pleased. She had obviously bought "The Starlight Crystal" with her own money.

"None," I said. "Since playing one of my games is the highest activity a human being can aspire to."

She smiled. "You talk just like your characters. Is Chaneen's identity the big secret that you told me about before?"

"No."

"What do you mean, no? I have to be close to cracking it."

"You're not. It's impossible to make real progress until you know Chaneen's identity for certain. You still have a long way to go."

Becky thought I was putting her on. "How big is this game?"

"What's the last world you visited?"

"Neptune," she said.

"You've hardly warmed up your computer. You're not even out of the solar system. This game goes to the ends of the known universe."

She was impressed. "You must be a genius. Where do you get your ideas?"

"There's a place in Fairfield, Iowa. I send them ten dollars and they send me back three ideas."

She frowned. "Really?"

"I'll give you their address. They give out ideas for books and movies, too. For twenty dollars they send you complete outlines. All the big producers in Hollywood use them."

She laughed. "You're so full of it, Tom Cleary."

"Please, call me Mark. Tom Cleary doesn't exist."

She turned away, shaking her head. "I can't believe Chaneen is the big queen. Did you base her on anyone you know?"

"Not many girls I know can stop the sun from rising with a wave of their hand."

"You just don't know the right type of girl."

I thought the comment suggestive, and this time my heart did skip. It was only then that I began to realize I liked her—silly, I know, since I had already made four trips to the store to see her.

"It's hard to meet them when you work in your room all day," I said, trying to be suggestive myself.

"Where do you live?" she asked.

"Over the hill." I added, "By myself."

"Probably in a huge house, with all those royalties you collect."

"My apartment's small. I couldn't swing a cat in it."

"Do you have a cat?"

"No." I tried to think of something funny to say. That's my downfall when I talk to girls—trying to think. I'm fine as long as I keep my mind a perfect blank. Except that my face has a tendency to go blank along with my mind, and it's not that expressive to begin with. "I had a dog once."

"What happened to him?" she asked.

"He killed himself. He ran in front of a car on purpose."

"Right. Your dog committed suicide."

"It happens all the time. They just don't keep statistics on dog suicides."

"Why would he do it?"

I shrugged. "He couldn't break my game, either."

She punched me lightly on the arm. "You nut. Tell me the big secret or I might copy your dog. Then my death would be on your conscience."

"Tell me your first name first."

She took a step away. "No."

I summoned my courage from the depths of my soul. "Have some ice cream with me, then."

I had caught her by surprise. "When?"

"When you get your break."

She hesitated, for several seconds actually. The feeling created by our light banter vanished. "I can't take my break for another couple of hours," she said.

"It usually takes me that long to look around the store." An awkward moment followed. She didn't speak, didn't look at me. I added, "Don't you like ice cream?"

"Sure."

"We could go for frozen yogurt instead."

"I only get a fifteen-minute break."

I knew she was putting me off, but I persisted anyway. I'm not a pushy guy normally, and I wasn't that upset, I just figured I might as well give it my best shot. I didn't want to end up like my dog. He had always been afraid to take a chance with his life, except when it came to crossing streets. The story I told Becky was true, most of it.

"You can have any flavor you want," I said. "Mint chocolate. Bavarian chocolate. Chewy chocolate."

"Chocolate gives me pimples," she said.

"Hell, get vanilla, then. I might even pay for it."

She smiled faintly. "You're funny."

"Then it's a date?"

She nodded slowly. "In two hours. And you're not going to stay in the store the whole time. I won't work."

I agreed to her terms. I walked out of the store feeling like a million dollars, my heart beating a million miles an hour. I didn't know why. She was obviously a klutz when it came to computer games. We obviously didn't have anything in common. It was as obvious as her big brown eyes. Boy, I thought, were they sweet. I hoped she didn't have a boyfriend.

I was back in exactly two hours. I had spent the time making up funny things to say. I actually wrote down several witty remarks on a slip of paper, which I stuffed in my pocket. But Becky was busy with customers when I returned. She kept me waiting another twenty minutes. I spent this time revising my witty remarks before I tore them up and threw them away.

Finally we went around the block for ice cream. Becky ordered one scoop of rocky road, which I tactfully pointed out had a ton of chocolate in it. I can't remember what flavor I had. It was cold, that's all I recall. We sat in a booth by the front window. Becky wanted to talk about my computer games. Her easy, flirty manner had returned, but she was evasive when I turned the questions on her. I wanted to find out more about her and began to suspect that she did, in fact, have a boyfriend. I considered asking her point-blank, but by then I'd decided to ask her out. I felt that even if she did have a boyfriend she might agree to go out with me if I didn't *know* she had a boyfriend. Not that she seemed like the cheating type, but, hey, she was human.

What was it about her that brought me to the point where I was willing to risk the ultimate humiliation a teenage boy can suffer—that of the big No? I don't know. She was cute, but so were a lot of girls, and never mind that most of them didn't go for ice cream with me on a regular basis. It wasn't her spunk that fascinated me either. Her allure was simpler. It was the way she touched me. Twice while we sat in the booth she reached over and tapped my bare arm. She did it to make a conversational point, but it had a deep effect on me, and once again, I didn't know why. The nerves in my arm didn't send a rush of pleasure exploding into my brain or anything silly like that. But the touch of her skin on mine felt good. It felt *right*. If I'd been bolder, I'd have reached over and touched her hand. But I didn't, and soon it was time for her to return to work. We climbed in my car and drove back to the store. As she climbed out, she thanked me for the ice cream.

"I wasn't sure you were going to pay," she said with a smile.

"If you had ordered two scoops, it would have been a different story," I said. She stood holding the passenger door halfway open, ready to close it. A part of me kept saying to wait till the next time to pop the big question, while another part argued that I might not have the same opportunity. The last voice was the more persuasive. I didn't want to go home and spend the next two weeks kicking myself for not just asking her and getting it over with. "What time do you get off work?" I asked finally.

She hesitated. "Six o'clock. I have to take my mother shopping."

She might have been trying to head off my question, I realized. She was perceptive. Fortunately, I had no such problem. I sucked in a deep breath, let my heart pound a few times, and blurted out the question.

"Would you like to go out sometime?" I asked.

She stared at me for a moment. "I can't."

"All right."

"I have a boyfriend."

"Okay."

She smiled. "I'd really like to. You understand."

Sure, I understood a lot of things. Life was a bitch. Life sucked. My insight into all matters of personal relationships was vast and unerring. I was a goddamn philosophical genius. It was amazing how intense my disappointment was. I couldn't believe it. I hardly knew her, I kept telling myself. I was never going to know her.

"How long you been going together?" I asked.

"Two years. He's a great guy. You'd like him."

"Would *he* like to go out with me?"

She laughed. "You crack me up."

"I'm just one big bundle of laughs."

She quieted. "Thanks for asking. You're a nice guy, Mark."

Nice. I hated that word. None of the football jocks in school had been nice. But they'd gotten the girls, oh, yes. I put the word *nice* right up there with "I like you as a friend" and "You have a great personality." I don't know, I wasn't bad looking. Looking in the mirror in the morning wasn't a painful experience. I had a nice friendly face, a lot of personality. Christ. Perhaps that was the problem, I thought. So many girls seemed to want guys who were going to be a problem. Sex and danger—they went together like peace of mind and insurance premiums. My hair was dark and curly, my eyes deep and intelligent. So I didn't have muscles? So I was underweight? So my heart always felt as if there was a weight on it? It was there inside my chest and beating. I felt things. I thought I felt a lot of things most guys never did.

"Well," I said finally. "It was fun while it lasted."

"You're still going to be coming in the store, aren't you?"

"Sure. It's a great store. I might try to get a job there."

"Not you. You're too good for that."

That was another thing about Becky that I had noticed from the start, something that had in fact given me the confidence to ask her out. She poked fun at me occasionally, but she had a curious respect for me, out of all proportion to my skill at constructing computer games. Not that it mattered now. I started my car.

"I'll see you around," I said. "Take care of yourself. When you're playing my game, you can get ahead best by looking behind."

"Is that the big secret?" she asked.

"No. It's Tom Cleary's."

Chapter Two

My disappointment and embarrassment stung for a week. Then they began to fade, and when they were all but gone, I did the worst possible and most human thing. I drove back over the hill to visit Becky again. She looked great. She was happy to see me. We went for ice cream again. This time she didn't keep me waiting, and her answers were no longer evasive. She spoke openly of her boyfriend, when I asked. His name was Ray. He worked in a bookstore in a mall that was near her store. He was a great guy. Yeah, yeah, I know, I thought. But I didn't know why I had asked. Curiosity, I guess. I wasn't thinking of killing poor Ray or anything.

I began to visit Becky regularly, twice a week, sometimes more. I bought more merchandise than I could afford. I felt I needed an excuse to go into the store. Becky always gave me her employee discount—fifteen percent, which was pretty good if it was something I really wanted.

As time passed, I grew bolder with her. Occasionally I'd ask her out, sort of as a joke, sort of to stick the knife in a little deeper to see when my blood would start to bubble out. She would always laugh and change the subject. I loved the way she laughed, except when what I wanted more than anything else was a yes. Yes, Mark, you may not have the greatest body in the world, but you turn me on and I want to kiss you. Every now and then I would say mean things to her, hoping that they would make me appear sexier. But they were never that mean, and she never listened to them, anyway, and I'd be left feeling about as sexy as the cover of one of my computer games.

I can't say she lowered my self-esteem so much as she knocked it off its feet. Each time I saw her, I soared inside, but never too far off the ground, because I remembered I had crashed at takeoff. The relationship was cursed from the beginning. She had a boyfriend. Why was I chasing a girl with a boyfriend? I asked myself that frequently. You see, I had no illusions that I was *not* chasing her. I was still hoping that her boyfriend would suddenly disappear.

It was toward the end of summer, when I had known Becky about three months, that I met Vincent. We bumped into each other in Becky's store. It was a typical visit for me. I asked her out and she responded by inquiring how my latest game was progressing. Becky was very concerned that I was working hard and getting ahead. She took special pride in the fact that I could do something few people my age could do, and that she knew me. Unfortunately, at that time, the gigabytes in my computer had swallowed my creativity whole. I would turn on my computer each morning and stare at the blank screen and pray for the invention of intelligent machines. I was stuck. I didn't know if my space heroes should go through a time warp or change clothes and try to defeat the local kung fu champ.

I happened to notice Vincent as I was leaving the store, just after I had said goodbye to Becky. He was standing in the software section. He had one of my games in his hand. I paused to see if he was going to buy it, and when he persisted in reading the back—apparently without coming to a decision— I decided to saunter over and say, "Hi! I wrote that game. Ain't I smart?" Actually, it wasn't ego alone that drove me. I often talked to people who browsed the software selections, to learn what they enjoyed. Market research, it's called. And if I did most of my research on pretty girls, that was Becky's fault.

There was something about Vincent that drew me to him besides "The Starlight Crystal" in his hand. He looked familiar. He was one of those people I felt sure I'd seen before, but it bugged the hell out of me because I couldn't remember where. His hair was longish and pale blond, and he had a few more muscles than I did, although we were about the same height. He looked up as I approached. His eyes were a piercing blue.

"Hi," I said.

"Hello," he replied. His voice was soft, his age a puzzle. He looked about my age, but the ease of his manner and his obvious self-assurance made him seem older. He nodded to the game in his hand. "You wrote this."

"How did you know?" I gestured to Becky. "Did she tell you?"

"Yes."

"When?" I had been talking to Becky for the last hour.

"An hour ago."

"You've been here all this time?"

"I wanted to talk to you," he said.

"About the game? Have you played it?"

"Yes. It's one of my favorites. You're very good."

I took pleasure in the compliment. "Thanks."

"I write computer games, too," he said.

"Really?" I was smart enough not to ask if he had sold any. If he had, he would tell me.

"Becky told me you think your graphics are weak," he said.

"It's true. They're very ordinary. You must have noticed."

"Yes."

I hadn't exactly wanted him to agree with me. "What's your name?"

"Vincent." He offered his hand. "You're Mark."

I assumed Becky had told him all about me. "Pleased to meet you, Vincent," I said, shaking his hand. "What kind of stuff do you like to do?"

"Science fiction. Fantasy."

"You're like me. You live around here?"

"Yes. Not far. I'd like to show you a game I'm working on." He hesitated. "Becky said you wouldn't mind."

I was surprised Becky hadn't mentioned Vincent to me when we'd talked. I didn't get a chance to ask her about it because at that moment she went into the back. I knew she had a ton of recently delivered DVDs and Blu-rays to sort.

"Sure," I said. "I'll have a look at it. How far along are you?"

"I'm almost done. The major graphics are complete. I just have to decide what the major conflict is going to be."

"What?" I asked, amazed, thinking Vincent must be in more trouble than he realized. The plot of a game had to be thoroughly developed and charted before the first lines of code could be written. Otherwise, the amount of time wasted on a wrong turn could be staggering.

"I'd appreciate your input," he said calmly.

"No problem." He struck me as safe enough. "I'm free right now. Do you want me to follow you to your place in my car?"

"If you would." He put the game back on the shelf. "I already have a copy of this at home."

"Vincent? Have we met before? You look awfully familiar."

He hesitated. "I come into this store a lot."

I chuckled. "To see Becky? I do. She's a great girl."

He smiled, a smile as soft as his voice. "I have a girlfriend."

Outside in the cool night air, I stopped worrying about

whether or not Vincent was in trouble with his game. He drove a black Ferrari, one of the fastest cars on the road. Following him in my twice-rebuilt Toyota, I figured that if I had a car like his, I could sell it and live comfortably for the next ten years. Or afford heart surgery and maybe be dead in ten days.

Vincent had his own place. I was impressed. We parked in a circular driveway and walked to the front door. The house itself wasn't spectacularly huge, but it was perched on top of the hill I crossed whenever I went to Becky's store. It had a wonderful view of the city lights far off. Also, the landscaping was exquisite; even in the shadows of night, I could see that the bushes and trees were well groomed. The fragrance of blooming roses filled the air. I envied him his side yard. One could take it straight into the hills and disappear. Despite my heart, I still enjoyed a good walk. A good slow walk.

"You really live here alone?" I asked after he told me the house was his.

"My girlfriend stays with me," he said, opening the front door without a key.

"Is she here now?"

"She'll be along later. If you stay, you'll meet her."

We stepped inside. I was surprised to see that the house had very little furniture. A couch, a bar, a chair, but no TV or dining room table. Aside from the lack of furnishings, the house felt distinctly unoccupied. Vincent must have sensed my thoughts.

"I haven't been here long," he said.

But he had been visiting Becky's store for a while, I thought to myself.

"Did you grow up in Los Angeles?" I asked.

"Yes."

"Your family must have money."

"Yes." He gestured toward the kitchen. "Let me get you something to drink. What would you like?"

I shrugged. "A Coke, if you have it."

"I do."

We sat at the bar and drank Cokes together, enjoying the view of the city lights. I quickly discovered that unless I spoke, Vincent would lapse into silence. Briefly I wondered if he did drugs, but he betrayed no hint of dullness. His blue eyes were remarkably shiny. I didn't feel in the least uncomfortable around him even when he was silent. He was one of those rare people who was in absolutely no hurry to have anything happen. I had to bring up the matter of his game. Nodding and carrying his drink with him, he led me to his bedroom. Here again the furniture was sparse. A mat on the floor took the place of a bed. He had no chest of drawers, and a glance into his open closet told me he didn't own many clothes. But his computer was excellent, top-of-the-line. Although I made my livelihood on a computer, all I had was a clone of his. I had picked it up at a swap meet. He gestured for me to have a seat in front of the screen and flipped on the machine.

"Is this your first crack at programming a game?" I asked as the computer booted up.

"No. I've done several games."

"Do you have any here?"

"No," he said.

"Why do you want to program games? You obviously don't need the money." I didn't imagine for a moment that he had paid for his Ferrari with software royalties. If he had, I would have heard of him. Then again, he hadn't told me his last name.

Vincent pulled up a chair beside mine. "I enjoy it. The games are excellent educational tools."

"I think most people just play for fun."

"You can learn while you're having fun," he said.

"Are you trying to teach something in particular?"

"You tell me after you've seen what I've done."

The password for loading his program was "Vincent." He took me right into the game, not into the code, which would have made no sense to me without several hours of study. Some days my own code was incomprehensible to me. The screen brightened with the smartly lettered title: "Decision."

"Interesting title," I said.

"Do you like it?"

"Yes, I like it. But I don't think it will sell. Forgive me for being blunt. I assume you want my honest opinion."

"I do," Vincent said. He was observing me closely to see my reaction to his creation. But he wasn't the least bit anxious.

I pressed a key, and a clearly defined and wonderfully drawn space station filled the screen. It was revolving with such real-life precision that I could hardly imagine the hours he must have spent to achieve the effect. I marveled at his skill. I had never seen anything remotely approaching his graphics—outside a movie theater, that is. It was only after a few minutes that the reason for his sophisticated graphics dawned on me.

"What is the RAM in this computer?" I asked. The RAM, or random access memory, determined how much space the computer had to work with at any one moment. The greater the RAM, the more exotic a program could be.

"Twelve gigabytes," Vincent said.

"But this game will run on a lot lower RAM, won't it?"

"Does it matter?" he asked.

"You can't be serious? How do you expect to sell it if only one in ten machines can run it?"

"I'm not worried about that right now. I just want to create the finest game I can."

"All right," I said, already thinking Vincent was hopelessly idealistic. "What's the game about?"

Vincent pressed a key, and the earth—also beautifully drawn and defined—appeared below the space station. An instruction box in the upper right-hand corner immediately informed me of the space station's armament: neutron beams, helium lasers, three hundred missiles tipped with five nuclear warheads each and packing a ten megaton punch. We were obviously talking

Star Wars here, SDI—Strategic Defense Initiative. I must admit I was disappointed. I had hoped Vincent's imagination matched his artistic vision. Nuclear war games bored me to tears. There were too many of them on the market.

Then I saw that the enemy was China. It made sense, in a way. Since the game was set in the future, it was reasonable to believe that China had advanced to the point where it could take on the United States.

"The United States and China are on the verge of war?" I asked.

"The whole world is," Vincent said.

"What's the goal of the game?"

"To win."

"Obviously, but what's your problem? Do you have a second space station in orbit?"

"I've only got the one."

"Right off, I don't think that's a good idea. Say the entire earth gets obliterated. It would be nice for our heroes in the space station to have a final enemy to face."

"I was trying to be realistic," Vincent said.

"You can have two space stations and be realistic. The game's far in the future. You could use ninety percent of the same code you've written for the American station to create the other one."

"I'd just like there to be the one."

"All right." I could already see he wanted my approval rather than my advice. But he didn't seem put off by my suggestions.

I pressed the next key. Immediately I was called upon to make a decision. Diplomatic solutions had failed, and negotiations had broken down. Both sides were readying their missiles for launch. My options were numerous: I could fire my lasers and destroy the enemy missiles in their boost phase; I could try to take out enemy subs off the west coast of the United States with my neutron beams; I could send a barrage of missiles down on the major enemy cities. After playing for a few minutes, I learned that I was limited to one option at a time and that for each measure I took, a countermeasure was taken by the enemy. For example, if I fired *three* missiles, *nine* foreign missiles would be hurled toward the United States. The discrepancy in numbers made sense because I did, after all, get to make the first move. Now I could let the nine missiles hit the United States and concentrate on taking out more foreign cities and subs, or else I could try to protect my country as well as the space station. I only had to play the game for a short time to realize that I—sitting inside the space station—was a primary target.

Scene after scene, the graphics of the game were exceptional. The logic of attack versus counterattack was also impressive. Vincent must have studied the theory of modern warfare in depth. At least I thought so at first, but soon—too soon— the game became unmanageable. Too many things were happening at once. I couldn't keep up. Also, countries that hadn't even suffered direct hits were being totaled up as casualties. I stopped to protest.

"What the hell happened to Australia?" I asked.

"It's dead," Vincent said simply.

"Why? Melbourne and Sydney haven't even been touched."

Vincent pointed to the total number of megatons that had been detonated. It was well past the ten thousand mark.

"Billions of tons of dust and smoke have been forced into the atmosphere," he said. "The greenhouse effect is now a certainty. The earth is going to freeze."

"That will take years."

"True. But Australia will be dead before then. The dust and smoke are radioactive."

"But that's ridiculous. You can't have a game like this. You should only focus on war day. No one can possibly win if you have to take into account factors like radioactive dust. The only ones who'll be left are the people on the space station."

"That's the problem I need your help with," he said.

"Just dump this radioactivity and greenhouse garbage."

"But I want the game to be realistic."

"That's noble of you," I said. "But you lose any possibility of a goal. No offense meant, but the player can't win this stupid thing." I paused. "Unless you've set it so that China can be knocked out quick and clean."

"I haven't."

"Then do that if you feel you have to keep it realistic. Also, you've got to put up an enemy station. It's just not fair that our side should be the only one with weapons in space."

"Could you help me make it work?" he asked.

"What?"

"Could you help me?"

"No. I mean, I'd love to, but I'm busy. Anyway, I don't think you need my help." I gestured at the screen. "I can't create scenes like this. You're talented. Fix this thing up so that it makes sense and get it to run on a lower RAM, and a major computer software house will give you a six-figure advance easy. Really, I'm envious."

"I'll split the advance with you," he said.

"Get off it."

"I'm serious."

I chuckled. Then I looked at his face and stopped. He was watching me intently. He meant it. But I didn't feel I was being pushed into a decision. Quite the reverse, I had the feeling he was trying to help me. Half of a six-figure advance would be a lot of money to me.

I didn't get a chance to answer him. I heard someone come in the front door just then. Vincent stood and called out, "Kara?"

"It's me, it's me." A cheerful English accent sounded down the hall. "There's a car outside. Do we have guests?"

"Just one," Vincent said. "Mark Forum is here."

Kara entered the room. I tried to stand, but I misplaced

my legs when I saw how pretty she was. Like Vincent, she was blond and blue eyed, but there the similarity ended. Vincent was calm almost to the point of serenity, but Kara obviously was charged. At the sight of me, she went up on her bare toes and pressed her palms together in a soft clap. Her face radiated pleasure.

"Is this the computer genius you told me you were trying to find?" she asked Vincent, keeping her eyes on me. I'm ashamed to say I forgot all about Becky at that moment. Kara's hair fell past her waist—a mass of tiny golden curls that clung to her like a warm embrace. Her mouth was wide. As she smiled, her red lips parted, revealing perfect white teeth. She seemed so delighted to see me, a complete stranger, that I didn't know how to react.

"This is him," Vincent said.

I turned to Vincent. "You were looking for me at the store?"

He nodded. "Becky told me you came in regularly."

Kara stepped farther into the room, her hand extended. I finally managed to get to my feet. She nodded to me, and I took that to mean I was doing fine. I felt as if I were being tested, but that was okay because I was passing with flying colors. I felt an immediate sense of ease and familiarity with Kara as I had with Vincent. Yet Kara looked and sounded like no one I had ever known. Her hand was cool and soft, her grip firm.

"I'm pleased to meet you, Kara," I said.

"Vincent showed me your games," she said. "They're clever. I was hoping he'd find you."

I shook my head. "I can't believe I'm so popular."

"In a select group," Kara said and glanced at her boyfriend.

"I was just showing Mark my game," Vincent said.

"Do you like it?" Kara asked me.

"Yes, I do. Very much."

"But it needs work, huh?" she said in a slightly teasing tone. It was strange, but I didn't know if she was teasing Vincent or me.

I shrugged. "I think a few changes would give it more commercial appeal."

Kara moved to Vincent and wrapped an arm around his shoulder. She kissed his cheek. "Can you help my big boy?" she asked me.

"Sure," I said. The word was out of my mouth before I realized it, but I had no regrets. I found them both fascinating. "But I couldn't possibly accept half your advance money, Vincent, if we get that far."

"Whatever you think is fair will be fine with me," Vincent said, raising his head. He had lowered it the moment Kara came into the room, almost as if he wanted my first meeting with his girlfriend to be private.

"Let's see how much work I actually do," I said.

Kara laughed easily and tossed her head, and as she did so, her long yellow hair rippled like small sunlit waves. I was romanticizing her, it's true. I did envy Vincent for having her as his girlfriend, but I wasn't jealous of him. Becky returned to my mind, and I was content with my thoughts of her.

"Now that we have that out of the way," Kara said, "what are we going to do next?"

"Do you want to work on the game?" I asked Vincent.

"I don't care," he said.

"Would you mind going for a walk and eating ice cream?" Kara asked, not waiting for an answer. "This is no time to work. It's time to get to know one another. Let's go for a stroll under the stars and stuff our faces."

Apparently Kara wore the pants in the relationship, although she had a dress on at present, a loose knee-length skirt that showed off her shapely legs. Whenever I think of Kara, I see her spinning around me in a short dress, brimming with enthusiasm and grace. Vincent never did answer her, except to lower his head again. It was decided. We would go for a walk and eat ice cream. It was what Kara wanted.

Kara had brought ice cream home with her, three pint containers, softening on the kitchen table. She handed us each a spoon, one for each of the three different chocolate flavors. She obviously wasn't worried about pimples, as Becky supposedly was.

We left by the side door, eating our ice cream, and stepped onto a path that led straight into the hills. It was a dark night, moonless, but I was able to distinguish the grade of the slope.

I was worried I would quickly become a burden to the expedition. There is something about climbing that is particularly hard on heart patients, and I hated to admit to Kara and Vincent what a weakling I was.

But the admission proved unnecessary. Kara stepped off the path so frequently to collect flowers or to investigate croaking frogs that I was given frequent breathers. Vincent was obviously used to her behavior and didn't hurry her along. It took us half an hour to walk three-quarters of a mile into the hills. Rounding a bend in the path, we saw the city lights stretching for miles into the distance on our right. Vincent raised a hand to stop us and stepped off the path. He disappeared into the very side of the hill.

"What the hell," I muttered.

"There's a cave," Kara said quickly. "Vincent and I often come here. He keeps a telescope inside."

"Is that safe? Someone might find it and steal it."

"Unlikely," she said. "The opening to the cave is well hidden. Even in the daytime you'd probably walk right by it."

"But Vincent said you only just moved here. How did *you* find it so easily?"

"Friends told us it was here," she said, moving to the edge of the hill and looking out on the city. The hillside was mostly gnarly shrubs and dead grass, with an occasional tree bent over and waiting for rain. The air was still, the dry heat disturbed only slightly by faint damp undercurrents that hugged the ground.

Kara sucked in a deep breath and let out a happy sigh. "This is so neat."

"It's quite a view," I agreed. "Where are you from?"

"Don't you recognize my accent?"

"It sounds English."

"It's Scottish, actually. But I've lived in this country so long, I'm losing my accent. Or gaining another one, depending how you look at it."

"How did you and Vincent meet?"

"The way everyone does."

"Which is?" I asked.

"By chance."

"I'm serious."

"So am I," Kara said and giggled. "Do you have a girlfriend?"

"No."

"No?"

"Well, there's this girl I like. But she has a boyfriend."

"What's her name?" Kara asked.

"Becky. She's the girl who told Vincent about me."

"She works in the electronics store?"

"That's her," I said. "She's neat."

"If you like her, go after her. Don't worry about her boyfriend. How much do you like this Becky?"

"I don't know, she's neat."

"You're repeating yourself. Sounds like love to me, Mark."

I was embarrassed. I couldn't believe I was discussing Becky, I hadn't even written about her in my journal. I was waiting until I had some good news to report.

"I've asked her out," I said. "I asked her out a few times."

"What did she say?"

"No."

"No means nothing. Does she get angry that you keep asking her?"

"No. We've become friends. She's very sweet."

"She's interested," Kara said. "Take my word for it. I'm a girl. If she wasn't, she would have told you to take a hike by now."

"I don't know. She could just be acting polite."

"What's her boyfriend do?"

"He works in a bookstore."

"What's his name?" Kara asked.

"Ray."

"Do you know which bookstore he works in?"

"Yes. Why?"

"Have you ever gone in to see him?"

"No," I said. "Why would I do that?"

"To see what you're up against."

"This isn't a competition."

"Sure it is. Don't fool yourself. Love is like everything else in this world. You have to fight for it. Look, do want my help?"

"Your help?"

"In getting Becky."

"Kara, I don't mean to be rude, but I hardly know you."

"This will be a good way for us to get to know each other."

"Isn't getting a girlfriend something I have to do for myself?"

"Why should it be?" Kara asked.

I stopped. "Why do you want to help me?" I asked.

Kara stared at me for a long moment. I was wondering if I had insulted her with my question because she didn't respond. Finally, however, she broke into a smile and fluffed up my hair with her hand.

"Because," she said.

"Because what?" I asked.

She took her hand back. "Just because."

The spot where Vincent was now setting up the telescope offered an unobstructed view in all directions. I could see that Vincent spent as freely on his optical equipment as he did on cars. He had a ten-inch Schmidt-Cassegrain, a telescope that twice folded the light collected by its primary mirror—a favorite of wealthy amateur astronomers the world over. I had always had a special interest in astronomy, but lack of funds had stopped me from seriously pursuing the hobby. Plus L.A. was no place to look at the stars. City lights and smog had done away with the Milky Way years ago.

"Can we look at the moon?" Kara asked as Vincent fiddled with the eyepieces after the tripod was set on a flat portion of the path.

"It isn't up yet," he said. "It's three days past full."

"But it'll be up soon," I said. When the moon was full, it rose in the east close to the time the sun set.

"I know," Kara said to Vincent, almost in apology.

"We'll look at the planets," Vincent said.

"You really should take this thing out to the desert where the air is clear," I said, not sure what the big deal was about the moon.

"We like this spot," Kara said. "Hey, can we see Becky's store from here?"

"Kara," I said.

"It's just about eleven. Maybe we can see Becky getting off work," Kara went on. "We could see her walking out to her car." She laughed. "We could use *high* magnification."

"We can't see the store from here," Vincent said softly, bent over the eyepiece and fiddling with the focusing knob. "Come here, Mark. I want to show you something."

"What is it?" I asked, moving a step closer.

"The space shuttle," Vincent said.

"*What?*" I gasped. "How could you locate the shuttle?"

"It's in orbit," Vincent said.

"I know that," I said. "But I would think it would take hours to find."

"It's not that hard if you know where to look," Vincent said. He gestured to the eyepiece. "Take a look."

It took me a moment to get my bearings as I pressed my

eye to the ocular. Vincent was using low magnification; the field of view was large, dense with stars despite the interference from the city lights. In the upper right-hand corner, a bright white star was moving steadily across the star field.

"How do you know it's the shuttle?" I asked.

"If it isn't, then it's a flying saucer," Vincent said. "Do you want to look, Kara?"

"No," she said.

"Take a look," I said, fiddling with the knob. I was attempting to elongate the point of light, trying to make it look like the shuttle I was familiar with on TV. I realized that was probably foolish without a major observatory's telescope.

"You two look," Kara said.

"It's moving out of the field of view," I told Vincent.

"Let me help you," he said, putting his hand over mine on the focusing knob. He pressed his face close to my nose in order to peer through the tiny finder telescope strapped to the side of the main instrument. The walk up the hill must have taken more out of me than I realized. Suddenly the entire star field blurred, and Vincent hadn't turned the focusing knob. It was me: my eyes, my blood, my damn heart. A wave of dizziness swept over me and I staggered back. If Vincent hadn't caught me, I would have fallen. The irregular beating of my heart often made me dizzy, but this was stronger than anything I had ever experienced. Vincent led me to a nearby boulder, supporting me with both arms, and helped me to sit down.

"Take long, deep breaths," he said.

I followed his advice, keeping my eyes closed. It wasn't long before the spell passed. A minute later I felt fine, although a bit foolish. If Kara hadn't been there, it wouldn't have been so bad. Showing weakness in front of a girl always embarrassed me. As I looked up, I found her kneeling anxiously by my side.

"Are you okay?" she asked.

"I'm fine." I chuckled. "It must have been something I ate. Really, I'm perfectly all right. It was nothing. What were we talking about?"

"Space," Vincent said. He knew it wasn't something I ate. But he didn't question me further because he also knew I didn't want to talk about it. So did Kara. As suddenly as the dizziness had come, so also came a rush of love for both of them, mysterious and illogical in its origin. They were both strangers, I told myself. Yet, already they were my friends.

We spent the remainder of the evening surveying the sky and eating ice cream. I suffered no further attacks. Saturn and Jupiter were both visible. Unlike the shuttle, the planets seemed to interest Kara, and she had no qualms about looking at them. We also searched for and found a number of globular clusters and nebulae. Vincent was skilled at plotting sidereal coordinates. He would look them up in a small reference book he carried—the telescope had a small red light attached that allowed him to read—and know where to aim the telescope after only a minute of calculations. He was so obviously my mental superior that I felt silly even thinking about helping him with his game. I asked him if his interest in astronomy had inspired his computer game. He said, "Indirectly," but didn't elaborate.

Sometime after midnight we took down the telescope, and Vincent returned it to its place inside the cave. I was curious to see the cave for myself, but Kara said to wait until daytime, or until we had a flashlight. I didn't get the impression they were hiding anything from me.

We parted in their driveway; I didn't go back into the house. Vincent gave me his phone number and told me to call him whenever I wanted. He shook my hand and left me alone with Kara. She walked me to my car.

"I'm glad you're helping Vincent with his game," she said.

"I just hope I don't screw it up," I said.

"I'm sure after you play it for a while you'll know what to do."

"We'll see." I opened my car door and got in behind the wheel. Kara stood to my left, slightly behind me. A breeze had come up from farther down the hill. It lifted her long hair and floated it behind her, creating the impression that she was wearing a cape made of gold. She seemed pleased to have met me, but unlike Vincent, she seemed to have a lot on her mind.

"I want you to think about what I said," she said.

"About Becky?"

"Yes."

"How could you possibly help me?"

"I'm full of ideas. Do you want me to tell you some?"

"No," I said. "Becky's happy with who she's got. I have no right to interfere."

Kara looked down at me. She was no taller than Becky, but she gave the impression of great stature. She didn't have Vincent's calm confidence, but she had something few girls her age possessed—a sense of mystery.

"Are you sure?" she asked.

"That I shouldn't interfere? Of course."

"No. That she's happy. How do you know? Have you ever asked her?"

"It's none of my business," I said.

Kara leaned over and kissed me on the cheek. Her lips were warm, her breath cool and sweet like chocolate ice cream.

"You're wrong, Mark," she said.

Chapter Three

The next evening found me back at their house. Vincent welcomed me warmly. Kara was out. When I asked Vincent where she was, he smiled faintly and said she was impossible to keep track of. I was disappointed, but only slightly. Vincent was excellent company, even if he spent most of his time with his mouth closed. Maybe that was what made him easy to be around. He had to be the world's greatest listener.

Except when it came to his game. He didn't reject my suggestions so much as he ignored them. At present, he said, he'd be happy if I simply played the game and learned how it worked. This made sense, up to a point. It was true one had to play a game for many hours, weeks even, to get a complete picture of its logic. But the major problems I had discussed with him the previous day were not going to disappear with an in-depth analysis. I told Vincent this, and he nodded—I had to assume he heard me—and that was the end of it. Then, at his gentle insistence, I played the game once more.

"Decision" both frustrated and intrigued me. The manner in which the enemy responded to each of my attacks was a lesson in cause and effect. The more elaborate my attack, the more clever the counter-measure. Playing the game, there was usually a point where I'd get a rush of adrenaline, my heart would pound, and I'd think, "I'm going to beat these bastards! I'm going to win!" But, of course, that was the problem. I couldn't win. No one could. The earth would be as good as dead before I could really get down to business. I never even got a chance to use all my missiles.

But I didn't get bored. I had a goal, one that I thought was achievable even with Vincent's current programming. So the earth got wasted, I thought. If I could finish a game with the space station intact, I felt I would have beaten it. Then I would feel justified in making Vincent rip into his code. "See?" I would say. "The operation was a success, but the patient died."

In the next two or three weeks, I visited Vincent five more times. Kara was present on all but one occasion. She would greet me at the door, usually in shorts and a T-shirt, and get in as much conversation with me as she could before Vincent would appear and we'd retire to do battle with the forces of evil. Our friendship deepened steadily. Kara and I talked about everything: music, the environment, politics. Kara was extremely liberal, very down on the military. I understood why she didn't want to look at the space shuttle. It seemed to her that every other shuttle put a new spy satellite in orbit. For the sake of our discussions, I would try to present the opposite argument—the need for a strong defense. Kara would hear none of it. She was stubborn. For his part, Vincent would only listen patiently to whoever was talking and then politely ask where we should go for ice cream.

I decided Kara had forgotten about Becky; she hadn't raised the subject since the first night. But at the end of my seventh visit, when we were waiting for Vincent to shower so we could go out, Kara suddenly brought up Ray, Becky's boyfriend.

"I've been to his bookstore a few times," she said.

"What for?" I asked, surprised.

"To see if he's half the man you are."

I admit I was curious. "Is he?"

Kara made a face. "He's a jerk."

"What makes you say that?"

"He tries to pick up every pretty girl who comes into the store."

"You're just saying that."

Kara reached over and took my arm. "Come on. I'll show you."

"What? I don't want to see him."

Kara pulled me to my feet. "You're going to see with your own eyes how miserable he's going to make Becky unless you stop him."

"Right now? What about Vincent? We can't just leave."

"Vincent won't care. Nothing bothers him."

"This is crazy."

Kara stared me in the eye. "Are you afraid?"

"Of what?"

"Becky?"

"No. It's not Becky you're dragging me off to see."

"I'm dragging you off to opportunity."

"Why drag me anywhere? Why not let me go when I feel ready?"

Kara backed off a step. She looked away. "I can't," she said.

"Why not?"

"Because."

"Because what?" I insisted. "Why do you even care what Ray does?"

She closed her eyes and took a breath. "If you could just see this guy."

"You sound as if you hate him."

Kara opened her eyes. "I know I'm not supposed to hate, Mark. I know it's wrong."

"Nobody's perfect."

"Vincent is," she said.

"Really?"

"Yes." She glanced at her watch, then at the setting sun. "But I'm not."

"Kara, why don't we—"

She came to a decision. She grabbed my arm again. "You're coming. Now. Don't say anything. Just watch and learn and thank me later."

I hoped Vincent took long showers. I gave in.

Kara drove a red Ferrari. She and Vincent must have purchased the cars at a two-for-one sale. She drove fast, fearlessly, and I thought each curve we went into would be our last. I realized I should never have told Kara where Ray worked. In fact, I couldn't even remember when I had told her. Maybe Becky had told her. I had been in to see Becky a number of times since I had met Kara and Vincent. Becky confirmed that she had spoken to Vincent about me, but she never mentioned Kara, and I hadn't brought her up.

It was after eight o'clock and just getting dark when we drove up to the mall where Ray worked. Kara jumped out of the car without locking it. One of these days, I thought, these two were going to get a rude awakening. I had quizzed Vincent once about where he got his money and had learned nothing more than it was in the family.

Kara had me enter the store first. She didn't want Ray to think we were together. That set off all kinds of alarms in my head. But I didn't argue with her. It wouldn't have done any good.

I had no trouble identifying Ray. My psychic powers were operating at peak performance. He had a name tag on. He was shelving books as I strolled past. He didn't ask if I needed help. I was disappointed to see that he was tall, strong, and handsome. It gave me a sinking feeling just watching him rip open the boxes of books with only his hands. He was not someone I wanted to annoy. He would have been soap-opera pretty if it hadn't been for his expression, which was very intense. On the other hand, he looked intelligent, like someone who was planning a future. He wore dress slacks and a tailored shirt—his family probably had money, too. His dark hair was cut short, almost a crew cut. Judging by his muscles, I decided he had probably played football in high school. Those days looked a couple years behind him now, though.

I walked by him without saying a word and hid behind the New Age section. I picked up a book on reincarnation and was halfway through the first page when Kara entered. I could see them both by rising up on my toes and peering over the astrology books. My major suspicion was immediately confirmed.

"Kara," Ray said, delighted. "I was just thinking of you."

"What?" Kara asked, laying on the charm. "You can think of me and work at the same time?"

Ray set aside his boxes and stood tall, puffing up his chest. "What brings you here?" he asked.

Kara let her eyes swim over the rows of books as if she was a dizzy blonde searching for one that didn't have too many words. "I'm looking for something inspirational," she said.

Ray pointed over his shoulder. "Our sex manuals are in the back."

Kara moistened her lips. "I already own enough of those."

Christ, I thought. It only got worse.

Ray grinned. "I bet you came by to see me."

Kara played with her hair. "Maybe. Maybe not."

"I know you did," he said. "Hey, I get off in an hour. You want to grab a bite to eat?"

"I can't. I'm busy."

"You told me that last time."

"What can I say? I'm a busy girl. I'm busy every day this week except tomorrow night."

Ray was encouraged. "I'm off tomorrow." Kara just gave him a blank stare. He added, "Do you want to get together?"

Kara thought for a moment. "What would your wife say?"

Ray laughed. He had undergone a personality transformation since Kara had appeared. He was full of fun now. "I'm not married. Whatever gave you that idea?"

Kara frowned. "You don't have a girlfriend?"

Ray didn't hesitate. "No."

Kara smiled with relief. "Where do you want to meet?"

"Why don't you give me your phone number?" Ray said.

"Because I don't want you talking to my boyfriend," Kara said and tapped him playfully on the chest. "I'll meet you here at six. I'll be hungry."

That was fine with Ray. Kara left the store moments later. I waited a few minutes before following. Ray gave me a curious stare as I walked by. Maybe he thought I was stealing a book.

Kara was sitting behind the wheel of her sports car, looking pleased with herself, when I caught up with her. Not saying a word, I climbed in and stared straight ahead.

"What's the matter?" she asked.

"Nothing," I said.

"I told you, Mark."

"I believed you when you told me. I didn't need a demonstration."

"He's no good. He's a liar and a cheat."

"He's a young man and you're a pretty girl and you threw yourself at him. You set him up."

"To prove a point. If you were going with Becky and I flirted with you like that, would you have asked me out?"

"No, I'm not Ray. But if I was Ray and I learned what you just did, I'd be angry."

Kara looked hurt. "You're mad at me."

I peered at her. She was still playing with her hair, but now she was tying it in knots. The strength of her reaction to my disapproval surprised me.

"No, I'm not," I said honestly. "I'm confused. I don't understand why you're going to all this trouble on my behalf."

"I want you to be happy."

"Why?"

"You're my friend," she said.

"Seeing you go out with Ray doesn't make me happy, Kara. What will Vincent say?"

"Nothing. He lets me do whatever I want."

"Are you really going to go out with Ray?"

"Yes."

"But you've made your point. He's a liar and a cheat. I told you I believe you." When she didn't answer immediately, I thought I understood why. "You're going to try to break them up, aren't you?"

"How could I possibly break up two people who are in love?" I shook my head. "I won't have anything to do with this."

She turned and took my hand. "Listen, Mark, I said that sarcastically, but I meant it. I can't ruin their relationship if it's strong."

"That's not the point. None of this is your business. You're trying to decide things for them, for me, and you can't do that. You can't play God, Kara."

She let go of my hand and sat back. Together, without speaking, we watched as the last shoppers left the mall. The issue remained unresolved between us. It was dark now, and the parking lot was all but empty. Soon the employees inside would finish locking up, and the last of them would drive away. Kara must have been reading my mind.

She pointed toward a red BMW. "That's his car."

"How do you know?"

"I know."

"At least if you go to a drive-in, you'll be comfortable."

She smiled faintly. "I could bring one of my sex manuals."

I had to chuckle. "Really, Kara, that was crude."

"For someone who thinks she's God?"

"I didn't mean it that way."

"No," Kara said, staring at the BMW. "You weren't far off."

Chapter Four

At ten o'clock the next night I watched the earth die once more. But this time it was different. As I slid back from the keyboard, the enemies didn't have a missile left to fire at me and my space station was still spinning, unharmed, with everyone on board alive. I hadn't realized how obsessed I'd become with the game. I let out a shout of triumph. Vincent wandered back into the room.

"I did it," I told him. "I survived."

He sat on the extra chair beside the computer. "How's China?"

"Smoking."

"How about the United States?" he asked.

"The same. The whole planet's fried. But I'm still here."

"Now what?" Vincent asked.

I shrugged. I had been hoping he'd at least congratulate me. Vincent had already become something of an idol to me. He was so cool. I was trying to earn his approval, I suppose, which made it difficult to criticize him.

"That's up to you," I said. "This isn't a satisfactory way to end. If even a portion of the U.S. could survive, there'd be hope the world could be rebuilt. Realism's fine, but despair is such a turnoff." I paused, squinting at the screen. "What's that?"

"Hope?" he asked and smiled.

As always, Vincent's graphics were superb—his world in ruin was particularly effective. The majority of radiation was, of course, invisible to the human eye, but Vincent had shown "hot" areas with pulsing waves of color. For example, New York City and Beijing, which inevitably suffered a dozen direct hits apiece, were throbbing with violet light on the globe below. But then, from seemingly nowhere, a number of barely defined glowing white balls began to cluster around the space station.

"What are those?" I asked.

"The next level of the game," Vincent said.

"Huh?"

"They are there to help you."

"I don't need any help. I'm safe."

"For the time being. But this space station isn't self-sustaining. You'll starve without regular supplies. You'll suffocate."

"Says who?"

"It's the way it is," Vincent said.

"What are these white balls? Are they aliens come to rescue me in their flying saucers?"

"They could be."

"You're going to have to do better than that," I said.

Vincent was not offended. "Tell me what you'd do."

I pointed to the screen. "First of all, if these are alien craft, you're going to have to picture them a lot more clearly. Frankly, I'm surprised. Visually, you're always top-notch. You know what these look like?"

"What?"

"Nothing," I said. "Balls of light."

"I didn't actually say they were flying saucers."

"That leads me to my second point. I don't care what they are. To suddenly have outside help at the end of the game is a cop-out. What are these white balls going to do, miraculously counteract all the radiation? You can't have divine intervention."

Vincent was interested. "Like angels?"

"Yeah. I mean, no. You don't want angels suddenly showing up and fixing everything that's wrong. You've got to win or lose with what you had to start the game."

Vincent nodded. "I agree."

"Then take these white balls out."

Vincent stared at the screen. So many of them had gathered about the space station that it had become hard to see. "But I like them," he said.

"Listen, this is a science-fiction game. You can't bring in supernatural creatures. You'll annoy the purists, and they're your biggest market."

"Then what if they are aliens?"

"Don't you know what they are?" I asked, getting exasperated.

"I'm asking what you would do with them."

"I've told you."

Vincent sat back and lowered his head. "Oh."

I turned off the screen. "It's getting late."

He looked up. "Don't you want to play anymore?"

I checked my watch. "It's after ten."

"So?"

I stood and stretched. Kara had told Vincent she was going out with Ray, and he had reacted exactly as she had predicted, by showing no reaction at all. She had left at five o'clock, although the mall was less than thirty minutes away. She said Ray was going to leave early.

"No, I don't want to play," I said and began to pace the floor. "Don't you care that your girlfriend's out with another guy?"

"Don't worry about Kara. She'll be all right."

"Aren't you jealous?"

"No."

"Why not?"

"I trust her."

He said it with such simple innocence that I felt guilty.

But truthfully, I had no reason. I had never even entertained the thought of what it would be like to have Kara for a girlfriend, to take her away from Vincent. As he watched me pace, I couldn't rid myself of the feeling that he knew exactly what I was thinking. And for that reason, he trusted me, too.

"Don't worry, Mark," he repeated.

"But do you know what she's trying to do?"

"Yes."

"She's trying to break up Becky and her boyfriend."

"Yes."

I stopped. "Do you think that's right?"

"It's what she wants to do."

"You didn't answer my question," I said.

He smiled. "I tried."

"Vincent—"

"All we can do is try to do what we think is right," he went on, gazing out his bedroom window at the city lights below. "What happens from that point on is not up to us. It's like the computer program in this game. You can choose what course to take, but the consequences of that course are already set."

"Is that your personal philosophy of life?" I asked in a kidding tone. I had never seen him so serious before. But maybe he wasn't being serious now. He smiled again.

"It's the way it is," he said.

"But about Kara. I think she's making a mistake."

"Are you afraid of her mistakes, or are you afraid that you

might try to profit from them and end up making your own mistakes?"

It was an insightful question. In fact, he had hit the nail right on the head. I didn't want Kara to succeed in breaking them up. If she did, and I went chasing after Becky and still didn't get her, then I would have no excuse. I would be unloved simply for who I was. Ray was a safety net that protected me from reality. What I mean is, I often fantasized about being with Becky, but I never believed I would be, not really.

Vincent was peering at me in the same way he peered through his telescope—completely interested, yet also completely detached. My life to him was like some remote occurrence, worthy of respect, but nothing to cry over. I can't explain how such a perception of him didn't make him seem any less warm.

"I'm afraid of hurting Becky," I said finally.

"Yes?"

I hesitated. "And I'm afraid that what you said is true."

He nodded. "It's the game."

I was confused. "What does it have to do with your game?"

He wasn't given a chance to respond. Kara popped through the front door right then. I hurried into the living room to greet her, Vincent following at a substantially slower pace. Kara gave me a quick hug in greeting and then slipped into the kitchen. I had to go after her.

"How was your date?" I asked.

"We had fun, but he's a jerk."

"Are you going out with him again?" I asked.

She placed her purse on the bar, her head down. Her clothes were sexy—a short leather skirt, black high heels. I noticed her lipstick was smeared.

"I don't know if it's necessary," she said.

I felt relieved, for the moment. I didn't imagine that Kara could have made Ray forget the love of his life in one evening, even though she had almost done that to me.

"It's not necessary," I said, as Vincent came up beside me.

"Hi, honey," she said to him, raising her head only slightly.

"Hi," he said.

We stood that way for a long moment, Vincent and I together, Kara on the other side of the room. The two of us against her, or so it seemed. I assumed Vincent was on my side. Kara appeared to be deliberating over something. I could always tell when she was thinking. She would look sad.

"What is it?" I asked finally.

She spoke to the wall. "I saw a picture of Becky in his wallet."

"You looked in his wallet?" I asked.

"I did," she said.

"What for?" I asked.

"To see if he carried her picture," she said. "He was paying the bill at the restaurant. I just grabbed it out of his hand. I told him I wanted to see if he was really twenty years old. When I stumbled across Becky's picture, he told me she was his cousin."

"I might have done the same thing," I said.

Kara shook her head. "You wouldn't have lied to me."

"Lying isn't my style," I agreed. She heard the reproach in my voice. She continued to look away.

"I won't do this if you don't want me to," she said slowly. "But if you don't, Mark, you'll have to stop me. Otherwise, I'll do it."

"Do what?" I asked, glancing at Vincent, worried. Vincent looked as if we were discussing how many cities I had just destroyed while playing "Decision." He appeared as calm as ever. Kara finally glanced over at me. Her mascara was smeared, and I wondered if she'd been crying. Yet, when she spoke next, her voice was steady.

"I plan to go into Becky's store tomorrow," she said. "I'm going to have her help me find a movie. Then I'm going to pretend to suddenly realize she's Ray's cousin." She nodded as my face darkened. "I'm going to tell her I was out with him the night before."

"I don't want you to do that," I said flatly, feeling hollow. My thoughts were not with Becky then, or how Kara's plan would ruin Becky's relationship with Ray. My mind was already grieving over the end of my friendship with Kara. For her even to conceive of such an act told me she could no longer be a friend of mine. It was ironic in a way. The whole magical mystery of my friendship with Kara had been the manner in which it had seemed to spring into being already firmly established.

But I had only been fooling myself. What I was hearing told me I hadn't really known her at all.

"Before you decide," Kara said, "I want you to do me one favor."

"I've already decided," I said.

"I want you to visit Becky tonight," Kara went on. "She's still at the store. She's working late."

"How do you know?" I asked.

Kara held my eye. "I know."

"You're a jerk," I said bitterly.

Her lower lip trembled. She nodded. "But he's a bigger jerk."

"I'll warn Becky," I said.

"No, you won't," she said.

"I will!" I swore. "And don't tell me you know what I'll do!" I turned on Vincent. "Say something."

"Are we going out for ice cream?" he asked.

"Vincent," I pleaded. "What about Becky?"

"She can come if she wants," he said. Then he smiled to let me know he was no fool, or maybe a bigger fool than I could imagine for being with Kara in the first place.

I left the house, got in my car, and drove. I didn't know where I was going until I stopped the car and saw Becky through the window of her store counting out a register. I just sat there, watching her without her knowing it. Then she turned off the store lights; she had been working alone. She stepped outside, and after she locked the door, she noticed me sitting in a car, watching her. But she didn't recognize me at first. She appeared to be frightened. Then suddenly she waved and hurried toward me.

"What are you doing here, you nut?" she asked, leaning into my open window.

"Thinking," I said.

"About your new game? I think I've almost cracked the 'Starlight Crystal.' My problem's been right in front of me all the time. I've figured out that the queen of the universe—" She paused. "What's the matter, Mark?"

"Nothing."

"What are you doing here?" she asked.

"I came to see you."

"I wish you'd told me ahead of time. I can't stay and talk."

"Ray's waiting for you?"

Becky hesitated. She never brought up Ray unless I did. "I promised him yesterday that I'd stop by his place on my way home tonight."

"It figures," I said. It sure did. Becky had probably made the promise to Ray before he set his date with Kara. I'd been wrong to complain to Vincent that Ray and Kara were out late. Ten or ten-thirty was early to finish a date. But Ray knew he had to be home for Becky's visit. I had no illusions that Ray was going to tell Becky where he'd been. I felt I knew him well, and we hadn't even been formally introduced. Becky put her hand on my shoulder.

"I wish you had stopped by this afternoon," she said. "I was craving ice cream."

"You don't need me to eat it," I said, my melancholy refusing to depart. Becky surprised me. She leaned over and kissed my cheek.

"But with you it always tastes better," she said.

"When are you working next?"

"Tomorrow."

I coughed. "How about the time after that?"

"Monday night. Three to eleven. Are you going to come by?"

"Sure."

"You have to promise. I'll plan on it."

"I promise," I said.

"We could go to McDonald's together. Is six good for you?"

"It's good."

Becky sighed. "I wish you were coming by tomorrow. I hate Saturdays. They're so long."

"Yeah," I muttered, my guilt swelling in my lungs. "I know."

I could have suggested she stay home. I could have told her the whole story. I could have unleashed all my missiles on Beijing at once and concentrated my lasers on the enemy submarines. Then maybe I would be a winner and there would be something left to show for it. Maybe Vincent had been right about it all being a game, right about his choice of titles—"Decision." It seemed the most important decisions I made were the ones where I decided to do nothing. Kara had me figured cold.

Yet that was all B.S. I didn't tell Becky that Kara was coming in to ruin her life because Becky suddenly leaned over and kissed me again on the cheek. That made twice in two minutes, and I couldn't remember when she had kissed me once. I loved it. I wanted a third, not necessarily right then, but Monday. Yes, I thought, Monday. Because of Kara, that was suddenly a possibility. An opportunity, as Kara had put it. Goddamn her. I wasn't just afraid of making a mistake. I was jumping at the opportunity.

"Good night, Mark," Becky said. "Take care of yourself."

"You, too."

"Monday?"

"I'll be here."

"Great," she said.

Chapter Five

Everything is inevitable once a decision has been made. Vincent said that and I believed him.

I didn't try to stop Kara. It was what she wanted to do. And even though I pretended to want to stop her, she was doing what I wanted, too. No wonder I felt so angry with her. I realize now that I only got angry when people did things that, deep inside, I knew I was capable of doing myself.

I didn't talk to either Vincent or Kara over the weekend. I waited until six the following Monday night before I visited Becky. As promised. What a hypocrite I was. On the drive to the electronics store, I kept hoping Becky had called in sick. But she was there, hard at work, even though she looked sick. One glance at her and I knew immediately that Kara had carried out her plan with cold-blooded efficiency.

"Hi," Becky said softly, glancing up from a box of DVDs she was shelving. There were circles under her eyes.

"Hi," I said. "How are you doing?"

She went back to her job. "Fine."

I was brilliant, I must say. "What's new?" I asked.

"Nothing. How are you?"

"Great."

"That's good," she said.

I squatted beside her, my conscience crying out to tell her that it was all a setup. My vocal cords didn't hear a word of it. "Is something wrong?" I asked.

"No."

"Do you want to get something to eat?"

"No."

"Something to drink?"

She stopped working and stared at a DVD cover for a moment. Her hands were trembling. "All right," she said.

She told the manager she was taking her break. We drove around the block to our usual ice-cream shop. We ordered Cokes and sat on a bench outside drinking them and watching the sky, not talking. The evening was warm and dry, but the sweat under my shirt was cold and sticky. I let Becky break the silence.

"I know I'm lousy company tonight," she said.

"That's okay."

"I had a bad weekend."

"Do you want to talk about it?"

She shook her head. "No."

"That's okay," I said.

"I broke up with Ray."

"You don't have to talk about it."

She sniffed. "I don't want to."

"That's okay."

"Thank you," she said, hanging her head. I put my hand on her back. If ever there was a time for an understatement. I couldn't believe what I said next.

"Don't thank me," I said. "I didn't do anything."

"Thanks for being my friend."

I forced a chuckle. "I'm not that great a friend."

She took my free hand and turned her damp eyes on me. "Yes, you are, Mark. When you come into the store, you always make me feel better. You make me laugh. I appreciate that. It means a lot to me."

"Well, I hope I never run out of jokes, then."

She smiled. "You're silly."

"A moment ago I was great."

"You are." She let go of my hand and took a sip of her drink, chewing on an ice cube, losing her smile. "He was such a jerk."

"Yeah."

"I should be happy."

"Yeah."

She set her drink down. "Do you want to go out?"

"Yeah. What? No. You just broke up. It wouldn't be right."

She snorted. She was angry. I had never seen her angry before. "Do you know what he did to me, Mark?"

"No."

"He went out with another girl. Friday night, when I was working late, he was out with another girl. Can you believe that?"

"You don't have to talk about it."

"I want to. He was out with this blond girl from Scotland. She came in my store the next day. She thought I was Ray's cousin. That's what he told her. Can you believe that?"

"Yeah."

"I hate him."

Becky was beginning to sound exactly the way Kara sounded when she talked about Ray. Minus the accent, of course, which Becky had so cleverly identified. It gave me a bad feeling.

"You shouldn't hate," I said.

She put her hands on her drink, but didn't pick it up. Her hands were trembling again. She swallowed the ice cube in her mouth.

"I know," she whispered.

She began to cry. I put an arm around her, and she sagged against my side, and I felt if she didn't stop soon I would tell her that Kara was *my* cousin. I would tell her anything to make the tears go away.

And I did. I told her the truth. Well, a big part of it. I told her I wanted to go out with her. It worked. She stopped crying. She asked me where we should go.

Chapter Six

The following evening I was getting dressed for my date with Becky when someone knocked on the door of my tiny apartment. I seldom had visitors. The knock startled me. In the instant before I opened the door, a horrible thought flashed through my mind that it was Becky come to tell me she had changed her mind, that she was back with Ray. I had been looking forward to seeing her all day. I had barely slept the previous night. My resting pulse was in the low one hundreds, but I was feeling no pain.

Until the knock at the door. But then, it was only Kara, and I didn't know how to feel. She looked properly chastised— and beautiful.

"Can I come in?" she asked in a meek voice.

"I was just leaving."

"I know."

"Ah," I said. "What do you want?"

"To apologize."

"I'd think you'd be pleased at the turn of events. I'm surprised you're not here to tell me what to wear."

She inspected my clothes. "You know, you wear the same size as Vincent."

"Oh, Christ."

"You look good, Mark."

"You just implied that I looked awful."

"I mean your face." She stepped inside and took my hand. She pressed it to my chest and stared at me with her bright blue eyes. It was only then I noticed that she wore contacts. "You look happy," she said.

I shook my head. "You have some nerve."

"Are you still angry with me?"

"Yeah."

"Are you?" she asked again.

"No." I shook free of her and searched for my car keys. "I've got to get out of here."

Kara checked her watch. "You're picking her up at eight o'clock?"

"No, about nine."

"Where are you going now?"

"Don't you know? You know everything else."

"I hope you're going to get some decent clothes."

I put a hand to my head and closed my eyes. "I *was* going to buy some new clothes," I muttered.

"Why don't you wear some of Vincent's?"

I whirled around. "Is that why you're here? To tell me what to wear? What to say?"

"I know you'll think of something to say."

"Thanks."

"Are you sure you're not still angry with me?"

Suddenly I began to laugh. I didn't know why. Maybe because it felt good. It burst out of me. I laughed and laughed. Kara joined me. Crossing the room, she gave me a big hug.

"You'll have fun," she said, pressing her cheek to my face.

"I should have you shot," I said.

"Not tonight. Later. I have to hear every detail of your big date." She pulled away and slapped me on the rump. "Come on, we'll go in my car."

"So you're going to chauffeur us?"

"You're taking my car on your date. It's much more impressive."

"I doubt that Becky is so materialistic she'll be impressed by an expensive car."

"Don't think, Mark." Kara took my hand. "Let me do that for you."

Vincent wasn't home when we drove up. Kara thought he might be up at the cave setting up his telescope. Naturally, his absence didn't prevent her from plowing through his closet. Vincent had more clothes than I recalled from my last visit. Most of them looked as if they'd never been worn. I suspected that Kara had been out shopping that afternoon.

"You shouldn't wear blue," she said, pulling out a black leather coat. "You have dark hair, fair skin. You're definitely winter. You should throw away all your blue shirts. They look like your mother bought them for you."

"She did buy some of them." Several of the shirts I owned went back to my freshman year in high school. Clothes had never been a priority with me.

"Well, you're not going out with your mother," Kara said, finding a pair of jeans and a red belt. I had never seen a red belt before, and I certainly couldn't see it around my waist. "You're going out with a woman. You've got to look sexy."

"It's almost eight," I said. "I don't have time to stop at a plastic surgeon on the way."

Kara was amused. "You're sexy, Mark. If it wasn't for Vincent, I would have seduced you weeks ago."

My heart did a nice natural skip that was infinitely preferable to the kind of thump caused by my defective valve. "Vincent might meet with an unfortunate accident on his walk back from the cave," I said hopefully.

She grinned and tossed me a handful of sex appeal. "Put these on."

"Wait in the other room."

"Of course," she said.

The clothes were just a bit loose; Vincent was more muscular than I was. Kara was pleased with the results, and I had to agree there was something to be said for the red belt after all, especially with the black leather boots Kara pushed on me next. I wondered if Becky would recognize me.

We walked up to the cave. We took it slow and easy. Kara let me stop and rest a number of times. I muttered something about being out of shape, and she just nodded her understanding. I felt a wave of intense love flow through me. And to think I had been furious with her only days before. I tried to figure it out but got nowhere.

Vincent had the telescope focused on the moon when we arrived. The sun had set, and the moon was about thirty degrees above the horizon, almost full. Kara was eager to look at it. Vincent didn't comment on my wearing his clothes. He seemed to be far away, serene as usual, yet preoccupied at the same time. He did ask about Becky, though.

"I'm going out with her tonight," I said.

He nodded. "You'll have fun."

"I hope *she* does," I said.

"Of course she will," Kara said, her eye pressed to the eyepiece. "Hey, Mark, you've got to see this. It's so big and bright."

Kara stepped aside and let me have a peek. I immediately reached for the focusing knob. Kara must have had sharper sight than I did. For a moment the moon was like one of those blurred balls of light in Vincent's game. The similarity struck me so strongly that for a moment I felt disoriented, as if I were seeing two moons at once. Then I noticed Vincent had his head pressed close to mine; he was fiddling with the smaller finder telescope strapped to the side of the main instrument. I thought my double vision must be a result of his shaking the telescope stand. Yet when I put my hand on the stand to steady it, the two moons didn't go away. My double vision actually intensified, and I had to step back from the eyepiece. I feared I was about to have a dizzy spell as I had the first night. But as quickly as it had come, it stopped.

"Are you all right?" Kara asked me.

I sucked in a deep breath. "I'm fine."

Vincent was also watching me. "Kara, why don't you show Mark the cave," he said.

"Yeah," I said. "I'd like to see this mysterious cave."

While Vincent stayed with the telescope, I followed Kara through the bushes to the opening of the cave. It was nothing spectacular, at least at first glance. The entrance was less than five feet high, so we had to stoop to enter. It was dark inside, naturally, but Kara carried a flashlight and flicked it on, revealing rough rock walls, an uneven dirt floor. The odor, however, struck me as unusual. The air inside the cave smelled fresh, like a forest after a spring shower.

"What do you do in here?" I asked.

"Talk."

"About what?" I asked.

Kara was walking in front of me, leading the way. She paused and glanced over her shoulder. "You'd be amazed," she said.

Not far into the cave, perhaps a hundred feet, it opened into an oval space approximately twenty feet across and with plenty of head room. This was not the end of the cave—it continued through a narrower opening on the far side of the room—but it was obviously where Vincent stored his telescope and talked to his girlfriend. The sides of the room were equipped with several natural rock ledges, perfect for sitting. The happy couple had placed a few blankets over these and set a small table and gas lantern nearby. As I stood and watched, Kara lit the lantern and turned off her flashlight. She gestured for me to sit on a ledge beside her.

"There's a draft in here," I said, pointing to the dark hole across from us. "Have you ever explored where that leads?"

"Not all the way."

"It would be interesting to find out," I said.

"Not now."

"You're right. I shouldn't even be here now. I'll be late."

"Becky will wait for you. She expects you to be late."

"I suppose she told you that?" I asked.

"Would you believe me if I said yes?"

"No."

Kara smiled. In the soft glow from the lantern, she seemed

years younger, a child, free from all cares. Yet it was not only the light. Overall, she seemed greatly relieved. She met my gaze.

"What are you thinking?" she asked.

"If I tell you, will you tell me what you're thinking?"

"Maybe."

"I'm not thinking anything," I said. "I just feel happy."

"It's the same with me." She drew in a breath and took in the cave with her eyes. "Do you notice how quiet it is here?"

"Now that you mention it. I can hear my own heart beating."

Her face suddenly went blank. "So can I," she whispered.

"Kara?"

She smiled quickly. "Nothing. What are you going to do tonight?"

"You mean you're not going to tell me?"

Kara turned businesslike. "You have to eat first. Take her to a nice restaurant. It doesn't matter what kind: Italian, French, Japanese—Becky didn't strike me as being picky."

"Not like she is with the kind of car I drive. Has it occurred to you that she might have seen your car in the parking lot when you visited her at the store?"

"I had to go there. You said you forgave me."

"I do," I said. "But what about the car?"

"I doubt if she saw it. But you can take Vincent's if it makes you more comfortable. Now, after dinner you can ask her what she wants to do. Leave that part up to her."

"I was thinking of taking her to a movie."

"You can't talk at the movies. You should talk to her. Besides, it will probably be too late for a movie."

"What if I bring her here and we talk?" I asked.

My suggestion seemed to startle Kara. "What?"

"I was just kidding. What's the matter?"

Kara relaxed. "There'll be plenty of time for that later."

"Time for what?"

"You know."

"What?"

Kara shrugged. "Seducing her."

I chuckled, embarrassed. I hadn't known that was what she meant. "Are you sure?" I asked. "It seems I missed my chance with you when you met Vincent."

"That was a long time ago."

"Really? How long have you known him?"

"Many years."

"When did you meet?"

Kara checked her watch and stood up abruptly. "You'd better go."

I stood and stretched. "But you just said she would wait for me."

She took me by the hand and pulled me toward the entrance. "Sometimes I'm wrong," she said.

Chapter Seven

I ended up being exactly on time. Becky wasn't even ready. She had no sooner answered the door than she dashed back into her bedroom. I didn't know why; she looked great to me. I was left all alone in her deserted living room. Her parents had gone out for dinner. I hoped we wouldn't end up at the same restaurant. I had a sneaking suspicion they wouldn't approve of me after the smooth-talking Mr. Ray.

It was while I waited for Becky that I started to doubt my date was really going to happen. I guess at heart I was a pessimist, a dreamer. I knew I was bound to wake up any second and everything would vanish. I'm not kidding, walking around the living room, I actually pinched myself to see if I was where I thought I was. Yet there was something other than my date with Becky that filled me with a sense of unreality. Something about the two moons I'd seen up on the hill. Despite my dizziness and their blurred shapes, they had both seemed so vivid and real.

"Hi," Becky said finally, coming up behind me and taking me by surprise. "How do I look?"

Her taste in clothes was vastly different from Kara's, much more conservative. She wore a simple summer dress, white and cool, covered with green flowers and singing birds. With her warm smile and her sweet welcome hug, I counted our date a success already. I hadn't wanted to spend the night mourning for Ray with her.

"You look like the queen of the universe," I said.

She laughed. "You know, when we come back here tonight you're going to help me crack that stupid game of yours."

"No way. Then you won't need me anymore."

She took me by the arm and led me toward the door. I was reminded of Kara leading me out of the cave. "I'll always need you to help me with something," she said.

We went outside to my car—to my black Ferrari. Kara had been right. Becky was impressed. She muttered something about the royalties I must be getting. I muttered something back about its being stolen.

We headed down to the beach. It was a crazy idea—the beach was twenty miles away. On the drive there, our conversation flowed easily. We talked about nothing of importance, the kind of talks I find are usually the most important. We even discussed the weather. It was hot. It had been hot all summer. But soon summer would be over. I kept glancing at the moon as we drove. Almost full, I thought. The love of my life was finally sitting beside me, but I couldn't keep my eyes off the moon. A sense of loss plagued me. It was the sight of the moon that brought the haunted feeling, but I didn't know why.

Yet I was happy. Vague forebodings can't compete with a real live girl. Becky was in good spirits. She cracked one joke after another, half of them at my expense. I didn't mind. We drove with the windows down, the wind in our hair.

I chose the restaurant. Becky put up a bit of a fuss—she thought it was too expensive. It overlooked the water, and the clientele coming out the front door carried gold toothpicks. Because I was driving a Ferrari, I told her, we couldn't very well go to McDonald's.

The meal was a new experience for me. We had three waiters attending us, and my cup of coffee was never allowed to slip below the halfway point. Becky ate lightly, a salad for a bunny, but I managed to choke down a thick steak. A man's meal, as they say. We left the restaurant with me totally stuffed.

Then the fun started, but it was not good clean fun. It was a nightmare.

Walking to the car, we spotted a couple of oil wells a little way down the beach by the water. We were in a classy neighborhood, but in southern California by the beaches, oil wells are not out of place. These two were cranking full speed, up and down. I innocently remarked how as a child I used to climb oil wells and ride them. Becky was instantly intrigued.

"Could we do that?" she asked.

"You mean now?"

"Yeah. It looks like fun."

"No," I said. "You'd get your dress all dirty."

"I don't care. I want to do it."

"There's a fence around each well."

"We'll climb it." She gave me a sly grin. "Scared?"

That got me. I'm sure it was a male ego thing. With my poor heart and all, I'd always been particularly sensitive about being regarded as a wimp. I figured we could climb the fence, and once Becky saw how big the wells were up close, she'd back off. I didn't stop to think how weird it was that she wanted to ride one of the oily monsters in the first place.

It was a short drive to the wells. Becky bounded out of the car and across the sand before I could put on the Ferrari's parking brake. She attacked the fence surrounding the wells. Kicking off her shoes, she was over it in a few seconds. I took a lot longer with my climb, even though she implored me to hurry. I figured having a heart attack would only spoil the evening.

The wells were remarkably quiet. They must have been of a recent design, although they were both coated with rust. The ocean air was to blame for that. They towered above us like hungry insects plowing the earth for fresh meat. A metal ladder led up each side. As kids we used to climb similar ladders and then crawl onto the head of the arm of the well. But even as a kid, I never climbed such a huge well.

"This is crazy," I said.

Becky put a foot on the ladder. "It'll be exciting."

"Why do you want to do this?"

"Why not? Are you coming, Mark?"

"I'll mess up my clothes." Or Vincent's clothes, I thought. Not that he'd care, probably.

"Come on," she insisted.

I followed her up the ladder. She had on pink underwear. I couldn't help but notice. The moon shone brilliantly across the beach. I half hoped a policeman would swing by and give us a strict scolding. As I looked down from near the top of the ladder, a wave of anxiety and dizziness swept over me and I had to grip the metal bar tightly.

"What do we do next?" she asked.

"Say a prayer. We should get down."

"How do you climb onto this thing?" Becky asked, gesturing to the rising and falling arm. I called it an arm, but as it swooped rhythmically by, driving its pipe deeper and deeper into the earth, it looked more like an angry fist.

"Carefully," I answered.

"Tell me."

"That's how you do it. You just catch it and climb on. But I warn you, if you panic and want to stop, it won't stop. We can't stop it."

She ignored me. She climbed onto the arm, initially pull-ing herself up with her arms, before throwing her legs over the top of the metal. I took the ladder up another few rungs. Becky was having a great time. Hugging the blasted thing with both arms, rocking up and down, she smiled over at me.

"This isn't so bad," she said.

"Just stay where you are. If you climb out toward the end, you'll feel like you're riding a tornado."

I'm a master of suggestion. Becky did exactly what I didn't want her to do, and then some. She crept *all* the way to the end, until she was straddling the arm just above the huge insectlike head. Her hair flew up in the night, and she threw back her head and laughed.

"I love it!" she said. "Come on, Mark."

"No."

"You've got to try it."

"Becky, please get down."

"I'm fine. Don't worry."

"You're going to get dizzy," I said.

Another suggestion. I didn't mean it that way. I meant it as a warning. But suddenly, as Becky stared up at the moon, the dizziness hit her. She began to panic. I knew exactly how she felt. I had warned her. That sudden overwhelming desire to have the world stand still. It hit her with irrational speed and didn't respond well to logic. Even though nothing had changed for her in the last few seconds, I knew she was now afraid she was going to die. She threw herself onto the metal arm, hugging it with both her arms and legs.

"Mark!" she cried. "I'm going to throw up."

"Hang on. You'll be fine."

"I'm going to fall, Mark. Help me!"

I responded too hastily to her panic. I should have tried to talk her down. By going to her rescue, I blocked her way back to the ladder. But I did it anyway. I had just eaten steak. I was a man. I had to save my woman.

I had little trouble climbing onto the arm of the well. Despite my lack of strength and endurance, I'm extremely well coordinated. But I had a full stomach, and the rocking motion quickly let me know it. Creeping toward the head of the arm, with the strength of the ride growing in intensity as I edged forward, I also began to feel as though I would vomit. Yet none of my fear for myself matched my fear of Becky's fear. Her leg grip was weakening. Her hips had begun to rock to the side. I glanced straight down into a mess of gears and motors. If she fell, she wouldn't have a soft landing.

"Mark!" she screamed.

"I'm coming. Keep your eyes open. Stare at the road, anything stationary. You're going to be fine."

I reached her in a matter of seconds. Now my problems really began. It was not as though I could ease her onto my shoulders and carry her safely back to civilization. Indeed, I couldn't budge her an inch. Her legs might have been losing their strength, but her hands were dug so tightly into the rusty lip of the oil well arm that her fingers were bleeding. She cried pitifully.

"I have to get down," she said. "Please help me down."

"You're going to have to let yourself slide backward. It's easy. Each time we swing upward, loosen your grip slightly. Tighten it as we swing down." Naturally, she sat with her back toward me; she had crept headfirst toward the end of the arm. I leaned forward and wrapped my arm around her waist, an arm I could ill afford to spare at the moment. I spoke in her ear. "Trust me, Becky. I will not let you fall."

She nodded her head weakly. She loosened her vise grip when we were going up. Slowly, painfully, we inched back toward the ladder, the center of balance, where the waves were kinder. It didn't take us long to reach our goal, although it seemed like forever. Once there, we had to deal with the next big obstacle to freedom and safety from the metal monster: I was still in her way. I had to climb off. I had to let go of her. But she wouldn't let me.

"I can't hold on," she gasped. "I'll fall off."

"I'll just have to let go of you for a second."

"No!"

I had no choice. She could cry all she wanted. In her condition, I knew there was no way she'd be able to climb onto the ladder without my assistance. Backing up farther, past the ladder, was therefore out of the question on my part.

"Just hang on," I said.

"No! Mark, no!"

I let go of her and swung onto the ladder in one smooth motion. It turned out to be easier than I thought. Unfortunately, Becky's dizziness had worsened. She didn't know what was up and what was down, and never mind that she was now close to the center of balance and was no longer rocketing into the sky every few seconds. I couldn't get her to swing her legs down onto the rungs of the ladder. I couldn't even get her to respond to my voice. She had buried her head in the metal arm. She was crying. I was afraid she'd go into shock next.

Just then I noticed a metal pole lying on the ground near the base of the oil well. The pole was attached to a fallen sign that carried a wise warning that this was a hazardous area. I left Becky and climbed down the ladder in a moment. I picked up the pole, dragging the sign on the ground. The gears of the oil well motor were sheltered from rain but were wide open to any determined vandal.

"Hang on tight, Becky!" I called. "I'm going to stop this thing!"

Becky stirred. She raised her head and glanced down. She didn't speak, but only retightened her grip. I shoved the end of the pole into the motor.

Instantly it was snapped from my hands. I was lucky the sign didn't behead me. It flew into the gears with the rest of the pole. Something cold whisked by the tip of my ear. An awful noise followed. It sounded like—well, a pissed-off oil well. A screech rent the air. Orange sparks shot out at my feet. The arm of the well crawled slowly upward and got stuck. And for that I was thankful—that the oil well hadn't jerked to a halt and tossed Becky off. The noise stopped, and the silence that followed was like a blessing from above. I leapt back onto the ladder, trying to ignore my labored breathing and the growing pain in my chest.

Helping Becky down to the ground proved simple. I knew exactly how she must have felt when the oil well stopped moving. Infinite relief. Yeah, I'd got trapped on an oil well once when I was only eleven. I had been alone. When I had finally got down, I felt as if I'd aged eighty years.

We sat without talking for a few minutes, trying to catch our breath. Naturally, I took forever to recover. The pain in my chest receded in tiny gulps. Becky stood and stumbled to the fence that surrounded the wells and leaned against it. She didn't have to reclimb it. For the first time I noticed a hole in the sand beneath the fence. I pointed it out to her, and she nodded without a word and used it to slip under the fence. She didn't have to worry about her dress now. She was a mess. I followed her shortly, feeling limp and spent. Becky wandered down to the water. Close to the edge of the waves, she plopped down in the sand, her head buried in her knees. I sat beside her. She had stopped crying, and I took that as a sign of progress. Until she spoke.

"He's probably out with her now," she said.

Of course I knew who the *he* and *she* were. I realized in an instant what was going on. Ever since I had picked her up, Becky had been unusually jovial, almost wired. She was trying to block it all out. I made a good block. So did risking her life. She really cared about Ray. The whole situation made me feel awful.

"I bet he's not," I said.

"How would you know?"

"I don't know."

She glanced up. Her face was dry. "I'm sorry. I shouldn't have said that."

"It's all right. How do you feel?"

Disgust wrinkled her features. "Like an idiot."

"It's good to feel that way every now and then. It keeps us humble."

"Have you ever felt this way?" she asked.

"Yeah."

"When?"

"When I first asked you out and you said no."

"I'm sorry," she said.

"Don't be. The feeling went away when you said yes."

She shook her head helplessly. "It hit me so suddenly. I felt so dizzy. I thought I was going to die."

"I know the feeling." I paused. "Do you miss him?"

She looked out over the ocean. She nodded. "Yeah."

"Do you want to go home?"

She continued to stare at the water, the waves. They were small but well formed, sleek curves of moonlit glass.

"Mark," she said, "what's the big secret in your game?"

"Your traveling companion on your quest is your worst enemy."

She frowned. "But you choose a different companion each time."

"It doesn't matter. They're always against you. You have to kill them at the first opportunity. Then you can make rapid progress."

"Why did you make it that way?"

I shrugged. "I wanted it to be unique."

"That doesn't seem like much of a reason. Is Chaneen, the queen of the universe, an enemy, too?"

"She's the only exception. But that's all I'll tell you. What's your first name?"

Her face changed, but I wasn't sure how. She appeared to go still, to turn inward. Without moving her head, she let her eyes stray to the moon above. My own eyes did the same, and for a moment I had the sudden conviction that Vincent was still on his hill with his telescope, looking at the moon. The conviction carried with it a peculiar sense of déja vu.

"I don't want to go home," she said softly.

"You're changing the subject."

She looked directly at me. "I want to go to your place."

"Why?"

"Don't ask why."

"But—" I wanted to say something about Ray without speaking his name. I wanted to tell her she had to get over him before she could get to know me. She didn't give me the chance. She leaned over and kissed me on the lips.

"You risked your life to save me," she whispered into my ear as she held her cheek to mine. "Can you tell me why?"

She didn't know that I could but wouldn't. Regrettably, my love for her was not the only answer. I was no better than my computer-generated characters. Because of me, Becky had gone up on the oil well in the first place. Because of Kara and me, she had broken up with Ray. I was her worst enemy. But I said nothing. I stood and brushed off my pants and led her back to the car.

We passed the wrecked oil well as we drove back to the main road. Someday, I thought, when I was rich, I would send the oil company a check.

Becky stayed late at my place, although not the entire night. We didn't talk much. We didn't have sex. We just lay beside each other on my bed and rested, listening to each other's heartbeats. Once during the night she pressed her hand to my chest and asked if I was all right. She must have noticed the irregularity in the beat. I told her I was fine. Then I thought of Kara, probably waiting up late to hear how the date had gone, and I smiled. I would tell her the same thing. It went fine, just fine.

Chapter Eight

The next morning Kara came early and knocked softly on my door. I knew who it was without asking. I shouted for her to come in. She peeked through a crack in the door before opening it all the way.

"Just wanted to be sure you were alone," she said.

Kara had on torn blue jeans and a black T-shirt. She plopped down on the bed beside me. I had only a white sheet and my underwear for covering. That was all. Yet I didn't feel uncomfortable. Kara kissed me on the forehead, her blond curls falling all over my pillow.

"We didn't see you last night," she said.

"Tell Vincent I'm sorry I didn't bring the car back."

"Vincent says you can keep the car."

"Right," I said.

"Really. You can stay at our house. We're going away on an extended vacation."

I sat up with a start. "Where are you going?"

Kara sat up slowly. "Far away."

"Where? For how long?"

Kara spoke gently. "I can't tell you where we're going. It's a secret. But we'll be gone a long time."

"Why can't you tell me?"

"I just can't tell you." She touched my hand. "You have to trust me on this and accept my answer: It's what Vincent wants, too."

"But I haven't had a chance to help him with his game. All I've done is play it. You two can't leave now."

Kara smiled a sad smile. I know she didn't intend it, but I suddenly felt as if I were her child, a child about to lose his mother.

"You helped him more than you know," she said. "He wanted me to tell you that."

"I'm not going to get to say good-bye to him?"

"I'm afraid not." She leaned over and kissed me again, this time on the lips. "Don't worry, Mark. Everything will be all right."

I had never cried in front of a girl, or in front of anyone, for that matter—at least not since I was a little kid. I didn't cry then. But I came so close to weeping that my eyes stung and I had to cover them with my hand.

"You can't go," I said, and there was so much wrapped up in those three small words it would have taken volumes to explain. But I think Kara heard and understood it all. Kara and Vincent's appearance in my life had been like a moon rising on a dark night. I couldn't bear the thought of going back to being by myself. Kara seemed to read my mind, as she so often did.

"You have Becky now," she said. "You don't need Vincent and me."

I stood and walked to the sink and drank a glass of water. I stared out the window, not caring about Kara's seeing my underwear. The sky was blue overhead, but there were clouds on the horizon. Maybe there would be a storm later that night, I thought, to cover up the moon. It was then I remembered my premonition of loss and recognized how accurate it had been.

"I don't have Becky," I said.

"Yes, you do."

"You haven't even asked how our date went."

"I know it went well."

"What would you say if I told you she almost died?"

Kara hesitated. "Really?"

"Yes."

"Then I would say it was probably you who saved her from dying."

I bit my lip softly, not enough to draw blood but hard enough to feel pain. That was the thing about physical pain. It was real. It was simple to understand, unlike other kinds of pain.

"I don't understand any of this," I said. "You come here out of nowhere, set me up with Becky, and then disappear back into nowhere. Were Becky and I your reason for coming?"

"Our reasons were complicated," Kara said.

"Will you ever come back? A simple uncomplicated yes or no would be appreciated."

"No."

I put down my glass of water. Actually, I dropped it. The glass shattered. Then my finger was bleeding. I didn't feel the cut—it was too sharp, too sudden. Kara stood and wrapped my bloody finger in a white paper towel that quickly turned red.

"Are you all right?" she asked.

"Yes."

"Did you have fun last night?"

"Yes."

She nodded. "I'm glad."

"I promised I'd call Becky when I woke up."

"You're awake now." Kara gestured to the phone. "Go ahead, let me listen. I fought for this, you know."

I dialed the number. I didn't know why I didn't wait. Maybe I was trying to keep Kara there longer. I felt as if she would leave any second and just be gone forever. I got blood all over Becky's numbers. She answered on the third ring.

"Hello, Becky? It's me, Mark."

She hung up the phone.

"What's wrong?" Kara asked, standing near the kitchen

sink. I stared at the dial tone sounding in the receiver. Yeah, stared at it. Then I slowly put the phone down.

"I don't know," I said.

Kara sat down beside me on the bed. "Dial her again."

"She hung up on me," I said.

"You might have had the wrong number."

"It was Becky," I said.

"Maybe she got disconnected. Try her again."

This time I punched out the number with my uninjured hand. It rang and rang—ten times. A big ten times.

"Maybe she's not home," Kara said.

"She was home a second ago." I set down the phone again. "She hung up on me."

Kara was concerned. "There must be some mistake. Try it again."

"No."

"Are you sure you dialed the right number?"

Becky had given me her number when we arranged our date. I had instantly memorized it, but now I studied the wrinkled slip of paper on the wooden stand beside my bed.

I read the number aloud.

Kara frowned. "That's right."

"How do you know her number?"

"Never mind. Today's Wednesday. She starts work at ten. She'll be going in soon. You have to talk to her."

"She doesn't want to talk to me."

Kara stood and began to pace. "Don't you want to know why?"

I swallowed thickly. It was turning out to be one lousy day, and I only had my underwear on. "I don't know."

Kara grew impatient. "We have to find out what's going on before I leave. I have to know."

"Maybe she went back to Ray."

Kara whirled on me. "Don't say that! Don't even joke about that!"

"I wasn't joking."

Kara grabbed my pants and threw them at me. "Get dressed. We're going to the store."

Chapter Nine

Kara drove. She drove as only she knew how—fast and dangerously. I tried to pass the time by not thinking. It was amazing how difficult it was. Time was my enemy now, I thought. But then, when was it ever a friend to anybody? It killed us all. My heart ached. I felt as if I was dying inside.

Kara parked around the block from the store. "Talk to her," she said.

"It isn't ten yet."

"She always goes in a few minutes early."

"Why do I have to ask her why she hung up on me? Why don't you just tell me? You tell me everything else about her."

Kara closed her eyes and sighed. "Because I don't know, Mark."

I got out of the car. I can't say the walk to the store did me good. I was feeling more than sorry for myself.

Kara was right. Becky had come in early. She stood behind the cash register, exactly as she had when we first met. But she took one look at me and immediately strode into the back where only employees were allowed. I followed her. I mean, I wasn't worried about getting fired. Fortunately the storage area was deserted.

"Becky," I said, "what's wrong?"

She stood with her back toward me, reeking of disdain for the woman who had borne me. "Why don't you ask your girlfriend?" she said, so quietly I could hardly hear her.

"I don't have a girlfriend."

"Ray says you do."

"She's not my girlfriend."

"Is she your cousin?" she asked.

"Becky, I can explain."

She turned on me and pointed toward the emergency door. It was one of those kinds with an attached alarm.

"Get the hell out of here!" she screamed.

I recoiled at the words. I had never heard Becky cuss before. "Could I first tell you my side of the story?" I asked.

Her anger had enlarged her eyes, and I felt so small in them. "Your *story*," she said bitterly. "This is not one of your stupid games. I loved Ray. He was my boyfriend. We were happy together. And then you came along and set him up with that girl, who set me up . . ."

Becky didn't finish. Her head dropped to her chest, and tears slipped down her face onto her shirt. She appeared to be as ashamed as she was angry, ashamed that she could have been stupid enough to fall for my scheme. I wanted to tell her it wasn't my scheme, but I didn't think she'd be stupid enough to believe my story, even though it was the truth. I decided it would be best if I just left. I could go buy a bottle of sleeping pills or a good strong rope, I thought. I stepped to the emergency exit and put my hand on the bright red bar. But before I could leave, I had to turn and say something. It seemed required.

"I had a great time last night," I said.

Becky nodded. "So did I."

"Goodbye," I said. She chose not to answer. I went through the door and into the sunlight. An alarm went off at my back. I kept walking. I considered walking all the way home, and to hell with Kara. But it would have taken me ten hours to get there, and I was already exhausted. I returned to Kara's red Ferrari. She was pacing in front of the car. A squad car swept by on the adjoining street, no doubt on its way to the store.

"How did it go?" Kara asked.

"She knows."

"She knows what?" Kara demanded.

"What you did. That I was behind it."

"That's impossible."

"Yeah," I said.

"But you weren't behind it. I was."

"I suppose you could explain that to her right now," I said. "But considering that I just left, it might look kind of suspicious."

Kara slapped the hood of her car hard. "Dammit! There's no way she could have known."

"Ray told her," I said.

Kara jumped at that. "How could Ray have known?"

"I don't know." I opened the door on the passenger side. "Please drive me home. I don't feel so good."

Kara slammed the door shut before I could get in. She was shook, and it showed.

"We have to find out what happened," she said. "Don't you see, Mark? I have to know before I can leave."

"Why don't you just leave and not worry about my love life? I'll send you a postcard that explains it all."

Kara's expression was pinched with pain. "You blame me."

I sighed. "No," I said honestly. "I blame myself. I blame God. He has a weird sense of humor."

"God," Kara muttered to herself. She stared in the direction of the store. It was a long stare. Her breath was ragged and her lips were trembling, and then she wasn't breathing at all and her lips were white and bloodless. "Ray," she whispered.

"I doubt he'll want to go out with you again," I said.

Kara broke out of her trance and grabbed my hands. There was real fear in her eyes now. "We have to go see him," she said.

"No, I don't think so. I think I should go back to bed."

Kara let go of my hands and hurried around to the driver's side. She hadn't heard me. "Get in," she said. "He'll be at the bookstore. We'll go there. He can tell me what happened."

"He might just kill you," I warned, opening the car door.

Kara didn't hear that, either.

We spent the drive to the mall listening to the radio. Every station was playing commercials. I felt so flat that I wondered if the music didn't just sound like commercials. My depression was so deep that there was no room for anger or blame. I tried to tell Kara it was all right, that she should just go off with Vincent and be happy on Saturn or Jupiter or wherever she was going. I tried to reach over and give her a reassuring pat on the leg. My hand bumped into the stick. She was shifting into fifth, running a red light at ninety miles an hour. If she was trying to kill us, I decided not to complain.

By the time we reached the mall, I had decided I'd better accompany her inside. She wasn't in favor of the idea.

"Are you crazy?" she asked.

"You're in no position to ask such a question," I said. "Why are we here? To ask Ray how he found out what you were up to? I warned you about that before. You met him at the mall for your date. You were driving a Ferrari. I drove a Ferrari when I went out with Becky. Who cares if it was a different color? It's a very unusual car for someone our age to have. If they talked, it could easily have come up. Then they could have become suspicious."

Kara shook her head. "She wouldn't have talked to him after she found out he was cheating on her."

"How do you know?"

"I know her."

"How?"

"Don't ask."

"But what if he called her?" I asked.

"Impossible. What happened to you this morning when you called?" Kara opened the door on her side. "Stay here. I'll be back in a few minutes."

"No." I stared at her. "No."

"You're the one he'll try to kill, Mark. There's more here than meets the eye. I have to talk to him alone."

"Then you can talk to him after I do."

Kara gave in. We went into the bookstore together. A young girl at the cash register told us Ray was working in the back. I tried to think of a nice way to introduce myself. Kara held my hand as we walked to the rear of the store. I shook her off. I wanted both hands free.

It didn't do me a bit of good.

We knocked on the door. Ray answered. He peered at us for a moment. Then his handsome face twisted into something that wasn't so handsome, and I caught a blur of fist out of the corner of my left eye. He was quick. I didn't even have a chance to raise my arm to block the punch. It caught me square on the nose. I dropped to my knees, blood spurting over my white

T-shirt. I had worn the same shirt while I had lain in bed the night before with Becky. My vision went as red as my blood, but the fight had already been knocked out of me. He was a strong son of a bitch.

Kara came to my rescue, which I thought fitting. She jumped at Ray and shoved him back into boxes of books. She was trying to calm him down, but she might have used too much force. He shoved her away with one of his powerful arms, and she landed on her butt. A pity. Ray now had the chance to punch me again. He came after me and all I could do was watch.

"Ray," Kara cried, "it's not him."

Ray hesitated. I prayed the blood on my face had made me unrecognizable and that he had a short memory. Then it struck me that he must have had an incredible memory to associate me with the night he had asked Kara out. It didn't make sense that he knew automatically that I was the one who had been out with Becky, unless she had described me to him, which seemed unlikely. Kara got to her feet.

"Leave him alone," she told Ray. "We just want to talk to you."

"This isn't the guy who tried to steal my girlfriend?" Ray demanded.

"Your girlfriend?" Kara said. "You told me you didn't have a girlfriend."

Ray was not ashamed. "You didn't tell me you had a scheming partner."

"I'm not a scheming partner," I mumbled.

"Who the hell are you?" Ray turned and asked me.

"A friend of Becky's," I said. I have lousy timing, I really do. Ray drew back his fist and stepped forward. Kara grabbed hold of his arm and rode it several feet in the air.

"You have to listen to us, you idiot!" she yelled.

Ray stopped to listen. Even with an open vein inside my nose pumping out my life's blood, I couldn't help but be fascinated by the way Ray and Kara related to each other, like an old couple who were fed up with each other. Obviously, though, I wasn't nearly as perceptive as Ray. He turned toward Kara and his jaw dropped open.

"What happened to your accent?" he asked.

"That's right," I said. Kara was no longer the sweet Scottish lass. Indeed, she now sounded exactly like someone who had been born and raised in southern California. Kara stared at each of us before answering. It wasn't much of an answer.

"Never mind" was all she said.

"Who the hell are you?" Ray demanded of her.

"Yeah," I seconded. Kara was not intimidated.

"Who the hell told you about me?" she asked Ray.

"Why should I tell you?" Ray said.

Kara sucked in a hissing breath, and it was filled with cold vapors. But it was not directed at Ray. She had turned away to face the wall. Ray glanced at me and I shook my head. Suddenly he and I were in this together. Neither of us could see Kara's face.

"He was here," she whispered.

"Who was here?" I asked.

"Are you talking about Frederick?" Ray asked. "You know him? I guess you do. Yeah, he told me about you two slimes."

"When?" Kara asked.

"Last night," Ray said. "He came in the store. He's my kind of guy. He got right to the point about you two, didn't mess around." Ray threw me a wicked look. "He told me to watch out for you."

I raised my hands in a gesture of submission and got up slowly. Ray watched me the whole way. Obviously, this Frederick didn't have a high opinion of me. Ray put his hand on his sport coat pocket, and it made me wonder just how bad the opinion had been. Yet at the moment Kara was more my concern. She had been upset before, but now she was trembling.

"Let's get out of here," I told her, gently touching my nose and coming away with a handful of blood. "Come on, Kara."

Kara slowly turned back to Ray. She moved toward him as if in a dream—the information about Frederick's visit had obviously shocked her. She took a deep breath, as if to steady herself.

"If Frederick comes back," she said to Ray, her accent apparently gone for good, "be careful. He's dangerous, more dangerous than you can imagine."

Ray snorted. "You can't tell me anything, bitch. I just met him but at least I know he's honest."

Kara nodded faintly. "As honest as a loaded gun."

Again Ray's hand strayed to his coat pocket. He stopped himself when he realized what he was doing. Kara smiled thinly at him and shook her head; then she crossed the room. She took my hand and we left the store—out the back way, through another emergency exit, setting off another alarm.

Once outside, Kara didn't stop to look at my nose or comment on the loss of her Scottish accent. She walked away swiftly, pulling out her cell phone as she went. I followed her as best I could, using the hem of my T-shirt for a handkerchief. But it's no easy task trying to chase after someone while keeping your head tilted back. By the time I caught up with her, she had already made her call and given up on getting an answer.

"Vincent's not home," she said.

"So?" I asked.

"He should be home. There's no reason for him to be out."

"Maybe he went to the store," I suggested.

She was upset. "Vincent doesn't go to stores!"

"Never?"

She grabbed my hand. It seemed she was always doing that, dragging me places I did not want to go. "Hurry," she said. "We have to go home."

"But I want to go back to bed."

"Mark!" she cried. "Vincent could be in trouble."

I stopped. "Is this Frederick really that bad?"

Her face seemed to fall all the way to her shaking knees. "Worse."

We hurried to the car. On the way to her house, I tried to find out about Frederick and about Kara's new nationality, but I got nowhere. I tried not to bleed on the Ferrari's upholstery. I wasn't really worried about Vincent, although I suppose I should have been. I wondered if Ray had, in fact, been carrying a gun in his jacket.

The door to the house was wide open. Kara barely stopped the car before jumping out and flying toward the porch. By now I had recovered somewhat. I caught up with her before she could enter.

"Me first," I said firmly, a hand on her arm. "No arguments."

Kara agreed. Leaving her on the porch, I stepped through the front door and into silence. Everything appeared to be normal, but nothing *felt* normal. The house rang with the hollow vibration that coffins must suffer after a visit from graverobbers. Yes, even before I saw it, the house reminded me of a coffin. An empty box that only sorrow could fill.

"Vincent?" I called.

I found it in the kitchen. It was all that I could do not to vomit. I was already covered with my own blood, but this blood touched me deeper, deep in that part where our mortality lives. For the second time in less than an hour I dropped to my knees. I would have prayed for another blow to my face to take the place of the pain I suffered in that moment, if only I believed the prayer would be answered.

The blood was all over the countertop, dripping drop by slow drop onto the floor. Right away I knew the surprise had been left there for me, as much as for Kara. It was obvious. Frederick's wicked stab was too personal to be understood in any other light. He must have known all about me, too. And what he knew must not have pleased him.

Sitting on the white-tiled countertop was a human heart— impaled on a shiny steel knife.

Chapter Ten

When the smoke finally cleared and Kara and I could think again and look with eyes that wouldn't close at the bloody sight, we decided the heart had not belonged to Vincent. It was old—it smelted of formaldehyde. It could have been stolen from a medical-school supply room, or even possibly swiped out of a high school biology class. But the blood was fresh, and God knew where Frederick had obtained it, although it was probably from an animal. It didn't have the consistency of human blood, and I had a fair amount of the latter available on my shirt with which to make a comparison.

Kara went to search for Vincent in the cave even though she knew it was hopeless. She didn't allow me to accompany her. She told me to stay and rest my heart. She had never before indicated that she knew about my heart trouble. I washed up and changed into some of Vincent's clothes. I sat at Vincent's desk and turned on his computer game. I don't know what I was looking for, maybe for some hidden message that would give me a clue to his whereabouts. It was Kara's belief that Frederick had kidnapped Vincent. But there was no clue on the computer, only the same old game. And the strange lights that came when the war was over. I played it through to the end just to see the lights. I was trying to figure out how the game was supposed to continue with them in the picture, when Kara interrupted me.

"He's not in the cave," she said.

She staggered into the room and plopped down on the chair beside me. She was through crying for the time, but she was still terribly distraught. She had insisted we burn the heart in the fireplace, although I wanted to save it for the police. The red stain from it still colored her hands.

"Maybe it's not as bad as it looks," I said.

"You don't know Frederick," she said.

"Tell me about him."

"I can't."

"Then you'll be telling the police about him."

"Is that a threat?" she asked, too spent to be angry.

"It's a good idea. Whoever this guy is, he's got to be weird. I don't understand you, Kara. I'm worried."

"The police can't help us."

"You don't know that," I said. "Give them a chance."

"You don't understand."

"Christ!" I swore, slapping my leg. "I am sick and tired of hearing remarks like that. You don't know. You don't understand. Only I know. *What* do you know? And what are you saving this knowledge up for? Vincent's welcome-home party? If this Frederick is as wicked as you and that mess on the counter indicate, then you won't be having that party soon, sister, unless you start talking to me or the police right now."

Kara looked at me with exhausted eyes. "You're right, Mark. It's time to tell all."

I sat back in my chair, surprised. "Who's Frederick?"

"It's a long story," she replied, not being evasive this time, her eyes straying to the game. Surprise crossed her face when she saw the lights gathered about the space station. "He put in the ships."

"Yes," I said. "Vincent said they were important."

"They are," Kara smiled faintly at the irony of something that I hoped she would soon reveal. "Everything is important. There is a reason for everything. Do you believe that, Mark?"

"On a good day."

She nodded. "You're like me in that way. You need proof, something you can see with your own eyes. Vincent's not like that. He trusts in the moment. He knows everything's going to be fine, and even if it isn't, he doesn't mind." She paused, a brief spasm of grief causing her right cheek to twitch. "But I shouldn't talk about the differences between you two. You both have incredible imaginations. You can imagine the strangest things and then bring them to life in your games, making them seem perfectly believable. I'm curious, Mark, were you ever able to win Vincent's game?"

"No. That's the problem with it. There is no way to win."

"Oh, but there is a way."

"What is it?" I asked.

She stared at the lights again. She appeared indecisive. "Never mind. I have to tell you about Frederick and Vincent and me."

"Please," I said, my impatience growing as rapidly as my concern. I didn't know why I hadn't called the police while she was hiking to the cave. In kidnappings I knew time was of the essence.

Kara nodded again at my prompting. She appeared to be on the verge of starting her tale when she suddenly reached out and touched my knee.

"How do you feel?" she asked.

"Horrible."

"What do you mean? Are you sick?"

"No. But with what's going on, how could I feel anything but horrible?"

"You don't feel dizzy or anything?" she asked. "Like you did when we were all together at the telescope?"

"No."

"You're sure?"

"Yes."

She relaxed slightly. "At least we have that going for us."

"I don't think I'm the one we should be worried about right now."

Kara gazed straight into my eyes. She had removed her contacts. I wondered if they had just been another prop, like her Scottish accent. Maybe now she no longer felt the need for them. Her eyes were no longer bright blue, but soft brown.

"That's not true," she said. "How you feel matters most of all."

"Who is Frederick?" I asked, tired of the riddles.

"My husband."

"What?"

"He's my husband, but Frederick's not his real name."

"Since when are you married?"

"I've been married a long time," she said.

I tried to digest the news. "This is some kind of joke, right?"

"No joke," she said.

"How old are you?"

"How old do I look?"

"My age," I said.

She considered a moment. "You could say that's a fair estimate." Then she changed the subject without expanding on the matter. "Mark, I have a story to tell you. Could you please just listen to it and not ask me what it has to do with our predicament until I finish?"

"What kind of story is it?"

"A science-fiction one."

"Don't tell me. You're from another planet. You're an alien whose flying saucer has run out of plutonium fuel. You need my help to break into a nuclear-power plant and steal uranium rods from the core so that you can get back home."

Kara was not amused. "What if that was my story? What would you do?"

"Nothing. I'd call the police and tell them that I believe a friend of mine has been kidnapped. But I'd probably keep an eye on you from then on."

Kara sighed. "The story I have to tell you is far stranger than the one of your alien."

"Is it a true story?" I asked.

"It depends on your point of view."

"Don't play games with me, Kara."

"I don't mean to, but my story is much like Vincent's game. Only it starts before World War Three. It's about a woman and two men. I have to tell it mainly from the woman's point of view. Could you please just listen? Please, Mark?"

"I'm listening," I said.

Kara stared out over the city. Even with the normal layer of Los Angeles smog, it looked peaceful. Of course a thousand people were murdered in L.A. each year. One more death was not going to change the destiny of the world, I thought. It was a bitter thought, a result of the frustration I felt at just sitting and doing nothing while Vincent was in danger.

"There was this girl," Kara began. "She was intelligent, pretty—she had a lot going for her. She had big plans for her life. She was going to go to college, then medical school. She planned to be a famous doctor and help people the world over. And she did end up attending college, but she never became a doctor. She married too young, to a man who was also ambitious, too ambitious to have time for his wife's dreams. It's an old story, I know, but it's also new. It happens all the time.

"Anyway, she married this guy and played the role of the good wife while he joined the service. I realize that doesn't sound like the beginning of an exciting career—signing up for a stretch in the air force. But this woman's husband was smart. The air force recognized his abilities. They sent him to school, and he earned degrees in both nuclear engineering and aeronautics. He rose swiftly through the ranks: lieutenant, captain, colonel. He was hardly forty when they made him a general. It seemed that nothing could stop his rise to power.

"Except maybe his wife. His wife was not happy. It's hard to say why. Being the wife of a general carries many benefits with it. She had a nice house, plenty of money, and friends, but she didn't love her husband. I guess that's reason enough not to be happy. What's even sadder is that she probably never loved him, not even when she married him. But if anyone asked her why she didn't divorce him, she couldn't have answered. She had a feeling, though, even before her thirtieth birthday, that it was already too late for her. That she would never be happy, no matter what she did.

"The husband was not satisfied with the marriage either. He knew his wife didn't love him, and it drove him crazy. But he wasn't any better. He didn't love her either. He didn't love anybody. He was too busy to love anyone. He had to save the world from the enemy. He was a military man to the core. As far as he was concerned, there was always an enemy out there somewhere to be destroyed.

"Still, he was extremely attached to his wife. He couldn't make a decision without her. But he never listened to her. I know this sounds contradictory. He would get an opinion from her, then argue with her for several days about how foolish that opinion was, and then do exactly what he wanted, regardless of what his wife recommended. Then, if things didn't work out, he would blame her for confusing him with all her talk. He blamed her for everything all the time, for stalling his career at every juncture. Even though he was a general in his early forties, he was far from satisfied. He wanted to be the most powerful man on earth. He wanted to be president of the United States.

"He didn't make it to president. But when he was in his late fifties, he was put in command of America's newest space station. There had been others prior to this one, but they didn't count for the general because they weren't armed. They had no missiles, no destructive lasers. But this new space station was loaded to the max. All by itself, it could have taken out the whole world.

"I have to pause here to say something about the political climate of the day. In a sense, it was better than what we have in our present society. China was the only major communist country left. There were far fewer missiles. Disarmament programs had succeeded in shrinking the stockpiles for thirty years. It gave the world a false sense of security. As a wise man once pointed out, you only need one bullet to blow someone's brains out. So we could only blow each other up once? We would still be dead.

"Anyway, this space station was supposed to be a secret, a kind of hidden life-insurance policy. God only knows who thought up the idea, but our general was its biggest supporter. The armaments aboard the station were deftly hidden. Officially, it was a scientific facility. What a joke. The missiles may have been hidden from the American people, but they were well known to the other side. And the space station made the other side very uneasy. For God's sake, it drifted right over China several times a day.

"Through quiet diplomatic channels, China tried to have it brought down. They were having enough troubles at home and didn't want a major confrontation. Our side said no, or rather, they denied there were arms on board. Of course, they wouldn't let the enemy board this innocent scientific facility to see how unarmed and safe it was.

"I say that sarcastically. In a way the space station was safer than any place on earth. Its lasers could destroy any incoming missiles, and it had a respectable force field that, once activated, made the station all but impervious to laser attack. Our general felt quite secure riding in it among the stars. He felt so secure he even brought his wife up to join him. Maybe he had begun to get a little worried about what he and his like-minded cohorts had started rolling down on good old planet earth. The other side refused to let the space station question rest. They issued an ultimatum: Take down that damn space station. You know how ultimatums are. They make everyone nervous. People do weird things when they're nervous. They don't think clearly. They begin to think things they've never thought before."

"Someone pushed the button?" I interrupted.

Kara nodded with effort. "Yes."

"Who?"

"I don't know. Their side. Our side. Does it matter?"

"What happened?" I asked.

Kara shrugged. Her voice came out weak. "There was a war and everyone died."

"Like in Vincent's game?"

"Yes."

"Did the space station survive the war undamaged?"

"No," Kara said. "It was damaged, and several crew members died in the battle. The force field didn't work as well as it was supposed to. The hull was breached in two places. Some people were swept right out into space. A few others were burned to cinders in seconds. But the station survived. The other stations—the actual scientific establishments—did not. They were blown out of the sky in the first five minutes of the war. They didn't stand a chance."

Kara paused again. Throughout her narration, she had kept her eyes fixed on the view out Vincent's bedroom window. She didn't look away now, but somehow, watching her as I was, I had the uncanny sensation that her view was no longer the same as mine. She was seeing the city through entirely different eyes. Nothing she had said had upset me. It was just a story, after all. But this look on her face disturbed me in ways the bloody heart in the kitchen had not. It was a look of total despair.

"The world was dead, Mark," she said finally. "Oh, there were some people alive, walking around down there, but they were goners. If the radiation didn't kill them, the coming ice age would. It would come fast. The bombs had thrown so much dust and smoke into the air that the people in the station couldn't even get a glimpse of the earth anymore. Yet there were these eerie orange glows in places. It was the fires burning beneath the smoke. There was no one to put them out. They just kept burning and burning, and you would stare at one of them and wonder if it was Paris or London or Los Angeles . . ."

Kara began to cry softly. I left her in peace. I couldn't very well console her by telling her that none of it had happened. She knew that. She wasn't crazy. But I did begin to wonder if the shock of Vincent's kidnapping had momentarily thrown her. I believed in the kidnapping. I had a burned heart lying in the fireplace for evidence.

But that look on Kara's face wouldn't go away. Nor would the disquiet it brought to my own heart. It was amazing, I thought, what she had said about the radiation and the ice age. Vincent had said the same things when he had first shown me his game—almost word for word. Another coincidence. They kept piling up like a growing snowball rushing out of control toward a blazing fire. Something had to break. I could feel it. Either the fires Kara was weeping over had to be put out or the snow would come, and never mind that in her story one brought the other.

"Kara," I said finally, gently, after a couple of minutes had gone by. "We've got to find Vincent."

She nodded and sniffed once. "We can find him."

"Do you know where he is?"

"No. You do."

"Huh?" I said.

"You can locate him."

"How?"

"I have to finish my story. Then you'll understand."

"But we don't have time for it right now."

"Please, Mark, you promised me you'd listen."

I took a deep breath and counted to ten as psychologists recommend. I could have counted to a hundred and turned blue and my anxiety still wouldn't have gone away. "Go on," I told her.

Kara sat up straight in her chair and gave me her full attention. Apparently the city no longer interested her, and I think it was because in her story it was no longer there. As she wiped away her tears, I thought how weird it was that I had taken only a moment to get used to her eyes being brown instead of blue. It was as if they had always been brown and I just hadn't noticed.

"The space station remained largely intact," she said. "About one hundred people survived. A shuttle had been docked to the station at the outbreak of the war, but the battle had damaged it beyond repair. It didn't matter. There was nowhere left to land it, and even if there had been, there was no point. The people on the station were alone. They knew they were doomed. The station was large. It was powered by nuclear fusion. It had gardens aboard for growing food and replenishing the air supply, but the station was not self-sufficient. It needed regular supplies from below under the best of conditions, and with the vast loss of oxygen that occurred when the hull was breached, the people aboard could count the days till they smothered. They began to count. One day. Two days. One week. The time passed slowly. That's how it is when you're waiting to die."

"Did some commit suicide?" I asked, trying to show I was listening. Kara nodded.

"Some," she said. "But not many. Bad as things got, most of the people never gave up. They kept waiting—I can't say what for. There was this feeling that pervaded the space station that it simply couldn't end this way. It wasn't right that humanity should just disappear. It was hopeless—yes, we all knew that. Yet we had hope."

"We?"

She nodded again. "We."

"Who is we?" I asked as carefully as I could.

"Me and the others."

"You were aboard this space station?"

"Yes," she said, not blinking.

"What were you doing there?"

"I was married to the commander of the station."

"I see," I said.

"You don't have to believe me now, Mark. I don't mind."

"Thank you."

"Should I continue?"

I shifted uneasily. "If you want."

"Do you ever pray?" she asked.

"Very seldom."

"Who do you pray to when you do pray?"

"God," I said.

"But usually only when you have a problem, right?"

"Yeah, I suppose. I don't think about it a lot."

"Well, we had a problem. By the second week our air had gone bad. It stunk. You'd take a deep breath and feel like you got nothing out of it. You'd want to take another one right away, but you knew the effort was using up more oxygen than the deep breath was giving you in return. It was hard to be alive.

"What happened, finally, was that everyone gathered in the hub of the station. The space was cramped, but at least at the hub there was no gravity. You can squeeze a lot of people in a small room when they can float on top of one another. It was getting near the end. Some people were already beginning to lose consciousness. We figured we had maybe another six hours before we passed out. We had a discussion—it was really quite beautiful. We decided that we would pray until we died. Not to be saved, but to say we were sorry for having destroyed our world. Now, someone might view that cynically. Naturally we would not pray to be saved. There was no chance. Still, you had to have been there. We were all scared. None of us wanted to die. We could say what we wanted, but none of us knew what to expect on the other side, or if there even was another side. Nevertheless, we chose what I thought a dignified way to go out. We accepted our portion of the blame for what had happened. We accepted our punishment."

"Did your husband take part in this prayer?" I asked.

"No. He was too busy."

"Go on."

Kara closed her eyes. "I remember that time as if it were happening to me right now. Our prayer was mainly within— we didn't have much breath left to speak it out loud. We were all Americans, of course, but there were a variety of races aboard the station, a variety of beliefs. When we first began, some prayed aloud, in different tongues. I remember how the sound blended together and became one sound, one voice talking to God. It was very special, but sad, very sad, too.

"Then everything began to settle down. The six hours began to pass. Except for the wheeze of labored breathing, there was silence. I think I dozed for a while. I drifted from my spot to the end of the hub. There the station was equipped with wide circular windows. When I opened my eyes I could see the moon. It was full, and as the station rotated on its axis, the moon appeared to go up and down, up and down. It was hypnotic. It was like staring up at the moon in the nighttime sky while riding on the arm of an oil well."

"What did you say?" I asked, startled.

Kara opened her eyes. "An oil well. The kind that goes up and down. You know?"

"That's what Becky did when we were out on our date. She jumped on an oil well and almost got herself killed."

Kara was not surprised. She closed her eyes again. "I can still see that," she said. "It was a last impression. It went deep. It was near the end. The air was almost gone. I could hear each breath drag through my chest as if I were old and ill. I was old then. I could hear my heart. The beats were slowing down. The time between each one seemed to take as long as it took for the moon to come up again. But I had my eyes open. I was conscious. I had stopped praying. I was thinking about my life. I was thinking about you."

"Me?"

"Yes."

"Why would you think about me?" I asked.

"I remembered you."

"From when?"

"From long ago." Kara opened her eyes. "Look at me, Mark. Who do you see?"

"Kara."

"And who is Kara?"

"I don't know." A cold sweat had sprung out on my forehead. Suddenly I had the inexplicable sensation of being cornered and lost at the same time. "You're my friend."

"How did you feel when you met me?"

"Why are you asking me this?"

"How did you feel, Mark?"

I paused. "As if I knew you."

"You did know me, even though you didn't recognize me. I knew you wouldn't. I took precautions. I dyed my hair. I bought contacts. I changed my voice. I wore makeup that changed the contours of my face ever so slightly. But I think if I had done none of those things, you still wouldn't have recognized me. I don't think any of us can see something we don't believe is possible. Do you understand?"

"No."

"Did Becky ever tell you her first name?"

"No," I said.

"She would never tell anybody."

"That's right," I mumbled. I was having trouble breathing. The dimensions of the room seemed to have altered. The walls were closing in on me, while at the same time they were dissolving into a nothingness that stretched forever. I glanced anxiously to the right and the left to reassure myself I was where I was supposed to be. Suddenly I was afraid to look at Kara. Just the sight of her filled me with terror.

"Look at me, Mark. Who do you see?"

It was like a mystical command. I didn't want to obey, but I had to obey. My head turned in her direction. She leaned forward so her face was only inches from mine, and her eyes were all I could see. Those sweet brown eyes that had caught my attention the moment I walked into the electronics store.

"Oh, God," I whispered.

"Do you know what Becky's first name is?"

"Kara."

"That's right." Kara nodded and sat back in her chair. "I'm Becky. I'm from the future, Mark. I've come back for you."

Chapter Eleven

I t would be shameful for me to say I knew all along. It would, in another sense, also be correct. I was completely infatuated with Becky when I met Kara. But even when I became infatuated with Kara, I *consciously* understood that there was no conflict. I just didn't stop to think about why I felt no conflict. That's all. I never stopped to look at Kara. I never stopped to look at Becky, for that matter. I was too busy daydreaming about them. That's how it is for me with the people I love. They become unreal to me. I guess I like them better that way.

Still, now I had a *real* problem. I believed Kara all right, without a shadow of a doubt. The eyes, the voice, the face, the body—everything was the same. But she was talking about time travel and I hadn't even bothered to write a time travel computer game because the topic was simply too far out. My mind quickly jumped to the possibility of Becky's having an identical twin. Just as quickly I discarded it. Kara knew Becky as no twin could know a sister. They were the same person, I knew, and the laws of physics were simply going to have to understand.

What did I do when she made her incredible revelation? I just stared at the floor and went straight to the heart of the matter.

"Who's going to win the World Series in the year two thousand and twenty?" I asked.

Kara nodded. "You believe me."

"I don't know."

"It's me, Mark. It's Becky."

"What are you doing this Saturday night?"

She didn't smile. "I won't be here."

"Are you going back to the future?"

"Not exactly." She glanced at her watch. "I have to finish my story."

"All right."

She was concerned. "Are you all right?"

"No. But you were about to die. Tell me what happened."

She closed her eyes again, and as she did so, she looked older. Not physically, of course, but the experiences she had gone through were there in her face, her voice. I tried not to think about what that meant. I hadn't always been happy during my short stay on earth, but I'd never blamed the planet. I didn't want it to die any more than I wanted Vincent to die.

I didn't stop to ask myself who Vincent was.

"I was staring at the moon and thinking of you," Kara began. "I was thinking about how you used to come into the store and make me laugh. This wasn't the first time I had thought of you in all those years. During the first few years of my marriage, I'd sometimes sit and daydream about you for hours. I used to wonder where you were, what you were doing. I did that until I was about thirty."

"Why did you stop?"

Kara looked uncomfortable. She kept her eyes closed. "That'll become clear as I go along," she said.

"Okay," I said, not reassured by her response.

"The moon appears brighter seen from space. You would know this. The light doesn't have to go all the way through the earth's atmosphere. Staring at it as I was, however, it suddenly appeared as bright as the sun, which it never does, even in deep space. Yet the light did not hurt my eyes. I can't explain why. It was a cool white light. It blotted out everything else, even my fear of death. It seemed to surround the entire space station, to fill my head. All I could see, all I knew, was this great white light. And I felt such joy then. I can't tell you how it was. Everything was fine. Everything was perfect. It was the Illumni."

"The what?" I asked.

Kara opened her eyes. "You mean, the who. The Illumni are a superior race from another star system."

I sighed. "I knew aliens were going to come into this somehow."

Kara laughed softly. "The Illumni are not like the aliens you see in science-fiction movies. They don't even have bodies. They have evolved beyond a need for physical form."

"But what was this light you saw? Their bodies?"

"Their ships."

"Why do they need ships if they don't have bodies?"

Kara paused. "I never thought of that. It doesn't matter. They were there to help us."

"They should have come a few weeks earlier."

"They said they couldn't. They didn't say why. Anyway, I take that back. They weren't there to help us, but to give us the chance to help ourselves. This is important to understand. The Illumni do not think the same as we do. I don't know if they even have thoughts as we do. I'm not even sure they have individuality as we understand individuality. It didn't matter which one I communicated with—it was as if I was talking with all of them at the same time."

"They spoke English?" I asked.

"I use the word *talking* loosely. The Illumni communicate telepathically." Kara smiled. "It's difficult to describe what it's like to make mental contact with them. It's so incredibly delightful. You feel like you're with your best friend. You can say—I mean, you can think—anything, and they'll understand."

"How many did you personally communicate with?"

Kara paused again. "Only one, I believe."

"Then how can you say that communicating with one was like communicating with them all?" I asked.

"That was the impression I received when I talked with the other humans about the experience afterward. Is something wrong?"

"I was simply entertaining the idea that there may have been only one of them," I said.

"No, there were definitely many. Close to a hundred I'd say. But you've raised an interesting issue. I can't overemphasize this. From their point of view, everything is the same, everything is one. I know that sounds like a trite philosophical concept, but when you're with them, in contact with them, it seems the highest of truths, the answer to all questions. But they told us that this state of unity is not something that can be imagined. What I mean is, without the Illumni present, it's a meaningless idea."

"Do they have a God?"

"I never asked them."

"Why not?" I asked.

"It never occurred to me. What do you think so far?"

"I'm intrigued, Becky."

She made a face. "Don't call me that. I hate that name."

"Why did you hate the name Kara when you were younger?"

"I didn't. I loved it. I loved it so much that I only wanted those who truly loved me to know it."

"That's bizarre. Please go on with your story."

"The Illumni saved us for the time being," Kara said. "They

restored our oxygen supply. They went a big step further than that. They took a small part of the earth that had been totally devastated in the war and made it whole again, with trees and rivers and hills to walk in. They transported us there. They gave us a tiny paradise where we could rest for a while and heal ourselves from the trauma of the war."

"Where on earth was this place?"

"Right here."

"Los Angeles?" I asked.

"Yes. Why? Does that surprise you?"

"Because you grew up in L.A. Were you the one who chose the spot?"

"No. But why shouldn't it have been here? Here is as good a place as any."

"I suppose. It just strikes me as an amazing coincidence. "

"Other people aboard the station also grew up in Los Angeles. "

"Fine," I said. "I shouldn't keep interrupting."

"I don't mind. You have such a sharp intellect. Your questions help me understand the whole thing better." Kara glanced out the window in the direction of our path into the hills and the secret cave. She smiled again and now it seemed the memory of better days was at hand.

"The Illumni are miracle workers," she continued. "You probably know this, but the Los Angeles basin, with all its aerospace industries, is a prime target in a war. This place was hit with God knows how many warheads. No one survived, and the hills you see here were burned to ash. But in a matter of days the Illumni caused them to bloom with grass and flowers. You should have seen the trees. They grew with each passing hour, with long slender blue and green and red branches. The leaves were like individual watercolor paintings. I used to pluck them and carry a handful as I went for my walks—they smelled like flowers. Even when they dropped to the ground, they never shriveled and died. It was like being in heaven."

"What did your general husband think of all this?" I asked.

"I didn't spend much time with him after the Illumni arrived."

"You went to court and got a divorce?"

"Had there been a court left standing I would have. But, no, I was busy with someone else. Do you know who that was?"

"Vincent," I said.

"In a manner of speaking. Mark, now we come to a very delicate subject. It's important that what I tell you next doesn't upset you. This is what happened but it's not what has to happen."

"I doubt anything could upset me after World War Three."

"How about your future?"

I shrugged. "I assume I went up in flames with everyone else."

Kara's expression was grave. "You weren't alive for World War Three."

I swallowed. I felt kind of sick. "That's okay. I never liked fighting anyway." Then I considered a moment. "Wait a second. How do you know what happened to me? You never had contact with me."

"The Illumni told me."

"How did they know?" I asked.

"They know everything."

"Are you serious? Everything?"

"I shouldn't say that," Kara replied. "I can't speak for them. But their knowledge seemed to me to have no limits. However, it was not as if they answered every question put to them. Half the time they didn't respond one way or the other."

"But they told you about me?"

"Yes."

"How old was I when I died?" I asked.

"It doesn't have to be this way, Mark. It shouldn't be this way."

"How old?"

"Twenty-nine."

I coughed. "The good always die young."

"Mark."

"Was it my heart?"

"Yes," Kara said.

"You've known about my heart?"

"Yes."

I nodded. I believed her. Actually, when I thought about it, I was surprised I'd made it that long. Twenty-nine. Christ, I had only about ten years left.

Then it really hit me, and it was not something I could laugh off. My eyes started to get all teary. It was totally humiliating. I didn't want to cry in front of Kara. But this horribly sad feeling swept over me right then, as cold as a gust of wind blowing off a glacier. I'd had it before, but not this bad. I wanted my mother. She had given me life, and now I wanted her to stop the future from taking my life away. But my mother was not there. She had never been there for me. Neither had my father. All I had was Kara. She reached for my hand and I let her take it and stroke it. I wanted to stop trembling. Only I couldn't stop trembling any more than I could have willed my heart to beat when it wanted to stop. My chest suddenly felt constricted, and I was afraid my heart was going to stop right then, that I was going to die in my girlfriend's arms before I had a chance to be her boyfriend.

But I didn't die. Kara held on to me, and slowly my premature grave was covered over in my mind and I was able to sit straight and not shake. I wiped at my face. I was embarrassed.

"I'm sorry," I said.

"It's okay," she said, her face pressed close to mine.

"It just hit me all of a sudden."

"I understand."

I forced a chuckle. "You know what they say about someone walking over your grave."

"No one's going to walk over yours," Kara promised, sitting back in her chair. "You're not going to die at twenty-nine.

Let me continue with my story. While we walked in our tiny corner of paradise, the Illumni came to us with an offer, a chance to save our world."

"By going back in time?" I asked, my breathing still not steady. I couldn't get rid of the feeling that I had just seen my tombstone, complete with inscribed dates.

"Yes. They made us a fascinating offer. They said we could go back to any point in our lives for exactly one lunar cycle— approximately one month—and try to change the course of our lives in such a way that the history of the world would also be changed. Remember, we're talking about fewer than a hundred people. It was—is—a tall order. Particularly since we were forbidden to try to convince the populace as a whole that we were from the future. For example, we can't bring out technology from the future or take advantage of the stock market or such things. We were told we had to work in secret."

"Did they tell you what would happen if you didn't?"

"No. But I received the impression it would be a serious mistake."

"But your telling me this story is a violation of that order."

"It wasn't an order," Kara said. "The Illumni never order anything. They cherish free will above all else. It was simply strong advice." Kara paused, worried. "Do you think I've gone against their advice? You're not the population."

"If they're as highly evolved as you say, I'm sure they'll forgive you."

Kara thought for a moment before continuing, tugging on her beautiful blond hair, which I now knew was really brown.

"Yeah," she said. "Anyway, I was alone on a hill when my Illumni made this offer. It both excited and depressed me. I didn't know what to do, which Becky to go back to. The Illumni really wanted us to influence, not the world, but the world through an earlier version of ourselves. Do you understand?"

"Yes. They wanted you to take care of yourself first."

"Exactly. I expressed my confusion to the Illumni. I can't say she told me what to do, but I do believe she guided me."

"She?" I asked.

"Yes. I think it was a she."

"The Illumni don't have bodies but they have gender?"

"Yes," Kara said. "What's wrong with that?"

"I don't know. I've never met an alien."

"Someday you will. As I was saying, the Illumni guided me in the direction of love. What could I do that would bring greater love to the world? This question seemed the only one worth asking. You see what I'm getting at? Before I opened myself up to this guidance, when I thought about how to save the world, my mind naturally went to the different ways to bring about greater peace between the superpowers. But in the Illumni's presence, such ideas appeared childish. I knew I couldn't go back in time and get Becky to quit her job at the electronics store and join a protest group." Kara paused. "Then you came to mind. I thought, what if I had married you instead of Ray?"

"You married Ray?" I asked, startled.

"Yes. He was the general. I thought you knew that by now."

"I didn't."

"You look shocked," Kara said.

"He's a jerk."

"I know," she said.

"Why did you marry him?"

"I made a mistake."

I shook my head. "This alien and time travel stuff maybe I believe you. But Becky getting married to Ray—that's horrible."

"Are you disappointed in me?"

"Yes."

Kara looked hurt. "Well, you didn't offer to marry me."

"What are you talking about? You wouldn't even go out with me."

"You asked me at a bad time."

"I asked you a dozen times," I said.

"If you had dressed a little better when you came into the store, maybe I would have said yes."

"Becky doesn't care how I dress."

"*I'm* Becky, Mark, I care."

I stopped. "You have a point there. You really didn't like the way I dressed?"

"I told you. You looked as if your mother had bought your clothes."

"Okay. Enough," I said. "I need a black leather jacket and a black Ferrari. What were we talking about?"

"Who I should have married. When I was with the Illumni, I thought that if I could go back in time and somehow get Becky together with you, I could change my life for the better and thereby make the world a better place."

"And then there wouldn't be a war?" I asked.

"Yes."

"That sounds a little farfetched to me."

"The Illumni didn't seem to think so," Kara said.

"Why did you think I would make such a difference in your life? Was it just a feeling?"

"It was a feeling and something more," Kara said. "Before coming back to this time, I had a chance to spend time with you."

"What? When? I thought the deal was that you could only go back in time once?"

"I got to spend time with you after the war."

"But I was dead," I protested.

"You were dead. You were dead and buried. But you were buried in a special manner. Mark, do you know how people sometimes have themselves frozen after they're dead in the hope that in the future a way will be found to revive them?"

"Yes. It's a ridiculous idea."

Kara hesitated. "Why?"

"Because of what is known as the 'ice barrier.' Practically every liquid in the universe shrinks when it is frozen. Water's unique. It expands. The human body is largely composed of water. When people have themselves frozen, the water in every cell in their bodies expands and ruptures every cell wall. These people don't simply need to be thawed out and revived, they need to be regrown."

"What if I were to tell you that ten years from now this ice barrier will be overcome?" Kara asked.

"Is that true? Was this discovery made before the war?"

"It must have been."

"Was it or wasn't it?" I asked. "If the discovery was made, you would have read about it."

Kara looked doubtful. "I didn't read about it, but then, I didn't keep up with science, except as far as it influenced Ray's career. But if there is an ice barrier, as you say, then it must have been overcome."

"How can you be sure?" I asked.

"When you died, you had yourself frozen," Kara said.

"I did? I did not. I would never do that. The idea disgusts me."

"Would it disgust you if you knew there was a chance you could be successfully revived in a future time when your heart defect could be fixed?"

"Yes," I said.

"Don't give me a hard time."

"A hard time? I'm the one you're turning into a Popsicle here."

"It happened, Mark."

It wasn't fair, I thought, having to argue with someone from the future. "All right," I said. "I had myself frozen. Obviously I defrosted when the bombs went off."

"Not at all. All frozen bodies were kept above the Arctic Circle. You were unaffected."

"Why?"

"It's cold up there," Kara said simply.

"Wait a second. What are you getting at here? Did your Illumni thaw me out so you could have another look at me and decide whether you wanted to go to the movies with me after all?"

"More or less. But it wasn't my Illumni who did the actual revival. It was another."

"Why?"

"I don't know."

"How old were you when I was defrosted?" I asked.

Kara hit me. "You have a nerve. You were a corpse! I looked great well into my fifties."

"I've always liked older women. How did I look?"

"Like Vincent."

"I don't understand."

"Yes, you do," Kara said.

Another time to stop and reflect. Another time to feel the pain in my chest, to cry at what might have been and what would be. But I did none of these things. Instead, I smiled, all the way down into my heart. I smiled because I had adored

Vincent the moment I met him. Because he was so neat. I didn't mind that I'd become like him. There was no one else I could think of that I would want to be.

Kara nodded in understanding. She was reading my mind again. The Illumni had obviously taught her a trick or two.

"I understand," I said.

"It was fun walking in these hills with you."

I was embarrassed. "I bet Ray loved it."

A shadow fell across Kara's face. "He didn't. But not until I saw that bloody heart in the kitchen did I understand how much it must have bothered him."

"Was there no one he wanted the Illumni to thaw out?"

"Please don't joke about this, Mark."

"I'm sorry."

"I have very little left to say, but what I have left is crucial," Kara went on. "With you by my side, my decision to return to the time that you first entered my life became even more apparent. Vincent agreed to go with me. Together we made plans to get you and Becky together."

Something about that didn't ring true. "But Vincent didn't approve of your plan to sabotage Becky's relationship with Ray."

"Why do you say that?" Kara asked.

"I thought it was obvious. He never really supported it."

Kara frowned. "He supported it."

I shrugged. "You'd know better than I."

"Maybe not. You're Vincent." Kara shook her head. "We

talked about it and he said he wanted us to be together for our whole lives."

"Maybe it was just the way you went about it that he didn't like. You know, trying to make the end justify the means and all that stuff."

"I don't know what you mean," Kara said, and I believed I might have insulted her.

"You sort of pressed the issue," I said as delicately as I could.

"What would you have done? I had only a month."

"I don't know," I said.

"No. Tell me. I want to know."

"Did you ask Vincent what he would have done?"

"I told you, we discussed it," Kara said.

"Yes. But did you ask his opinion?"

"Of course." Kara hesitated. "Well, he knew what I was going to do. He didn't try to stop me."

"Maybe he didn't want to interfere with your free will," I said, the strangest feeling coming over me at the comment, as if I had just solved the riddle once and for all. A pity I didn't know what the riddle was. "Please finish your story."

"Very well," Kara said, apparently content to let the matter rest. "We decided to go back to a month ago from today. I felt that Becky would have known you long enough by then. And if a bad situation were to arise between her and Ray, she'd go out with you. The Illumni told us that when we came back we'd be the same age as you two. It makes sense, I suppose. The Illumni had no inhibitions about giving us spending money for our trip. We brought back a sack of precious gems. Vincent and I sold them right away and bought this house and the cars."

"Do you know the principle upon which their time machine works?"

"No."

"Damn." I was disappointed. "Not even a clue?"

Kara smiled. "Have you seen *The Wizard of Oz*?"

"Who hasn't?"

"Remember the part at the end when the good witch helps Dorothy to return home? Dorothy closes her eyes and repeats, 'There's no place like home. There's no place like home.' Basically that's what we did. We focused our minds on this time. We had to do it in that cave on the hill. Maybe that's where the Illumni keep their time machine. Vincent and I came into this time from out of that cave. I remember it was a sunny day. The city was alive with millions of people. It was great to be back."

"Is the Illumni time machine present in the cave now?" I asked.

Kara raised an eyebrow. "An interesting question. I never thought about it. We never actually saw it before we left, although we felt it at work. I suppose it could be there even now. The inside of the cave does have a timeless quality about it."

"Wait a second, I'm confused. If the time machine is not there, how are you going to get back to the future?"

"I'm not going back," Kara said.

"But you spoke of going away on a long trip. Weren't you talking about returning to the future?"

"No. Do you know what it means to violate causality?"

I was familiar with the topic from all the science fiction I had read. It was the main problem scientists had with the concept of time travel. It was why they thought it was impossible. Simply put, the problem read: How can something go back to the past and affect its future in such a way as to prevent its backward journey through time? Science-fiction writers tended to phrase the dilemma by asking how someone could go back in time and kill his own grandmother. If the man in question kills his grandmother at a young enough age, then his own mother will never be born, and then he'll never be born. The end result being, of course, that it would then be impossible for him to kill his grandmother in the first place. It all got very confusing.

"Yes," I told Kara. "I'm familiar with the paradoxes. But from what you've said, the Illumni are giving you a chance to change what's to be, and never mind how the future is affected."

"That's right," she said. "But think what that means. There can be only one Kara in the future. She'll be someone else. I hope she'll be a happier Kara in a happier world. But there'll be nowhere for me to go *back* to."

"But what will happen to you?" I asked.

"I will cease to exist."

"When?"

"When the moon is full."

"The moon is full tonight!"

"I know."

I was upset. "You're going to die?"

Kara smiled sadly. "I don't think there's any death, not anymore. In some time, someplace, I'll always be alive. Don't grieve for me, Mark. We're going to be spending the rest of our lives together."

"But it won't be with the you who's you," I protested.

"What would you prefer? The future I lived? The one you didn't get a chance to live?"

"I'll still die when I'm twenty-nine," I said. "Becky's not a heart surgeon. She can't save me."

"The Illumni don't agree. They say the ultimate cause of physical weakness is unhappiness. You'll be happy with Becky."

"But the defect in my heart is congenital," I said. "It's not simply going to go away."

"I didn't say it would. But you have the defect now and you're alive. The reason you died at the age of twenty-nine was that the loneliness of your life finally wore you down. Trust me on this. Trust the Illumni. With me in your life, your heart will go on beating for many years to come."

I shook my head. "I can't believe you're just going to be gone."

Kara was reflective. "Neither can I."

"When exactly will it happen?"

"I'm not sure."

"Will you just dissolve?" I asked.

"I honestly don't know."

"Are you scared?"

"I'm scared of Frederick and what he's done," Kara said. "Fred is Ray's middle name. They're the same person. He's obviously come back to wreck my plans."

"Why?" I asked.

"The Illumni must have given him an opportunity to try to save the world also. I'm sure he would have jumped at it. But you've got to understand the Ray I know. He's ruthlessly ambitious. Do you know what he said to me after the war, when the entire world lay in ruins? He said we should have hit China with everything we had as soon as our space station was assembled. Then we would have won decisively. That's the kind of mentality we're dealing with. He only understands force. He sees an enemy everywhere, including in his own home. Throughout his career, he blamed me for his failure to become president. For God's sake, he wouldn't have made it to general without me! I think I see what he's come back for. He's determined to set Ray on what he believes is a straight road to the top. He wants to be president. He wants to be in a position to order a first strike. To do all this, he thinks he must keep Becky away from Ray."

"Don't you have that backward?" I asked. "He deliberately went to Ray and told him what we were up to."

Kara dismissed the objection with a wave of her hand. "He

did that out of jealousy. He hates me now. He saw how I went off with Vincent. Don't think for a second that he's fighting to save me for himself. He hates you even more. That's why he came after Vincent."

"Why didn't he come after me directly?"

"He probably doesn't know where you live."

"How did Ray find Vincent so easily?" I asked.

"He may have come out of the cave and bumped right into him."

"Will he hurt Vincent?"

"I'm not sure," Kara said. "Ray was willing to destroy the lives of millions of people. The bloody heart he left in the kitchen doesn't exactly encourage me."

"Why did he do that?" I asked.

"To let me know he was on to me. To scare me."

"Why are we sitting here talking? We're wasting time. You said you knew where Ray took him. Let's go after him."

"I didn't say that. I said *you* knew where Vincent was."

"But I don't know."

"Of course you do. You're Vincent. That's how I know Frederick hasn't killed him yet. You would have felt it. But there's something more. Remember when you were looking through the telescope and your head brushed close to Vincent's? Remember your dizziness? That was the result of a momentary blending of your minds. The Illumni warned us about that. You notice I've had almost no contact with Becky. When two of the same person are together, all kinds of strange things can happen."

"But Vincent and I sat together for hours," I said.

"Vincent's mind is far more developed than mine. He's able to put up a wall against the blending. Even so, strange things happened to you guys on at least two occasions that I saw."

"What does this have to do with our predicament?"

Kara stood. "We're hiking up to the cave. Once we get there you're going to sit and close your eyes and get into Vincent's mind. It will be easy. He'll let you in. I'm sure he knows where Frederick has taken him. What he knows, you'll also know."

I climbed to my feet. I looked out the window. The day was moving on. Night would be coming soon, and with it the moon. There was a painful question that needed to be asked.

"Kara," I said. "If all you say is true, is it necessary to save Vincent? I don't mean to sound cruel, but he's going to be gone soon anyway."

Kara shook slightly at the question, but her eyes remained fixed on mine. "I can't leave without Vincent by my side. You asked earlier if I was scared. I didn't really answer your question. But I think you know the answer. You have to help me find him, Mark."

Chapter Twelve

Inside the cave, in the inner chamber I had visited before, Kara lit her gas lantern against the oppressive dark. But no light penetrated the black hole at the rear of the chamber. No light penetrated my heart. I had to face my fears. I knew who I was. I was Mark Forum. Kara was asking me to be someone else. It did not matter that it was someone I loved. Kara understood. When we were comfortably seated, she tried to reassure me.

"The Illumni taught us that the cause of all fear is the presence of a second," she said. "What they mean is that if one sees any difference anywhere, there is always the possibility of danger. The Illumni don't fear anything because they are one with everything. I realize, of course, we can't pretend to be in that state of unity. But the fact that it exists gives me comfort. I hope it does the same for you. You are not going to experience anything foreign when you go into Vincent's mind."

"Are you sure he'll let me in?" I asked.

"You're already in. It's merely a question of remembering what has yet to happen. What's the difference between you two? He's only had more experience than you, nothing more. Close your eyes, Mark; it will be easier that way."

I did as she suggested. "What do I do?" I asked.

"Be still."

"Do you want me to blank out my thoughts?"

"No. The Illumni say that's impossible. We can never force our minds to do anything. They'll do just the opposite. Try not to think and you'll have more thoughts. What you should do instead is give your mind something more pleasant to dwell on than what it is already caught up with. Then there will be no force involved. Be with the thought of Vincent, that's all. It's a pleasant thought. He's a great person. He's a more evolved form of your present self. Be easy, Mark, and imagine Vincent as you remember him. His smile, his carefree manner. Be with him. Be him."

I began to protest. I was too wound up with all that was going on to relax. I wanted to jump up and run out of the cave and find a gun and hunt Frederick down. But just as the idea of arming myself passed through my mind, I couldn't help wondering what Vincent would have said. And no sooner did I wonder than I thought I heard him laugh. Or saw him smile at least. Then I suddenly did see him smile. It was so vivid he could have been standing in front of me. Or standing with his back to me, with me peering over his shoulder into a mirror.

Two mirrors, I corrected myself. Each placed in front of the other, with us between, reflecting back and forth down a tunnel of endlessly rebounding images. I saw them clearly. They took shape in my mind like pictures projected on the back of my eyelids. I felt myself step into one of the tunnels, a long dark passageway with a faint white light at the far end. I felt myself begin to fall, slowly at first, as if I had grown wings to help ease my descent. I was vaguely conscious of my body remaining in the cave beside Kara, but it seemed I had become so still I was no longer breathing. I had turned to stone.

I was aware of speed without the jarring effects of motion. I fell and fell down the long corridor, and with each passing second the light at the end grew brighter. But it was not a white light as I had thought at first. Nor was it exceedingly bright. At present the tunnel was not leading out of my body and into the presence of a glorious being. It was just leading me into another body.

Suddenly my descent stopped. I jumped without moving. My place with Kara was lost. The tunnel disappeared. I opened my eyes.

I was in a motel room. My hands and feet were bound. I was lying on the floor with my head pressed at an uncomfortable angle against a wall that needed paint. A dusty mirror on a chipped and splintered chest of drawers hung above me. I twisted my head to the right, feeling pain in my neck. There was someone on the bed.

It was Ray.

He was the same age as he was in the bookstore. His body language, however, was not that of a twenty-year-old kid. He had a cigar in his right hand, and the way he gestured with it as he talked was an exercise in arrogance. I'd disliked Ray when I watched him pick up Kara in his store, but this guy was worse. And to think he'd had five hundred warheads waiting at his fingertips.

He had, however, made a few changes in his appearance. His hair was lighter. He also appeared to be wearing contacts. I could not remember Ray's eyes being green. I tried to think of him as Frederick. It made it easier for me to keep everybody straight in my head.

The smoke from his cigar filled the room with a foul smell. I coughed weakly. My mouth was gagged with an old rag. It was difficult to breathe. I was in Vincent's body. But where was Vincent? Where were his fearless thoughts? I was alone.

"You know what's wrong with people like you?" Frederick was saying. "You only have guts when you don't need them. I've seen it a thousand times. You go to rallies and burn the American flag. But if a thief breaks into your home, suddenly you want a little frontier justice—someone with a gun. You call the cops. You should be able to take care of your own problems. That's what I do. You should have learned to take care of yourself. You see, Vincent, you're my problem now. That's the cold reality of the situation. What do you think I should do with you?"

I told him, through my gag, to go to hell. It came out like a pathetic mumble. Frederick took pity on me. Wearing a jovial sneer, he climbed from the bed and knelt by my head. He had on a black sport coat. I couldn't help but notice the slim switchblade tucked in his coat pocket.

"You speak?" he mocked me. "I thought you were beyond all insults."

I told him to go do something to himself that the Bible wouldn't have approved of. He got the gist of it. His face broke into a grin.

"Vincent, there's hope for you after all. If I remove your gag, do you promise not to scream? Neither of us would want that, would we? I would have to shut you up quick, and that could get kind of messy."

I nodded. He undid the rag at the back of my head. At last I could breathe freely.

"Hi," I said, cautioning myself to move carefully.

"What did you just say?"

"Nothing."

"Come on," he insisted. "What was it? You've bored me the whole day. Now you're going to talk."

"What would you like to talk about?"

"Where's your double?" he asked.

"Beats me."

He belted me in the face. He was every bit as strong as Ray, which made sense. Ten times as fierce. Twice in one day, I couldn't believe it. I tasted blood.

A numbing pain swelled in my head. I couldn't be sure, but it felt as if he'd broken my nose.

"Where is he?" he demanded.

"How should I know?" I gasped.

"You know I'm going to find him."

"What do you want him for?"

"I want to pull his arms out of their sockets. What do you think I want him for? You guys are trying to steal my wife."

"Your wife is trying to get away from you. Why don't you just let her go and we'll all be a lot happier."

Frederick grinned again. "I'm afraid I can't do that. There's this thing called pride. It's the difference between a guy like me and a guy like you. I have a lot of it. I couldn't live knowing she was with somebody else."

Kara *had* underestimated him. I realized then that he intended to kill Becky as well. It should have been obvious. What better way to keep Ray away from her while Ray moved toward the presidency?

"You won't find either of them," I swore at him, my own pride overcoming my earlier caution. "They've been warned. They'll hide until your month is up and you turn to dust."

Anger and doubt wiped away his grin. "You lie! Kara

would never have gone against the Illumni. Even if she had, Becky would never have listened to her."

"Kara only told Mark the truth. He told Becky. She listened to him. She knows about you. You'll never find her."

Frederick was livid. He leapt to his feet and began to pace the floor. "I'll get Kara. She'll know where they are. I'll beat the information out of her if I have to."

"You'll get nothing from her," I said. "She's too smart for you. She always has been. Without Kara, Ray will be lucky if he rises above wiping up latrines in the air force."

Frederick kicked me in the face. Lying on the floor as I was, I had an interesting angle on the approach of the foot. He had on black leather boots. It must have been a style preference from the future. The toe of the boot caught me square in the right cheek. This time there was no question of something breaking. The bone in my cheek shattered. My head was jerked cruelly to the left where it smacked the wall. The motel room receded to a blurry red distance. Blood poured over my face. I felt Frederick grab me and shake me roughly.

"She was mine, you son of a bitch!" he swore. "You had no right to her."

I tried to smile. I could feel the teeth falling out of my mouth. "She told me you were afraid of the dark."

He shook me harder. "Where are they?"

"She said you sleep with a pink night-light on."

He pulled out his switchblade and held it to my throat.

"Tell me where they are this second or I'll slit your windpipe!"

I swallowed thickly, feeling the touch of the cold blade through the stream of warm blood that poured down my neck. I could see the situation was already hopeless. The only reason he hadn't killed Vincent so far was that he wanted information about Becky and me. It may have had something to do with being in another person's body, but I felt no fear of Frederick. Vincent might have been with me more than I knew. All that was transpiring seemed inevitable.

"Tell me where we are first, and then I'll tell you where they are," I muttered.

A look of comprehension crossed his face. He threw me back against the wall. "They're trying to get to me through you!" he cried.

"Fair's fair," I whispered.

Frederick began to pace the room again. Even with my thoughts spinning, I saw something about his personality that should have immediately disqualified him from commanding a nuclear-armed space station: He was a goddamn lunatic.

"She doesn't care what she does to me!" he yelled. "She hates me. And what did I ever do to her? I'll tell you what. I saved her life. I had to drag her up to the station. And did she thank me? No! All she did was whine about what a temper I have. Temper! I'll show you temper. I'll kill all those bastards. I'll make them burn. I'll kill her!"

Frederick suddenly reached for me again, grabbing me by

my messy shirt and hauling me to my feet, his knife held hard and tight in his other hand.

"Tell me where that bitch is right now before I stick this through your skin!" he yelled.

I forced another smile. I could feel Vincent coming near, like the rolling approach of rain from a distance. But before he could reach me and become one with me, I had to get in my last dig.

"She said you were lousy in bed," I muttered.

Frederick slit my throat. He dropped me to the floor like a soggy bag of potatoes and kicked me in the side with his boot. Then he wiped off his blade on his pants and stormed out of the motel room. I gulped in a thin breath and swallowed red fluid.

I began to die.

But first I had a life to live. Things to remember that were yet to be. Of course it was only through Vincent that I could recall what I had done with the next ten years of my life. He was with me now in full. I felt his presence in my soul like the soft chant of the words: "There is no fear where there is no second."

Truly I felt as one with him. I was not afraid. I began to remember living the life I would have lived if Vincent and Kara hadn't come back in time.

I was standing in the electronics store. I had just said goodbye to Becky. Just before I opened the door to leave, I thought I saw a young man standing in the software section with one of my games in his hand. I turned to get a better look. But there was no one there. I wondered if I was beginning to see things. I stepped outside, into the dark.

Home in my apartment, I worked on my next game. But during the night, when I was in bed, a horrible pain filled my chest. I got so scared I called the hospital. They told me to come in immediately, but then I got even more scared and decided to stay in bed. I thought of my mother and father. I thought of Becky. Eventually the pain in my chest subsided and I was able to sleep. I dreamed.

I dreamed I had the best friends in the world. A guy and a girl, both of whom had blond hair that shone in the sun like gold. We would do everything together: go for walks, look at the stars, eat ice cream. The girl always ate chocolate ice cream, like Becky. It was the best dream I ever had, and when I woke up I was sad that it was over. But my chest felt better, and my life went on.

At least my life went forward. I saw Becky less and less often. She had a boyfriend. I didn't want to bother her. I tried to concentrate on my work, and in my self-imposed isolation, I developed my skills beyond what I had imagined possible. I began to write the most incredible computer games, with graphics and plots that few could match. Half my plots were taken from my dreams, from the conversations I continued to have with my two nightly visitors. They would tell me stories and I'd listen. They didn't come every night to me, but whenever they did, it hurt to say goodbye.

Becky quit her job at the store. We talked a few times on

the phone after that, but then I heard she was getting married. I didn't call her anymore. It didn't upset me that she didn't tell me about her marriage. I understood. She didn't want to hurt my feelings. She knew how I felt about her. Later, though, even when she was married and moved out of the area, I was tempted to try to find her again. I could never get her out of my mind.

I grew old, not in years, but physically. My health began to fail. I was rich from my computer games, but none of the specialists I saw could help me. I knew I was going to die young.

I bought a house in the hills that overlooked the area where I had grown up. The house reminded me of the two friends who visited me in my dreams. But even they began to visit my dreams less and less often, and after my twenty-ninth birthday, they came no more. I felt truly alone. But I did not forget them or the stories they told me. I began to collect what they had said in a book. There was a cave in the hills not far from where I lived. It was there that I wrote most of the book, especially at night, when the moon was bright in the sky.

I was outside the cave entrance when my heart gave out.

The pain started in my chest, as it always did, like a dull weight that grew steadily in intensity until breathing was a strain. This time, however, sitting perfectly still and taking long gentle breaths did not ease the pain. It just kept growing. Soon I could barely move.

There was a gas lantern beside my notebook on a fold-out table. The table stood not far outside the entrance to the cave, on a dirt path that wound up into the hills. It was by the flame of the lantern that I had done the bulk of my work. My eyes automatically fixed on the flame as the breath inside me choked. I couldn't exhale. I could not bring in fresh oxygen. My body shook with minute convulsions. But the flame remained steady. It was protected by the glass cover of the lantern. It was safe from the wind, I thought, but what about the world? I believed much of the story I was writing, the tale the two golden-haired friends had told me in my dreams. I knew the winds of change were going to bring bad times for the earth. My main purpose in writing the story was to warn the world. But now, as my death approached, I felt that my story was incomplete. It was without hope. Everybody died. Suddenly I didn't want anyone to find the story after I was gone and think that I had died without hope.

I needed to destroy my story.

Gasping in air that could no longer feed my blood-starved heart, I reached out and managed to topple the gas lantern onto my notebook. The fuel in the container at the bottom of the lamp spilled out. Quickly it was ignited by the flame, and soon tall orange flames were licking across the tabletop and turning back the pages of my story, turning to the last pages and leaving them in ash. The flames leapt from the table and into the dry grass. The whole hilltop, I realized, would go up in smoke—the bushes and trees would be consumed. I don't know why, but I smiled then. Perhaps it was because I understood that now others would be able to find the cave. It had always been a special place to me. Or maybe I smiled because I knew that no one would find my body. I would become ash like the pages of my story.

I fell from my seat, onto the ground, rolling over on my back and staring up at the moon. It was so bright to me then, as bright as the midday sun, although its light was cool and soothing. Red flames began to dance around it.

They were hardly any different from the red blood that poured out of my cut throat.

Suddenly I was in two places at once: a cheap motel room and a burning hilltop. I was two people: Vincent and Mark. But we were soon to be one. The only thing that separated us now was that while Vincent was already in the light, I was just beginning to move toward it.

The flames touched the sleeve of my shirt. My heart gave a final agonizing squeeze and stopped. My head rolled on the motel floor. My lungs took a final gulp of my blood and were smothered. It didn't matter: I had no fear. I kept my eyes fixed on the moon. I could see it in the motel ceiling as well as in the night sky above the burning hilltop. I began to rush toward it with incredible speed. The moon, the white light. How obvious it was to me then that the Illumni should have appeared to come out of the moon. That they had come to Kara on a blissful wave of light.

Kara—I remembered her then. Just as I was about to drown in the white light, I remembered her and I saw the space station.

Chapter Thirteen

M ark," Kara was saying. "Wake up. It's late. You have to come back. Mark, it's Kara. Can you hear me?"

I opened my eyes. The small flame of the lantern shone before me. Shadows stood patiently behind us on the cave walls. Our shadows, waiting for us to make a move. My eyes were damp.

"Did you reach him?" Kara asked.

"Yes," I whispered.

"Do you know where he is?"

"Yes."

"Where?"

I faced her, and in doing so I caught a glimpse of the cave opening. It was dark outside. The whole day had gone by and Kara had stayed by my side.

"He's with the Illumni," I said.

"What?"

"Frederick slit his throat. He's dead."

Frederick could have put the knife into her. Kara sucked in a breath and did not let it go. The light in her eyes went out. It was as if the shock had momentarily driven her soul from her body. Then her face crumpled and her head dropped to her chest. I put my arm around her. For a long time we sat there, making no sound at all. I didn't have to try to blank out my thoughts. My mind was empty.

Finally Kara stirred. She stood and walked to the far side of the chamber, where the cave continued through a narrow dark hole. Kneeling by the opening, she stared into it, at what I didn't know. When she finally spoke, the tone of her voice made me shiver. It was flat and cold.

"Frederick could do nothing if he didn't exist," she said.

"It's done," I said. "Another murder will help nobody."

She glanced over her shoulder. In the yellow light from the lamp, the lines of grief on her face were sharp and deep. She looked wicked.

"You forget the advantages of causality," she said.

"The Illumni didn't send you back in time to kill."

"They didn't send me here to fail either!" she snapped, jumping up. "He has to be stopped. He'll kill Becky. He'll kill you."

"You don't have time to find him. Vincent was in some motel room—I don't know where it was."

"You know I'm not talking about Frederick," she said.

I realized in a rush what she meant to do. "Kara," I pleaded. "Listen to yourself. He's a twenty-year-old boy. He hasn't done anything wrong."

"You don't know him!" she yelled. "He killed millions. In the war, when it was over, he kept shooting off our missiles. He used them all up, on small villages even, where the people's only crime was that they were born on the wrong side of the lines on his map. He has to be stopped."

"He didn't start the war, Kara."

"He didn't stop it either!"

"And you think you will by killing Ray?"

She put her hands to her face. She lowered her voice. "I cannot leave without Vincent. I told you that."

"He's gone." I stood. "But I'm here. I'll stay with you. We'll stay in this cave. Vincent would tell you the same thing. Don't do it, Kara."

She took her hands down from her face. She gripped her right wrist with her left hand. It was shaking and she couldn't stop it, just as I wasn't going to be able to stop her.

"I loved him more than the moon," she said miserably. She dropped her hands to her sides and took a step toward the cave entrance. "Good-bye, Mark. Maybe I'll see you later."

I tried to grab her as she hurried by, but I was weak from my lengthy trance. She pushed me away, and I hit my head on the wall of the cave and fell. The shadows jumped. I looked on in disbelief. Even though Kara was gone, there were still two shadows. Waiting.

Kara must have broken into a dead sprint the moment she stepped onto the path outside the cave. By the time I reached it there was no sign of her. I knew it was hopeless to try to catch her. The moon had just risen, and its light was bright on the hill. I wondered how much time she had left. I struggled down the path as best I could. Less than halfway to the house, I heard the start of a car engine, the burn of peeling rubber. Maybe a cop would stop her and give her a ticket, I hoped.

That morning we had driven Kara's car to the electronics store and the bookstore. Vincent's black Ferrari was at my apartment. I was stranded without wheels. Sitting in the kitchen where we had found the heart, I considered my options. I could call the police. I was sure I could think up some story to convince them that Kara was dangerous. But there were problems with the idea. In all probability, the police wouldn't be able to locate her right away. And I couldn't send them to guard Ray because I didn't know where Ray was, not for sure. Even if he was at the bookstore, I couldn't see the police putting a ring of armed men around him just because I asked them to. More than any of these things, however, I hated the idea of turning Kara over to the authorities. I didn't want her to be in jail when her end came.

Then there was the idea of calling the bookstore. I dismissed it almost immediately. Frederick had already spoken to Ray. Ray was already on his guard. If I gave him further warning, there was no telling what he'd do to Kara when she showed up.

In the end, I called Becky. It seemed logical. I had no illusions about trying to get Becky to enter Kara's mind. Ray would be dead by the time I could explain the whole story, never mind the fact that Becky wouldn't believe a word of it. But I thought Becky, being Kara, would know what Kara would do next. Whispering a prayer that she wouldn't hang up on me, I dialed Becky's number.

"Hello?" Becky said, the first ring hardly over.

"Becky, it's Mark. Ray's in danger."

There was a long pause. "What do you want?" she asked.

"Remember that girl who came into your store? The one who went out with Ray?"

"Yeah. What about her?"

"It's a long story, but you've got to help me. You've got to come to where I am."

"How is Ray in danger?"

I had to move carefully. If I gave her too much information, she would call Ray. She might call him anyway, I thought.

"Becky," I said. "Until this morning, you and I were good friends. Hate me tomorrow if you must, but for tonight, just for tonight, I'm asking you to trust me. Please?"

There was another pause. "Where are you?"

I gave her directions to the house. She told me to give her thirty minutes. Hanging up the phone, I wished to God she had a Ferrari.

It wasn't an easy half hour to kill. The horror of Vincent's slit throat came back to haunt me. If I hadn't pushed Frederick, would Vincent still be alive? Useless questions to ask, I realized, those that began with the word *if.* Except in a universe where the effects of causality could be overruled. My guilt remained, unsoothed by the beautiful white light I had beheld at the end of my trance. Kara was right. It was not something that could be imagined, or even properly remembered.

I went into Vincent's bedroom. I had left the computer on while Kara and I hiked up to the cave. I restarted the game, finally understanding why Vincent had given it the name he had— "Decision." But what had he wanted me to decide, I asked myself? Colored indicators on the screen flashed on and off, asking what weapon I wanted to fire first, what submarine or city I wanted to destroy. They were keyed to the number pad: one through ten. Then it hit me. The answer had been obvious from the beginning. I pushed the numeral zero. The space station vanished and was replaced by one word in big white letters: CONGRATULATIONS.

The only way to win the game was to not play.

Becky took forty minutes to reach the house. I was outside waiting for her by that time. I didn't even give her a chance to turn off the engine. I jumped in beside her. Her brown eyes looked at me with open concern.

"Where's Ray right now?" I asked.

"Why?"

"Just tell me."

She checked her watch. "It's nine-thirty. He's working tonight. I'm sure he's closing. He'll probably be there till ten."

"Drive me to the mall right now."

"What's going on?"

"Kara is upset with Ray. She might hurt him."

"Kara," she muttered. "Who's Kara?"

"That girl who went out with Ray. Let's go. Now!"

Becky backed out of the driveway. She was *not* a fast driver. She must have picked up the habit later, in a car of the future that did a cool three hundred miles an hour, or in a marriage that drove her to live dangerously. I implored her to use greater speed.

"Becky," I said as we drove down the hill and into the city. "I have to ask you a strange question."

"What's gotten into you, Mark?"

"Believe me, it's been a weird few days. I want you to think before you answer my question. If you were mad at Ray, so mad you wanted to kill him—how would you do it?"

"Mark!"

"Please, I need to know."

"Why? You're not going to hurt Ray, are you? It's over between us, thanks to you. Haven't you hurt us enough?"

"I told you," I said, trying to keep my voice calm, "it's Kara who will hurt Ray. You have to tell me how she will do it."

"Have you lost your mind?"

I paused. "Yes. I think I may have lost it."

We lapsed into a strained silence. Becky was finally picking it up, running a red light and cruising through a stop sign. I let her concentrate on her driving. I was lost in my own pain. From the time I got out of bed that morning, it was impossible to imagine how I could have screwed up worse. I had lost my girlfriend, been beaten up, gotten killed, and driven my future wife to murder. I didn't know which was the greater sin. Each act seemed a part of the same big monster. I knew what Vincent would have said: it was meant to be. But Vincent was dead. I couldn't hear him anymore. Since I had come out of my trance, I couldn't even *feel* him inside me. It was as if I had left the better part of myself in the light when I stepped back into the world.

I felt Becky's hand on my knee.

"Are you all right?" she asked.

"No."

"What's wrong?"

"I'm dying," I said, feeling sorry for myself.

Her face wrinkled in anxiety. "Are you sick?"

"Yes."

"What's wrong?" she asked.

I shrugged. "What's right? You hate me. You and Ray hate each other. Kara hates Ray. Ray probably hates Kara."

"I don't hate you, Mark."

"You certainly don't love me," I said.

Becky took back her hand. She ran another red light, this time without looking both ways. She seemed to be thinking.

"Can you tell me why you did it?" she asked finally.

"I didn't do it," I said. "But I let it be done."

"Didn't you realize how much it would hurt me? Didn't you care?"

"I care. I think that's why I let Kara go ahead with her plan."

"Who is this Kara?"

"She's just a girl I know," I said.

"Why did you say you're dying?"

"I have a bad heart. I've had it since I was a child."

"Why didn't you tell me?" she asked.

"I didn't want you to feel sorry for me."

"You still should have told me."

"Why would you care?" I asked, suddenly tired of being Mr. Nice Guy. "The only time you were interested in going out with me was when your boyfriend was unfaithful. Some girl you are. You really know how to pick them. You know what Ray's goal is? To become president of the United States so he can blow up China from outer space."

"Who told you he wants to be president?" she asked, surprised.

"You don't even like the way I dress."

"How do you know all this?"

I stopped. "You really don't like my clothes?"

"They're okay. But sometimes you look as if—"

"My mother dresses me," I interrupted.

Becky frowned. "How did you know I was going to say that?"

"Kara told me you would."

"Who is this girl?" she asked for what seemed like the tenth time.

"Tell me your first name and I'll tell you who she is."

Becky hesitated. "It's Kara."

I looked at her. "You only tell those you really love your first name," I said.

She was amazed. "How did you know that?"

"Did you want to tell it to me?" I asked.

Becky stopped at a red light. There were no cars coming in either direction. Kara was probably adjusting the telescopic sight on her rifle. The bookstore had been closed awhile. Still, I didn't hurry Becky. She bit her lower lip.

"Last night," she said. "I told you my first name while you were asleep. I didn't think you heard me."

"I didn't."

She reached over and put her hand on the back of my neck. "But you knew my name before I told you," she said. "How?"

I looked out the window. The moon continued to rise in the black sky. "I dreamed it," I said.

"I'm sorry."

"What are you sorry about?"

Becky leaned over and kissed me. "I just feel sorry, that's all. About everything, I guess. I wish you didn't have a bad heart."

"So do I." I held her tight for a moment before letting go. "We have to hurry."

Chapter Fourteen

The parking lot at the mall was all but deserted. There were only three cars visible. One of them was Ray's red BMW. I could see no sign of a red Ferrari. I wondered if Kara was already inside the store blowing away her old boyfriend. Becky interrupted my thoughts.

"I would just run him over," she said.

"What?" I asked.

"You asked me how I would kill Ray. I'd just run him over as he walked to his car."

I studied where Ray had parked his BMW. He probably didn't want people opening car doors into it. It was about a hundred and fifty yards of open asphalt from the back door of the bookstore. I estimated that distance would take him twenty seconds to cover at a full sprint. I reminded myself that Kara's car could accelerate at g-force.

"Are you sure?" I asked.

"The other day, when I learned he had gone out with another girl, I spent an hour fantasizing exactly how I would do it, where I would park and stuff."

"Where would you park?"

Becky pointed to the far side of the mall, over a quarter of a mile away and poorly lit. "On the other side of Mervyn's department store. You see how the corner of the store is all windows? If you parked beyond those windows, you could see Ray when he came out."

I squinted my eyes. I could see the windows, but not if there was a car on the other side of them. I considered having Becky swing around the store, but then decided it would be better if Kara was unaware of us. I had this thought of first letting Kara come out into the open before pouncing. I think I had seen too many cop movies. Becky was watching me.

"This girl's not really going to try to kill Ray, is she?" she asked.

"It's a possibility. That's all I can say." I gestured to the back of the mall. "Let's put your car behind that Dumpster over there. I want to get out and walk."

Becky did as I requested. Once out and up on our feet, I began to check around for a secret way into the mall. Like I would find one just because I needed it. Right. Becky figured out what I was trying to do.

"Why don't we just go knock at the security door?" she asked. "The guards all know me. I used to come by to see Ray after hours all the time."

I agreed to the idea. I still wasn't sure what I was trying to do, but I thought if we could get to the other side of the parking lot via the inside of the mall, then we could hide out where neither Ray nor Kara could see us, and make sure they didn't kill each other. If we just walked across the parking lot, I knew Kara would see us.

Becky had to pound on the security door to get someone's attention. One look at the guy who finally answered the door told us why. He was a couple of years older than we were, and dressed in a uniform, but his pupils were as big as the moon in the sky. He reeked of marijuana smoke. His grin took up most of his face.

"Becky!" he said. "Are you here or do I just think you are?"

Becky nodded. "I'm here, Ted. What are you up to?"

Ted waved his hand. Then stopped to make sure it hadn't fallen off the end of his arm. He burst into a laugh.

"Just killing clocks, babe. Got to put in the clocks to get paid."

"You mean, you're killing time," I said.

Ted shielded his eyes, as if the mere sight of me dazzled him as much as the sun. "Hey, who is this guy? Is he really here?"

"No," Becky said. "But could you let us in? We have to talk to Ray. It's important."

"Sure," Ted said, letting us go by. "Just don't steal anything. I'll have to pay for it."

We left Ted sitting in front of his four security TV screens. He had *E. T.* running on all of them. Walking through the center of the mall with no one around was spooky. I asked Becky to take off her leather-heeled shoes. The slightest sound echoed the length of the mall. Ray's bookstore was on the ground level, not too far from the Mervyn's Becky had referred to.

"I don't want Ray to see us," I said to Becky. "Is there a store near the bookstore that we could go through to get to the parking lot?"

"The stores are all locked from the inside," Becky said, gesturing at the iron gates that covered all the display windows. "But I doubt that Ted locked the hallways that lead to the bathrooms. The janitors clean the johns after hours."

"Where are they?"

"On the far side of the bookstore," Becky said.

"Great. We better go up to the second floor and come back down farther along. I don't want Ray spotting us sneaking past his store."

"Can't we just warn him that this girl is dangerous?"

"No," I said.

"Why not?"

I couldn't very well tell her that Ray was even more dangerous than Kara. Especially when I didn't know if it was true. But I was worried about Frederick. Where had he gone after slitting Vincent's throat? To talk to Ray? How much time did Frederick have left? A day? A month? There was so much I didn't know.

"That would just make things worse," I said. "Trust me."

Becky smiled at me. "I trust you, Mark."

I got her drift. "This is not like my game," I said quickly.

"You mean I'm not the queen of the universe?"

"Ask me later," I said, not sure what I meant.

We ran up a flight of stairs and down one on the far side of the bookstore. I hoped Ray was still at work in the back.

As Becky predicted, the door leading to the bathrooms on the first floor was unlocked. The rest rooms were at the far end of a long, drab hallway. Beyond them was an emergency exit. Just our luck, I thought. We couldn't open the door without everyone knowing it. We'd probably even bring Ted running.

We hurried to the end of the hall. Two wires—one red, the other blue—were attached to the hinge of the door. I checked my watch. It was ten after ten. The time for subtlety was past. I ripped the wires out. Becky jumped, but no alarm went off. Holding my breath, I cracked the door an inch and peered outside. Ray's BMW was still there.

"He hasn't left," I said.

"That's weird," Becky said, sounding far away.

Preoccupied, I hadn't noticed the change in her voice. I shifted my angle. Now we were too close to the wall of Mervyn's to see through the corner windows Becky had pointed out.

Mervyn's was to our right, the bookstore to our left. I pulled back from the door. It was only then I noticed that Becky had slumped to the floor and was sitting with her eyes half-closed. Her last comment had not been in response to mine, I realized.

"What's wrong?" I asked, kneeling beside her. She rubbed her eyes with her hands, blinking.

"I just had the strangest feeling."

"What?"

"I can't describe it."

"Did you feel split in two?" I asked.

"Yes. Sort of."

"Close your eyes, Becky, quickly. Tell me what you see inside your head. Where are you?"

Becky didn't question my order. It was almost as if she had no choice in the matter. She was being sucked inside in the same way I had been when I fell down the long tunnel into the cheap motel room. She sat silent for several seconds. Her breathing deepened. Slowly her confused expression turned to one of contentment.

"I'm in a forest," she said, her voice soft and dreamy. "I'm with you and we're happy. The trees are pretty. They're all different colors."

She was talking about the Illumni's slice of paradise, I realized. Kara must be reminiscing about her time with Vincent. I considered having her open her eyes to see if there was a parking lot on the other side of the trees, but I was afraid it would take her out of Kara's mind.

"What are we doing?" I asked.

"We're talking, but we're not moving our lips. You can read my mind."

"Can you read mine?"

"No. It's not necessary. You look different."

"Do I have blond hair?" I asked.

"No. You're glowing."

"What?"

"You're lit up like a lightbulb," Becky said.

"Are you?"

"No. But I'm happy."

"What are we discussing?" I asked.

"I don't know. I don't understand it. But it's nice."

"Is Ray there?"

"No. He's dead. I wish he was . . ." Becky's voice trailed off. For a moment she appeared confused; then a look of realization crossed her face. The problem was, I wasn't sure if it was Kara's realization or Becky's. Faintly, I heard the sound of a door open and close to our left. Becky suddenly leapt to her feet.

"No!" she shouted, her eyes flying wide open.

"What is it?" I asked, grabbing her arms.

"We have to stop him!"

"You mean Kara? We have to stop Kara? Is she here?"

Becky shook her head as if she were trying to shake out of it. "I don't want him to die," she cried.

"Who?"

"Please stop it!"

"Becky, who's going to die?"

"No! I can't tell you. You're not real."

Before I could respond, many things happened at once. But even before that, I had the crazy idea that Ted the security guard must also be from the future.

You're not real?

What did that mean?

I knew the door opening and closing outside must have been Ray leaving his bookstore. I didn't respond to it immediately because I still didn't know for sure if Kara was in the area. Or Frederick, for that matter. Plus I had to deal with Becky. Above all else, I knew I had to protect Becky. But that's the trouble with having a number-one priority. You strain so hard to accomplish it, it gets away from you. Becky struggled free of my grasp and ran out the door.

"Becky!" I called after her.

She had a jump on me and she was fast. By the time I got through the door, Becky was already a dozen feet into the wide-open parking lot. Ray was off to her left.

He was also farther away than Becky from the headlights that suddenly ripped around the corner of Mervyn's department store. They were aimed straight for him.

It was Kara's red Ferrari.

When Ray saw the headlights barreling down on him, he froze. It was only for a moment, but Kara was sparing her clutch nothing. The rev of the engine vibrated across the entire lot. The car was coming at him like a missile launched from Vincent's space station. By the time Ray could get himself moving, the Ferrari was probably up to sixty miles an hour—and it was accelerating. Ray glanced at the door he had just exited, then at his car; back and forth his eyes darted. I thought his choice was clear. He had to head for the door to the bookstore. It was closer. But he chose his car instead. As he ran toward it, there was no question he realized the seriousness of his situation. I never saw a guy move so fast.

Unfortunately, a shopping cart got in his way. It was ironic. There wasn't even a supermarket at the mall. The nearest one was around the block. Probably some shopper from the space station had brought it over because they hadn't liked Ray either. They probably wanted to see what he would look like as a kid with a couple of retreads burned over the back of his skull. The shopping cart was one of those silver metal kind, but it was practically invisible in the dark. Ray hit it with a bang and down he went, the headlights of the Ferrari shining in his eyes like twin lasers locked on target and itching to be fired.

His sudden fall threw Kara off as well, though. The headlights might have flashed bright in Ray's eyes, but then they swept to his right, more in the direction of the mall. Kara was an excellent high-speed driver, but she had overcompensated for Ray's tripping. At the speed she was going, it was understandable. The Ferrari was easily up to eighty by now. Even though the parking lot was big, the car was out of control.

Then there was Becky. In all the excitement, I had momentarily forgotten about my number-one priority. I had forgotten to tell her when I called from Kara and Vincent's house that she should wear bright clothing. Becky had on black jeans and a black cotton sweater. She made the shopping cart look like a neon sign. Kara probably didn't have the slightest idea her other self was there, in spite of the fact that they had just mind-melded. Certainly she was so many years removed from the days when she loved Ray that Kara couldn't imagine that Becky would suddenly bolt in the direction of her fallen boyfriend—that Becky would risk her life to save Ray's.

"Becky!" I cried. I didn't freeze as Ray had. I was up on my toes in an instant and running. I was pretty fast, too, for a heart patient. I almost caught her. But she had that goddamn head start and I didn't have on my goddamn running shoes. The goddamn car was coming so goddamn fast. I almost saved her. For a second, as the roar of the engine and the glare of the headlights drowned out all else, I saw her in my mind's eye crying helplessly on top of the oil well. I had saved her then, I thought. Why couldn't I save her now? All I had to do was reach out and pull her to safety. The car would pass and the world would survive. It seemed so simple. But I think that is how it is with all miracles in life, and all tragedies. They are so simple they can't be comprehended, even as they transpire before your eyes.

"Becky!" I cried as I leapt for a handful of her sweater. I leapt as far as I could, with every bit of strength in my body. But I had been born weak. I missed. I landed face first on a hard ground, which scraped the skin from the end of my nose. White lights swam over my head, harsh and blinding. A squeal as from a tortured animal rent the night. Kara had slammed on her brakes and the hard ground was now scraping away melting rubber. Too late, and not enough.

I heard a cry. A human cry. My love. I heard the two of them scream in unison. Then there was a horrible thud followed by an even more horrible silence. I tried burying myself in the hard ground, but it would not have me. I suppose it was against the rules to die twice in the same day. I had to get up and live. I staggered to my feet.

The Ferrari had hit Becky. Of that there was no doubt. She lay crumpled in a heap no less than thirty feet from the glaring headlights of the now stationary car. The force of the impact must have thrown her through the air. There was blood on the ground near her head, a small puddle not much different from the color of the black asphalt. I tried not to see it. I looked at Kara instead. She stood just outside the open door of her Ferrari, her fingers in her mouth. I wanted to tell her to turn off the blasted headlights. They were beginning to hurt my eyes. I wanted to tell her that she shouldn't have pushed so hard for everything to work out.

"Kara," Kara said. It didn't sound funny. I watched as Kara

walked slowly toward herself. I was watching again, I was not acting. I was never going to learn. But those goddamn headlights. I couldn't see a thing beyond the glare of them.

Kara knelt in the light and took Becky's head in her hands. I wanted to tell her that she shouldn't move her, that Becky might have a spinal injury. But then I figured Kara would know exactly what bones Becky had broken and how long it would be before the moon rose too far into the sky. The dark puddle beside Becky's head continued to grow. My feet began to take me toward them, one step at a time.

"This was not supposed to be," Kara told Becky, her voice gentle and forgiving. It was confusing to hear forgiveness in her voice instead of apology. But then it made perfect sense.

Ray stepped into the tunnel of light cut by the car's high beams.

He had a gun in his hand.

"Kara!" I screamed.

Ray pointed his weapon in Kara's direction.

"Don't move!" he ordered me as I attempted to place myself between them. I stopped cold. Fury had twisted Ray's face beyond recognition. For an instant I wasn't even sure it was Ray. It could have been Frederick. But the doubt only lasted until he spoke again. He gestured to Kara with the barrel of the revolver, which Frederick had no doubt given him. "Who are you?" he demanded.

Kara carefully eased Becky's head onto the pavement. She

stood and faced Ray. There was blood on her hands. Perhaps she should have held them up for Ray to see. Perhaps he would have taken pity on her if he had been told it was her blood. But I should have known she'd ask no pity from him.

"I am nobody now," she said.

Ray shook his gun. "You bitch!"

Kara sighed. Then she drew in a deep breath and looked at the sky. Not at the moon, but at the few stars that were visible. And it seemed to me that she was remembering all the times, throughout the long course of their unhappy marriage, that he had called her a bitch. Finally she lowered her head and stared him straight in the eye.

"You bastard," she said.

Ray shot her in the chest. Kara dropped to the ground.

The chase by the Ferrari and the confrontation with Kara appeared to have left Ray a bit dazed. I had to get to him before he could turn the gun in my direction. I'm not sure if he would have tried to shoot me if I hadn't attacked him. But now that I was jumping him, I was the enemy. I had to be destroyed. I leapt onto his right side, both my arms wrapped around his neck. I probably should have played football. It was a hell of a tackle. Ray went down with me riding on top of him.

"Son of a bitch!" he swore as the side of his head hit the pavement. Pleased with the effect the blow had on his personality, I let go of his neck and grabbed his hair near his right temple and slammed his head into the pavement again. Ray's grip on his gun loosened. It fell out of his hand onto the pavement. I immediately reached for it. I was in too much of a hurry and succeeded only in knocking it out of my reach.

"Dammit," I said. Ray appeared to be only semiconscious. I decided it was worth the risk to jump off him to get to the gun. I almost made it. But he was not that unconscious. He grabbed my ankle and hauled me back just as my fingertips were brushing against the barrel. It really pissed me off. I reacted instinctively. I kicked him in the face several times. He finally let go of my foot and I made another lunge for the gun. This time I got it. Pivoting on my knees, I raised it in his direction, directly into the glare of the lights.

"Hold it right there!" I ordered.

Either Ray thought he was Superman or else he had already started his dive before I could tell him to stop. He crashed into me with the force of a freight train. This time it was my head that hit the pavement. A dark purple light swelled inside my brain. I saw stars. I saw galaxies. But I didn't let go of the gun. Feeling Ray clawing at my hand for it, I swung my right knee into his crotch. He was tougher than I thought. These ex-jocks—he probably wore a cup even in the bookstore. He just grunted and kept trying to grab the gun. The weight of his body on my chest was suffocating. He was wriggling my finger away from the trigger. I was losing the fight.

Suddenly the gun went off. One of the Ferrari headlights exploded in a crash of glass and went out. Then there was another shot. This one didn't appear to hit anything. It also sounded different. It wasn't until I heard Ted the security guard shout out that I understood the second shot had come from another gun.

"Hold it right there!" he ordered Ray.

"Go to hell!" Ray swore.

Ted put his revolver to Ray's head and pulled back the hammer. "What did you say, buddy?" Ted asked.

Ray stopped fighting with me. Slowly he turned his head to look at Ted's loaded gun. "All right," he said in resignation.

Ted had the two of us get up. He had sobered up some since we last saw him, but he still had a long way to go. He made both of us put our hands above our heads. His eyes kept straying uneasily to Kara and Becky. Kara had fallen beside her younger counterpart. She was bleeding freely from a chest wound. Neither girl was moving.

"What's going on here?" Ted cried.

"That girl ran over Becky," Ray said bitterly.

"This bastard shot Kara," I said, lowering my arms.

"Don't call me a bastard," Ray yelled, also taking down his hands, and balling them into fists.

"Shut up, both of you," Ted said, moving close to Becky. Keeping his gun pointed at us, he knelt beside her and felt for a pulse at her neck. He had tears on his face. He moaned. "We've got to get Becky to the hospital."

I turned to Ray. "You take Becky. I'll take Kara."

"Who's that girl?" he demanded, pointing to Kara. I noticed Ray didn't react to the sameness of names. Becky must not have told him her first name yet. His question was interesting in another respect. He had gone out with Kara, yet he was asking about her as if he was missing something, which of course he was.

"It's Becky's twin," I said.

"Becky doesn't have a twin," Ray growled.

"Look at her!" I said. "They're identical."

Ted allowed Ray to step to where he was standing over Kara. It was as if Ray was seeing her for the first time. I could relate to that. Kara had been right about its being impossible to recognize what you think is impossible.

"Jesus Christ," Ray whispered, his face white in the glare from the remaining headlight. Ted almost dropped his gun when he saw the similarity. I used the opportunity to move to Kara's side. She lay on her back, her eyes closed, her breathing ragged. I touched her cheek. It was as cold as marble.

"Kara," I said. "Can you hear me?"

"Yes," she whispered.

"What should I do?"

She coughed weakly. Her eyes remained closed. "Take me home."

"Where's that? Kara? Kara?" She lapsed into unconsciousness. I pressed my hand on the messy hole beneath her right breast. Sticky warmth spread around my fingers. The bleeding was not going to be stopped without an operation, if it could be stopped at all. Yet the fact she was alive at all meant an artery couldn't have been hit. I looked up at the others. "We're running out of time," I said.

"We should wait for the ambulance," Ted said.

"Did you call an ambulance?" Ray asked.

Ted thought a moment. "No, I forgot."

Ray nodded to me. "Okay. You take Kara. I'll take Becky. Do you know where the nearest hospital is?"

"Yes," I said.

Ray knelt and carefully lifted Becky from the ground. She hung in his powerful arms like a broken doll, her long dark hair sticky with clots of blood.

"I'll meet you there," Ray said.

"Yes," I repeated. I watched him put Becky in the backseat of his car. I watched Ted climb into the front seat. I watched them drive away before realizing that the hospital was not the place for me to go. I remembered a remark Kara had made about the Illumni's time machine.

"We never actually saw it before we left, although we felt it at work. I suppose it could be there even now. The inside of the cave does have a timeless quality about it."

Causality. It had been both Kara's friend and her enemy. The Illumni had given her a chance to change her future, but in another sense they had taken away her place in the future. There could not be two of them, she had said. It made sense. It also made sense that if Becky died, Kara would cease to exist in all possible futures. I didn't like the odds. Becky's head wound was grievous. I had little faith in what the doctors could do for her. But Kara, I thought, stood more of a chance to survive.

A timeless quality?

I wondered if the laws of causality applied inside the cave. And if Kara was inside when Becky died—if Becky died—if time's hourglass would not turn over one more time, and leave Kara alone. It was an interesting question. It could be both girls' only hope.

I lifted Kara into the backseat of the Ferrari. Her blood soaked the front of my shirt. She clasped my hand as I strapped her in.

"What time is it?" she asked.

"It's still early," I said.

Chapter Fifteen

My heart had so far withstood the stress of the evening's events, but there was no way I was going to be able to carry Kara the three-quarters of a mile from the house to the cave. It was all uphill. Necessity is the mother of invention. In this case it was also the ruin of a fairly expensive paint job. When I got to the house, I kept right on driving. A knee-high wooden fence was all that separated the yard from the hills and the start of the path. It was the first thing to fall to the bumper of the Ferrari. The boards cracked beneath the wheels, and Kara moaned in the backseat.

"Hang on," I said. "We're almost there."

The path wound dangerously and was mostly made up of loose dirt. Traction was a problem. My main concern, however, was the width of the path. There simply wasn't enough space to accommodate the car.

I had to make the space. Many bushes paid. They tore at the sides of the Ferrari as I ground them into the dust. A couple of young trees didn't go down so easily. I had to floor the accelerator and ram them. We were lucky I didn't drive off the edge.

Vincent's telescope was standing in the center of the path. I almost knocked it down as well. I guessed that Frederick hadn't given Vincent time to put it away. I didn't stop to think that Vincent would never have had the telescope out in the daytime, when he had in all probability been kidnapped.

Ray's bullet had not gone all the way through Kara. There was no bloodstain on her back. Not knowing the type of bullet in Ray's gun, I didn't know if that was a good thing. Her blood was all over the backseat, but she was still conscious. She peered out the window.

"What are we doing here?" she asked weakly.

"I've brought you home," I said.

I hated to pick her up again. She tried not to let me know how painful the wound was, but I could see her clenching her teeth so she wouldn't scream.

"Don't drop me," she said.

"Never."

When I finally got her out of the car and was standing in the middle of the path with her arms draped loosely around my neck, I marveled at how light she felt. Perhaps I could have carried her all the way up the path. She felt as if she were made of space, and I gripped her hair to make sure she was not leaving me too soon. The moon was high in the sky and I stared at it anxiously.

"Not yet," I told it. "Give me a few minutes."

I carried her into the cave. The way was dark, but we reached the inner chamber quickly. The lantern was still lit. I assumed I had forgotten to blow it out. I laid Kara on a stone ledge and rolled a blanket beneath her head. It was cool—I wished there was a second blanket. I made another feeble attempt at putting pressure on her wound to stop the bleeding. She waved me away:

"It's too late for that," she whispered, her eyes shut, her cheeks damp with perspiration.

"You're not going to die," I said.

"Becky is going to die."

"You don't know that for sure."

She opened her eyes, smiled faintly. "I remember all the times you used to say that to me. You were wrong, you know." Her eyes strayed to our shadows on the walls. Her smile vanished. "But so was I."

"It wasn't your fault."

"From the very beginning, it was all my fault." She nodded, her eyes glazed and staring. "Becky will die soon."

"You're with her?"

"Yes."

"Is she at the hospital?" I asked.

"Yes. They're in emergency."

"Is Ray with her?"

"Yes," a voice said at my back.

Frederick came out of the black hole at the far end of the chamber. There were bloodstains on the leg of his pants. He had not changed since he cut Vincent's throat. He still had his knife. He held the blade out for us to see as he strode casually our way. Kara tried to sit up, but couldn't manage it.

"Don't push," I whispered to her.

"Now who do we have here?" Frederick asked, stopping a couple of feet away.

"My name's Mark Forum," I said.

Frederick nodded. "We've met, haven't we?"

"No," I said.

"Yes, we have," Frederick insisted. "You visited me in the motel room this afternoon. You said something about me being less than a man."

I shrugged. "You know how it is when you're in another body. Things don't always come out the way you mean them."

Frederick slowly smiled. "You're very funny."

"Thank you," I said.

Frederick slid his blade beneath my throat. "Entertain me."

"Fred," Kara said quickly.

"What?" he asked.

"You know what's happened?" she asked.

"Yes," he said.

"Then you know you've won," Kara said. "Becky's finished. I'm finished. Leave Mark alone."

Frederick shook his head. "No, I don't think so. Too risky. He might try to mess with Ray. I can't chance that."

"I promise I won't," I said. The knife against my Adam's apple didn't feel any better the second time around. There were disadvantages to being in one's own body. I tried not to swallow. I was acting cool, but inside I was ready to pee in my pants. I could handle the sight of blood as long as it wasn't gushing out of my jugular. All of a sudden twenty-nine sounded like a ripe old age to me.

"And you expect me to believe you?" Frederick asked me.

"He expects you to do what you were trained to do," Kara said. "You're supposed to protect people."

Frederick was not impressed. But he did temporarily withdraw his knife from my throat. My eyes darted about the chamber for a possible weapon. I noticed a coil of rope sitting on the ledge across from us. I assumed Frederick had used a piece of it to tie up Vincent. I didn't imagine I'd get too far trying to whip Frederick to death with it. The only other thing was the lantern. I ran through an elaborate scenario in my mind whereby I threw the fuel in Frederick's face and set it on fire. All I needed was a Phillips screwdriver and five minutes of undisturbed work on the base of the lantern. I had no illusions about attacking Frederick directly. I figured I would last about three and a half seconds. Even though he looked exactly like Ray, I knew he was meaner and stronger. He regarded Kara critically.

"You're bleeding," he said.

"You shot me," she replied.

"Are you in pain?" he asked.

"No," she said.

He nodded. "You're in a lot of pain. But you're only one person. This guy's only one person. You saw what kind of pain the country went through."

"The world went through," Kara corrected, shifting uneasily as a spasm went through her body that she couldn't hide. "You think killing Mark's going to stop the war?"

Frederick sneered. "Did you think killing Ray would stop it?"

"You're the one who attacked us," Kara said. "I was content to leave you alone."

"Does leaving me alone include stealing my girl?"

"I'm not your girl," Kara snapped. "I don't belong to you."

"Don't worry," Frederick said. "I don't want you."

"Then what do you want?" Kara asked. "Why did you come back in time? You've been with the Illumni. You must know force won't work. It can't save the world."

"The Illumni never told me that," Frederick said.

"You lie."

"They never said a word to me about nonviolence,"

Frederick said. "Just the opposite. They told me I had to be strong. That I had to make strong decisions if I was going to change things."

"Right," Kara said sarcastically. "Cutting a young man's throat is a sign of strength."

"He wasn't a young man!" Frederick shouted. "He was a stinking corpse. He'd been dead for thirty years. I just put him back in the ground where he belonged."

"Where you belong, you mean," Kara spat back.

There followed a much-needed silence. Frederick moved back a step and contemplated his shadow on the wall. Kara briefly closed her eyes. Lying down as she was—not to mention the fact that she was bleeding to death and that Frederick was carrying a switchblade—she should have been at a distinct psychological disadvantage in their argument. But she was holding her own, and I would have admired her for it if something hadn't begun to trouble me. Frederick was a maniac—there was no question about that. Yet Kara had a bit of him in her. Her solutions to problems had always been dramatic—one might even say violent. This was not to say she was in her nasty husband's league, but it was easy to imagine the two of them arguing for the next forty years . . . all over again.

"How is Becky?" I whispered.

"She'll go any second now," Kara whispered back, her eyes still closed. She arched her back slightly and sucked in a tight breath. The drops of perspiration on her face were as big as tears, and I had no handkerchief to wipe them away. She was speaking for the two of them.

"Are they going to operate on her?" I asked.

"The doctors have given up on her," she said.

I had expected as much; nevertheless, the words cut like blades. "Is she unconscious?" I asked.

"Yes."

"Is there any possibility of her regaining consciousness?"

"I don't think so," Kara said.

"Could you make her regain consciousness?" I asked.

Kara paused. "Maybe."

"Is Ray still with her?"

Kara opened her eyes and glared at her husband. He glared back at her. "Unfortunately," she said.

"It will do him good to watch her die," Frederick said. "It will make him strong."

The cruelty of the remark went beyond anything imaginable. It did not make sense that this man could have been the same man the president of the United States had put in charge of the most powerful military installation America had at its disposal. The war must have done this to Frederick, I thought. Seeing his country burn from outer space and being unable to stop it. Something must have snapped inside him. It was as if a demon peered out from behind his eyes.

Yet he must have been ready to snap. He must have been beaten before the war began. Throughout her description of her life, Kara had said he was always a demon, always at fault. The only one at fault in their marriage. I wasn't ready to defend him, but I did know from my brief experiences that there were always two sides to a story. Or maybe I knew it because Vincent had told me when we were together. For the first time since exiting my trance, I felt him close to me, like a warm feeling deep inside me. An idea that had been slowly forming in my head suddenly became crystal clear.

"May I make a suggestion?" I said.

"Can it," Frederick said. "You're history."

"Listen to Mark," Kara said. "He's smarter than both of us put together."

"I've been listening to you two," I said, watching Frederick for a sign of interest. "And something has occurred to me. You two don't like each other very much."

Frederick chuckled. "He's smart, all right."

Kara touched my hand. "What do you mean?"

"I mean," I said addressing them both, "that you've forgotten you once loved each other."

Kara looked sad. "I don't think I ever loved him."

Frederick chuckled again, although this time it was obviously forced. "Forget the amateur counseling, Forum. It ain't going to save your skin."

"I am worried about saving my skin," I admitted. "But I saw someone tonight who wasn't. It was Becky. You say you know what happened in the parking lot. I assume you were able to see through Ray's eyes. If that's true, then you must know that Becky leapt in front of the car in an effort to save you."

"It swerved and hit her accidentally," Frederick snapped back.

"Did it?" I asked Kara.

Kara hated to admit the truth. "No. It was no accident. She did try to save the bastard."

"Well, I'm touched," Frederick said bitterly, moving close again. "I'm really touched. Some dimwitted teenager jumps in front of a speeding car and I'm supposed to give up my plans to win the war this time."

"But you can't win the war," I said.

Frederick snorted. "Don't lecture me. If we had hit them hard at the beginning, they wouldn't have hit back. It's as simple as that."

I realized I wasn't going to win an argument with him concerning nuclear strategy. "Let's forget about the war for a minute," I said. "Your wife is lying here with a bullet inside her. Don't you feel anything?"

Frederick scowled at Kara. "She's not my wife."

"Oh, swell," Kara whispered. She was having trouble breathing.

"She is your wife," I told Frederick. "You married her when you were a young man. And right now that young man is with Becky in the hospital. Do you know how he feels?"

Frederick wanted to snap at me, but chose to say nothing

instead. I was encouraged. I mean, we were talking about a guy who planned to slit my throat any minute. Something I said had touched a chord in him. Or maybe it was his watching Kara. He couldn't take his eyes off her. The flesh around his mouth quivered. Kara squeezed my hand.

"You don't know what we've been through together," she said, blood appearing at the corner of her mouth. She wiped it away and grimaced at the sight of it on the back of her hand. She added, "The wall between us is too thick."

"There are things neither of us will ever forget," Frederick agreed. "How do you feel?" he asked Kara.

"Weak," she whispered.

"It's your own fault," Frederick said.

"Thank you," Kara said.

"Ray and Becky have nothing to forget," I interrupted, afraid to let them get started again. "They haven't lived yet. Why don't you ask *them* what you should do."

"I know what to do, Forum," Frederick said. "I've done it. I just have to finish it."

"Do you really want to kill me?" I asked.

Frederick bristled. "It has nothing to do with what I want. It's what has to be. Ray has to be left to fulfill his destiny. He could go down in history as the greatest hero this world has known."

"Please," Kara said. "Spare us your visions of destiny." Yet she was interested in what I was proposing. "You want us to go into their minds?" she asked.

"Yes," I said.

"What for?" Kara asked.

"Your bodies have come back in time," I said. "But you're still locked in a horrible future. I think you've got to come all the way back."

Frederick snorted. "If you think I'm going to sit here and close my eyes while you run off to the police, you must be out of your mind."

I gestured to the rope on the other side of the chamber. "You tied me up once today and I didn't get away."

Frederick shook his head vigorously. "This is idiotic. Someone in your position telling me what to do. You should be on your knees praying that you die as painlessly as your twin."

I couldn't argue with him. I had no good reason why he should listen to me. All I could talk about was a fresh perspective, when he was obsessed with how many megatons he could float over the enemy. Kara spoke up.

"Perhaps we should do it," she said.

"No," Frederick said. "You're just trying to trap me."

Kara coughed up more blood. "What are you afraid of?"

Frederick was angry. "I'm not afraid of anything."

"I am," Kara said softly. "I'm afraid of dying. But I wonder if Becky is."

"Becky's in a coma," Frederick growled.

Kara raised an eyebrow. "You *are* there."

Frederick nodded reluctantly. "How could I help but be there?"

"Then let's go all the way," Kara said. "What have we got to lose?"

"What have I got to gain?" Frederick asked, and I think he was scared. I could understand. It was almost easier to die than to become someone you couldn't remember, or someone who had once been dead.

For the first time since Frederick had entered the chamber, Kara's expression softened. "You're going to have to face the end soon," she said. "It doesn't matter what you do to Mark. Or what Ray does."

"I've faced it before," Frederick said proudly.

Kara nodded. "It was hard."

"It was hard," Frederick agreed, turning away and staring at the black hole that led deeper into the earth. "You left me at the end. I'll never forgive you for that."

"I didn't leave you," she said. "You just didn't come with me to the prayer." She raised her arm feebly. "We can do it again. This time we'll do it together. What do you say?" She choked. "I can't go on bleeding like this forever."

"If you go to her, you'll just black out," Frederick said.

Kara looked at the ceiling. The glaze across her eyes had thickened. Her warm brown irises were now cold and colorless. Yet she seemed to be looking far away and seeing clearly.

"I don't think so," she said.

"You're talking nonsense," Frederick said.

She looked at him. "Maybe."

"Kara," he said.

"Please come with me, Fred," she said.

He was suddenly confused, this all-powerful general who had laid waste to millions of lives. "But you hate my guts," he said.

She tried to smile. She didn't quite make it. She was in too much pain. "Yes," she said. "But I wish I didn't. And I wish you didn't hate me. Maybe that's the real reason the Illumni sent us back in time. For this wish." She bit her lip. I knew she tasted blood. It was now pouring out the side of her mouth. Her right lung must be drowning in it, I thought. "Will you come with me?" she asked.

Frederick appeared to forget me for a moment. He knelt at Kara's side. "Nothing will change," he said. "You said it yourself. You're finished."

She nodded. "But what about us?"

The word startled him. "Us?"

She touched his cheek. "Us."

Frederick blinked. There could have been something in his eye. He didn't seem able to get it out.

"All right," he said. "I'll go with you to them. But your boyfriend is going to wait for us with a noose around his neck."

"I don't mind," I said.

Frederick had me lie down in the most uncomfortable position, flat on my belly with my arms behind my back. He tied my hands and feet together so that I was strung up like a bow. He kept his knife beside him the whole time he worked on the knots. He did an admirable job of choking off the blood supply through my wrists and ankles. He had probably been an outstanding Boy Scout as a child. But as he said, I was not in a position to make demands. I kept my mouth shut.

It was weird to see Frederick sit close to Kara and shut his eyes. It wasn't that he was in any physical danger from Kara or me, but in another sense he was placing himself in a vulnerable position. He would be opening himself up to feelings he hadn't felt in decades. Maybe he wasn't such a steel-hearted son of a bitch after all.

I didn't know what was going to happen. But if Becky did die and Kara didn't evaporate, I was going to have to get Kara to a hospital soon. I wondered what would happen if I took her to the same hospital where Becky was. The doctors would probably think they were seeing a ghost.

"Mark," Kara called softly, unable to raise her head and look at me. "I don't know if I should say goodbye."

"Don't," I said.

"Let's begin," Frederick interrupted, trying to make himself comfortable on the floor. He was too big to sit on a stone ledge. His expression was fixed in concentration. Briefly I saw the old general in his face: determined, cunning, burned out. Then his expression shifted in a less rigid direction and I imagined I saw Ray. But only for a moment. Then the breath seemed to leave his body, and his face became set like that of a dead person. The same thing happened to Kara. I let a few minutes go by. The tension was unbearable. I didn't know if, when Kara had left, her gunshot wound had closed the door behind her.

Then I noticed a sweet odor in the air. It reminded me of the first time I had visited the cave, the smell of a forest after a spring rain. But now it was stronger. It was almost as if the cave was attached to a corner of the paradise the Illumni had created on future earth. The fragrance was drifting out of the hole on the far side of the room. I took it to mean we were running out of time.

"Kara," I finally said.

"I am in the hospital," she replied after a brief pause. To my surprise, although her voice was still soft, it was clearer than it had been before she went into her trance. She sounded like Becky.

"How is Becky?" I asked.

"I am floating above her," Kara said. "She is unconscious."

"How can you speak if you're in her mind and she's unconscious?"

"She is floating above her body," Kara said.

The implications of Kara's comment took a minute to hit me. Becky was alive, but she was outside her body.

"What's happening?" I asked.

"There are wires hooked up to her," Kara said. "There are

monitors. The top of her head is covered with a towel. There's blood. Becky is watching from the ceiling, watching her body. The doctors are watching—there's nothing anyone can do now. They've let Ray come into the room. They're talking to him. They tell him his girlfriend is going to die."

Kara fell silent. I checked on Frederick. His face was still flat and lifeless, but his right cheek had begun to twitch.

"What's Ray doing?" I asked Kara.

"He's sitting beside Becky," she said. "He's very pale. He keeps looking at a screen. It measures Becky's brain waves. The waves are almost flat. There is little brain activity." Kara paused. "Becky is worried about Ray."

"The Becky who is outside her body?" I asked.

"There is only one of us outside," Kara said. "There is only one of us. Ray is upset. I want to tell him I'm all right. I can't tell him. He is beginning to . . ."

Kara felt silent again. I was surprised to see Frederick had rolled onto his side. It was hard to believe, but he was slipping into the fetal position.

"He's beginning to cry?" I asked Kara.

"Yes," she said. "It's sad. Wait. Something has begun to beep."

"The monitor attached to her brain?"

"No," Kara said. "Another one. One attached to the heart. It's beeping. Ray is trying to get the doctors to do something. They don't want to. They tell Ray it's hopeless. Let her go. Ray is arguing with them. He is—oh, no."

"What?" I asked.

"He's shoved one of the doctors to the floor. But the man is okay. He gets up. He's not mad at Ray. He's a nice man. He understands. He tries to comfort Ray. I'm trying, too, but I can't. He can't hear me. I touch him and he can't feel me. He's so sad."

"Are you sad?"

"Only for him," she said.

Kara fell silent for a third time. The fragrant breeze blowing in through the black hole grew stronger. The smell was intoxicating. It made Kara's earlier description of the blue and red trees easy to imagine. Had the circumstances been less hellish, I could have believed heaven was near at hand. Kara spoke again.

"The monitor is beeping faster," she said. "The heart—the heart is going to stop!" Kara's whole body jumped. Her voice got loud and excited. "Tell him I am all right! Tell him I will see him again!"

"What's Ray doing?" I asked. Frederick had buried his face in the floor, but now his body was shaking, too.

"He's begging her not to leave him," Kara said. "He can't stand it. He's holding on to her. The doctors are trying to pull him away, but he won't let go. He's afraid no one's ever going to love him the way Becky loved him."

"Does Becky love him?" I asked.

Kara was long in answering. "Yes."

"Does he love Becky?"

"Oh, yes," she said. "He would give his life if she could go on living." Kara suddenly became very still. When she spoke next, her voice was faint. "The beeping has stopped."

Ten seconds went by. Twenty seconds. I counted them. I was praying. If Kara continued to live now that Becky was dead, it meant that my theory was correct, that the inside of the cave was unaffected by the laws of causality. When my count reached one hundred, Kara and Frederick opened their eyes together. Frederick sat up and dusted off his shirt. Kara strained to roll onto her side. She reached out to touch him. He turned and looked at first her hand, then her face. Their eyes met.

"It was horrible," she said.

"Yes," he said.

"It was beautiful," she said.

He touched her hand. The hard lines of the general's face were gone. "What did all these years do to us?" he asked.

"What we let them do," she said.

"Was that really us?"

"It was us."

He nodded. "I had forgotten how it used to be."

Kara smiled. "In the hospital I just wanted to tell you I was all right. Now I can."

He gestured to her wound. "Can I do anything for you?"

"Yes," she said. "Kiss me goodbye."

He kissed her. I couldn't help but watch. My eyes were damp. When Frederick was done, he stood and took out his knife.

"I suppose I owe you one, Forum," he said.

"Think nothing of it," I said, knowing he had not taken out the blade to threaten me.

He knelt by my side and cut the rope. I couldn't get over the change in him. He looked twenty years younger. Of course he was in a body that was only twenty years old. He offered me his hand when he was through setting me free.

"You have guts," he said. "I think we could have been friends."

I shook his hand firmly. "Maybe we will be."

He understood. "Don't tell him about me."

"I won't," I promised.

Frederick stood. He turned to Kara. "I came out seconds behind you and Vincent. You didn't know that, did you?"

"I didn't," Kara said.

He looked at his watch. "I have to go now." He turned away.

"Ray," Kara called.

He stopped. "Yes?"

"You're my favorite general," she said.

He smiled faintly. Then he nodded in my direction and turned and disappeared into the black hole. I wasn't sure where he was going, but I knew it would be foolish to try to follow him. I hurried to Kara's side.

"You're alive," I exclaimed.

Kara was staring at the spot where her husband had vanished. "Not for long," she said.

"That's not true. Don't you understand? Becky is dead, but

you're not. Time has let you slip by. I'll get you to a hospital." I slipped my arms under her. "You're going to make it."

She stopped me. "Becky's not dead."

"What? You said her heart stopped."

"It did."

"Did the doctors restart it?"

"No," Kara said. "They couldn't if they tried. But her brain is still alive."

I understood what she was saying. Even when all respiration halted, the brain still took five to ten minutes to actually be destroyed.

"Where is she now?" I asked.

"She's still floating above her body."

"Will she leave when everything inside it is dead?"

Kara finally looked at me. "When I join her."

I shook my head. "No. You're going to stay in this cave. This is where the Illumni put their time machine. Becky's death won't affect you. You'll go right on living. Then I'll take you to the hospital."

Kara was sad for me. "Mark, this cave is just a cave. There is no time machine."

"What do you mean?"

Fighting against her pain, she tried to sit up. "Take me outside."

"No! The laws of causality don't apply in here. You're not going outside. I won't let you."

Kara touched my cheek. Even hurt as she was, she was so beautiful. I remembered the first time I had ever seen her, when I walked into the electronics store. She had been so full of life.

"Please," she said. "I want to see the moon before I go."

Tears filled my eyes. I closed them and the tears welled over my cheeks. I could bear anything, I thought. Even the end of the world. But this was too much. My heart was breaking—physically, I could feel it tearing apart inside me. How could the Illumni do this to me? How could they take both Kara and Becky?

"No," I moaned.

She cupped my face in both her hands. "Look at me, Mark. Who do you see?"

I did as I was told. "Becky."

"Who else?"

"Kara."

She smiled. "And someone else."

"Who?"

"Take me outside," she said. "I will show you."

I lifted her carefully. I had thought her light before; now I could scarcely feel her body in my arms. It was difficult even to focus on her, as if she were somehow becoming transparent. But I might have imagined this. Quickly I carried her from the cave and out onto the path. The moon was now directly overhead and surrounded with a wide white halo. Her right arm hung around my neck. With her left arm she pointed to the moon.

"See," she said.

"What?"

"There's the moon. There's me."

"So?" I said.

Kara snuggled against my cheek. "It feels so good to hold you. It's like holding Vincent. I was never afraid when he was with me. I'm not afraid now."

"Why did I choose that name—Vincent?"

"The forest where I met you again after all those years looked like a Vincent van Gogh painting. The colors were so vibrant." She smiled to herself. "I chose the name for you, Mark. It was a good name."

"I always liked it—Chaneen."

"So I'm the queen of the universe at last," she said, pleased.

"You have always been my queen. Can't I take you to the hospital?"

"I am at the hospital. I'm floating in the same way the moon floats in the sky."

"I don't understand."

"It doesn't matter," she said. "It's not your time yet. That won't be for a long time. I love you, Mark. In the years to come, you must never forget that. Don't be sad, and you'll live forever." Kara kissed me gently on the lips. She hugged me tight. "I love you more than the sun and the moon put together."

"Even with my lousy clothes?"

She smiled. "Look at the moon and close your eyes, Mark. Don't let go of me."

I turned my gaze. The moon was so bright. Even when I shut my eyes, I could still see an impression of it in my mind. An impression that went deep, like the last thought at the time of death. It grew in both size and brilliance as I focused on it. Soon it was as bright as the real moon outside my body, brighter even, and I almost forgot the real one for a moment. But then I opened my eyes and lowered my head. And I was standing alone on the outside. And Kara was gone.

Epilogue

Ten years have gone by since that night. A lot has changed. A lot has remained the same. I don't know if that's good or bad. I'm twenty-nine years old now. Before I can talk about the last ten years, though, I must finish with that night and the following day.

I went back to my apartment. I had to hitchhike home. The Ferrari I had driven to the cave was gone. At the apartment, Vincent's black Ferrari was also gone. I could understand why, sort of. Becky was dead. There was no Kara in the future to come back in time and buy the cars. Consequently, they were never bought. I just thought they were because I had a good memory. But then again, at least one of them must have been bought. One of them *had* killed Becky. But who had killed Becky? Kara? She couldn't have because if she had then she wouldn't have been alive to kill her. On the other hand, Kara must have killed her because no one else did.

The logic got awfully sticky, and it only got worse the longer I thought about it. Nevertheless, I will give my thoughts on the matter after I deal with the official investigation into Becky's death.

The next morning I heard a knock at my door—exactly as I had the previous morning. This time, however, I didn't yell for the person to come in. I got up and put on my pants. It was a good thing I did. It was the police. Apparently Becky had talked to Ray about the computer games I wrote. The police had contacted my software company, and they had given the police my address. Now the police wanted to talk to me. It seemed they were getting conflicting stories about what had happened the night before. They offered me a ride to the station. I took it and wondered if they would give me a ride home.

Ray and Ted were at the station. Both looked awful. I was surprised to learn they had been arrested. Actually, I could understand why they had arrested Ted. The police had probably taken one look at his stoned expression and figured they'd found the pipeline—or rather, the bloodstream—for half the Colombian cocaine in southern California. But I had to sit down when I learned Ray had been arrested for manslaughter.

The detective in charge of the case was old and tough. His thin hair was as white as his starched shirt, his red face wrinkled and cracked from the sun. He held his spine ramrod straight and when he shook my hand he hurt my little finger. He looked and talked like a cop, and had I been told he had shot a few people in the line of duty, I would have assumed they were teenagers. He gave me a dirty look as I sat down. His name was Lieutenant Cocker.

"Were you at the scene of the crime last night, Mr. Forum?" he asked, wasting no time on small talk.

"What crime is that?" I asked innocently. I needed information. I didn't know how Ted and Ray's stories were in conflict. Ted sat to my right, Ray to my left. Lieutenant Cocker pointed to Ray.

"I've already told you," the lieutenant said. "This young man has been arrested on a charge of manslaughter. Are you saying he's innocent?"

I had to move carefully. "Who's accusing him of killing Becky?"

"I am," Ted spoke up. I turned toward him.

"Did you see him run over Becky?" I asked, grateful that the detective hadn't tried to get my story in private. I could only assume I wasn't under suspicion.

"No," Ted said. "But he was there."

"What about me?" I asked. "I was there."

"But you were on foot," Ted said quickly, taken aback by my remark. "Ray was the only one who had his car there."

"How did you arrive at the mall?" Lieutenant Cocker interrupted.

"I went there with Becky," I said. "We were in her car."

Lieutenant Cocker nodded impatiently. "We found Becky's car parked on the other side of the mall from where she was run down. But what are you stalling for? Tell me what went on last night."

I was reluctant to speak when I wasn't sure if Ted's obvious memory loss was a result of cosmic causality or simply dead brain cells.

"I don't understand what you're asking me," I said. "How does Ray's story conflict with Ted's?"

Ray had been sitting quietly with his head bowed. Now he sat up angrily. "What the hell are you talking about?" he demanded. "You saw what happened, Mark. That Kara bitch ran Becky down in her red Ferrari."

"What red Ferrari?" Ted asked.

"The one with the headlights that were shining on the two girls!" Ray snapped. "Christ, how wasted were you last night, Ted? The car was sitting right in front of your eyes."

"What two girls?" Ted asked. "Becky was the only girl there."

"When you got there," Ray said, making a vain effort at a patient tone, "Kara was lying on the ground beside Becky. They were both bleeding."

"Why was this Kara also bleeding?" Lieutenant Cocker asked.

Ray glanced at me and lowered his head. "I don't know."

"There was only one puddle of blood on the ground," Cocker said. "What do you have to say about that?"

Christopher Pike

"Nothing," Ray replied, clearly confused.

At last I thought I understood. Causality *was* at work, but in a strangely limited fashion. Only the three of us in the present—Becky, Ray, and I—could remember the true sequence of events in which our future selves were involved. Otherwise, to other people, Kara, Frederick, and Vincent hadn't even existed.

"I'll tell you what happened," I said to the detective. "I saw it all. Becky and I were walking across the parking lot. Ray had just gotten off work. He was over by his car. We were trying to catch up with him. Then this other car came out of nowhere. It hit Becky and drove off. Ray didn't have anything to do with it."

Ted frowned. "But Ray was beating you up," he said.

"That's ridiculous," I said. "He was just upset. We all were. We weren't fighting."

"But what about Kara?" Ray asked. "Becky's twin sister?"

"Becky doesn't have a sister," I said.

"Yeah, she does," Ray said indignantly. "The girl looked just like her."

"We've spoken to Becky's parents," Lieutenant Cocker said dryly. "There is no sister."

Ray was ready to throw a fit. "But I went out with this girl on a date!" he shouted.

"Why would you go out with your girlfriend's sister on a date?" Cocker asked.

"I didn't know it was her sister," Ray said.

"But you just said this Kara looked like Becky," Cocker said.

476

"She did," Ray said. "I just didn't notice it at first."

"Lieutenant," I said reasonably, "this whole experience has the three of us in a state of shock. Ted and I were good friends of Becky's, but Ray was the closest to her. They'd been going together a long time, and suddenly she was lying on the ground dying. You can see how he could begin to have hallucinations."

"But Kara came into my store!" Ray cried. "She came in with you!"

"I think if you check with Becky's parents," I said to Cocker, ignoring Ray for the moment, "you will discover that Becky's first name is Kara."

"It is?" Ray asked.

"They already told me that," Cocker said, unimpressed. He eyed the three of us suspiciously. "But I still don't buy how all your stories could vary so much." He gestured to Ted. "What do you have to say about Forum's version of what happened last night?"

"It sounds good," Ted replied cautiously.

"Is it true?" Cocker asked.

"I told you," Ted said. "I wasn't actually there when Becky got hit. It just looked like Ray had done it."

"Why?" Cocker insisted.

Ted searched his memory and appeared to get lost. "He was carrying something. It made me think he—I don't know."

"What was he carrying?" Cocker pressed.

Ray was watching Ted intently. He was worried. Only I

knew that Ted was remembering the ghost of the gun that wasn't there. Already I could see my theory would have to be modified. Maybe nobody else was going to remember Kara and Vincent and Frederick, but their shadows were inside a few heads somewhere. Ted had seen Ray and me fighting for the gun that the future Ray wasn't going to be coming back in time to give Ray.

"It could have been a gun," Ted replied.

"Did you see a gun?" Cocker asked.

"No," Ted said.

"Were you carrying a gun?" Cocker asked Ray.

Ray hesitated. He glanced at me. "No," he said finally.

Lieutenant Cocker sighed. "I should lock the three of you up and let you sit for a week and then see what you have to say." He pointed at Ted. "I'm letting you go by the kind permission of the letter of the law. My men were there to investigate a hit-and-run, not to search for drugs. But I think you'll find that you are now unemployed and that the paraphernalia you kept at the mall has gone up in smoke. You are free to go. I don't want to see you back here anytime soon."

Ted got up and fairly ran from the room. Lieutenant Cocker was not through. He stood up from his desk and walked behind us. Ray sweated out the move. But I figured, what the hell. The evidence Cocker needed to convict either of us had never existed. Not now, anyway.

"Both of you are lying to me," Cocker said. "You're a lot

better at it, Forum, than Mr. Gardener here, but you're not good enough. Now I want to know what happened last night, and I want to know the truth."

"Are you placing me under arrest?" I asked.

"Not yet," Cocker said.

"If you were to arrest me, what would the charge be?" I asked.

"Obstructing justice. Possible manslaughter."

"No one's saying I hit Becky," I said.

"Don't fool with me, Forum," Cocker snapped.

I decided he was trying to intimidate me. "I already told you the truth," I said. "A car came out of nowhere and hit Becky and drove off."

"And you have no idea what type of car it was or what the driver looked like?" he asked.

"Absolutely none," I said, throwing a look Ray's way. "It was dark, wasn't it, Ray?"

Ray held my eye for a moment, "Yeah," he said slowly. "It was pitch-black. Neither of us saw a thing."

Cocker chewed on that for a minute. "And now you're agreeing with Forum, is that it, Gardener?" he asked.

Ray nodded. "Looks like it."

"Get the hell out of here, both of you," Cocker said, moving back to his desk. "But just know one thing. If I find the tiniest bit of evidence that could be used to nail either of your asses, I'm going to go out and buy myself a big hammer. Do you get my drift?"

We both told him that we did. Ray followed me down the long hallway that led out of the police station. He didn't speak until we were standing in the parking lot beside his car. His grief was with him still. The circles under his eyes were dark and deep.

"What gives, Mark?" he asked.

"I can't tell you," I said. I raised my hand as he started to protest. "If I did tell you, you wouldn't believe me. Trust me."

"Why should I trust you? Becky died last night. She's dead. I can't believe I'm saying it, but it's true." He put his hand to his head to steady himself. His skin was pale and damp. "I can't take this," he moaned. "The whole world's gone insane."

I put my hand on his arm. "You felt that way last night when her heart stopped. You felt so upset that you had to lash out at something, anything. You pushed a doctor to the floor."

He stared at me in amazement. "Who told you that?"

"Becky. She told me something else. That she was all right."

"When?"

"When she died."

"What are you talking about?" he asked.

"Magic. I know that sounds foolish, but I can't explain it any other way. Just know that before Becky left she wanted you to know that she was all right and that you were her favorite general."

A strange light touched Ray's face. "She used to tell me that I would be a general one day," he said.

"Then you will be. She was a special girl. She and Kara both were. You weren't hallucinating. Kara was real. Her hitting Becky was just an accident."

"I know," he said. "She was trying to hit me."

"Because she thought you were guilty of something that you hadn't done." I let go of his arm. "You'll be able to take it better the next time."

"The next time what?" he asked.

"The next time the whole world goes insane," I said. "You'll know not to lash out like you did at the doctor. I have faith in you, Ray."

He gave me an incredulous look and then shook his head. "You're crazy, you know that, Mark?"

"So are you," I said. "I wonder what Becky saw in either of us."

Ray offered me a ride home. I took it. He shook my hand as he dropped me at my apartment building. He promised to keep in touch. Maybe he forgot, I don't know. I never saw him again.

But I don't think he ever forgot Becky. Or what it was like to hold her in his arms and watch her die. For the sake of the world, I hope not.

My life went on. I never went back to Becky's store. I never stood at the door and glanced over my shoulder and imagined I saw a guy with pale blond hair holding one of my computer games. I seldom dreamed of Vincent and Kara. I remembered them—that was enough. My programming skills improved dramatically, particularly my graphics. I copied Vincent's style. It came easy to me. I didn't consider it plagiarism. I started to make good money, and by my twenty-second birthday I was making great money. I wrote a program called "Decision" then. The reason I waited three years to write it was so that the industry could develop computers with RAMs big enough to hold the game's many complexities.

The game was an instant success. In fact, it became so big that I gained celebrity status. The major talk shows wanted me as a guest. The game was talked about in high schools and colleges across the country. The first nonviolent video game, it was called. Teachers used it to teach nuclear age morality. Kids played it even though they knew they couldn't win. Privately, I found it all very amusing. I just didn't see myself as a modern-day prophet. I cashed my royalty checks and stayed out of the limelight.

With my newfound wealth I was in a position to see the finest heart surgeons in the world. But I never made an appointment. The more I thought about the Illumni's comment on health and happiness, the more profound it seemed. Maybe I was just afraid of dying on the operating table, I don't know. I'd still wake up in the middle of the night with pain in my chest, but I stopped feeling sorry for myself, or feeling unloved, which I think is the same thing.

I lived alone, as I had always lived alone. Occasionally I

dated different girls, but I knew nothing would ever come of it. That is the problem with finding the perfect girl. You can't find her twice. That is not to say that Kara was without her faults. No one knew them better than I. Except perhaps Vincent, whom I miss as much as Kara. I think about him a lot. He was so kind, so at peace. I ask myself who he really was. I mean, I know he was me, but *which* me was he? It may seem a silly way to put the question, yet I wonder if it is not *the* question.

You see, I think Vincent had no faults. None.

Ten years later I'm still trying to understand what happened.

Kara talked about superior beings from another planet. I could see how she thought that. She was in outer space when bright lights suddenly swept in and rescued everybody. But from that point on, her story was filled with one inconsistency and coincidence after another, and I don't think she even realized it. Several I brought up at the time of her explanation. The Illumni supposedly had no bodies, but they needed spaceships to get around and had gender distinctions. She only communicated with one, and that one happened to be female. The Illumni took a single spot on earth and turned it into a virtual paradise, and that spot just happened to be where Kara grew up. Given Kara's basic premise of a highly advanced alien culture, none of this is impossible, but it makes me wonder if she wasn't missing the sun because it was so bright. What I mean is, the truth might have been so overwhelming and yet so simple that it just escaped her.

Several points puzzle me. One is that I, as Vincent, wasn't even on the space station—much less alive—and yet I was able to come back in time. Kara explained this away by saying that I had been frozen and stored in ice above the Arctic Circle, where no atomic bombs exploded. At the time it all sounded awfully convenient to me. Why was I the only one who was thawed out? How exactly did the Illumni bring me back to life? They weren't God. They were supposed to just be friendly aliens.

I think Kara was wrong. I think the Popsicle Mark Forum Theory was given to her or perhaps created by her. Not intentionally to mislead her, but to give her a framework from which to interpret certain events that couldn't be understood unless the Big Thing was understood first. In other words, I think Kara missed something important the moment the Illumni showed up, and because she missed that, nothing she said about subsequent events can be accepted as truth.

What exactly was going on with Kara and Frederick when the Illumni appeared? They were dying. Then suddenly, miraculously, a bright light came to their rescue. No, not just one bright light—about a hundred bright lights. One for every person on the space station. I find that an amazing coincidence. An alien space ship filled with the exact number of aliens to personally attend to each dying crew member of an American space station.

From the start, something about the description of the Illumni reminded me of something I had read about in magazines and books. A bright white light. A peace beyond description. People who suffer a near-death experience talk about things like that. There have been dozens of shows on TV about it. People get in car accidents or almost drown or get hit by lightning, and suddenly they're thrust into a realm of blissful light where their lives are reviewed so they can see where they've done well and where they've screwed up. Granted, Kara didn't exactly describe this, but the parallel is striking. In fact, it's almost unnerving.

Who were the Illumni? *What* were they?

I realize I'm treading into the area of philosophical speculation, and believe me, I have no desire to do so. I know I will only get lost. Nevertheless, I'm willing to go a little further, with the understanding that I will not be arriving at any definite conclusions. I'm not an Einstein who can think in six dimensions at once. I'm just a survivor of strange times. In a sense, I am also a survivor of death.

I was in Vincent's body. Frederick cut Vincent's throat. Then I reviewed my entire life, even the end of it, while I simultaneously experienced the end of Vincent's life. It was the most horrible thing to go through, yet it eventually brought me to a place of wonderful joy. In the end, before Kara called me back, I went into a bright light. I *was* the bright light. There was no difference. There was only one. Then I saw the space station. Yes, it's true I responded to Kara when she called to me. The question is, to *which* Kara did I respond? The one waiting by my side in the cave?

Or the one dying aboard the space station?

This is getting confusing. Let me just say what I think and be done with it. I'll phrase it in the form of another question. If one version of our future selves could come back in time, why couldn't an even more distant future version also come back?

Who was Vincent? I think he was one of the Illumni.

Who were the Illumni? I think they are ourselves.

I think Vincent was myself from a far more distant future than even Kara could dream of. I also think he was that part of me that exists in the dimension beyond life. I realize these statements appear to support entirely separate points of view. But do they really? I was dead when Kara wished me back to life. I had been dead for close to thirty years. And suddenly I was up and walking around in a flower-strewn meadow that sounded suspiciously closer to heaven than to Los Angeles on the best of days. Then what did I do? As Vincent, I went back in time with a girl who was anxious to change her past so her future could also be changed. But as Vincent, I didn't sweat a thing. I didn't interfere because I knew that what was to be would be.

Several other points lead me to believe Vincent was no ordinary time traveler. Kara said repeatedly how highly developed Vincent's mind was, and I could see that for myself. When Becky glimpsed Vincent—via Kara's memories—she saw him lit up like a lightbulb. In the same vision, Becky said it was Vincent, and Vincent alone, who possessed telepathic powers. Also, and perhaps most important, before she ran out the door to her death, Becky said I was not real. Still caught in a portion of her trance, I think she had mistaken me for Vincent. And in that trance, I don't think Vincent was a flesh-and-blood creature.

Of course, it could be argued that Becky should have been able to see Vincent only as Kara remembered him. Nevertheless, Becky's remarks, made in a state of complete ignorance of the travel experiment, may have been more accurate than anything Kara told me.

What's the main problem with time travel? Causality? The paradox of going back in time and killing your grandmother is a piece of cake compared to the problem of immortality. We have bodies. They are supposed to wear out and eventually stop working. But if you've got a time machine, and if you're careful, you never have to die. Yet just before Kara died, she said there was no time machine. In fact, by her tone, she implied that there had *never* been a time machine. The cave was just a cave, she said. I think she was right. *I think, in the end, Kara understood precisely what I am talking about right now.* She pointed to the moon. To the white light. That's me, she said. And she was happy.

Who were the Illumni? Vincent once referred to them as angels.

I'm sorry. This analysis will have to be left incomplete. I'm getting tired. It's late, very late. My time has finally come. The night I saw as the end of my life has arrived. I'm sitting at my table on the side of the hill. The moon is out. It's bright—it's a full moon. I have my gas lantern nearby. The orange flame burns without flickering beneath the glass cover. I warm my hands above it. My fingers shake, although the night is warm. I'm trying to finish my story. It's not easy. I know I shouldn't complain, but I'm having chest pain. It comes in waves, like my memories of Kara and Vincent.

I still don't understand why things happen the way they do. I wish this story could have been a happy story with a happy ending. I did not want Becky and Kara to die. At funerals, ministers often say we're only here for a short time before God calls us back home to heaven. Perhaps they, too—like Kara—have it backward. Perhaps we're never really here when we're born, and we never really leave when we die. That makes sense if there's time travel. If I had a time machine, I could keep pushing the buttons and go around and around the calendar like the stars in the sky. I could live forever, but maybe then I would never get anywhere. I would only become a dream of what I could have been, a shadow of who Vincent will be.

I don't want to die. In spite of all I've been through, death still frightens me. I'm alone. I wish Kara were here. If my heart should suddenly stop, there'll be no one to freeze my body to keep it for the day it could be revived. That's another reason I don't believe everything is the way I was led to believe. As far as I know, there is still no way to keep water from expanding when it turns to ice. Not that I blame Kara. I feel nothing but gratitude for her.

The city appears very peaceful from where I sit. Bathed in the light of the moon, it looks like a surreal black-and-white painting that I would gladly hang on my bedroom wall and look at each night before retiring to pleasant dreams. But I know it will not always be this way. Tonight I'm worrying about myself, but I can honestly say that I usually think more about what's to become of the world. Unfortunately, of all the many incidents that Kara predicted, the one thing that rang terribly true was the impending cataclysm. I see it in the headlines of the newspapers. I hear it in the voices of the politicians. But I'm not without hope. I can close my eyes and sit so still that the outside voices all but disappear. Then I see and hear something quite different. A hundred white angels flying quietly through the nighttime streets, stopping at a house here, an apartment there, and whispering into the ears of their sleeping counterparts, "Wake up. Wake up. The moon is in the sky."

I have to put down my pen. I have to close my eyes. The pain in my chest is getting worse. Perhaps I have not remembered my love as well as I should have. It is not easy to stay happy living on memories alone. My heart is tired. It needs to rest.

But I'm not going to burn this manuscript, as I burned the one before. This time I have not come to the end in despair.

I feel Vincent near me. I sense Kara. They come to me from another time and place, where there is only happiness. I feel as if two angels stand behind me and touch my head. It may be only my imagination, but I do not think so. They are real, like my story, although these two do not whisper to me. They stand silent. They have already told me all there is to tell.

I know I will see a light when the dawn finally comes. The cool white light of the moon, shining forever in a starry universe that goes on forever, or the warm light of the sun, burning brilliantly in a sky all its own, a sky that lasts only a day.

I know I will either live or die.

I wish I could say which it will be.

TURN THE PAGE FOR
A SNEAK PEEK AT
CHRISTOPHER PIKE'S
BRAND-NEW NOVEL:

CHRISTOPHER PIKE

#1 NEW YORK TIMES BESTSELLING AUTHOR OF THE THIRST SERIES

WITCH WORLD

A NEW SAGA BEGINS...

ONCE I BELIEVED THAT I WANTED NOTHING MORE THAN love. Someone who would care for me more than he cared for himself. A guy who would never betray me, never lie to me, and most of all never leave me. Yeah, that was what I desired most, what people usually call true love.

I don't know if that has really changed.

Yet I have to wonder now if I want something else just as badly.

What is it? You must wonder . . .

Magic. I want my life filled with the mystery of magic.

Silly, huh? Most people would say there's no such thing.

Then again, most people are not witches.

Not like me.

I discovered what I was when I was eighteen years old, two days after I graduated high school. Before then I was your typical teenager. I got up in the morning, went to school, stared at my ex-boyfriend across the campus courtyard and imagined what it would be like to have him back in my life, went to the local library and sorted books for four hours, went home, watched TV, read a little, lay in bed and thought some more about Jimmy Kelter, then fell asleep and dreamed.

But I feel, somewhere in my dreams, I sensed I was different from other girls my age. Often it seemed, as I wandered the twilight realms of my unconscious, that I existed in another world, a world like our own and yet different, too. A place where I had powers my normal, everyday self could hardly imagine.

I believe it was these dreams that made me crave that elusive thing that is as great as true love. It's hard to be sure, I only know that I seldom awakened without feeling a terrible sense of loss. As though my very soul had been chopped into pieces and tossed back into the world. The sensation of being on the "outside" is difficult to describe. All I can say is that, deep inside, a part of me always hurt.

I used to tell myself it was because of Jimmy. He had dumped me, all of a sudden, for no reason. He had broken my heart, dug it out of my chest, and squashed it when he said I really like you, Jessie, we can still be friends, but I've got to go now. I blamed him for the pain. Yet it had been there before I had fallen in love with him, so there had to be another reason why it existed.

Now I know Jimmy was only a part of the equation.

But I get ahead of myself. Let me begin, somewhere near the beginning.

Like I said, I first became aware I was a witch the same weekend I graduated high school. At the time I lived in Apple Valley, which is off Interstate 15 between Los Angeles and Las Vegas. How that hick town got that name was beyond me. Apple Valley was smack in the middle of the desert. I wouldn't be exaggerating if I said it's easier to believe in witches than in apple trees growing in that godforsaken place.

Still, it was home, the only home I had known since I was six. That was when my father the doctor had decided that Nurse Betty—that was what my mom called her—was more sympathetic to his needs than my mother. From birth to six I lived in a mansion overlooking the Pacific, in a Malibu enclave loaded with movie stars and the studio executives who had made them famous. My mom, she must have had a lousy divorce lawyer, because even though she had worked her butt off to put my father through medical school and a six-year residency that trained him to be one of the finest heart surgeons on the West Coast, she was kicked out of the marriage with barely enough money to buy a two-bedroom home in Apple Valley. And with summer temperatures averaging above a hundred, real estate was never a hot item in our town.

I was lucky I had skin that gladly suffered the sun. It was soft, and I tanned deeply without peeling. My coloring probably helped. My family tree is mostly European, but there was an

American Indian in the mix back before the Civil War.

Chief Proud Feather. You might wonder how I know his name, and that's good—wonder away, you'll find out, it's part of my story. He was 100 percent Hopi, but since he was sort of a distant relative, he gave me only a small portion of my features. My hair is brown with a hint of red. At dawn and sunset it is more maroon than anything else. I have freckles and green eyes, but not the green of a true redhead. My freckles are few, often lost in my tan, and my eyes are so dark the green seems to come and go, depending on my mood.

There wasn't much green where I grew up. The starved branches on the trees on our campus looked as if they were always reaching for the sky, praying for rain.

I was pretty; for that matter, I still am pretty. Understand, I turned eighteen a long time ago. Yet I still look much the same. I'm not immortal, I'm just very hard to kill. Of course, I could die tonight, who's to say.

It was odd, as a bright and attractive senior in high school, I wasn't especially popular. Apple Valley High was small—our graduating class barely topped three hundred. I knew all the seniors. I had memorized the first and last name of every cute boy in my class, but I was seldom asked out. I used to puzzle over that fact. I especially wondered why James Kelter had dumped me after only ten weeks of what, to me, had felt like the greatest relationship in the world. I was to find out when our class took that ill-fated trip to Las Vegas.

Our weekend in Sin City was supposed to be the equivalent of our Senior All-Night Party. I know, on the surface that sounds silly. A party usually lasts one night, and our parents believed we were spending the night at the local Hilton. However, the plan was for all three hundred of us to privately call our parents in the morning and say we had just been invited by friends to go camping in the mountains that separated our desert from the LA Basin.

The scheme was pitifully weak. Before the weekend was over, most of our parents would know we'd been nowhere near the mountains. That didn't matter. In fact, that was the whole point of the trip. We had decided, as a class, to throw all caution to the wind and break all the rules.

The reason such a large group was able to come to such a wild decision was easy to understand if you considered our unusual location. Apple Valley was nothing more than a road stop stuck between the second largest city in the nation—LA—and its most fun city—Las Vegas. For most of our lives, especially on Friday and Saturday evenings, we watched as thousands of cars flew northeast along Interstate 15 toward good times, while we remained trapped in a fruit town that didn't even have fruit trees.

So when the question arose of where we wanted to celebrate our graduation, all our years of frustration exploded. No one cared that you had to be twenty-one to gamble in the casinos. Not all of us were into gambling and those who were simply paid Ted Pollack to make them fake IDs.

Ted made my ID for free. He was an old friend. He lived a block over from my house. He had a terrible crush on me, one I wasn't supposed to know about. Poor Ted, he confided everything in his heart to his sister, Pam, who kept secrets about as well as the fifty-year-old gray parrot that lived in their kitchen. It was dangerous to talk in front of that bird, just as it was the height of foolishness to confide in Pam.

I wasn't sure why Ted cared so deeply about me. Of course, I didn't understand why I cared so much about Jimmy. At eighteen I understood very little about love, and it's a shame I wasn't given a chance to know more about it before I was changed. That's something I'll always regret.

That particular Friday ended up being a wasteland of regrets. After a two-hour graduation ceremony that set a dismal record for scorching heat and crippling boredom, I learned from my best friend, Alex Simms, that both Ted and Jimmy would be driving with us to Las Vegas. Alex told me precisely ten seconds after I collected my blue-and-gold cap off the football field—after our class collectively threw them in the air—and exactly one minute after our school principal had pronounced us full-fledged graduates.

"You're joking, right?" I said.

Alex brushed her short blond hair from her bright blues. She wasn't as pretty as me but that didn't stop her from acting like she was. The weird thing is, it worked for her. Even though she didn't have a steady boyfriend, she dated plenty, and there wasn't a guy in school who would have said no to her if she'd so much as said hi. A natural flirt, she could touch a guy's hand and make him feel like his fingers were caressing her breasts.

Alex was a rare specimen, a compulsive talker who knew when to shut up and listen. She had a quick wit—some would say it was biting—and her self-confidence was legendary. She had applied to UCLA with a B-plus average and a slightly above-average SAT score and they had accepted her—supposedly—on the strength of her interview. While Debbie Pernal, a close friend of ours, had been turned down by the same school despite a straight-A average and a very high SAT score.

It was Debbie's belief that Alex had seduced one of the interviewing deans. In Debbie's mind, there was no other explanation for how Alex had gotten accepted. Debbie said as much to anyone who would listen, which just happened to be the entire student body. Her remarks started a tidal wave of a rumor: "ALEX IS A TOTAL SLUT!" Of course, the fact that Alex never bothered to deny the slur didn't help matters. If anything, she took great delight in it.

And these two were friends.

Debbie was also driving with us to Las Vegas.

"There was a mix-up," Alex said without much conviction, trying to explain why Jimmy was going to ride in the car with us. "We didn't plan for both of them to come."

"Why would anyone in their right mind put Jimmy and me together in the same car?" I demanded.

Alex dropped all pretense. "Could it be that I'm sick and tired of you whining about how he dumped you when everything was going so perfect between you two?"

I glared at her. "We're best friends! You're required to listen to my whining. It doesn't give you the right to invite the one person in the whole world who ripped my heart out to go on a road trip with us."

"What road trip? We're just giving him a three-hour ride. You don't have to talk to him if you don't want to."

"Right. The five of us are going to be crammed into your car half the afternoon and it will be perfectly normal if I don't say a word to the first and last guy I ever had sex with."

Alex was suddenly interested. "I didn't know Jimmy was your first. You always acted like you slept with Clyde Barker."

Clyde Barker was our football quarterback and so good-looking that none of the girls who went to the games—myself included—cared that he couldn't throw a pass to save his ass. He had the IQ of a cracked helmet. "It was just an act," I said with a sigh.

"Look, it might work out better than you think. My sources tell me Jimmy has hardly been seeing Kari at all. They may even be broken up."

Kari Rider had been Jimmy's girlfriend before me, and after me, which gave me plenty of reason to hate the bitch.

"Why don't we be absolutely sure and invite Kari as well," I said. "She can sit on my lap."

Alex laughed. "Admit it, you're a tiny bit happy I did all this behind your back."

"I'm a tiny bit considering not going at all."

"Don't you dare. Ted would be devastated."

"Ted's going to be devastated when he sees Jimmy get in your car!"

Alex frowned. "You have a point. Debbie invited him, not me."

On top of everything else, Debbie had a crush on Ted, the same Ted who had a crush on me. It was going to be a long three hours to Las Vegas.

"Did Debbie think it was a good idea for Jimmy to ride with us?" I asked.

"Sure."

I was aghast. "I can't believe it. That bitch."

"Well, actually, she didn't think there was a chance in hell he'd come."

That hurt. "Love the vote of confidence. What you mean is Debbie didn't think there was a chance in hell Jimmy was still interested in me."

"I didn't say that."

"No. But you both thought it."

"Come on, Jessie. It's obvious Jimmy's coming with us so he can spend time with you." Alex patted me on the back. "Be happy."

"Why did you wait until now to tell me this?"

"Because now it's too late to change my devious plan."

I dusted off my blue-and-gold cap and put it back on. "I suppose this is your graduation present to me?" I asked.

"Sure. Where's mine?"

"You'll get it when we get to Las Vegas."

"Really?"

"Yeah. You'll see." I already had a feeling I was going to pay her back, I just didn't know how.

ABOUT THE AUTHOR

CHRISTOPHER PIKE is a bestselling author of young adult novels. The Thirst series, *The Secret of Ka*, and the Remember Me and Alosha trilogies are some of his favorite titles. He is also the author of several adult novels, including *Sati* and *The Season of Passage*. Thirst and Alosha are slated to be released as feature films. Pike currently lives in Santa Barbara, where it is rumored he never leaves his house. But he can be found online at christopherpikebooks.com.

SIMON TEEN

Simon & Schuster's **Simon Teen**
e-newsletter delivers current updates on
the hottest titles, exciting sweepstakes, and
exclusive content from your favorite authors.

Visit **TEEN.SimonandSchuster.com** to
sign up, post your thoughts, and find out what
every avid reader is talking about!

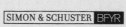

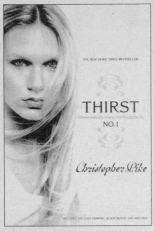

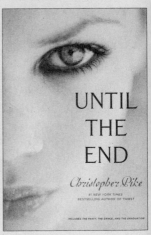